Night Warriors
Histories, Book 1

Brenna
Lyons

The
Blutjagdfrau
Chronicles

FIREBORN
PUBLISHING

Fireborn Publishing Copyright

Statement

The Blutjagdfrau Chronicles
Includes:
Choosing a Mate © 2011/2015 by Brenna Lyons
Starting a War © 2011/2015 by Brenna Lyons
Blutjagdfrau Lost © 2013/2015 by Brenna Lyons
Raised to be His Own © 2011/2015 by Brenna Lyons
Print ISBN: 978-1-943528-18-9
First Fireborn Publication: October 2015

Cover Artist: Brenna Lyons
Photo Credit: 123rf
Editor: Kathryn Lively
Logo copyright © 2014 by Fireborn Publishing and Allison Cassatta
Licensed material is being used for illustrative purposes only. Any person depicted in the licensed material is a model.

PUBLISHER

FIREBORN
PUBLISHING

PO Box 5216
Haverhill, MA 01835

Glossary of Warrior Terms

Beast- Beasts are what humans erroneously refer to as vampires. The stories humans tell are obviously not correct, but you can't expect a human to get everything right.

Blutjagd- The "blood hunt." Warriors crave battle with the beasts, as the beasts crave blood. Warriors are tied to beasts in that they sense many of the beasts' special powers. A Warrior can feel the use of coercion, feeding, and other controls of humans. They also feel other Warriors engaged in *Blutjagd*, the death of beasts and Warriors in their range, and the presence of nearby beasts that are not fully ghosted. Rigorous battle training will quell the *Blutjagd* for short periods of time.

Elder- One of the original beasts, the Stone stealers who were damned for their crimes against the Stone and the Warriors. The elders are gifted with powers turned beasts are not, including the ability to reproduce with a *Blutjagdfrau*, the ability to turn other beasts, and the inability to be killed by anyone but a Warrior.

Endspiel- The point in printing when a Warrior must either seal printing or go insane. A Warrior who feels printing may not progress should break printing long before this point. Note that they are rarely smart enough to do so.

Fluch- The Warrior's curse, passed from father to son or daughter. The *fluch* may be removed from a daughter but never a son. If the *fluch* is not removed in the *Zeremonie der Freiheit* by the time the menses begin or the *Zeremonie des Schutzes* is performed before freeing, the daughter is cursed to become *Blutjagdfrau*, a female Warrior. Because elders target *Blutjagdfrau* as mates, Warrior fathers will go to any lengths to free a daughter not marked by the Stone.

Ghosting- A talent that both beasts and Cursed Warriors learn to harness. Ghosting can hide the physical form of Cursed Warriors or beasts and all they hold or carry from each other and humans. In a lesser strength, it can "blur" the image of the user so that humans do not note the passage in particular but still see a person there, which avoids accidental collisions. Even a ghosted beast cannot hide uses of power that a Warrior can track. Warriors sometimes ghost in tandem to remain visible to each other but not other Warriors or beasts.

Krankheit- The "sealing sickness." In the final stage of the transformation between human and Cursed Warrior, at or about the sixteenth birthday in males and a year after the start of menses in females, the sickness strikes. The young Warrior will suffer nausea, vomiting, a high fever, disorientation, dizziness and may become incoherent. It is usually the only time in a Warrior's life that he or she becomes ill, save morning sickness in a *Blutjagdfrau*.

Printing- Like imprinting, a Warrior becomes tied to his mate for life. He cannot choose another if she's lost, cannot be unfaithful while she lives, and cannot ever divorce or otherwise dissolve the union. A printed Warrior is the most stable of men, unless his mate or children are endangered or lost. Then, he will suffer the printing madness and may have to be killed by his house. Likewise, a Warrior who breaks printing, even early printing, will suffer for it. A Warrior who breaks printing too close to Endspiel will face the madness.

Veriel- The Mad Elder. The Destroyer of Lives. The Mad Deceiver, who led the traitors and freed the elders from the Stone. The most hated and hunted of all the beasts. Fixated on one woman, he would destroy the world to own her. Or... At least, that's what the stories say of him.

Warriors- Also called Cursed Warriors, Krieger der Nacht, Soldat der Nacht or Sons of the Stone. The Warriors were an ancient race of protectors who spawned the beasts and now are driven to hunt their former brothers to extinction.

A Note from the Author:

The muse is a noisy creature, and her whip stings. I mention this to explain the stories you're about to read. When I'm writing in a series world, the muse will get fixated on an unanswered question or "what if" raised elsewhere in the series. All of these stories grew out of discussions like those with the muse.

I've warned readers, on occasion, to read another story before you read a particular one. I won't be doing that today, but I will say that these stories were written to appeal to readers who already have a fair grounding in the series. If you don't, certain turns may seem abrupt to you...jarring, but Night Warriors fans will be able to follow the changes easily.

Happy reading and welcome back to the Night Warriors world!

Brenna

Choosing a Mate

Note from Brenna:

I always have to know how things started. When the muse answered that question, I made some startling discoveries. The very first beast war started when the gods escalated the war in their realm by choosing humans to be their vessels on Earth. The first few "Stone-chosen" were named for the blood marks they possessed.

Happy reading!
Brenna

"You know why this is necessary," Syth prodded her.

Ani nodded miserably. Their Goddess Mother had proclaimed that the war could only end with children from her line. The gods had named her Raga, Mother of Peace and vessel of the Stone Goddess. Though both of the males originally chosen for her had been lost to them, producing children was essential to that end.

If only that didn't mean bedding with a man not Goddess-crafted for her, she might not be so nervous about it. As it was, Ani knew that she would never have happiness in her life.

Damn Reg!

"Are you prepared to do this, Ani?" her brother asked.

She peeked up at him, reassured by the fact that he looked no happier with the situation than she was.

Syth stroked a hand along her cheek, hooking her long hair behind her ear. "If I could return Ori to you, I would. You know that, I hope."

She swallowed a sob at the reminder, then nodded.

Ori had won the battle for her bed and had gifted her with a single, sweet kiss in promise of the mating to come. But that mating had never come to pass and, courtesy of Reg, never would.

Damn Reg!

"Ani, today or another day, this must happen," Syth reminded her.

"Then it should be today." She was glad to hear she sounded surer than she was about it.

Syth offered her a comforting hug and took her elbow in his hand, leading her down the corridor and to the chamber where their remaining numbers waited for her "pleasure" in choosing a mate.

There will be no pleasure. That was nearly a given.

Ani realized she was being peevish. Of course, there would probably be pleasure. *Krieger* were known for their sexual prowess. Whichever male she chose would do that, out of duty, if for no other reason.

But there will be no love. She'd been fated to love whichever of the two destined won her bed.

And she had loved Ori, much more than she had ever loved Reg. Ani pushed that thought away. Ori was the past. Whatever *Krieger* she chose was her future, love him or not.

She paused at the archway and took a calming breath. Syth offered a squeeze of her elbow in support.

He released her as she entered the chamber. It could not appear that he'd led her decision in any way.

Ani nearly turned and ran at the sight of them. She'd known this was coming, but she hadn't been prepared for the reality of it.

The men showed no distress at her reaction. None of them commented on the step back she took before she managed to smooth her jangled nerves.

There was no instruction given. The Goddess Mother's plan so fouled, there was no tradition for what was about to happen. No one had foreseen it to suggest where to progress from the ruins they'd been dealt. In the end, Syth had conferred with the *Krieger* remaining.

Only two possibilities had been advanced to her for a decision. Since it was Ani's body and her children at stake, no one had argued that the ultimate choice should fall to her.

The first had consisted of Ani taking each of the men into her body in turn until she caught pregnant with a child...or two. Three... As many as she would be have proven willing to carry and from as many of the men as remained unprinted when she sought out males to fill her bed. Syth would have raised the children as his own, and none of the others would know who had truly sired them.

Beyond the horror for her of taking all the *Krieger* in turn, that possibility presented the very real possibility that all of the men would be driven mad by the idea that the child she bore was his own and she with it. She secretly believed it more likely that some would be driven mad and some not, further fragmenting their waning ranks.

The other was the only possible solution. Ani would choose from among the remaining men and take only that chosen man to her bed to sire her children.

Not that the plan was perfect. Ani was the first to admit that there were problems with it. If her chosen one printed on another woman, he would be forced to leave her or go mad in wanting the other. Beyond that, he would not be able to perform sexually with Ani if he was printing on another. If that happened, she would have to choose again and release her first male to his chosen.

There was little possibility that any of the remaining men would print on her. But, short of isolating her chosen from all the other women in the world, how could they avoid the problem?

She conceded that there was no way.

Though she'd stood immobile for so long, none of the men prompted her to continue with this farce. Syth had decreed that no one was to speak to her unless she spoke first and seemed to want an answer. There would be no coercion, no convincing her. There would be no appeals of Ani's final choice. They would all accept it as law, as if the Goddess had chosen the man for her personally.

Still, approaching them took all her fortitude. Though she'd seen Syth nude while he bathed, she hadn't seen another man in such a state. Now, she was faced with six of them, all more than double her size.

Ani wanted to look them in the eyes, but that wasn't the point of this display. She knew their faces, and when Syth had asked, she hadn't been able to simply choose one as more appealing than another that way.

To this moment, she wasn't certain which of the men had suggested she choose the most appealing...package. She supposed it didn't really matter who had suggested it. Since Ani had been unable to choose a favorite by face, she had to choose by some differing quality about them.

All of them were tall, broad men. All had thick, black hair that reached at least to their shoulders. All had dark eyes, ranging from deep blue to brown and even black. All had training scars of varying lengths and in varying places. There was only one thing left that would matter to a woman, according to the one who'd suggested this manner of choosing.

Choosing a mate by the cock that appeals to me most. I must be mad to have agreed to this.

But she had agreed to it.

That a given, Ani started at the closest man. His cock was as long as her hand and fingers combined...not so long that she worried about his depth harming her, but he was thick enough that she was afraid he might be an uncomfortable fit.

The next was slim and long. *Too long.* The urge to compare his length to that of her forearm was enough proof that Ani would shy from it when she had promised to embrace the one she chose. She moved on.

The third was of average length and girth, and Ani considered him a moment longer. She conceded that comfort was the only concern she had to worry about. Any of them would be an avid lover, passably talented, and produce the children the Goddess needed of them.

But I must consider them all. If any of them feel slighted, it could have catastrophic results.

She moved on, trying to push away the realization that all of them were hard for her inspection. Was it excitement that whoever she chose would get to bed with her? Was it just another battle to them?

The next was both long and thick. Not as long as the second but as thick as the first, easily. Ani started to move on, dismissing him that simply.

Not so simply. His cock jerked, slapping wetly against his belly, and she looked again. The slit in the head was beaded with clear fluid, and more of the same dotted his lightly-furred abdomen, where the head had struck. At her inspection, it jerked again.

She took a calming breath and moved on.

Focusing on the other cocks was difficult. Her gaze strayed to that one, again and again. Ani forced herself to consider them all. The fifth was the longest and thick, though not as thick as the one before. The sixth was less than a finger width longer than the first and narrow, as well.

She ranged the line again, not to compare dimensions but to compare their readiness. Only two of them had sacs that appeared hard and full, indicating—by her meager understanding—that they were aroused fully at the moment. Only the one was weeping fluids for her.

What did it mean? Had it been so long since he'd had a woman beneath him that he was in aching need of one?

The heat at her back meant Syth had drawn near. While he would not interfere, she was certain it was a gentle reminder that she was essentially baiting these men.

"I wish to consider...several further?" Ani hadn't meant to make it a question. It shouldn't have been. She was the one that would choose.

"Which?" Syth inquired. "And do you wish the others to leave?"

"Yes." She was certain she wouldn't be choosing several of them already. "They should leave." At least then she would only be faced with three cocks and not six.

At her brother's silence, Ani darkened. She had to name the three that would stay, and that meant doing so by connecting faces to the parts she'd been examining so closely. *For the rest of my days, I will know what every Krieger's cock looks like.* It was mortifying.

Her face burning in embarrassment, she looked up.

The third one was Len. His name meant *mountain*, but he was the one of average proportions.

Pol was the fifth; though his dimensions frightened her, his sac was tight and heavy in arousal.

Baroo was the fourth...the one whose cock was weeping fluids so avidly. She had to know why that was before she made any further decisions.

"These three," she breathed. "Len, Baroo, and Pol."

The other three tipped their heads in acknowledgement and withdrew to the next chamber, probably to dress. She winced at the thought that more than one of them was probably relieved that she hadn't tied him to her.

The three she'd asked to examine further shot looks that seemed to question silently at each other. None of them voiced their concerns, whatever they were.

They are not permitted to. There was something liberating in that.

Now that she'd asked to consider them closer, Ani didn't know how to accomplish it. She could hardly ask the questions she wanted to. Could she?

I have every right to.

"You are all very...ready," she noted.

Three brows furrowed, and sideward glances passed between them, but none of them commented.

Ani worked her lower lip between her teeth, nearly squirming in place.

Syth cleared his throat. "Did you mean a question in that, Raga?" he asked formally, using her title instead of her name. "You must be specific in your asking."

Her face flamed. "How often...? How often do you each typically...?" She swallowed hard. "Mother take it. I cannot do this." She turned to leave, the precursors of tears burning at her eyes.

Syth made no move to stop her. Part of her wished he would. Another was relieved he wasn't doing so.

Her hand was on the archway when one of them spoke.

"Often, Raga."

She spun back to them, her heart hammering. By the way Len and Pol gaped at him, she guessed that Baroo had spoken.

"Ask whatever you wish of us. If you choose to bed with one of us... It is your right." He tipped his head and offered a solemn and serious look.

Len and Pol nodded and grumbled their agreement.

Her heart hammering hard against her ribs, she took careful steps toward them. "How often do you?"

Len looked as if he would rather not answer that question. "As often as I have the opportunity to. With training and my other duties, nearly daily still."

"Thank you." Her mind reeled at his answer.

Pol went next. "More than daily. I have a fierce hunger."

She suspected he was boasting, hoping she wanted a virile man. He wanted to impress her. Ani knew *Krieger* bedded with women often, and she didn't care for a boastful man. "Thank you." She hoped it didn't sound as cold and clipped as it felt.

Ani looked at Baroo.

He met her gaze solidly. "Typically close to daily. I have gone as far as three hand of days, but I prefer not to wait longer than one or two."

She didn't hesitate. "And the last time you lay in a woman?"

Baroo didn't flinch from the question. "A day ago."

"Then you are not...?" The words stuck in her throat.

He waited patiently for the question, his eyes soft and inviting.

That gave her the courage to ask it. "Then you are...content not to bed a woman today...or soon, if needs be? You are not crazed to bed?"

"None of us would force you to bed, Raga." His voice was soothing.

"That was not what I asked," she huffed.

Baroo cocked his head to one side and stared at her for a moment. Just when she would have rephrased the question for him, he answered.

"No. I am not crazed for a woman."

The others hastened to add their agreement.

He wasn't crazed for a woman, but he strained and wept sex fluids. Ani launched into her next question before she could convince herself that it was inappropriate.

"Is..." She motioned to his cock. "Is that...personal...to me?"

Baroo looked down at himself, seemingly confused. "All the men are erect, Raga."

"That did not help," she grumbled.

"Be specific," Syth reminded her.

Ani swallowed hard and looked up at the three men. Their reactions to her question were varied. Len seemed to be studying cracks in the ceiling. Baroo silently invited her to ask. Pol smirked in a way she found most irritating.

"Please leave," she snapped at him.

His smile disappeared, and he tipped his head, following her orders without question. No matter why he was aroused, Ani would not spend her time bedding with a man she loathed.

There was a tense moment of silence. Finally, Ani forced herself to speak.

"You react more acutely than the other men do," she explained to Baroo. "Is it because of me? Do you feel something for me personally?"

Her heart pounded in fear that he would say it wasn't personal, that he felt nothing for her personally, that none of them did.

Baroo stared at her for a long moment. None of the men spoke. They barely breathed.

"Yes. Very personal," he offered. His muscles tensed, as if he feared she would tell him to leave next. Or perhaps he feared Syth and Len would accuse that he was swaying her with his words.

Ani took a step toward him, daring to lay a hand on his chest. A gasp left his mouth, and his cock jerked. His muscles tightened down another notch.

"Len can leave," she managed. "I have made my choice."

Len withdrew a step. "Thank you for your consideration, Raga. May you have many strong sons." The blessing imparted, he left the chamber.

* * * *

Baroo found it difficult to think clearly. Pol's plan to impress Ani with his size had failed him, and Baroo had captured Ani's attention without breaking the rules set out for them.

It was unbelievable. It was a gift or a blessing. Surely, the Goddess Mother had led her chosen daughter to Baroo personally.

"What is your wish, Raga?" her brother asked.

Baroo's cock had opinions on the matter, but it was the Young Mother's leisure and not his own urgency that mattered.

Ani didn't seem to know how to answer that. At last, she spoke in that same tentative tone she'd used when questioning their sexual exploits.

"You said I was fertile now." The way her voice faltered at the end said she was unsure.

Or she wishes she was. Baroo answered before Syth could. "I do not require immediate consummation, if that is your fear. As always, your choice is law."

Syth's voice was something of a rebuke. "Ori did not press for immediate consummation either."

He didn't need to say more. A moon later, several of the remaining *Krieger* still cursed Ori for a fool that had wasted his single chance to sire children.

But not Baroo. Baroo thanked the blessed Goddess Mother that Ori had been so unaware of the danger he faced. If Ori had not been lost to her, Ani would have no need of another, and Baroo would surely die in wanting her.

Ani pressed closer to him, shivering at her brother's warning, and Baroo shot the Stone lord a warning glare for it.

"I watch my back better than Ori did," he informed Syth.

A stiff nod of acknowledgement was his only answer.

Baroo continued. "What would please you, Raga? Anything that will put you at ease with me."

A wan smile pulled up at her lips. "It would please me to have you call me Ani."

"Ani." He'd always thought of her as Ani. Reminding himself to call her by her title had taxed his mind, a mind that was usually mired in lust any time he was within touching distance of her.

He could mark the moment when that lust had taken hold of him first, and he'd suspected that either the Goddess Mother had chosen him for Ani then...or that the trickster god Veriel had sought to drive a wedge in their ranks by cursing him with unrequited feelings for the Young Mother.

"You must make a choice, Raga," her brother insisted. "This is unkind to Baroo."

It wasn't. Every moment with her in his arms was a gift he would treasure forever. Baroo opened his mouth to say so.

Ani looked up at him, her smile strained. "Would it be unkind to ask to speak for a bit?"

"Not at all." If they grew to know each other better, she might feel for him what she'd felt for Ori. The concept of a life loving her while she could not return the feeling was the only horror deeper for him than Ani choosing another in his place.

Syth walked away, then returned and pushed Baroo's wrap at him. As if that reminded Ani that he was unclothed, she backed away and went a stunning shade of red.

She turned toward the corridor to her chambers and stammered out something about waiting for him in her work room. With that, she was gone.

Running from me. The thought hurt.

Ani needs time. I will give her as much as I can bear to.

Syth's warning made his heart stutter. "We do not have the leisure of time, Baroo. My sister has chosen you. If you feel as you say you do about her, bind her to you quickly and give her the heirs the Goddess Mother wishes...before Reg can act again to stop it."

"As soon as Ani is comfortable with the idea of sharing a bed with someone other than Ori," he vowed. He prayed that day would come soon.

Syth snarled at him, but whether it was at Baroo's use of Ani's given name or at his warning being ignored was an uncertain thing.

* * * *

Ani chose to lounge on the furs. There were other places to sit in the chamber. She wondered if Baroo would choose to share the furs with her or to sit apart from her.

He said he was affected by me personally. Would that mean he would hint at more or not do so, as to put her at ease with him?

All my life surrounded by males, and I understand so little about their ways. Of course, Ani hadn't been permitted to mingle with the *Krieger* since her blood began to flow.

Baroo strode through the archway, dressed again as the men did for training. He looked around the unfamiliar space, pausing at each possible place to settle. At last, he stepped to the foot of the furs and folded down onto the stone floor, his legs crossed beneath him.

It took Ani a moment to realize she was staring at the edge of his rough hide wrap. Was she hoping for a glance at his cock?

I should look away. She didn't.

"I can remove my wrap, if you wish."

Ani looked up, mortified that he was teasing her about her interest. It didn't appear that Baroo was teasing. She wriggled, uncertain if his candor was better or worse than the idea that he might be making fun of her.

"Or not," he conceded.

She nodded. But where to go from there? Ani wasn't certain what to talk to him about.

Baroo had his own ideas. "How did you choose the three?"

Ani stared at him. "How?"

He took his time answering. "When you named Len, I thought for certain..."

"What did you believe?"

"If you had been choosing for moderate length, Len, Vin, and Hir were of a type. If you wanted a longer man, Kor, Pol, and I would have been your choices. If you wanted a thick man, Hir, Pol, and I would have been your choices. If you wanted a man with less bulk, Kor, Len, and Vin would have been the obvious choices. In no way do the three of us match up."

Her face was burning at the recitation of their dimensions.

"You were not choosing by those sorts of attributes. Were you?"

Ani shook her head slowly.

"How did you choose us, Ani?"

He has a right to know. "I choose you and Pol because of your avid excitement. I wanted to know why you responded as you did."

"But you dismissed Pol without asking that question."

She cleared her throat. "I...uh... I dislike Pol."

A smile quirked up his mouth, and Baroo's throat bobbed in what was probably laughter. "An excellent reason to dismiss him."

Before Ani had a chance to fully appreciate his comment, she burst out in laughter. Baroo shot her a sly little look that made her laugh harder. He didn't speak again until she'd recovered.

"Why Len then?"

Ani bit lightly at her lower lip, uncertain how to discuss it.

"I see," he mused.

"Do you?"

"His length and girth are much less formidable. That was the reason. Was it not?"

* * * *

Ani's shock would have been amusing if Baroo wasn't so worried that it would continue to be a problem for them. He had to put her at ease.

"The differences are not as striking as they seem."

Her look spoke her disbelief.

"Women accommodate all lengths and girths." In fact, the village women often said they enjoyed the larger men, which was no doubt the reason Pol had believed Ani would choose him, based on his size.

But those are older, experienced women, most of which have borne children. Ani would be tight, untried. Perhaps, she would find his size uncomfortable, but there was no way to know it until she was willing to bed with Baroo at all.

Calming her was necessary. If she was fearful when they bedded, chances were she *would* find their joining painful.

Ani nodded solemnly, her eyes large and trusting. Her gaze slid from his face to the edge of his wrap.

15

"Are you certain you do not wish me to remove my wrap?" *Or to remove it yourself.*

She didn't look away. "No."

"As you wish." *Damn, but getting her to relax to the idea of bedding will not be easy.* And just the thought of it had him hard and weeping, and had for days.

Her eyes blinked, and her brow furrowed. "I meant... No, I am not certain."

"About?" He prayed it was as simple as him removing his wrap now and not uncertainty about a woman's ability to take varying dimensions.

Ani peeked up at him. "Syth says I am being cruel to you. I do not mean to."

He smiled. "Nothing you have done is cruel, Ani. Your brother should not speak for the sensibilities of other men."

She hesitated and then motioned to the furs beside her. His heart skipping in anticipation, Baroo rose, stepped to the furs, and folded down beside her.

Ani reached a shaking hand to him and touched his chest as she had earlier. Her gaze assessed his reaction, her eyes widening at the little moan of delight he let pass.

"This is personal to me," she breathed.

"Very personal," he repeated.

The moment she collapsed into her brother's arms, weeping over Ori's fate, burned in his memories. She'd screamed, ranted that she would never willingly bed with Reg after what he'd done, and she'd sobbed until her face and eyes were swollen and red.

At that moment, Baroo had wanted to tear Reg limb from limb. He'd wanted to be the one holding her, the one inhaling her feminine scent. He'd wanted to be the one to take Ori's place in her heart and bed, and that feeling had never faded and likely never would.

She explored, testing the feel of muscle beneath her small hands. Her hand retreated, and Baroo took a calming breath. It caught in his throat at the feeling of her hand delving beneath his wrap.

With exaggerated care, Ani trailed her fingertips up his inner thigh, ruffling his leg hair and waking his nerves to bliss. Her fingers curled in the mat of male hair, traced the outline of his rigid sac, and started up his length.

"Yes," he urged her, his breathing ragged.

He didn't doubt that it was Ani's touch in particular that affected him. He'd had women sucking him or riding him that affected him less than she did with an innocent, questioning touch.

"Oh, yes, we should," she whispered.

"Only if you truly wish to," he vowed. "Not because you are fertile. Not because of anything your brother has said or done."

But the fact that she was fertile was impossible to ignore. Baroo wanted his seed nestled deep in her and growing nearly as much as he wanted to draw his next breath.

Her massaging hand said she wanted something.

"Do you wish to watch me release to your hand, Ani?" Given much more of her, his climax was a surety. Whether she watched him or not, he was going to spill soon.

I want her to watch it. If she didn't finish him, the urge to do so for himself and let her watch was strong.

Her nod was quick and jerking, her eyes wide.

Baroo untied his wrap and pulled it away, exposing himself to her. Her hand was tiny and pale, compared to his sun-touched length. Her fingers only just met around his circumference.

A small sound that might have been distress or pleasure left her lips. They parted slightly, and her breaths were short and quick. Ani's scent rose to an enticing high.

The climax built in the root of his cock. As if Ani sensed it, she tightened her fist around him and milked hard toward that end. Baroo groaned, letting himself go, fighting his eyes open to take in every expression as she watched him shoot.

17

He stifled his sounds to low, intimate ones Syth was unlikely to hear but Ani would. If the Stone lord overheard sounds of passion, he might believe the task of conceiving Ani's first child accomplished.

Her eyes widened at the rush of his seed, but she didn't pull away. Baroo's cock spasmed against her grip, and his climax went on. Her lips parted in an "O" of surprise.

At last, it ended, and she continued to stare. Ani was so still, Baroo wasn't certain what to make of the reaction. He spoke her name softly in the attempt not to startle her.

Ani drew her hand back, her breathing coming in little gasps and catches. Baroo wanted to hold her but feared that reaching for her would send her running.

"Calm, Ani. All is well."

She didn't acknowledge his comment. Her hand shaking, Ani reached out and trailed her fingers through the ribbons of cum on his chest and abdomen.

"Why do you let me...?" Her face went crimson, and she averted her gaze.

Baroo reached out and cupped her chin in his fingers, urging her gaze back to his. "You chose me because my reaction to you is personal. Every touch is a joy to me, Ani. What would be the sense in denying myself that joy? Or denying you the chance to touch and learn?"

"Even when I am not certain of more?"

"Even then."

Ani squirmed, looking hopelessly confused.

"You need time to consider what you have seen." Baroo didn't question it.

"Yes." Ani vaulted to her feet and ran for the archway to her personal chamber. She stopped there, peeking at him around the edge of the rock. "Will you return to your home, Baroo?"

He shook his head slowly. "No, Ani. I will be here when you wish to speak to me again. Here or in your bed. Whichever you prefer."

"Here...for now." With that, she fled to the comfort and familiarity of her bed.

Baroo took his time, wiping away the leavings of his release. Yes, he was staying here with her. After what happened to Ori, Syth had decreed that Ani's chosen wasn't to leave her.

The man in question appeared in the archway to the corridor. He scowled down at Baroo. "I take it none of that went inside her," he grumbled.

"For a man with the Goddess-given place of protecting his sister—the Goddess Mother's vessel, no less—you seem awfully quick to push her into bed with a man she isn't comfortable enough to offer herself to. Her choice is law, you realize."

Syth visibly calmed himself. "The Stone says Reg and the other traitors have allied themselves with Veriel and the traitor gods. Traitors allying with traitors." He shook his head. "It defies all reason."

Baroo stared at him, trying to find the words to ask what this meant.

"Training on how to defeat the traitor beasts begins tomorrow. You will have half sessions. I believe you know how I expect you to spend the remainder of your time."

Trying to convince an innocent woman to accept me in her bed. The whole thing flew in the face of the rules of sanction.

* * * *

An oppressive silence fell over the training chamber, and the hair on the back of Baroo's neck rose in warning. He straightened and turned toward the archway.

Ori stood there, staring at Baroo as if he was deciding between beating him to a pulp and burying a blade in his gut. At his move toward Baroo, the other *Krieger* parted to let Ori pass.

19

The older man stopped an arm's length away from him, a tic working in the back of his jaw. "Baroo."

He tipped a curt greeting, unwilling to avert his gaze for any reason. There was no question why Ori was singling Baroo out. He'd heard Baroo was Ani's new chosen, and this was some sort of challenge, no doubt.

"Practice," Ori ordered. "Now."

Baroo waved him ahead, unwilling to give Ori his back. His opponent's eyes narrowed, but he complied, his gait tense and primed. There was little doubt he meant to pummel Baroo if he could. There was less doubt Ori wanted to kill him.

Out of the corner of his eye, Baroo saw his usual sparring partner, Len, move to Syth's side.

Syth started talking, but Baroo's mind was only half on the instruction. Beasts could be taken by a heart shot with a sacred weapon or by completely severing the head with the same. The heart shot would be easier. There were other ways to weaken them, but the usual killers would not.

He named the god each former *Krieger* had allied with. Syth explained how the beasts had been created by the hollowing out of the former *Krieger's* soul and the gods in question pouring a portion of their own souls in their places. It was unnatural. It created monsters. And it made the gods themselves vulnerable, while making their formerly-human proxies all the more powerful. It had been a calculated gamble, trapping a portion of their god-souls in the beasts to try and win the greater war.

All the while, he and Ori sized each other up. They'd sparred before, though they weren't often paired. But this time would be different. This time, the fight was personal.

Syth called for sparring practice, and Ori closed on him. The first few hits came hard and fast. Baroo landed the first that would be considered a killing blow on a beast.

Ori backed off two steps, taking slow, deep breaths while the pain in his chest eased. He didn't give the traditional nod of readiness. Instead, he launched at Baroo with a look that said Baroo would be taking the next blow.

He didn't. Ori went down hard, but it wasn't a killing blow for a beast. Baroo's move to take that blow ended with Ori flipping Baroo beneath him. They rolled and struck blows, struggling for the superior position.

"You think you are worthy of her?" Ori growled at him.

Baroo struck him across the face, bloodying Ori's lip. "No man is worthy of her, and you know it."

Syth called a halt, and they ignored him. Baroo threw Ori off and flipped to his feet. Ori swept them, and tried to do the same. Baroo took his knee and came up over him, bringing his fist down into Ori's heart hard.

The man beneath him grimaced, panting in the agony Baroo had left him in. Baroo waited for another attack that didn't come.

Ori stared at him. When he spoke, there was no question it was a warning. "If you put her through what I did, I will personally slit your throat. If you hurt her, I will make you live as I do now."

Baroo took to his feet and offered his hand to help Ori up. "I would kill myself before I would give Ani a moment of discomfort." He started to turn to Len.

"You train with me, Baroo," Ori informed him.

A smile pulled up at his lips. "So you can repay the damage I have dealt you?" he taunted.

The older man pushed his way to Baroo's face. "No. Because no other man in this chamber is as committed as I am to making certain you survive what is coming for you intact. We have something in common, you and I."

Love for Ani. He nodded grimly. "It gives you no rights," he informed the damaged lord.

"I know that. I accept it."

Baroo offered his hand in agreement, and Ori took it.

"I will not be soft on you."

Baroo didn't smile at that. "If you were, I would kill you myself."

* * * *

Ani snapped awake with a shout of horror. Burying her face in her hands, she tried to banish the visions of what Reg did to Ori. She hadn't seen it, of course, but the thought of his scarred body bothered her just the same.

Perhaps it was because the attack had been carried out in her name. Perhaps it was the horror of the things traitors did to achieve their goals. Either way, she wished Syth had told her they'd killed Ori. Of course, that would be a lie and beneath *Krieger* honor.

Baroo appeared in the archway between her work room and her bedroom. He lowered his blade slowly. "May I enter, Ani?"

"Yes." She wanted Baroo's arms, the solid reality of his protection and comfort.

He strode to her, laid his sacred weapon on the table beside the bed, and settled beside her.

Baroo didn't ask what her nightmare had been. He probably didn't have to ask it. She'd confided it to him their second day together, when they'd spent hours talking and looking at each other, neither daring to touch.

On their third day together, they still hadn't consummated. They'd talked for a while that afternoon; they'd kissed and touched. Baroo had released her arousal with his hand, whispering sweet words while she clung to him, needing more that she was afraid to ask for. Needing him but still too afraid of losing him to commit to bedding fully.

She'd retreated to her bed at the sight of him tasting her cream from his fingertips, his eyes hot in meaning even a virgin like herself could follow. His mouth would have come next, and Ani hadn't been certain she would deny him after that.

His arms encircled Ani, and Baroo eased her to his chest and both of them to the bed. "Sleep, Ani. I will protect you."

But sleep was the last thing she wanted. He was nude for sleep, and he was erect. Ani wanted more than being held and comforted. She wanted him touching her, tasting her...thrusting inside her.

Ani stretched upward, sliding along his body to bring her lips to his. Baroo angled his head to one side and sealed their mouths together.

He didn't ask what she wanted. He'd told her to let what came between them happen naturally. If she found herself unsure or uncomfortable or frightened, she was to tell him to stop or leave him for a time as she had earlier.

There will be no stopping. Enough of playing the rabbit. Baroo is mine, and I am his.

His lips parted hers, and he progressed to the deep, passionate kisses he'd introduced her to earlier in the day. Ani wrapped her arms around his neck and tugged. Baroo complied, covering her with his solid length.

Her heart stuttered at the weight on her, at his knee working up between hers, pushing her legs wide to admit him. She thrust her hips up, moaning at his muscled thigh touching her so intimately.

Baroo pushed up at her sleeping tunic slowly, probably believing she would startle and call a halt. It slipped past her waist, and his cock left wet trails along her belly.

Ani gasped and pulled her head back at the sensation, her body in a riot. She wanted to beg him to continue, wanted to touch, wanted—

The tunic has stopped moving. Baroo thinks he has pushed me too far.

"Yes," she breathed. "Please, Baroo."

His kiss was less restrained at that. The tunic passed her breasts, and he broke off the kiss. Just when she thought he might abandon his own rules and question her, he lowered his head and sucked one rigid nipple into his mouth. Ani found breathing difficult, but somehow she managed to drag in enough air to expel some of the tension building in her with a shout.

Baroo moved from one breast to the other, growing more avid. The tunic slid off the ends of her extended arms and left them skin to skin.

It was glorious. Ani wished she'd had the courage to do this days earlier. She pulled at Baroo and worked her slit against his thigh, needing more, needing all of him.

He grumbled curses into her breast, his breath hot and fast against the wet nipple. Baroo raised his head, his eyes narrowed. He opened his mouth as if to question her, snapped it shut, then dove in for another heated kiss.

His hand left her cheek and reappeared on her thigh. He cupped it and drew her leg wide around him. Ani wound her tongue around his and fisted her hand in his shoulder-length curls, doing her best to encourage him with her limited knowledge of what appealed to him.

His weight shifted, and his other leg pushed between hers. The broad head of his cock painted trails up and down the length of her seam. The teasing was too much, and Ani pressed down until the top curve was nestled between her nether lips.

It wasn't enough. She tore her mouth from his. "I need you, Baroo. Now. Please."

His hands circled her hips and lifted to position her. Before she could ask again, his cock was deep inside her.

The sensations were so striking, Ani couldn't identify any given one clearly. She was full—from the curls teasing her seam to the crown nestled inside her—stretched tight around his girth. There was a throbbing pain, a matching pleasure radiating up her abdomen and down her thighs, and the delight of his fingers massaging the curve of her ass.

"So beautiful," he breathed. "So perfect."

Ani moved her hips, pressing her buttocks down into his grip, massaging her inner channel with the length of his cock.

"Oh...definitely perfect." Again, he looked as if he meant to question her. Baroo didn't.

His hips slid back until only the head of his cock breached her. His forward move filled her even more fully than he had the first time. Ani moaned and arched into his hold. Her fingers curved in a purely instinctual move, driving her fingernails into Baroo's back.

From his groan, she guessed it was enjoyable to him. He moved again, withdrawing and thrusting deep. Her hands tightened, and he started moving faster.

In moments, he was driving hard into her. Ani pulled him deeper, only mildly aware of the fact that she was drawing blood on Baroo in the process. If his sounds were any indication, she had no reason for concern.

The sensation of the knot being pulled tight inside her returned, and she prayed for forbearance to the Goddess Mother. When she'd climaxed to Baroo's hand, Ani had nearly fainted in pleasure. This was faster, hotter, and Ani was certain it would shatter her into pieces.

The sensation of release was powerful and breath stealing. Her mind muddled, Ani couldn't say when her gasping breaths turned to screams and pleas for more. One moment, she was unable to fill her aching lungs...or perhaps trying to overfill the same. The next, her sounds were echoing off the chamber walls.

Baroo lodged his cock deep inside her, and he joined in Ani's sharp sounds. The heat of his seed shocked her into another spate of vocalizations she couldn't name. The world around them went hazy and indistinct, and she held to Baroo as the only sure thing she could attest to.

Clarity came back a little at a time. The first thing that made sense to her was Baroo. His hands stroked at her hair, and his voice feathered against her lips, soothing sounds that she couldn't properly put meaning to.

Ani opened her eyes, staring up at him, stunned. Syth had told her how enjoyable bedding could be, but she'd believed he was exaggerating to put her at ease. She was glad he hadn't lied about it.

* * * *

It was difficult to tell if Ani was happy about what had happened between them or not. Of course, Baroo knew she'd enjoyed the act, but her shock attested that something had caught her unaware.

"Are you well, Ani?" he asked gently.

She gasped out a weak little "yes," and aftershocks massaged Baroo's still-erect cock.

Before he could rein himself, he was pushing deeper inside her, reveling in her body's reaction.

Ani's fingernails bit in hard, leaving new tracks on his back. Raga, but that was good.

It was something of sacrilege to think of the Goddess Mother by her name when she was embodied in Ani, her essence split between the Stone and the woman. It was appropriate to defer to the Walking Goddess, but reconciling that was difficult for Baroo. On one hand, it was hard to think of Ani as anything but the sensual woman he desired so much. On the other, there was no denying that he was lying sheathed in a goddess. What else could one call this enticing woman?

Ani pressed kisses to his chest and throat, making his cock ache to continue.

"Are you certain?" he asked, breaking his own counsel.

She is fertile. With any amount of agreement on her part, Baroo would be inside her every moment day and night she was willing, training be damned. Not even Syth would drag Baroo from Ani's bed for training, if the Young Mother proved agreeable to conceiving her first child.

My child! All her children would be Baroo's, if he had any influence in it.

Her breath puffed into his ear, and she nibbled at the lobe. "Sure of you."

"Sure enough to carry my child?" It was probably already too late to avoid that outcome, but he wanted to hear it. If Ani said she was willing to carry for him, he'd last all night, at least.

"Yes. Your child. Our child. Raga's child." Her voice was a temptation, and her body heated around his length.

"Mine. Ours." He pushed away the sacrilegious thought that Raga had nothing to do with what was between himself and Ani. He would see Ani's face when he looked at his children, not the Goddess's.

Baroo rose, lifting Ani onto the column of his cock, her legs spread around his hips. She shivered in what her body's reactions said was delight. Little gasps bathed his throat in heat, and her nipples pulled at the hair on his chest.

They thrust against each other, a hard grinding that forced his cock as deep as it would go. There was no withdrawal, as if both of them wanted the feeling of him lodged in for an extended stay.

Her sounds were sweet and low, and her hands closed on his shoulders. Ani tested the feel of moving over him, faster and slower, but always deep.

Ani's eyes slid shut, and her head rocked back on her slender throat. Baroo bit back his release, forcing himself not to climax at the early contractions of her muscles around him. When her body released, so did his, in hard wracking spasms and a flood of cum.

"Mine," he repeated. Ani was his and no one else's.

"Only yours," she assured him.

That quickly, he was ready again.

* * * *

Baroo opened his eyes, smiling at the sight of Ani. After their third joining, she'd fallen asleep, his cock snug inside her. Duty had demanded he let her recover from their passion when his cock had screamed and pounded at his nerves for more.

Hours later, her body was a pleasant blanket. Though the urge to wake her for more was insistent, the comfort of her body pressed to his and the sealing they'd accomplished after she'd promised to be his were enough to stay his hand.

Then again, considering the fact that his hand was currently curved around her delectable little ass, why would he want to move it? That thought in mind, he laid his head back and let his eyes close.

But sleep wouldn't come. His nerves were on edge. Baroo slid from beneath Ani, needing to be prepared, though he had no idea what he should be prepared for. He pulled the furs over her and stroked a finger across her amulet, promising his protection silently.

Back on his feet, Baroo retrieved his sacred weapon, moved to her work room on silent feet, and looked around for some sign of danger. He cursed himself as ten types of fool. Syth was near and protecting their sleeping backs. He would have one of the other *Krieger* with him. What could pose a danger to three *Krieger*?

Still, he was uneasy for a reason he couldn't name. Baroo donned his wrap and sheathed the weapon. Edgy and battle-ready, he returned to Ani.

Baroo couldn't name the feeling at his back, but it set off warnings in his skull so intense, he whirled that direction, his sacred weapon out. It sliced a line across Pol's chest, shocking Baroo.

28

Goddess Mother, I have killed him. Pol must have felt the same warning and come to protect them. He must have been the one aiding Syth that night.

Baroo opened his mouth to curse vehemently, then snapped it shut at the sight of the black blood, coursing down his former brother's chest. The smell of it was akin to death and sickness instead of the copper tang of human blood.

He is no longer human. Was this what the beasts were?

Pol smiled a fang heavy smile, answering that question, and disappeared into a fine smoke before Baroo could take a killing blow.

"Traitors be damned. Syth!"

Ani came awake with a start at the shout, scrambled to the head of the bed, and pressed the furs to her chest. Her face went dark, and she coughed harshly, most likely at the smell. Her eyes blinked and teared up, reinforcing the determination.

In the blink of an eye, Pol was back...along with Reg and Nul. A heartbeat behind their arrival, Syth and Ori rushed in from the work room archway.

The three beasts ignored Baroo for a moment and focused on Ori. Reg smiled, baring the inhuman fangs that proved he was the young beast Veriel now, just as Syth had imparted to them in training.

"The gelded fool," Veriel greeted Ori.

"The traitor coward," he returned the greeting.

"Close your eyes, Raga," Syth ordered. "A woman should not see what is about to happen here."

Out of the corner of his eye, Baroo saw Ani bury herself beneath the furs.

That accomplished, the Stone lord turned to Pol. "Name which god damned you."

He didn't smile at that. "He gifted me, and my god is Lorian."

"He poured a portion of his unclean soul into your empty one, and you accepted it. Believe me, you are damned as no other ever will be."

"He made me a god," Pol insisted. His gaze shifted to the lump of shivering woman on the bed. "And now I will take what was intended for me."

"Raga chose me," Baroo snapped at him. *Ani chose me. None of them will touch her.*

Ori laughed shortly. "As young Veriel lost to me, but the second never sees it that way, I suppose."

"Second?" What was Ori talking about?

"There are always two to vie for Raga's attentions. I was watching for Pol to go traitor after he failed with Raga. I saw him meet with the traitors and returned here to warn Syth."

Baroo glared at Pol. He'd been so poor a loser he'd turned traitor? Baroo would have sworn he knew Pol better than that, until this moment.

The beast in question didn't seem troubled by his betrayals. He tipped his head and raised clawed hands, signaling a test of skills to follow.

Syth cocked his head to one side, as if considering something of great importance. "You all want a turn with her?"

Baroo stifled the urge to crack the hilt of his sacred weapon off Syth's skull for saying something so foul in front of Ani. He listened for a whimper from her that didn't come.

The Stone lord continued in a cold tone. "Which first?"

Lorian and Veriel answered in the affirmative together. The two glared at each other.

Baroo bit back a smile at Syth's handling. He was pitting the beasts against each other.

Syth wasn't finished yet. "And why exactly is Draden here? As I recall, he was never Raga-chosen to seek Her vessel's attentions."

Lorian glared at the aforementioned beast, then at Veriel. It was clear he agreed with that sentiment but hadn't been given a choice. "Sacrifices must be made to reach goals," he offered coolly.

"You want to gut him." Syth took a step toward the line of beasts. "They want to gut you, as well. And Veriel will...once he has used you to fight us. He will gut you both and leave you to die."

Lorian opened his mouth to protest, but Syth wasn't done yet.

"You were not the first Raga-chosen, Lorian. You think Veriel has not already convinced himself that you have no right to bed with Raga? You think he really plans to share her with you?" He made a mocking sound.

Veriel's eyes narrowed in warning.

"Did I ruin your surprise for them, Veriel?"

Baroo let his grin show. It would only infuriate them to see it.

Veriel's look promised death. "Remember what the gods promised. Help me kill the *Krieger*, and the world is ours."

"And Raga?" Lorian asked.

There was a moment of silence. "We take her together."

That prompted a whimper of fear from Ani, and Baroo felt his fury like a bonfire. He would have thought it was a trick of the mind, had he not felt similar reactions emanating from both Syth and Ori.

There was no time for Baroo to state his intention to kill them. In the next moment, all three *Krieger* were engaged in battle. Predictably, each singled out what he saw as his worst enemy. Draden attacked Syth, Veriel went for Ori, and Baroo found himself engaged with Lorian.

Baroo wasn't certain if Lorian suffered from being new to his damnation or was overconfident in his fighting style. Either way, the beast was impaled on Baroo's blade in a matter of heartbeats.

It wasn't enough. He shook the beast free and turned, burying his weapon into Veriel's heart through his back, smiling at the crunch of bone on metal.

Baroo looked up, meeting Ori's gaze over the beast's shoulder. It was only then that he realized the other *Krieger* had taken a matching blow to the chest. There was no saying who the kill belonged to.

It does not matter. There is still one alive.

Or not...

Baroo didn't need to see Syth strike the blow to know Draden was dead on the Stone lord's blade.

* * * *

Ani shivered in the stillness. Though she prayed the *Krieger* had defeated the beasts, there was no way to know.

Unless I look.

But Syth had told her not to look at the battle.

There is no battle. It is finished. And she had no idea if Baroo had survived it.

Her heart ached at the thought. She had no idea if her love was alive or dead. A scream built in her throat, and she threw the fur back, needing to see him alive.

Three *Krieger* heads turned toward her, and she sobbed in relief at the sight of Baroo. He lived! As long as he lived, all was right with the world.

Their eyes widened, and Ani looked down at herself, gasping at her nudity. Though Baroo and Syth had seen her unclothed, Ori never had. She pulled the furs up to her shoulders, glancing his way shyly.

Slowly, patiently...Ori withdrew his blade and cleaned it on Reg's clothing. He sheathed it, bowed his head to her, and then averted his eyes.

"A part of me will always love you, Raga, but I cannot be the man you need, either as Raga or as Ani. I know this for a fact. I withdraw to the far reaches of our territory. May you have many strong sons with your chosen."

Words stuck in her throat, and Ani forced them out. "May you find someone that brings you peace."

A weak smile pulled up at his lips. "If you say it will be so, I believe."

With that, he turned to Baroo and offered his hand. "You are worthy of her, brother. Your sons will be great warriors that even the traitor gods cannot stand against."

Baroo took it in a *Krieger's* greeting. "Have no mercy on them, and may we fight together again."

"I will hold you to that."

In the next instant, Ori was gone without a backward glance. Baroo shifted from foot to foot, his gaze moving from the downed beasts to Ani to Syth.

Her brother smiled. "Take her to the bathing chamber, and wash away the blood of battle and of lovemaking. The others and I will dispose of the beasts."

Baroo started to lift Ani from the bed, still wrapped in the furs. "My thanks."

"Baroo?"

He hesitated and looked over his shoulder at Syth. "Yes?"

"Do not appear for more than food or bathing until my sister is well past high cycle and bearing your son."

Ani's move to protest such an order died at Baroo's lips meshing with hers. He drew back, laughing darkly.

She shot Syth a warning look. "I believe we will. I also believe we will lie to you about when I leave high cycle. You deserve no better."

If her words angered or embarrassed her brother, he showed no sign of it. His laughter followed them out of the chamber and down the corridor.

Starting A War

Note from Brenna:

Thousands of years before "Crossbearer Turned," Raga was handled in a very different manner. Was it better or worse? Who but the gods can say?

Happy reading!
Brenna Lyons

"Ragan?" her brother asked, looking up from the weapon he was sharpening. Gatin's eyes narrowed, and he focused on the hands clenched in her dress.

"It is time." Her body burned, opining that it was more than time. She'd tarried, fearing what she knew she had to do.

His brow furrowed, his jaw tightened, and he grunted his agreement. "I will assemble them."

She took her leave with a tip of her head to him, rushing to her bed and the momentary safety of it.

It would only be a short reprieve. Before the sun set again, Ragan would be on that bed, spread wide for the thrusts of one of the men. The thought of it heated her woman's sex and chilled her blood at the same time.

Enough. I was born to this, gods-chosen to carry his seed. Whoever he is...

Ragan had picked the two secretly, months earlier. She'd thought choosing the two would be difficult, but as prophesized, only two had called to her and drawn her eyes.

The men hadn't been told which two she'd chosen, or even that she'd done so. She'd watched them, hidden by a drape at Gatin's side.

Only Gatin knew that she'd chosen and who she had. He'd waited for Ragan to request the proving, patiently allowing her to come to acceptance of the fact that her body would cease to be her own when the victor claimed her.

The ceremonial gown was of the lightest material she'd ever seen. It hid nothing. Her beaded nipples and woman's curls were nearly as clear as if she stood nude. The dampness from her core made the material it touched clear instead of opaque, showcasing the blood mark on the front of her thigh.

That was what proved she belonged to the victor to come. As if in confirmation, the blood mark throbbed in time with her heart and sheath.

Gatin's voice sent a shiver down her spine. "Ragan? They are here."

"A moment." She tied the ceremonial sash around her eyes, a symbol of her acceptance of the gods' will in her mating. "Come, Gatin."

The drape whispered, announcing his approach. Her brother took her hand, guiding Ragan through the drape and down the corridor to the training room.

She held her breath, letting it out on a rush at the sound of the tandem gasps of surprise. They'd seen her. Now they would fight for her...perhaps to the death.

* * * *

Oren forced a breath, his heart hammering in excitement. He'd assumed Gatin had called them to offer further instruction, not to fight for the Mother Warrior.

They hadn't seen Ragan since she'd been a child of four. From the moment the eldest Warrior, save her brother, had reached fourteen, Gatin's sister had been sequestered in the belief that the Warriors would kill each other to possess her.

A slow perusal of her nearly naked body confirmed that. No wonder she'd been sequestered. Even in the heavy gowns most women wore, she would be stunning. Oren didn't doubt he'd have killed for her then, let alone now.

Gatin's voice boomed out. "The gods call to Ragan to seek the mate intended for her. She has called to both of you. By the right of combat shall the will of the gods for Ragan be decided."

Oren shot a sideward glance at Piet. They were close in strength and prowess. It would be a hard fight, but Oren had no intentions of losing it.

Then again, neither will Piet. Oren glanced at Ragan out of the corner of his eyes, his cock coming to aching readiness. Gods, but the woman had a body any man, human or Warrior, would kill for.

And we might. If the loser didn't lose consciousness before he'd suffered enough damage to kill him, the victor would be the only one left alive.

If I lose, grant me death. Something told Oren he'd want her for the rest of his life, even if Ragan wasn't his to touch.

I will not lose her. She will be mine and only mine.

Gatin's voice drew him back to the present challenge. "Draw your weapons and take your places," he ordered.

Ragan shivered at that pronouncement. Her spine stiffened, as if she was preparing herself for the battle she wouldn't see.

It was a kindness that her eyes were covered. A lady shouldn't have to see two men tear each other to pieces, Mother Warrior or not.

It also insured she could show no preference between the combatants. Moreover, she couldn't sway the fight by calling out warnings to one or both of them. Since the gods had called Ragan to both of them, her urge to do so would be fierce.

Gatin stepped in front of his sister, drawing his weapon. If either of the combatants approached Ragan before the decision was made, Gatin would cut him down and give his sister to the other.

Oren focused on Piet, just as Gatin ordered them to fight the gods' duel.

Piet came at him hard, and Oren blocked blow after blow. Ten passes in, neither of them had made inroads toward a win.

With each clang of metal on metal, Ragan winced. Her shivering became more pronounced, until she pressed to Gatin's back, seeking the solace her brother offered.

The master trainer didn't relax his stance, but his lips moved, most likely in calming words for her. Something about it stoked Oren's *Blutjagd*. Gatin wasn't a rival male, but he *was* a male protecting the woman Oren wanted for his own. It was intolerable.

He lunged toward Piet, intent on killing him, if that's what it took to claim Ragan as his own. His younger Warrior brother faltered, attacked, then faltered again. Oren didn't question the reason for it. There was nothing in his style that Piet would recognize, nothing that would give clues to what Oren intended to do next.

Where the change came from, even Oren couldn't say for sure. The mark of Ori burned hot on his skin, seemingly answering that it was called the gods' duel for a reason. Ragan would be mate to the victor, but on another level, the god whose mark the Warrior victor carried would lay with the Goddess Mother whose mark Ragan did.

Perhaps the fire is Ori's fury? It was possible. The whims of the gods were not Oren's to decipher.

Sweat broke out on his skin as he moved faster, striking blow after blow. Piet held his own for a time, but his fire was inferior to Oren's.

It took three slices of Oren's blade, before he managed to rein in the *Blutjagd* enough to let Piet fall. He took two steps back, glaring at the younger, daring him to rise and die like a man.

Piet seemed prepared to do so. With his blood pouring onto the floor, he planted a hand to push himself up. Oren tensed to kill him...then relaxed as consciousness fled Piet's body, and he slumped to the floor.

Oren turned to Gatin, surprised to see the master trainer raising his blade in warning. For a moment, Oren worked at that. He'd won the gods' duel. He wasn't supposed to fight Gatin for his mate, as well.

A jerk of Gatin's head to one side had Oren's face burning in understanding. He looked down at himself, miserably noting the bloodstained hands and weapon, the splatters of the same on his clothing.

A Warrior mate should never see such things. Guiltily, he admitted he'd been so intent on her that he'd neglected her gentle nature.

I must not do so again. With a nod of thanks to Gatin, he went to the pots of water the master trainer had indicated.

Oren scrubbed his hands and arms, careful to remove every drop of Piet's blood. He stripped off his clothing, certain that Gatin would see it washed or replaced for him while Oren claimed his mate.

He tended to his weapon, lowered it to the table, then lifted it again. Oren couldn't state why he was taking his weapon with him, but he theorized it was the burn to protect his mate driving him to do so.

As an afterthought, he moved to the last clean pot and dumped it over his head, scrubbing at his skin. Ragan deserved the best he could offer, not a dirty, sweat-soaked man rutting on her. That accomplished, he turned to Gatin.

The master trainer sheathed his weapon, drawing Ragan to his side with a kiss on her uncovered chin. "Your mate, Ragan," he whispered.

Her shaking hand extended, and Oren folded it into his own. Something soft and completely at odds with his fighting fury lit in him, and Oren wondered at it.

Gatin motioned to the corridor he'd drawn her from. "The second chamber," he instructed. "Everything is prepared for you." With that, he withdrew to Piet's side, most likely to determine if the young Warrior would live or die.

Oren guided Ragan as he'd been directed, noting her shivering and her ragged breathing. "You have nothing to fear from me," he promised.

She nodded, but her trembling increased as they neared the chamber.

The sight of the fur strips laid over the bed had him hard in anticipation. He knew what was intended, of course. Oren imagined all the Warriors, save Gatin, had played at the scene with the women who sated their sexual fires, dreaming that the Mother Warrior would one day be his.

But those had been experienced women, and that had been a game. Ragan was an innocent, and she was frightened. To possess her body, he would have to seduce her mind and heart.

He trailed kisses from the sash to the tip of her chin, drinking in her gasp of surprise. "You fear what I mean to do," he noted.

She hesitated and then nodded.

"I will not harm you." Oren planted a lingering kiss at her throat. "Do you trust that is true?"

"Yes." It was more a breath than a word, and Oren smiled at that.

"There are things I must do," he soothed her.

Her muscles tightened down a notch. "I know."

"You will love them," he vowed.

Her head moved slightly, in what appeared to be a negative response.

Oren hung his weapon over the foot of the bed, then lowered her to the surface. Ragan positioned her body in the center, looking small and fragile.

She is fragile. In a moment of realization, he gleaned that the true test was not the test of blades, but rather the test of self-control to come.

He eased her arm up, wrapped one soft fur strip around it, and knotted it down loosely. He tied the other end to the far spindles of the headboard.

Ragan played her wrist against the fur, her nipples peaking against the fabric of her gown. After a moment, she extended her other arm for him.

Oren smiled, tying the fur on that side. Gods, she was going to look so good, spread for him this way.

She will look good, regardless.

It was time to make her love the restraints. Oren lowered his head, taking one perky nipple in his mouth. Ragan gasped in surprise, her arms tensing.

Her body rose against him, and a moan of delight left her lips.

He left that breast and moved to the other, his hunger sharpening at the way the gown went clear with the addition of his saliva. Ragan tipped her body, seeking his mouth with the unattended nipple.

Oren didn't hesitate. He let his hunger guide him, nearly maddened in the need to possess her fully, though he'd only just learned she was his. On that thought, he moved down her body, tasting her skin.

Ragan tried to spread her legs, but the dress was cut narrow, and she couldn't spread them more than shoulder-width.

He glanced at his weapon, a plan taking shape. "Do you trust that I will bring you pleasure, Ragan?"

"Yes." There was no hesitation that time.

"Be still and let me free you."

Her brow furrowed, but she nodded.

Oren slipped his weapon from the sheath, his mouth going dry. He licked his lips, then plunged the blade through the tight material between her thighs.

Ragan let out a little squeal of distress, and he answered with a soothing noise. Oren yanked the blade downward, cutting the dress from thigh to ankle. He returned his blade to the sheath, grasped the edges of the shredded fabric, and tore it to mid-breast.

She bit lightly at her lower lip, seemingly uncertain.

"Spread your legs and let me please you," Oren instructed.

Ragan did as he bid. Oren guided them wider, tying down the first...then the second. He took his time, surveying every fingerwidth of her lush body.

Oh yes! This is a gift from the gods and nothing less.

* * * *

Her mate settled on the bed between her ankles, and Ragan tensed. This was it...the moment her mother and brother had told her would come. His male rod would sheathe inside her, planting his seed deep.

Though she'd never seen or otherwise experienced the claiming, she knew she'd bleed as she did at her woman's time. Ragan only hoped the pain would be comparable to the cramping she felt then and not to the ripping pain of injury.

Fool! He will tear away my maiden's barrier. Of course it will hurt as any injury would.

His hair tickled at her thigh, and she jerked against the fur. The soft, warm stroke over her blood mark could only be his tongue. Ragan squeezed her eyes shut tight, drinking in every touch greedily.

He did touch...and taste. The victor moved inward, to the sensitive line of her inner thigh. Then he moved up, his lips and tongue exploring what was his by the right of combat and by the virtue of her blood mark.

His breath teased at the center of her body, and she arched up in shock. The anticipation was maddening. Would she feel his lips first? His tongue? His calloused fingers? Or his rod? Not knowing was torture.

His mouth came first, suckling gently at a fold of skin far to the front of her body. Pinpoints of color danced inside her closed eyelids, and she gasped.

She hadn't expected so much pleasure. They'd never told her she'd feel any at the claim, let alone blinding pleasure.

Ragan wanted to move against him, but the fur bonds prevented more than the smallest movements. It was both frustrating and invigorating. She was at his mercy, and he was playing her body like a fine instrument.

She wished she knew his name to spur him on, but it was tradition that she would not know the identity of her mate until the claiming was complete. Ragan cursed the sash preventing her from seeing him, even as her body heated at the idea that she was being so handled by an unknown man. There was something wickedly appealing in the possibility that it was either of the two.

He retreated, and she begged him to stay, shamelessly asking for more. A hum of male satisfaction vibrated against her slit, and she bowed up with a cry of need.

His tongue stroked and taunted, and she fought the fur strips all the harder. Her body tightened, reaching for something she couldn't name but suspected was the thrust of his rod into her conspicuously empty body.

That sensation didn't come, but another did. Sparks of pleasure flared into a bonfire. Her muscles burned then melted. Screams that she recognized as her own voice, anguished but not in pain, echoed off the stark stone walls. It was a formless begging for the one thing she needed above all else.

As if he could interpret her sounds and movements, her mate pulled back then returned, his rough fingers spreading her tender folds for the thrust of his rod.

For a hand of heartbeats, they were both still and silent. Her body rioted in sensation.

Pain... It was excruciating but so overpowered by other feelings she couldn't properly determine how much it hurt or how to react to it.

Stretching... The fullness of his rod touched Ragan in places she hadn't realized existed until that moment. She wanted to feel more of it, to feel all of him. For reasons she couldn't name, she knew he wasn't seated fully yet.

Pleasure... The bonfire still burned and sparked. The muscles of her sheath surrounding his length undulated, bringing whispers of new pleasures with them.

Ragan forced her hips up with a scream, seeking his full length. She babbled words intended to be pleas for more but that might not have communicated her wishes. In her scattered state, they might have told him nothing.

As if belying that, he seated himself deeper.

Her breathing went ragged, until she feared she might collapse in a faint. Her hips rose and fell, forcing him in and out fingerwidths.

"Yes," he urged her. "Take what you need from me, Ragan. Give me all of yourself."

She would have thought such a thing impossible hours earlier. She wasn't supposed to give herself to him; the victor was supposed to claim her. Her body would cease to be her own and become his to play at.

Realization heated her blood. Her body *was* his to play at, but not because he'd taken it by force, as she'd always believed he would. Her mate had brought her to such pleasure that she'd willingly conceded to him, that she'd begged him to take her body.

Ragan thrust her hips up, pulling at the bonds. Her mate growled out a curse, wrapping his big hands around her waist, supporting her weight to allow her to move with ease.

"Come again for me, Ragan. Come again, and I will do as you wish."

She wasn't certain what he meant, but she sought the rhythm her body set, gasping at the buck of his rod within her. Was she pleasing him with her movements?

A moan from him answered that. "Oh, yes," he breathed. "You are so close."

Knowing she had the power to affect him as he affected her was a heady drug on her already affected senses. Ragan moved faster, taking him as deep as the bonds and his hands allowed.

Her breathing turned to ragged gasps and then to little sounds she had no name for.

"Come to me, Ragan. Come for me."

The tightening in her belly gave way to a drumbeat of pleasure. She screamed, her body shattering into disjointed sensations.

One of them was the heat coursing into her. *His heat. His seed.* She moaned at the feeling of rightness about that.

"You are mine, Ragan," he growled.

Her inner muscles tightened in pleasure at the truth of that statement. "Yes. Yours. Only yours."

He leaned over her, untying the sash that covered her eyes. The material slid away, and Ragan blinked her eyes in the sudden brightness of the chamber.

His face took shape slowly, and her heart stuttered in excitement. "Oren." She hadn't thought she had a preference, but her heart called her a liar. From the moment she'd sighted the two men and identified them to Gatin, Ragan had hoped Oren would be the victor.

* * * *

Her smile warmed his heart.

A fierce jealousy followed. Would she have smiled thus for Piet, had the younger man been the victor?

Oren slid back and thrust into her, staking his claim. The fierce need to have her see his face as he claimed her drove him on.

He reached to release her hands, wanting to feel her touch as he drove into her.

"No."

Oren met her gaze, wondering at her refusal.

"This way first," she requested.

He started to question that, his voice dying off at the cycling of her hips against him. Gods, but he'd nearly shot off when she'd taken him this way blind. Now she was doing it with full knowledge of whose cock pierced her, and it was twice the thrill.

"Say it again, Ragan," he grumbled.

"Say..." She gasped, riding his cock.

"Say you are mine," he ordered.

"Yes. Yours. Oren, please."

His name on her lips broke the last of his tenuous control. Oren thrust hard and fast, fascinated by the sweet expressions and sounds Ragan vented.

The explosion of climax rolled into the sweet caress of the seal of printing. Oren went still...deep inside her, groaning at her swiveling hips.

Mindful of her needs, he eased out of her. Blood mixed with their fluids flowed out of her body, staining the ceremonial dress. Oren spread her slit, rapt on the sight of the proof of his claim pooling on the linens.

Ragan moaned, tipping her hips. "Oren?"

"Gods, but you're beautiful." How he managed to form the words was a mystery to him.

She raised her head, performing a silent assessment of him.

"Have you seen a man before?" he asked.

Her cheeks darkened to an enticing red. "I have seen the men stripped to their bathing cloths."

"Unclothed?" he asked.

"Only Gatin...when I was young."

Oren smiled at that. "Before he had a man's body," he guessed.

She nodded.

He reached across her, releasing the first of the fur restraints. Ragan stared at him, questioning the move with narrowed eyes.

"I will hang the ceremonial gown in announcement. Then I will take you to the heated springs." He licked his lips at the idea, and she shivered in seeming delight. "We will touch, Ragan. We will taste. You will come to know my body, as you will know no other man's."

"Only yours," she gasped.

* * * *

Ragan panted in intense pleasure, her hands tightening against Oren's shoulders. It had been three days of decadence, and still it showed no signs of stopping.

The Stone, in its wisdom, had called her to claiming at high cycle, as it called all Raga to claiming at their time. Oren would not leave her bed until she'd passed the moon phase and carried his son.

He stirred the heat inside her in long, slow glides of his cock. She shivered at the word. Oren had been diligent in stoking her fire, as well as in her education in the delicate delights of love.

"Oren!"

She startled at the sound of her brother's voice, and Oren pulled her to his chest, shielding her body from the doorway behind the shelter of his own. Her mind numbly processed that Warriors always protected their mates in the shelter of their bodies, even in battle.

"What is it?" he growled back.

"It has happened. We need you."

Ragan wondered at the tightening of Oren's muscles, but she didn't have time to question it.

He set her off his body with a series of grumbled curses. Oren panned his gaze up her body, his eyes hot in promise. "Dress, Ragan."

The order stunned her. Until her high cycle passed, neither of them would dress. "But–"

He silenced her with a kiss. "Quickly, now. Do not remove your amulet, for any reason. Do not leave our chambers. Promise me."

Oren was her mate, and his only concerns would be for her safety. Were they under attack? Who could be so foolish?

"Ragan," he reminded her.

"Yes. I promise, Oren."

He brushed another kiss against her lips and launched through the drape, his sacred weapon in hand. He was nude, but since he had no clothing in their chamber, she suspected Gatin meant to offer the use of some of his own.

Ragan stared after him, her heart pounding, though she couldn't say why it was. The chamber suddenly felt empty...too empty.

She went to the chest Gatin had given her when she'd gone into seclusion, pulling out her mother's best gown. *I have better,* a niggling corner of her mind reminded her. But there was something comforting in her mother's gowns, and she desperately wanted comfort now.

Dressed, she looked about for something to do. Her hands were shaking too wildly to work her loom with precision.

I should make something for Oren. She'd avoided it, until the claiming was complete, afraid that whatever she worked at would prove a poor match for the temperament of the victor.

I don't have to weave it now. I can make plans for what I will weave. That in mind, she went to the loom and considered what she knew of Oren.

The fires of the gods burned hot in him. That was no surprise, considering he wore the mark of Ori. But he wasn't hot-tempered. She dismissed the rougher fabrics and darker colors that simply.

The memory of his hands, calloused but so tender against her skin, kindled the doused fire in her well-used body. It would have to be a soft material, both in color and weave. She searched out her best, smiling at the plans taking shape in her mind.

The sound behind her warmed her heart. She'd known Oren would return to her as quickly as he was able to. Ragan turned, her smile fading and her blood cooling at the sight of two of the other Warriors.

Piet and Tral stood between her and the drape to freedom. Anywhere else she ran would be further into the underground corridors of her home.

And further from Oren and Gatin. No, she had to stand her ground or make her way toward the training areas and the village beyond.

Oren made me promise to stay here. She swallowed hard. She would have to try to hold her ground.

Regan didn't question them. With her heart pounding in her throat, she wasn't certain she could form words if she attempted it.

"Lady Ragan," Piet offered smoothly.

Despite her promise to stand her ground, she took a step back. There was something cold and calculating in his look.

They invaded my chambers! Only Gatin and Oren were permitted here.

Ragan might have argued to herself that Gatin and Oren sent them to protect her, but she knew it for a lie. If anyone was left behind to protect her, it would be one or both of the aforementioned men in her life.

They mean to claim me for their own...or fight a new gods' duel in mockery of the first. Gatin had always told her the Warriors would kill each other for her if she didn't remain sequestered. Now Piet had seen her. Likely, he'd told Tral about her attributes.

Why had the men been so inflamed by seeing her in the ceremonial dress? Surely, a simple announcement that they were to fight for her would have sufficed. Or she could have been presented in clothing that didn't bare her so completely.

Why had the loser of the match not been immediately killed? Had it never occurred to them that a man enflamed to attempt murder for a woman would not submit to defeat so simply?

Piet took another step toward her, and Ragan ran aground on her loom.

"Why so frightened, Ragan?" he purred.

She grasped at anything she could use against him. "Oren will kill you this time. If you touch me, he will–"

His smile went wide and mocking. "I will do so much more than touch."

Her stomach lurched at the idea. If he forced himself on her, whose seed would plant? What would

Oren do, if he wasn't certain he was the father of the child she carried after this night?

Ragan raged at it. *How did they get past Oren and Gatin, in the first place?*

Piet continued. "First me. Then Tral. You belong to all of us, Ragan. That is the way of it."

She shook her head, woozy at the concept. She didn't. Gatin had assured her she was intended for only the strongest...only the master hunter among the Warriors. Why would her brother lie about such a thing?

He wouldn't! She knew Gatin would never submit her to something so foul.

Piet made a move to pull her to him, and she swung the shuttle in her hand. He moved, of course. He was a Cursed Warrior. She was simply a gods-chosen woman. Instead of the shuttle connecting with his face, her wrist did.

The shove didn't come from him. Invisible hands forced her backward. The loom splintered against the stone wall, fouling the work on it and tangling Ragan in the threads.

She looked up, gaping at the sight of Piet pulling himself back to his feet, across the chamber from her. So he had been thrown, too?

But why? Had the gods protected her? She'd never heard of so outward a sign of their will.

The amulet! Oren told me not to remove my amulet. The amulet was bathed in the Stone's glow of power. But the amulet didn't react in such a way to Oren and Gatin.

Perhaps it would only react to one who meant her harm. The gods would know such intent.

Her examination of the events came to a crashing halt when Piet let loose a bellow of rage and ran for her. Tral stood his ground, one eyebrow raised as if in amusement at what Piet was attempting.

Ragan fought the threads, grumbling complaints when they pulled at her, slowing her attempts to escape him.

A battle cry brought her head up. Oren appeared from nowhere, the drape swinging in his wake. In the time it took Piet to pivot toward him, her mate's sacred weapon was planted in the center of his opponent's chest.

Gatin was beside him in the blink of an eye. Tral moved to flee further into the keep, but he made it only a step. Oren swept Gatin's spare weapon from its sheath and threw it, planting it as neatly in Tral's chest as he'd planted his own in Piet's. Both slain Warriors fell.

Ragan opened her mouth to ask for Oren's help in freeing herself, but the stench hit her solidly. She'd never smelled something so foul. The gorge rose in her throat, pushed up by her gagging.

In the next instant, Oren was there, gathering her to his chest. Gatin cut the tangled mess of threads free, releasing her to wrap herself around him.

"The rest have fled," Gatin whispered.

Oren sighed. "Three dead then. That leaves us with three to kill."

Ragan shuddered at that. There were six who'd intended to rut on her?

"All on your blades," Gatin replied in seeming awe.

A movement drew Ragan's eyes to her brother. To her shock, he knelt on the floor, his head lowered in submission to Oren. Before she could question it, he spoke.

"I greet you, Oren Elder Killer. You are indeed a most worthy mate to Raga."

Ragan's head spun. *Elder? What is an elder?*

Her gaze strayed to the dead Warriors and the thick, black blood that oozed from their wounds. *They aren't Warriors anymore. What are they?*

Blutjagdfrau Lost

Chapter One

Rajicorin ran, leaving the new Beasts far behind. A roar of her name sent her stumbling into the bushes at the bend in the trail. She pushed up and set off again, sobbing in the realization that Jotem's voice had become something to fear.

"Raji! Come back to me!"

To a Beast? To the King of Beasts?

The sky before her lightened to bands of pink and orange, promising safety. *Safe enough to find Goven.* Beasts couldn't walk the day. Goven had told her as much when he'd foreseen this day.

He hadn't foreseen Jotem turning against us. He is the strongest. We are surely lost.

Not yet. There is still our young one. He will be his father's downfall.

It was a meager consolation at best.

"Raji!"

Rajicorin. I will never use the name Raji again.

"Do not make me chase you, Raji," he warned. Jotem was closer, clearly chasing her already. "Raji, do not do this!"

Under other circumstances, she'd say he was panicked, but not now. *Why didn't he refuse?* True, the others had held a blade to her throat, but they hadn't dared kill her.

Or had they? Stealing her from Jotem's bed carried a sentence of death. Threatening her life certainly did. The rogues had nothing worse to fear by following through, she supposed.

"I will find you, Raji. I will find you."

Tears burned at her eyes. Now that he was a Beast, nothing would stop Jotem.

If I stay here. Every word of her training said she should seek her brother Goven's protection.

Something more insistent whispered to her. *{Go. Run. As far as you can.}*

Rajicorin blinked in the first rays of the rising sun, her lungs straining to keep up the pace, though Jotem couldn't continue his pursuit until sundown. The fork in the trail was only moments away.

Right. A right turn would take her to the huts that made up their village and the safety of Goven's arms.

{Left. If you wish to live to hold your son, go left.}

Right. Go to Goven and safety.

{Left, Rajicorin. Nowhere is safe that is within reach of the Beasts.}

Goven—

{Stay and you will be dead in less than two moons.}

Raji stroked a hand over her growing womb. If she left, she would have nothing but the clothing on her back.

{And your amulet.}

If the stories Goven told were correct—and Rajicorin didn't doubt her bother—the amulet would keep the Beasts from tracking her.

The foreign voice continued. *{You also have the sacred weapon you took from the ground.}*

Jotem's blade. Rajicorin clenched the hilt in her sweat-soaked hand. She'd nearly forgotten she'd taken it when she ran. Over the years, Rajicorin had learned more than a little about using it, but she didn't doubt she was no match for what was coming for her.

{Left!}

That trail was less used, and she skidded on the loose stones. They drew blood on one knee. Rajicorin ignored it, scrambled to her feet, and forged on.

{The river. They cannot track you if you swim.}

Questioning the voice didn't occur to her. It was reasonable, calming...

Rajicorin plunged in and paddled to the middle, where the water moved fast. There was no roughland for a quarter day's walk. If she stayed in nearly that long, it would be unlikely anyone could track her.

In less than half the time it would have taken her to walk the distance, Rajicorin emerged far downstream and on the opposite bank. She rested there for only a moment. Then she hid the signs of her escape and headed into the thick trees.

* * * *

People. Rajicorin watched the group from the safety of the trees.

She'd never seen such a mixture before. Some wore animal skins. Others wore wovens. Still others, like herself, wore a mixture of both, but none in the style she wore, of course. Her clothing alone would mark her village, if anyone in this group was familiar with her kind.

Rajicorin shook away the shaft of fear that thought engendered and focused on them again.

There were babes carried in slings, in backpacks, and in parents' arms. Some of the young were clothed in bits of cloth or fur. Others were naked. Likewise, the adults wore varying amounts of clothing from women with only waist wraps to women clothed to their ankles and wrists.

There were a few hide shelters like the Warriors would use when traveling. Only body-lengths away, there were stick shelters. Then simple tarp roofs over open camp sites. Behind them, she spied people moving in and out of caves.

Refugees from the battles. There was no other explanation for such a diverse mixture.

A twinge of regret settled in her chest. Somewhere, more than a moon of walking behind her, Goven and the other Warriors were fighting those battles. *And fighting the Beasts.*

When Rajicorin had followed the voice of her protector, she hadn't considered what Goven would think. How long had it taken her to lament leaving without word to her brother? A quarter moon? Half?

By now, Goven probably believed her dead. Did he believe she'd been killed by the new Beasts? Perhaps drowned in the river?

There was no way to know unless she went back, and since the voice had not led her astray yet, Rajicorin trusted that going back to her village would be disastrous.

{Go to them.}

To the Warriors? Why now? Why bring her all this way to—

{Go to the group below.}

Her heart pounded in terror. These people had seen battle, and she was a stranger. They might kill her on sight.

{Go, Rajicorin. Go to them.}

She rose on shaking legs. *She has never caused me harm, never led me astray.* Rajicorin repeated it to herself as she picked her way down the hillside.

A child sighted her first and ran for a group of adults, shouting in the language those to the south of the village used. The adults turned in her direction. The men rushed toward her, drawing their weapons. One of the women snatched up the child and retreated further into the group.

Rajicorin drew the sacred weapon, her opposite hand going to her son. They stopped short, and she backed away. If she could make it to the trees, she could disappear.

"Wait. Please, do not go." An ancient, stooped woman rushed toward her, waving the men back. She halted an arm's length away, and her gaze went to Rajicorin's womb.

"Zasha, come away," one of the men urged her.

She ignored him. "You fled the battles?"

Rajicorin nodded. She'd fled battles, but not the ones Zasha was referring to.

"You carry?" she continued.

"Yes. I do." Would they see that as a burden? Rajicorin prayed the worst she faced was being turned

59

out. She'd lived alone for a moon, but that would be much more difficult as her son grew larger.

Zasha approached. She stared at the weapon Rajicorin held. At last, she held out her hand. "Come. Warm yourself. Our goddess ensures your safety here."

Rajicorin hesitated and then lowered her weapon. "My thanks," she managed.

The men parted and let them pass. By their expressions, Rajicorin guessed they wished to offend their goddess rather than let her into their camp, but Zasha obviously had some measure of power in this society.

At the fire, Zasha offered a bowl of soup and flat bread. Rajicorin took them with a word of thanks. It was difficult to eat slowly, but she forced herself to do so. If she ate at the pace her stomach demanded, the others would surely know how weak she was.

And I would sick up all I manage to eat. Her son needed sustenance, not empty promises.

"Your weapon," Zasha began. "I have heard of such blades."

Rajicorin looked around, fearing an attack in the making. Her grip on the bread eased at the sincere interest. The men crouched, seemingly waiting for a story. She went back to the food. The old woman would get to her point in time.

"The blade is the type carried by a dark giant," Zasha informed her people. "I saw one when I was a child. He was tall as a hut and strong as a horse."

"You must be a great sorceress to have killed a dark giant and stolen his blade," another woman said.

Rajicorin swallowed a mouthful of bread and shook her head slowly. "The blade was my mate's. He is...was the strongest of the Warriors."

One of the men gaped at her. "You were the mate of a dark giant?"

The term aptly described Warriors. "Yes. He was a dark giant." *Darker now than he was before.*

Zasha reached out as if to touch Rajicorin's womb, then snatched her hand away. "You carry a dark giant's young one?"

"My son is a Warrior, as was his father before him." *What his father is now is of no concern to these simple people.*

"But a giant?" she pressed.

"Yes. A dark giant." Rajicorin hoped their silence was a good sign.

"Then you must be a sorceress," one of the women attested. "Everyone knows only a sorceress can bear a dark giant's young."

What? Before Rajicorin could question that belief, a man interrupted her.

He pointed to her. "She is. See there? She wears a magic amulet."

Rajicorin faltered, uncertain how to answer that. Proclaiming herself a magical creature could have unexpected results.

"Is the amulet magic?" Zasha asked.

{Tell them. What else would they believe the power to hide you from Beasts is?}

"Yes." A niggling fear worked its way up her spine. "In my hands, it is magic." It wasn't a lie. The amulet alone wasn't enough, and if they believed it only worked for Rajicorin, they might not try to kill her for it.

"My daughter suffers a fever, sorceress," one woman called out. She waved a half-grown girl toward Rajicorin. "Can you do something? Can you save her?"

Rajicorin set the nearly-empty bowl down and reached for the child. There was no question the cut on her arm was infected, causing the fever. Luckily, it could be treated.

"I must lower the fever and draw out the poison." She considered her words carefully. "I believe she can be saved without loss of her arm." *But it might come to that.*

The mother clasped her hands before her mouth, tears pooling in her eyes. One of the men wrapped an arm around her.

"I need someone with knowledge of plants," Rajicorin continued.

"I have such knowledge," Zasha offered. "I am Zasha, the healer of Mantagi tribe. What should we call you, sorceress?"

All of her titles and names stuck in Rajicorin's throat. Jotem and the other Beasts were searching for her. She had to leave all she could of her former life behind as quickly as possible.

"Sorceress?" Zasha prompted.

"I have enemies, Zasha." It was only right to tell them. "They will be searching for my name on the wind, spread by careless lips. For your own safety and that of my son, I must ask you to call me 'sorceress' and nothing more."

The stillness around her was so complete, Rajicorin felt certain they would cast her out without even letting her heal the young one.

Zasha nodded. "Names have the power to track and bind. I understand, sorceress. It will be as you wish."

"I must hide myself completely," Rajicorin admitted. "I will trade my services for a change of clothing to aid in that."

A gray-haired woman stepped toward Rajicorin from the crowd. "If you save my daughter's daughter, you will have all you require to hide yourself and protection within our tribe. As leader of Mantagi tribe, you have my solemn word in binding, sorceress."

"I will do all I can," Rajicorin promised. She turned to Zasha. "I will tell you which plants I need. In the meantime, I will need strips of leather, ash, honeycomb, and fresh water boiled."

"Now," the leader snapped.

Men scrambled to comply.

* * * *

"It is a boy," Zasha confirmed.

Rajicorin groaned in pain, weary from hours of labor. "What is his aspect? Show me."

Zasha placed her son in Rajicorin's hands, then eased the wrap from his chest, baring the blood mark.

"Kor." *Ah, my young cub.*

"Sorceress?" Zasha asked.

"His name is Korji, Zasha. The Goddess has decreed it. It means...the bear's paw."

She touched the blood mark with unsteady fingers. "You read the marks left by the gods."

The pain tore through Rajicorin, and she curled around her son. Zasha took Korji and laid him on a stack of furs she'd prepared for him while Rajicorin labored. The healer returned to check her progress.

It is simply the afterbirth. Just that. By the gods, Rajicorin had never realized it would hurt so much to pass that bit of nothing.

Zasha's gasp brought her head up, and Rajicorin started at the old healer. Her heart stammered at the pale face so intent on the waning labor.

Another pain belied that, and Rajicorin cried out in shock. "What is this, Zasha?" she pleaded.

"Another babe is descending."

Her heart stuttered at that pronouncement. *Another?* Was the second male or female?

Her protector was silent.

"If you wish to live to hold your son, go left."

Son. Singular. She would have said sons. The second is female. And I will not live to hold her.

Silence persisted between herself and what Rajicorin had always believed was the Stone. *Have I been misled all this time?*

"Sorceress? What ails you?"

"Prepare to leave here, Zasha." *Either way, it is the only safe course to take.*

"What are you saying?"

63

{Instruct her. Do it now. Hold nothing back.}

The contraction nearly doubled Rajicorin. She panted, pushing her daughter toward an unkind world stalking her already. When the pain eased, Rajicorin started talking.

"You must heed my words, Zasha. There is little time." A contraction silenced her. In the waning waves of agony, Rajicorin blurted out more. "I am dying, and you must be well away before that happens."

The old woman chuckled. "You are not dying, young one. Many women believe they are dying in the throes of the worst."

"And some do," Rajicorin snapped back at her. There was no time for arguments. Why couldn't Zasha see that?

Another pain ripped through her. There was no mistaking the warm flow of blood coursing down her thighs. *I will not live to hold her.*

Zasha faltered, her smile disappearing. "You know this to be true? It is certain?"

The words stuck in her throat, and Rajicorin ejected them with more than a little bitterness. "I was promised only time enough to hold my son. Not my daughter."

"It may be another boy," she dismissed the idea.

The pain was crippling, and Rajicorin struggled to talk through it. "The second young one is a girl. Her name is Ahdia."

Zasha started to protest, and Rajicorin waved her off.

"Pack quickly, and then I will tell you what you need to know."

Pain after pain crested and retreated, while Zasha gathered everything she could fit in her small cart together. At last she returned to Rajicorin's side.

"Time is short," she wheezed. "Listen closely. You must take the young toward the setting sun until you reach the river. Follow it upstream to the crossing place by the great forest."

"She is coming, sorceress. Please, attend to—"

"There is no time! Cross the forest to the village of the dark giants and seek one named Goven. He is leader of the village. If he does not live, find the one called Stone lord."

The next push widened the tears, and Rajicorin groaned, too tired to scream. "Say it," she begged. Breathing became difficult, and Rajicorin licked her dry lips.

"To the river, through the great forest...the cursed lands." She shuddered and then continued. "Find one named Goven or Stone lord. She is nearly here."

"I know. Hide the marks the young ones bear...especially my daughter's mark. At all costs, hide Ahdia's mark, until she is returned to my village. Let no one but Goven or the Stone lord see them. Tell him that the young ones need his protection now, show him the blade and amulet...and tell him my name."

Zasha looked up from between her spread legs, blood coating her to the elbows. "But, sorceress. I do not know your name. You cannot speak it."

"It may draw my enemies to me, I know. When the amulet leaves my body and goes to Ahdia, they will come anyway. That is why you must be far away tonight...before they come for my children."

"Tonight? But...the young ones—"

"Are safer moved tonight than here when the Beasts arrive. They are Warriors. They will survive the flight to Goven. My amulet will hide Ahdia from the traitors of my people; the amulet must never leave Ahdia's body. Never, or they find her.

"You must find my people, Zasha. The dark giants. Without me..." She screamed at the tearing sapping the last of her energy. "Korji will need them—the Warriors—to teach him. Ahdia will need them more. To protect—"

She screamed, feeling as if she was being cleaved in two by a sacred weapon. *Or a Beast's claws.* "Pro-

pro-tect her. Ahdia is most important. She must be protected, at all costs. At all times."

Zasha didn't question that. "One more push, sorceress."

"Rajicorin," she breathed. "My name is Rajicorin, Zasha. If they ask it as a test, my mate called me Raji." *Please, let that be enough to convince them.*

The pain came again, and Rajicorin bore down with a scream of agony. Silence fell, then shattered to the scream of one babe and then a second.

Rajicorin stared at the blood-soaked infant in Zasha's hands. "The amulet," she breathed. "Leave me...quickly now. Remember what I taught you."

If the gods were protecting them, they could be in the village and under Goven's protection within the season. If Zasha remembered and followed Rajicorin's directions, all would be well.

A tear slid down the healer's face. "No. You have labored the child alone while I prepared to flee. Let me care for you," Zasha pleaded.

"Take the amulet and weapon and go. Quickly, Zasha. They are coming. I feel them."

Zasha nodded and laid a kiss on Rajicorin's forehead. "As you wish. May your gods protect you and see you home to their shelter."

With that, Zasha was gone and the last vestiges of Rajicorin's Warrior life with her. She would be well away before the Beasts arrived to seek the child Rajicorin had delivered into the world.

Rajicorin pressed her hand to the empty space where her amulet had so recently lain. *It isn't mine anymore. Ahdia needs it now.*

The single horse moved away, and Rajicorin let her eyes slip shut to the waning fire. She dozed lightly, chilled. Though the night cold was biting, she hadn't asked for something to warm her. Zasha would need all the wraps she could carry for the task ahead.

Rajicorin woke once, noting the fire burning low.

Again...in near darkness and silence. She let her eyes slide shut, wondering why she was still alive after all this time.

"Raji?"

It was a dream. It had to be a dream. *Or a nightmare.*

"Raji, by the gods, answer me."

It was Jotem's voice, but she knew the Beast was no longer her beloved husband. She'd known it when he chased her to the river in the attempt to kill her.

Opening her eyes was too difficult. She slurred out her answer without doing so. "The gods have abandoned you." *And me. Why did I not die before he arrived? Perhaps I was meant to waste his time, so Zasha may escape him.*

"Yes, they have." There was something that sounded of defeat in that. After a moment of silence, he spoke again. "Where is our son, Raji?"

"My son," she insisted.

His Blutjagd flared high at her challenge. "Let me protect him. I will take him safely to Goven and let your brother raise him. He will be safer there than with me."

Her heart pounded at the offer, false as it was. "As you would have protected me?"

"I would have, had you let me. I am not like the other Beasts."

She used much of her waning strength to lever her eyelids up. "You threatened me."

"I did no such thing. I was my frustration and fear for you speaking. You must believe me." He certainly sounded frustrated now.

Frustrated by his failure to track Zasha. If he knew how to find them, he wouldn't be wasting time questioning her about their route.

Ask questions. Keep him talking while Zasha escapes.

Realization that she was making this decision without the Stone's interference—for once—made her heart sink. The gods really had deserted her. Rajicorin prayed they'd abandoned her to shield another...the only one truly in need of their protection. "Why should I?"

Jotem crouched beside her, holding a cup in his hands. He offered it to her, and Rajicorin shook her head in refusal. He paled another notch, his expression pained at her refusal.

"Where is he, Raji? Please, I must know where our son is."

She shook her head again, abruptly glad she didn't know for certain.

"Raji, please."

"I do not know," she gasped out. Rajicorin let her eyes slide shut again.

"I would do anything for you, Raji. Surely, you must know that."

"Then hold me while I die." One part of her cried out in horror at such a thought. Another argued it would delay his pursuit of Zasha and prayed it would take hours for her to die. Days, perhaps.

"You wish that of me?" There was a soft note at odds with the Beast she knew him to be.

For once, Rajicorin didn't try to hide the longing for the husband she'd lost. If he refused her, it would break what was left of her failing heart. "Yes. I do."

"I would deny you nothing. Nothing that I have the power to give."

Jotem crawled onto the sleeping roll with her, drawing Rajicorin into his arms. She'd wondered many times what the skin of a Beast would feel like...Jotem's skin. He wasn't cold. His skin was warm as a summer night, chasing away a bit of the chill the blood loss had brought upon her.

His touch was tender, and his body fit hers as it always had. With her head on his shoulder, sleep started to embrace her. Rajicorin just hoped she wouldn't wake cold and alone.

"Never," he breathed. "I will not let you die alone."

Chapter Two

Seventeen years later

"It is past time, little tease."

Ahdia stiffened, turning to face Tul slowly. How many times would she have to tell him she wasn't interested?

He continued, oblivious to her rising anger. "Where is your brother?"

"Close." But she didn't need Korji to fight off the likes of Tul. Though her brother would revel in the humiliation he would heap on the cave-dweller, Tul wouldn't be more than a few minutes' worth of fight for either of them.

He took a swaggering step closer to her. "My people believe an unprotected woman belongs to any man strong enough to take her as his own."

His people were barbarians even among the gathered barbarians.

Her fury spiked at the fact that he meant to try it...with her. Adhia could stop him. That was a given.

Korji will gut him, if Tul still stands when he arrives. And Korji will come. She was angry, and they could always feel each other's anger.

She reminded herself that Tul had laid a challenge. "My people are more civilized. Even if you managed to take me, my brother would kill you for it."

Even if you succeed, physical satisfaction is all you will gain from it. It was commonly held that only a dark giant or sorcerer could fill her belly with children. Though Tul's tribe no doubt felt strength in numbers would suffice, it was certain to fail. They would be better served finding a human woman to lie with them.

"And find my entire tribe standing with me."

She curled her lip at his threat. *Ten men. If Korji fails to kill them all, I would willingly give myself to Tul.*

No. She wouldn't, and there was no chance of Korji losing against ten men, let alone losing if Ahdia had even her legs free to aid him in the fight.

"I am not willing, Tul. That is all you need know. Any move to test that will end in your death."

His smile was cold and hard. "Then we will not return to my hut." Tul stressed the last word, as if reinforcing that he found living in such a structure like the other refugees beneath him.

{He is not accepting your refusal. Beware.}

Ahdia took a step back into a fighting stance Korji had taught her. The voice had always advised her well, and Ahdia had come to believe it was nearly omniscient.

She'd heard the voice since the year her blood started to flow. Zasha postulated it was Ahdia's mother's spirit speaking from the magic amulet she wore. It had been her mother's before hers, and Rajicorin had given her life to deliver Ahdia to the world and the amulet to her daughter to protect her.

Ahdia didn't doubt Zasha was correct. The stories of her mother said she was a great sorceress, bride of one of the dark giants from the cursed lands. The stories said that when the lands fell lawless and too dangerous to travel, the sorceress alone had escaped their boundaries, carrying the great giant's young.

Raji, guide me. It was forbidden to speak the sorceress's name aloud. Names had power, and her mother's name was bespelled to draw her enemies to the sound. The most Ahdia and Korji dared was to speak it in their minds, and she rarely thought the full name, even in urgency.

Zasha postulated that Ahdia started hearing her mother's voice when her blood flowed, because it unlocked her own sorceress's powers. Communing with the dead was a woman's gift. Not that of a child or man. Had Ahdia someone to train her magic, Zasha felt Ahdia would be very powerful indeed.

{Now!}

Tul barreled toward her, foolishly trusting his bulk in battle.

Korji is larger than you, and I have bested him more times than he likes to admit. Her first kick took his ribs, and she sidestepped his charge.

Tul turned, wincing at the movement. He came for her again, lumbering. Her punch knocked him flat back, and she danced out of his range.

It was a smart move. Her punch wasn't as strong as her kick, and he rolled to his feet. His glare announced his intention to have her rough and fast, if he defeated her.

That will never happen. Tul wasn't the first man to try it. Like the others, he would not try again, whether he lived or died.

Perhaps I should do permanent injury to his male parts.

Ahdia dismissed that idea. His people liked a good fight. Her defeating Tul would wound his pride and reduce his status among his own. Her killing him in a fair fight would be no more noteworthy. Any move perceived as cowardly on her part would invite retaliation from his kinsmen. Though she and Korji could kill his entire tribe, that would make them outcasts from the larger refugee group that included more than a dozen smaller tribes. The peace between them was tenuous already.

Tul's smile raised the hair on the back of her neck. Ahdia didn't need Raji's voice to interpret it.

She burst into motion, kicking one of the two males behind her in the face and driving the other back. Blood coursed from the former's broken nose, and the other tripped on his own feet and scrambled up again.

Ahdia followed directly into a back kick to Tul's already-injured ribs. There was no question what the three intended. They'd ambushed her with the thought of subduing her with numbers and rutting on her as a group. His tribe had shared females between their men before.

I will die first. I will kill them first. Her smile spread. *I will geld every one of them, the peace be damned.* With three against one, any way she triumphed would be fair fighting.

The one she'd driven back came for her, and Ahdia swept his feet. Tul was moving again, and she kneed his genitals, dropping him to the ground with a high-pitched scream that tapered off to wheezing sounds.

A movement over her shoulder sent her that direction with a harsh curse. Three men weren't enough for Tul. He'd brought—

Ahdia gasped in surprise at the block pushing her arm away from target. She looked up past a woven wrap...and up...and further up into the fierce eyes of a dark giant.

Her heart hammering in terror, she stared at him. Which was he? Friend or foe?

The sun. What had Zasha said about them? *Raji said those who were not traitors walked the sun in glory.* But had she meant it literally or figuratively?

He reached for her, and Ahdia reacted, kneeing him as she had Tul. The giant didn't double over or cry out in pain. He didn't even move his huge hand to cover his battered parts. His face darkened, and his expression promised retribution.

Perhaps dark giants have no proper genitalia. Or was it different from that of human men? Perhaps Korji was only intact—though enlarged—because he was half sorceress.

That thought in mind, Ahdia turned to run.

A second giant blocked her path, his hands up in a calming gesture. This one was older. He had patches of silver over his ears and threads of it through his shoulder-length curls. "Be still, little one," he requested.

No! She had to reach Korji. Ahdia still had no idea if these giants were the answer to her prayers or their end in the making.

Where is he? Korji would have felt her anger. He'd never failed to appear to protect her before.

The old giant extended a hand to her, and she struck it away. The one at her back tried to restrain her, and she elbowed him in the ribs. It didn't slow him any more than the knee to his groin had. In a heartbeat, he had her hands clasped behind her back, her body crushed to his.

The cock laying heavily against her lower back attested that the dark giants were indeed equipped as she knew men to be. Certainty that he meant to use his tool against her fired her resolve, and she fought his hold. His cock hardened further.

"Woman, be still," he growled. "You know well enough we only mean to protect you."

"D-do you?" Ahdia stuttered out.

The one before her cocked his head to one side, his brow creasing and his lips turning down. "Where is your lord?"

"Lord?" What was he talking about? The refugees had no lords. Each tribe had individual leadership, often the matriarch or patriarch of the group. Sometimes it was the strongest fighter or most successful hunter. Ahdia's tribe had a matriarch.

"Who cares for you?"

Ahdia glared at him. "I am no child in need of a nurse."

"Where did you get the amulet?" There was an edge of something fierce in that.

She swallowed hard, glancing around for signs of Korji coming to her aid. There was a third dark giant, but it wasn't her brother. He strolled from the tree line, wiping his bloodied hands on what looked suspiciously like the remains of Tul's chest wrap. Her heart pounded at the indentations in the grass where the three cave dwellers had fallen in battle. There was blood on a flat rock where Tul had lain.

He closed on her position, and Ahdia shied away...further into the chest of the one holding her.

"Where?" the old one reminded her of the question.

"My-my mother."

His expression hardened. It was frightening. And it was more. Emotions she couldn't name overwhelmed her. She had to escape him.

Escape them all. "Release me." It was the only warning she would give.

His eyebrows arched. "The amulet—"

"Release me!"

"The amulet—"

"Belongs to me. I must never remove it." Panic took hold of her, and Ahdia bucked against the one restraining her. "You cannot have it. You cannot have me."

Something in his expression changed. "Still her."

The one behind her snaked his leg around hers, pinning Ahdia tight to his erection. Though she wiggled and twisted, there was little chance she could escape him, and he was only one of three.

The one questioning her made a sound that drew her gaze. "I will have the truth," he warned.

"My mother," she repeated. It was the truth.

His gaze trailed to her chest, and the lines in his brow deepened. He grasped the edge of her chest wrap.

"No," she pleaded. Ahdia tried to pull away, but there was nowhere to go in the giant's grip.

He twisted the leather and yanked it back, uncovering her to the upper curve of one aureole. His eyes narrowed.

She looked down at herself, realization making her dizzy. He was staring at the mark on her breast, the mark he'd likely seen the edge of in the gap of her wrap while she'd been struggling for freedom.

A whimper of fear escaped her throat. Zasha had told her the mark had to stay hidden, even among women bathing together. Ahdia was never to show it. Like her mother's name, it would reveal what she was to an enemy.

"Who is your father?"

* * * *

The woman paled. She trailed her gaze from Warrior to Warrior, trembling hard. Just when Taigh would have prompted her, she decided to answer his father's question.

"I do not know. I know only that he was one of your kind—a dark giant. I was never told his name."

Taigh shot a look at his father, seeking answers that were not in the older Warrior's eyes.

Gyr's voice gentled a bit in deference to her fear. "Why were you not told? Did your mother not know it to impart it? Or...what did she fear in saying the name?"

"There is power in a name," she replied simply.

"What does that mean?" his younger brother Vesh asked, looking up from his careful cleaning of the attackers' blood from his hands.

"There are names you dare not speak, because names have a power. My mother spoke of it."

Taigh's heart pounded at the warning, though it was nonsense the barbarians taught their young. *Still, there must be a reason her father's name has been hidden.* "Who is your mother then?" Perhaps that would give a clue to her sire. Not all the women lost to them in the first days of the Beast War had been recovered. One might have lived but been separated from her mate.

She straightened. "She *was* the great sorceress."

"Sorceress?" There was no such thing. It was more barbarian stories. What game was this? What had she been told and why?

His father took over the questioning again. "What sorceress?"

75

"*The* sorceress. The greatest sorceress ever to walk the world of men. When the cursed lands fell lawless and her mate, the greatest of the giants, was taken, the sorceress alone escaped with her talismans of power and knowledge of the future, her belly swelling with the great dark giant's young."

Though the tale made no sense to Taigh, Gyr gasped, his eyes widening in understanding. "Raji. Your mother was Raji."

The change in the woman was startling. Her *Blutjagd* burned bright, and she fought for her freedom, screaming out her fury. She managed to free an arm from Taigh's grip and punched Gyr solidly across his cheek, sending the lord sprawling.

Taigh attempted to restrain her gently. When that failed, he released her legs and forced her to the grass beneath him. Pinning her wrists wasn't as easy as he'd anticipated.

The woman tried to head butt him, and he ducked her attempt. She writhed against him, enflaming his cock further. Visions of using this position for more carnal purposes, the woman moving against him thus, fired his lust.

Taigh pushed those errant thoughts away, wondering at his lack of control. She wasn't impassioned now. His duty was to handle her, to calm her, if such a thing was possible.

"Be still," he ordered her. "We mean you no harm."

She jerked her elbow into his jaw with jarring force. Taigh tightened his grip, reeling at her strength, well aware he would leave bruises on her.

It cannot be helped. A gentle hand will not hold her tight enough.

Her shrill voice bit at his ears.

"You said the name! You said it to draw the traitors. You called them. You. Serve. *Them.*"

"Traitors?" Why did nothing she say make sense? Did she mean the elders? They were traitors and definitely lawless.

She got a leg free, and Vesh captured it before she could use it to attack.

The rising *Blutjagd* to his left drew Taigh's attention. He looked up, gasping at the sight.

The young Warrior wore a waist wrap and rough foot wraps that came to his knees but nothing covering his chest. A blood mark stood out in stark contrast to his tanned skin, and long hair whipped in the wind, bits of color woven into four long braids that lay along one side of his face.

"Korji," the woman screamed. "Traitors."

A sacred weapon drawn, he launched down the hill toward them. Vesh released her leg with a battle cry and moved to intercept him.

"Is the man your twin?" His father asked urgently.

Vesh and the young barbarian met in battle, moving so fast a dust cloud rose around them from the lush grass. Her voice brought Taigh's gaze to her again.

"I will tell you nothing, traitor." Her expression said she meant every word.

"Did. Your. Mother's. Womb. Shelter. You. Together?"

Taigh knew by Gyr's tone and expression that his father would not be denied an answer. "Please. Answer him," he urged her.

"Korji will kill you," she vowed.

Gyr ground his teeth loud enough for Taigh to hear it over the battle. "Unlikely, but your answer of that question may save him yet."

She shot a pained look at the barbarian Warrior, paling, most likely at the sight of the blood coursing down his arm.

He is a Warrior. It is likely no one has stood long against him in battle since he was cursed.

Vesh drew another wound and received one in return.

She opened her mouth, closed it, clenched her jaw, then blurted out an answer. "Yes. We shared the womb. Do not kill Korji. Please. My brother means only to protect me."

Gyr bowed his head to her and rose. "Do not kill him," he thundered.

Taigh gaped at him, stunned by the order. What madness was this? Lost one or not, a Warrior who attacked another was a danger to all.

He probably believes we are attacking his sister. What Warrior wouldn't kill another, in such a case?

His father bolted to the battle, showing his speed and grace. The woman's brother was well matched to Vesh, but he was unequal to the skill and determination of a first cursed lord with decades of battle behind him.

In a hand of heartbeats, he was face down on the ground, and Gyr was binding his hands. Still, he struggled, cursing them in three languages, none of them the language of the ancients.

The woman made another bid to escape, and Taigh tightened his grip again, wringing a gasp from her. She dug her knee into his ribs.

Gods, I have to stop this. "Am I correct in assuming your brother will not accept healing or food from us?" he asked, a plan taking shape.

Her expression called him a madman.

Taigh jerked his head in Korji's direction. "If you make me bind you, who will care for him?" It was coercion of the worst sort, but he had to stop her somehow.

She peeled her gaze from his and stared at her twin miserably.

"Give me your vow and—on your soul—mean it to be true," he ordered. "Do not run from us or attack us, and I will guarantee your safety."

"And the word of a traitor is worth how much?" There was a note of defeat in that.

"We are not traitors. I have no idea why your mother told you not to speak her name, but—" He stopped short at her tensing muscles. "What is it?"

"Since she died in childbirth, she told me nothing directly, giant."

"I am sorry for your loss."

She didn't seem to know how to respond to that. "One does not miss what one does not know."

Taigh tipped his head in acknowledgement though he disagreed. Clearly, this woman had missed not having parents. He wanted to ask who had raised her, but that was a matter for another time. "Do I have your vow?"

"If you truly are not traitors...and you do us no harm, you have my vow that I will not run from you or attack you. If either condition proves false, I will gut you with the dark giant blade you carry."

He fought the urge to laugh at that. "We are called Warriors," he informed her.

She sniffed in dismissal. "You look like a giant to me."

"Korji—"

"He looks like a giant to me."

Taigh swallowed a laugh at her candor. Her brother would look like a giant to her. Like all Warriors, he was three of this fiery young woman.

A woman who likely has a lord-father ready to gut someone who takes advantage or presumes to touch. A lord-father who believes her dead. Taigh eased off her with a fine measure of guilt for his early reaction to her. It was a reaction that would have seen him on the end of her father's blade.

She pushed to her feet and dusted herself off. Without looking back at him, she loped up the hill toward her brother.

* * * *

Ahdia sprinted the last few body lengths to Korji's side and started assessing his wounds.

"What vows have you made?" he asked urgently. "What have you done?"

79

His panic was understandable. Breaking vows and turning traitor were nearly the worst offenses a person could commit, even if you made the vows under duress. Worse, Zasha said the dark giants and sorceresses could bind a person with a vow.

She pressed at the deeper of the cuts, avoiding his eyes. "If they are not traitors and do not harm us, I will not run from them or injure them. Nothing more."

He breathed a sigh of relief. "And if they are traitors?"

"You know the answer to that, Korji." But she was certain the three giants would defeat them easily. Not for the first time, Ahdia wished she'd inherited her mother's full magic and had been trained to use it.

"But you already know them to be traitors," he growled. His arms tightened, making the bleeding worse.

Ahdia smacked the muscle above the cut. "Stop that. Healing you will be difficult enough without you reopening the wound every time I move to stitch it."

"Ahdia, explain this to me," he commanded.

She looked at the young giant who'd restrained her, replaying his words. He'd sounded sincere, but she supposed those practiced at lying often did. "They do not believe in the power of a name," she imparted.

Korji launched up, and the eldest giant forced him down. Her brother ground his teeth. "They spoke the sorceress's name? We must leave then. Now. Before the sun disappears from the sky."

"No."

He stared at her as if she'd gone mad.

I am not certain I am sane.

"If he spoke the name, they will come when the sun sets," he reminded her.

Forming words was abruptly difficult. "Only if Zasha interpreted the sorceress's stories correctly. What if she was wrong, Korji?"

He gaped at her.

"Make the same vow I did," she pleaded.

His eyes narrowed in warning that his anger was barely in control. "To what end?"

"Make the vow, and they will cut your bonds."

The youngest giant snorted in disbelief. "I will not. He nearly took my throat."

"Quiet," the eldest barked.

"Yes, my lord."

Ahdia took a calming breath. "If they refuse to release you at your vow, I will know them to be traitors."

She could feel the tension rising in the youngest giant and shot him a nervous glance. The one who'd restrained her growled foreign words at him, and the younger went red-faced...and calm.

The eldest seemed to consider that. "I should warn you that we kill vow-breakers."

"So do we," Korji grumbled. "What is the rest of your plan, sister?"

"We stay here this night. In the very place the name was spoken. If the attack comes—"

"We die," he snapped at her. "You know the traitors mean to kill us. To kill *you*, Ahdia."

Her heart ached. "What choice have we?" Tears burned at her eyes, and she tried to blink them away.

Korji leaned toward her, and Ahdia wrapped her arms around him, letting the tears fall. Sobs wracked her overworked body. It had been a long day with too many adversaries.

"I will make the vow," he breathed. "On my life and on my soul. Now, release me, so I may comfort my sister."

The eldest giant lowered his head. "And I give my vow that I would give my life for either of yours. I welcome you home to our world...Korji and Ahdia, beloved young of Rajicorin and Jotem." With that, he cut Korji's bonds.

Ahdia fought the urge to bolt. He'd said the name again. Worse, he'd said the secret name Zasha had uttered only once, in the early morning, before a long day of travel.

The name that was to save us, if we ever found the giants our mother meant us to find. We were only to speak the name when we reached them.

The rest sank in slowly. *Jotem. He knew our father.*

She looked up at them, several hand of questions fighting for supremacy. The young giants' shock told her the answers would not be to her liking.

Chapter Three

Taigh stood in the shadows, watching Ahdia interact with her brother in the light of the still-bright fire.

Ani's children live.

And yet nothing was certain. They didn't trust the Warriors. They'd packed to run from the battle they anticipated coming. They'd refused food and drink from the Warriors with a look that spoke of fears of poison or drugs that would incapacitate them. They wouldn't even share their stories.

What would the Warriors do if Korji and Adhia refused to return home with them? There was no way to force them to, and their loss would be catastrophic.

With their father turned Beast, Korji was the head of their small household. Not even the Stone lord could order them to return to the village. If they refused to return, the only choice Taigh could see would be to move the village to the brother and sister.

Ahdia's eyes closed, and her head dipped. It was nearly sunrise, and she'd likely been awake since the previous one. If she had trusted the Warriors, she might have rested instead of remaining awake and vigilant through the night.

Korji didn't chastise her for it. Instead, he wrapped his bandaged arm around her and pulled her to his chest. A strange song hummed from between his lips, and Ahdia went lax against him.

Taigh watched, spellbound. He wanted to be the one soothing her to sleep, the one humming the song she so obviously loved.

Stop that! Whatever was wrong with him, it had to end.

* * * *

"Sunrise," the eldest giant pointed out in a voice low enough not to disturb Ahdia. "Answer me, Korji. Do I have your trust?"

His eyes burned in lack of sleep. "When Ahdia is at risk, I trust no one." He expected the old man to protest that.

Instead, he laughed heartily. "Very good, Korji. Whoever trained you did a fine job of teaching you to protect your sister."

Korji grunted his agreement. He started to arrange himself flat on the ground, using his sleeping furs to cushion his head. Ahdia snapped awake and blinked in the light. She met his gaze and sank to the ground, giving in to her need to sleep again.

"Rest, young Warrior," the giant invited. "We will watch your sleeping back."

His eyes heavy in exhaustion, Korji pulled his blade, wrapped an arm around Ahdia's waist, and nestled the weapon to his sister's back. If this was a giant trick, he would be prepared to fight them off. No one would take Ahdia from him. No one would endanger her and live.

* * * *

"Do you think they have always slept that way?" Vesh asked.

Taigh looked around at him, trying to follow his brother's reasoning. "Perhaps. They shared infant furs. Why wouldn't they?"

"It's just...odd, isn't it?"

The implied insult rankled him. "How would you know? We don't have a sister, and we know no other twins."

"I suppose," Vesh conceded.

Taigh calmed himself. "They were not raised in the village, Vesh. Survival may have demanded this. Remember the men who attacked her."

"I suppose," he repeated.

Their father interrupted them. "Taigh, take first sleep shift. Vesh, you have watch. I want to move when they wake."

"If they are willing, you mean," Taigh reminded him.

Gyr's eyes narrowed, and his jaw tightened down a notch. "If I have to take them along as prisoners, I will do so. They vowed not to harm us and not to run from us, as long as we didn't harm them or prove to be traitors. They set no exception on leaving here."

"They didn't say they would, either."

* * * *

Ahdia drifted in and out of sleep, drinking in the sun's warmth. She knew she should wake and go about her work, but lying in the shelter of Korji's chest was too comfortable for words.

Grass teased at her bare arms, and she sought out the reason she was sleeping without furs or a mat. Memories of the grass pressing into her back, Taigh laying over her, their bodies moving against each other gave way to other musings.

Living in the refugee village, Ahdia had seen people in all sorts of sexual situations. She'd never personally had an interest in what they did, but she'd seen it.

There was no mistaking the many things she was considering and the fact that she could place no other man in Taigh's stead. Her nipples came to points against her leather chest wrap, and her core wept hot fluid down her thighs.

Being held in Korji's arms while she thought such things felt wrong, and Ahdia started to extricate herself. Korji's arms tightened, and he came awake with a growl. Their gazes locked for a moment. He released her with a sigh and sank to the grass again, his blade clenched in his fist.

Ready to defend me. Ready to gut anyone that touches me.

Ahdia went to the trees to relieve herself and then returned to the fire. It was hard not to stare at Taigh's sleeping form. The dream images of him as a lover were still potent and not fading as dreams normally did.

I will not look at him. It must be some sort of trick. Even if it wasn't, the last thing she wanted was to encourage him.

The youngest giant, the one they called Vesh, cleared his throat and held food out to her.

Though her mind said she should show them a modicum of trust, her heart pounded and her hand shook. "I shouldn't," she admitted. Korji would be furious with her for chancing a potion or poison.

As if the elder giant understood her concerns, he cut meat from the carcass and ate some. Then he passed the bowl to her and offered a nod.

Her stomach growled, and Ahdia took the bowl with a whispered word of thanks. She sank to the grass an arm's length from Korji and started eating. Though she'd cooked for Korji the night before, Ahdia hadn't been able to stomach much of anything, due to her apprehension.

She was halfway done with the offered meat when shame forced her to speak. "My apologies for calling you traitors."

Vesh gaped at her.

The elder giant was still for a long moment. Finally, he sighed. "You protected yourself, Ahdia. Korji protected you. I would ask nothing less than such diligence. The fact that you felt the need to protect yourself against us was...unfortunate."

Ahdia nodded and scooped her hair behind her ear, a nervous habit she'd had since before her blood had started to flow. At a loss to understand her unease, Ahdia went back to eating.

"Does it mean something?" Vesh asked.

She looked up from the food, but there was no indication what he was looking at. "Does what mean something?"

"The decorations on your ear."

"Vesh," the leader of the giants grumbled.

Ahdia straightened and resisted the urge to touch the cuff and beads. "I am a healer for my..." *These are our people, and yet they are not.* "...village. I know herbs, what my mother taught Zasha and what Zasha already knew of the art. The cuff tells all who see it that I am a woman of high standing."

The old giant's eyes hardened. "Yes. You are that."

Something in his tone warned that she'd angered him. Ahdia pretended not to notice it and went back to the food, though her appetite had largely fled.

He paused and then continued. "You are a woman of high standing in our village, as well."

"And will returning me to them win you some sort of reward?" She kept the query light and questioning, stifling the challenge she wanted to make it.

He didn't react ill to the question as she'd feared he might. "Not in the way you mean. It will mean an end to the war with the Beasts that walk the night."

Ahdia took her time, chewing the meat while she considered his words. She swallowed slowly. "How? What difference will I make? I am a healer, not a fighter." Did the traitors need some sort of healing? Was her magic of some importance, as her mother's had been?

Vesh snorted, and the elder snapped a foreign word at him that had the young giant averting his eyes and red-faced in what she'd assume was embarrassment.

He answered before she could decide to question what he'd said to the younger. "We do not expect you to fight, Ahdia." He hesitated, his calculation palpable, then met her gaze, looking decades older than he had moments before.

The change sent shards of fear through Ahdia. How old was this giant? How desperate to get what he felt was best was he?

"I fear there are some that feel this war is hopeless, because we lost Rajicorin's young. Your return alone would be a balm on old wounds."

"It is more than that," she guessed.

"So many things. Your brother..."

Ahdia glanced at Korji.

"He was expected to be a great leader among us."

"A man of standing?" Her heart leapt at the idea. A man of standing would have a greater chance of attracting a woman. Korji sorely needed a woman in his life.

"Yes. A Warrior, but a great Warrior. And you would be a wonderful addition to our village."

Ahdia focused on him again. "Because I am a healer or because I am a child of Raji?"

"Both...and more. We do not produce many women. We protect those we do produce fiercely."

Because they need them as mates. "I should warn you. I am a leader of my village. I take orders from no man. Not even an ancient giant who feels it is his right to lord over me." The terms he'd used the day before made more sense now, and Ahdia didn't like the painting of their lives it was creating for her.

There was a moment of silence. Then the giant started laughing. "So much like your mother. Rest assured, the only man who would be expected to give you orders would be your brother, and I imagine you have already struck some agreement between you."

"And if some man in your village took an interest in me?" Ahdia raised her eyebrow in challenge. "Would he expect to have similar rights I would have to beat out of him?"

Vesh went a stunning shade of red that either said he found her impertinent or was interested in her himself.

Too bad, pup!

The elder tipped his head back. "Our men tend to order their women when the woman's protection depends upon it. Beyond that, their relationships are very individual."

Protection... Rajicorin spoke to Zasha about the giants seeing to her protection. She wondered what the term meant to them but dared not ask it.

"Will you accompany us, Ahdia?"

"I will consider it." *Do we need their protection, now that we are adults? Should the end of their war fall on us? We have no part in it.*

It doesn't matter. The only chance I have of creating a child is with a dark giant. She stifled the urge to look at Taigh again. *The only chance Korji has of finding a woman is with them.* Since she currently had no pressing need to be a mother, that was the more important concern.

"Do you have questions for me?" he invited.

"Many, but most will hold until Korji wakes to join in the discussion."

"Those that will not wait that long?"

A smile pulled at one side of her lips. "What is your name, giant? I have heard the others called by name but never you."

His expression said he was troubled.

Names have power. If he is afraid to give me his, perhaps I cannot trust him.

"Gyr."

Her heart rate eased. "Gyr. Thank you."

Chapter Four

"Will you share your stories of your mother with us?" Gyr asked.

Korji's arm muscles tightened against her back.

Ahdia pretended not to notice. "I will, if you promise to share your memories of my parents in return."

"Agreed." He motioned for her to continue.

Finding a place to start wasn't difficult. Zasha had told the tale many nights. What she hadn't done was spoken the name, but Ahdia intended to. That resolved, she began.

"Rajicorin was a sorceress, gods-chosen and gifted with magic to tame even the dark giants she lived among. In time, two of the giants came to love her and fought to possess her. Of the two—the stronger of the two and strongest of them all—bested the other, and Raji took him to her bed as consort and carried his young."

Vesh looked as if he was about to protest something, but Gyr waved him off, and the young giant fell into a brooding silence.

"Carrying a giant's child is difficult. It is enough to sap a sorceress's great magic, even one as powerful as Raji was. It is enough to kill a human woman." She glanced at Korji, wincing at his stoic expression. Gods knew, that one fact had made his life with the refugees intolerable. Perhaps he would find a suitable giant wife...or a sorceress to love him.

"The defeated giant turned bitter, seeing her belly grow large with his foe's young. He knew Raji would have to choose between using her magic to save herself and her young or using it to control him and those giants he had convinced to steal the source of her magic, a mystical stone that kept peace in the land." Ahdia hesitated, anticipating yet another protest that the story had been miscommunicated.

Gyr nodded solemnly. "I know the Stone well."

That sent a thrill through her heart, and she continued. "Raji saw the deed but could not stop them. She ran for help, but the great goddess she served told her the only way Raji would live to hold her son would be to flee with her remaining magic and hide herself with the refugees from the war.

"Once the great giant's son was delivered of her, her magic could grow strong again, and she could return to tame the unrest and secure the Stone. Until then, the only magic she dared use was to carry the giant's young and hide herself from them."

"What happened?" Taigh asked, his tone reverent.

"She ran as the goddess commanded. The traitors followed. They warned they would never stop searching for her.

"Raji could not use her own name, for fear that the night-walkers would hear it on the wind or from their spies. Her sorceress's robes were replaced with rough skins and furs, and she joined a band of refugees whose goddess demanded protection of women and children.

"Raji hid her great magic. She hoarded it to carry the giant's child. Instead, she made simple healing potions and was beloved by all, in her own band and others they encountered."

"She died in childbirth," Taigh offered at her pause.

Ahdia nodded, her heart heavy. "The great goddess is... She is something of a trickster. She does not always tell all, and her puzzles are most dire."

"What puzzle?" Gyr asked urgently.

Something in his expression made her heart pound. "Raji pushed her son into the world. By his mark, she knew the goddess had named him Korji, and Raji gifted him her sacred blade and called him 'protector.'

"But Korji did not sleep the womb alone. Raji saw the puzzle then. She recognized the cost of bearing the

91

great giant's young without her full magic to sustain her."

Taigh's face went shades paler.

"She did not question that the other babe was a daughter. Raji named her Ahdia without waiting to see her mark or even her gender revealed.

"There was no time to waste. Raji had fled with magic enough to deliver one of the giant's young into the world. Not two.

"The moment she knew there were two, she knew she would die bringing forth the second. And she knew the second was not a son. The subtle shades of the puzzle were unfurling to her."

Ahdia paused, and a tense silence settled over the giants. She continued to her greatest heartbreak.

"Raji instructed Zasha to prepare to flee with the young, while she labored alone. At the birth, Zasha was ordered to take the amulet from around Raji's throat and place it around Ahdia's." She touched the amulet. "It was meager magic, but it would hide Ahdia from the traitors until Zasha could deliver the great giant's children to their father's people."

"But she never did that," Gyr interjected.

"Zasha left that night with a rough cart full of everything she could carry. She took the babes, Korji swaddled with his mother's blade and Ahdia the amulet strung about her neck. She fed them on milk from her goats.

"Zasha followed Raji's directions, but the invaders who had forced her from her home had stretched across the path to the giants, and she fled. When they'd been driven back, she tried again, but the forest was full of magical creatures set free by the traitor giants, using the Stone's power."

"Creatures?" Vesh scoffed.

Ahdia glared at him. "Some call them shades that live in shadows and take form only to kill. Others call them demons and say they have red eyes and great claws and fangs. It is said they tear the flesh and consume body and soul."

"They do," Gyr confirmed. "There is some truth in every description of them...and more."

Ahdia retreated to Korji's chest, her breathing strangled. Of everything she'd been taught, she'd wanted to believe that part false.

"Finish...please," Gyr requested.

"Zasha was a common woman with no great magic and only the single amulet between them. And she was old. In the end, she could not reach the giants. She had no magic to fight armies and creatures."

There was a moment of silence, and Gyr started to speak.

* * * *

His father started his story in return, and Taigh focused on it, hungry for any small details he might have missed before.

"Rajicorin...Raji was born marked by the Stone, as all the elder Warriors were, traitors and not." He paused to uncover the mark of Pol on his own chest.

"The young ones are unmarked?" Korji asked, fingering his own mark in seeming confusion.

"Taigh is marked." Gyr paused and nodded to indicate that Taigh should uncover the mark just above the top of his waist wrap. That accomplished, he continued.

"He carries the mark of Syth, the Stone lord. When Goven, the current Stone lord, dies, Taigh will be the Stone's protector."

"But the Stone was taken by the traitors," Ahdia protested. She shot an unreadable look at Taigh, then focused on his father.

Gyr sighed. "They took the Stone to release the Beasts—what you call creatures—and to claim the power, but after that, the Stone becomes poison to them."

She pressed to her brother's side. "Go on. My apologies for—"

"None needed. You have questions. Ask them."

"What is my mark then?" she continued. "Korji was named for his, I know."

Taigh perked at the question. He hadn't seen the mark his father uncovered, and he burned to know her aspect.

"Tes. Your mark is the mark of the stars of the sky and wishes fulfilled."

A shy smile curved up her lips, and Ahdia pressed her fingertips to the mark. "My thanks," she breathed.

Taigh's cock went hard that simply. Visions of her pert breast with the blood mark standing in stark contrast to the pale skin was enough to drive him mad in wanting.

Gyr darkened a notch. "The term sorceress was...misleading. Raji knew herbs, and she was blessed by the Stone, but her magic was no more than that of any Warrior. Less than most."

Korji bristled at that, and Gyr waved him down.

"To an outsider, it would seem like great magic, I admit." When Korji didn't protest, Gyr continued. "Raji would be faster than one who was not a Warrior...stronger than other women her size. She would be able to hide herself as to appear invisible to the naked eye. Yes, it would appear to be great magic indeed.

"The gods, as you noted..." He tipped his head to Ahdia. "The gods enjoy their games. Women born with the mark of Ani, your mother's aspect, may take one of two men as mate. She will be drawn to both of them and they to her."

"And they fight to possess her?" Ahdia asked sadly.

Gyr hesitated and then nodded. "The two were named Jotem of the Fire and Persh of the Sun. Jotem bested Persh and took Raji to his bed."

Korji sneered at that. "In any civilized village, women choose. They are not taken as treasures from a battlefield."

"She did. Though fathers...or older brothers, when a father is dead, may disapprove of a match, those who take a woman unwilling die for it. Raji was most willing to become Jotem's mate."

Seemingly mollified, Korji motioned for Gyr to continue.

"They were very much in love—Raji and Jotem. Soon after they sealed printing...bound themselves as one, you were conceived.

"Persh went mad in wanting Raji for himself, and he convinced four other Warriors to join him in his quest for the Stone's power. But the Stone lord's magic protects the Stone. There is only one way to take it."

"And Persh did so," Raji guessed.

Gyr stared at her for moment, then shook his head. "He could not break the magic. He and his band distracted Jotem and stole Raji from their bed. They—"

Korji launched to his feet, his hand going to his sacred weapon. His *Blutjagd* burned hot. "My mother was no traitor," he bellowed.

Everyone tensed, and Ahdia went pale, her slight form shaking. The urge to take her away and calm her was strong, and Taigh stifled it with more than a little difficulty. In Korji's fury, it would be a death sentence.

Gyr motioned for peace. "No. She was not a traitor. Raji could not have freed the Stone any more than Persh could have."

"Then who did?" Ahdia's voice was low and tremulous.

Korji's *Blutjagd* died out, and he sat, drawing Ahdia across his lap as if she were a child.

She is being soothed. That is good. But jealousy that someone else was soothing her still ate at Taigh.

Gyr cleared his throat and began again. "The traitors held blades to her and threatened to kill Raji if Jotem did not free the Stone to them. His love for her was the only thing greater than the Stone lord's magic."

Ahdia pressed a hand to her mouth, and a sob escaped. Korji's arms encircled her and held her to his chest. He whispered to her, words too low for even a Warrior's hearing to track.

"In releasing the Stone, Jotem knew he would lose Raji forever. The price of claiming the Stone's power is becoming the Beast that hunts the night. I can only guess that he believed Raji living without him, in the hurt of his betrayal of our people, would be better than suffering her death.

"Becoming a Beast means losing all kind feelings. A Beast will kill brother, son...even his own wife."

"So, you thought Jotem killed our mother," Korji concluded.

From his tone, Taigh could tell Korji didn't consider Jotem his father. He winced at that, trying to imagine life without family.

Gyr didn't comment on it, though disrespect to an elder was punished severely. Perhaps the lord was letting his own hatred of the betrayer influence his decisions. Or perhaps, he was trying to build trust with Korji.

"We are certain he tried. We found Raji's track. They must have chased her. She ran...scrambled. She bled. They drove her to the river. When she didn't return, we assumed the worst had befallen her."

Korji nodded solemnly.

"The Stone would tell us nothing, but the Stone loves her games. Perhaps we should have known then that Raji was not dead, but if the Stone wanted her hidden away, She would have blocked our attempts to find your mother."

There was silence around the ashes of the fire. At last, Gyr spoke again.

"You must allow us to protect you." He motioned to Korji. "And to train you as a Warrior."

Korji started to protest, and Ahdia cut him off.

"You know we must."

"Ahdia—"

"It was our mother's final command to Zasha. It was her final wish for us. You know that is so. Would you defile—"

"Never." He shot a suspicious look at the three Warriors. "But I do not trust them."

Taigh bristled, then forced it back. It was a wonder that they'd trusted the Warriors this far.

Gyr tipped his head in acceptance. "You wear the amulet already. You know not to remove it?"

Ahdia hesitated, then nodded solemnly. "I do."

His shoulders eased. "Then I must bless it."

Her look of confusion said the stories passed down to her from her mother hadn't included that point. The idea of her unprotected and trusting an amulet this long sent Taigh's heart pounding.

"It is..." Gyr ground his teeth, most likely in frustration. "Magic. It makes the Beasts unable to touch you or to feed on you."

"No," Korji ordered. "You will cast no magic over my sister."

Ahdia gaped at him, and he continued.

"We have no magic to fight their spells." He winced as if in realization that such a statement would show weakness, if the Warriors really wielded magic, as they understood it. "If you let them cast their magic, we cannot undo what they do to you with it."

"Raji wished it," she reminded him stubbornly. "You remember what Zasha taught us, Korji."

"We do not know what sort of protection she meant. They have already *protected* you without their magic." He glared at Taigh, then turned his warning on each of the others in turn.

"Have they? How did they come upon me unseen? Until that moment, both of us would have sworn such a thing was impossible."

"It is called ghosting," Taigh offered.

Ahdia turned to him, her expression earnest. "Is it magic?"

She thinks of all of our powers as magic. "Yes. It is."

"You see?" she challenged her brother. "Magic. Just as I said."

He glared daggers at Taigh, his *Blutjagd* burning lightly in his skin. "You cannot know what our mother intended. How much has been proven wrong so far?"

Gyr motioned for his attention, and got it from both of Raji's children.

"Protection has a single meaning to our kind. If Raji used the term, she meant this."

"You see?" Ahdia repeated.

Korji grumbled curses, then nodded his agreement. "I hope this is not an error, Ahdia."

"I will speak the words in your—"

"No." It was Ahdia interrupting Gyr that time. She shook her head in an adamant show. "Not you." She pointed to Taigh. "That one will cast the spell of protection."

Gyr shot a startled look at him, and Taigh felt his cheeks heat. He had no idea why Ahdia had singled him out.

"Why Taigh?" his father asked with false calm that warned of judgment to be passed.

Ahdia blushed deeply. "You are a very old giant."

Vesh snorted in laughter, swallowing it down at a warning look from both his father and brother. He shifted nervously, most likely envisioning the trial their father would deal him for the insult.

"An old giant will be cunning," Korji explained for her. "He will know magic and deceptions a younger giant would not."

"And why not Vesh?" Gyr pressed, motioning to the younger of his sons on this journey with him.

Ahdia didn't hesitate. "He is young and undisciplined. If my life depends on this magic, I wish an old *enough* giant to perform it well."

Vesh scowled at her, no doubt irritated now that she'd said something negative about him.

Taigh felt a smile curve his lips up. Undisciplined certainly described Vesh. He wouldn't have been with them at all if their father hadn't wanted to get extra training in while they investigated the bursts of *Blutjagd* at the edges of their senses.

Gyr nodded. "A sensible choice then," he complimented Ahdia. "Very well. Taigh will speak the words, in your language, so you will know what will be said when he touches you to...cast the spell."

Before Taigh could comply, Korji added a warning that made his heart stutter.

"If one tone of it differs on the second utterance, I will gut you as a traitor, giant."

Taigh nodded. *Gods, how do I get myself into these situations?* "By the gods who forged us all, I grant you the protection of the House Pol. Any and all of our kind and kin shall lay down life to preserve yours from the evil that walks among us. Walked blessed among us, now."

Ahdia seemed to consider the words carefully. She met her brother's brooding gaze. "I see no trick in that," she offered carefully.

Korji grunted his agreement, settled Ahdia on the grass, and crouched beside her, his hand on the hilt of his weapon.

Taigh took a calming breath, then crossed the distance between them and knelt before her. He laid one hand along the curve of her chin, his fingers tangling in her hair. "I will speak the words and seal the magic with a kiss on your forehead."

"Is that necessary?" She looked to Gyr for an answer.

"It is," he confirmed.

Ahdia straightened. "Very well. It is then."

But she didn't meet Taigh's gaze, a sure sign that she didn't like the idea. That stung.

Taigh spoke slowly and clearly, well aware of the threat hanging over him. The final word left his lips, and he leaned toward her, pressing his lips to her forehead.

It struck without warning. The bolt of power started at his lips and rushed over his sizzling nerves, sending Taigh overbalancing backward in surprise. His cock went hard and thick, and he trembled in wave after wave of lust, grinding his teeth, flat on his back on the grass.

A roar of fury and the tang of *Blutjagd* scorched him. The ground shook as his father and brother forced Korji to the grassy hillside.

"Ahdia," he bellowed. "What have you done with Ahdia?"

With? Not to? Taigh forced his eyes open, staring at the crushed grass where she'd been sitting moments before.

* * * *

The young Stone lord's magic left fiery trails over her skin, sensitizing Ahdia to the world around her— the faint rustling of the wind, his scent, and his heated breath.

Then they were moving. Apart. Down. She sprawled on the hillside, her senses in a spin and her breathing ragged.

Her lungs were full of Taigh's scent, the crisp musk and magical essence of the man. The memory of his touch took on a life of its own, seeking out places that made the cleft between her thighs weep and heat in want of him.

Korji let loose a battle cry, and she rolled away from the fight instinctively, letting the careless toss of her weight tumble her downhill.

Hide. I need to hide. But she could barely move.

Bodies hit the ground, wrestling for superior position.

Hide!

At once, it stopped. There was a moment of blessed silence.

"Ahdia! What have you done with Ahdia?" Korji was desperate, panicked... It was a sound she couldn't remember hearing from him before.

She forced a gasping breath and levered her eyes up. All four men were staring at her, their expressions ranging from stunned to frightened.

No. They are looking through me. Ahdia didn't question that none of them could see her. As if in confirmation, gazes roamed, searching for her location.

Where am I? The grass beneath her hands indicated that she was still on the hillside.

What am I? Dead? A phantom? A shade? Surely, she wasn't a creature. Beast.

"Ahdia!"

She opened her mouth to reply, but only a gasp emerged.

Korji tried to throw the giants off, but they held him down. "Ahdia!"

I have to make him see me. See me, Korji! See me!

Her brother's eyes widened. At his first move toward her, the giants let him loose, and he scrambled to her side. His shaking fingers traced her jawline.

"Where were you? Where did they send you?"

Ahdia shook her head. "No-nowhere. I was here, but you could not see me."

Korji turned on the giants, fury rising off his skin like a steam. "What did you do, giant?"

"Ghosting," the one called Taigh rasped out. He levered himself to sitting, pain etched on his features.

She did the same. "You did...what did you do?"

"I was not my doing, Ahdia. You wished to be unseen."

Speaking was abruptly difficult. Ahdia nodded.

"And you wished to be seen again," he pressed.

"Yes. Seen." She swallowed hard. "I have giant magic? Or is it sorceress magic?"

"Warrior powers," he correctly gently. "You both do."

Gyr stared down at them. "And you will both learn to use those powers."

Chapter Five

"Like this," Vesh instructed. He swept his blade toward Korji, as he had countless times in the last three days of giant training in battle.

Seeing it coming, Korji ducked it and brought his own blade up to the young man's throat. For a moment, they stared at each other.

"Be aware," Gyr began his corrections again. "If you go for the throat, you may force the Beast to ground, but you will be unlikely to kill him, unless you have a sword forged in the Stone's fire to remove the head entirely. A heart shot is the best killer with a sacred weapon. Better, when we return to the village, I will have them forge you a second. That way, you can pin the Beast to solid form with one and use the other for the heart shot."

Korji lowered his arm. "I have other blades. I could pin him with one and use the other to kill."

"No," the old giant countered. "You cannot. The magic of the Stone is the only thing that can pin the Beast to solid form or kill. Another weapon can bleed but never kill. It lacks the magic to do the job."

Korji turned to look at him. "What happens if I remove the head completely with another weapon?"

There was a moment of silence.

Gyr sighed in a way that said he found Korji's endless questions tiring. "I have never tried it, but the stories say it will not cut full through and will only force the Beast to ground to heal again."

"Not useless then but not a killer."

"Yes, but the Beast will try to kill you and quickly, because you are a son of Rajicorin and marked by the Stone...and because you protect your sister. Battle is not the time for foolish chances."

His anger ignited at the rebuke. "I am never foolish in battle."

103

"If you were not, Vesh would never have laid a blade on you." There was a bite of something harsh in that.

"Because I was injured in—"

Gyr moved abruptly, coming face to face with him. "You are a stronger fighter, Korji. Had you any decent training, my son would never have laid a blade to you. But hear me now. You remember how quickly I defeated you?"

Korji nodded. It had been embarrassingly fast, so much so that he was glad no one from his village but Ahdia had witnessed it.

"I am not the greatest of the Warriors, Korji. Most Warriors are not better than a Beast elder. To survive against the elders and command respect among the Warriors, you will have to be a greater Warrior than I am. That means a level head. That means training. That means learning everything we have to teach you and learning it well, before you find yourself in a test of true battle again."

Korji considered that. It certainly sounded like a solid plan of action. "I understand."

"For your life, I hope that is true."

Out of the corner of his eye, Korji saw Vesh move toward him. He brought his fist up into the young giant's nose, followed him down to the grass, and planted his blade at the boy's heart.

Gyr laughed heartily. "Very good, Korji. Now you are learning. Be ever vigilant and be ruthless when you strike."

He pushed to his feet, keeping his blade ready to strike at Vesh. Still, he watched Gyr out of the corner of his eye. *Ever vigilant. Ruthless. This is what they prize. I will be sure to remember that.*

* * * *

Ahdia watched Taigh from the tree line, savoring the way his body moved. She'd never seen a more beautiful male.

{He is yours. All you need do is claim him.}

Her mouth went dry at the thought of that. Though women chose when they wished to enjoy a man, Ahdia had never made that choice.

Even if she'd dared expose her goddess mark to a male who wasn't a dark giant, Ahdia had never found a man appealing and wanted to bed with one before.

Now she found herself plagued by dreams of Taigh, dreams in which they shared all manner of intimacy. The lack of relief from it was maddening. Why else would she watch him this way?

Watch, but I still dare not touch him.

{Dare to touch him, Ahdia. You will not regret it.}

Taigh turned from the fire and headed into the forest only a few arm's lengths to her right. He seemed oblivious to her presence. That allowed Ahdia to follow him unseen. He made his way through the growth silently, and Ahdia thanked the goddess that she was just as silent as he.

The stream they were using for water made its way lazily down the hillside, bubbling around rocks. At first Ahdia thought he'd come to bathe in the cool water as she'd done earlier, but that wasn't Taigh's aim.

He settled on the grass close to the stream and seemed to be watching the water flow by. It was several long moments before Ahdia noticed the low sounds escaping his lips.

She moved to the left slowly, carefully avoiding making a noise that would reveal her presence to him. Ahdia swallowed a gasp in the realization that Taigh had opened his waist wrap.

His cock was hard, and he was stroking it within his fist, relieving his male drive as Korji did when the need became too much for him. It wasn't a small cock as the males in the refugee village had. It was easily the size of Korji's, she'd estimate.

Ahdia watched his hand moving over that beautiful tool, her mouth going dry. The moisture all over her body seemed to have moved to her slit, and an ache set up low in her belly, ebbing and flowing with the up and down motion of his hand.

She licked her lips, wondering if Taigh would be just as avid if her channel engulfed him instead of his hand.

{Or more avid.}

Her face flamed at the taunting suggestion. *Oh, Raji! Please do not tease me so.*

{Go to him, Ahdia. Remember that Zasha was ordered to find the Stone lord and deliver you to his care. He will care for you most diligently. He will gladly fill you with his tool. He will use his lips and mouth and hands to—}

Stop that! But the visions were already circling in her head. Ahdia pressed the heel of her hand to the tightening in her womb, her breathing coming in sips of precious air.

Taigh's sounds grew coarser, and sweat rolled down his face. Just when Ahdia felt she might faint in lack of air, his cock erupted, sending a copious amount of his male fluids to the grass.

He dropped to his back, panting in the aftermath of his release of need. His fingers stroked along the underside of his tool, drawing her eyes to the sex-bruised length and the thatch of dark curls at the base.

There were drops of his fluids at the head, shimmering in the slowly setting sun. Her mouth watered. What would he do if she went to him and tasted him as the females seeking babes would sometimes taste Korji, seeking to use the magic of his giant's cum to ripen themselves for a child with the men they desired?

The vision of the two of them entwined, Taigh feasting between her legs as she feasted between his, seared her, and Ahdia turned for camp, needing to right her senses before she did something so rash.

She walked the forest for some time, trying to banish the visions Raji provided for her torture, but they persisted. Ahdia took her time, gathering herbs for her healing while she considered what this meant.

Raji had never led her astray before. Was this her mother's way of telling Ahdia it was time to go to a man's bed? Was she telling Ahdia that Taigh should be that man? She certainly hadn't sent visions of Gyr or Vesh to Ahdia.

She headed for camp, certain that the sign should not be ignored.

"Where have you been?" Gyr demanded when she'd no more than set foot inside the clearing.

Ahdia looked at the herbs in her hand, then glared at the old giant, challenging him to be so unobservant for a moment longer.

Korji laughed heartily. "I told you Ahdia would not be harmed." He hooked his hands behind his neck, clearly gloating.

Gyr vented his fury at her brother. "Dark is coming. With the dark come Beasts that want to take or end your sister, Korji. As we approach Warrior lands, we approach the Beasts. I suggest you take more care with her."

Ahdia's patience snapped, and she threw the herbs in Gyr's face. "I *suggest* that you learn your place. I am a woman of high standing and not yours to order." With that, she turned, bumped past Taigh, and headed to their shelter.

A moment later, she realized Taigh's scent clung to her and she peeked back at him. He stood there, conferring with his father by the fire.

Ahdia considered that for a moment before she stepped into the shelter. Going to Taigh's bed gave his father no more say over her life than he had now. That being the case, she fully intended to exercise her right to choose him to stoke her inner fires.

Korji ducked into the shelter, still chuckling.

Now I have to ask Korji to do the unthinkable...guard me while I do what he has never had the opportunity to do.

Chapter Six

"No, Ahdia," Korji pleaded. "Not the dark giant. Not now."

Ahdia paused in her preparations, at a loss to explain her need to go to Taigh's bed. "There is a magic between us. Perhaps it has always been thus with sorceresses and dark giants."

The magic was no lie. There had to be some reason for the dreams that had tortured her, night after night. They were always dreams of Taigh, always dreams of his sex—potent, tactile dreams.

"You are a sorceress now?" There was a hint of amusement in that.

Though Taigh insisted Ahdia was giant—*Warrior*—as well, she was miniature, compared to the others. As such, there was little chance he was correct in that, and Raji's story beckoned.

"Ahdia? Are you a sorceress?"

"They say I have a magic." Taigh was adamant about it. Ahdia touched her mother's amulet, wishing yet again that she understood the magic she was supposed to wield.

"And what do you say?" he challenged.

She turned to him, searching for the words to define herself. "I will never be the sorceress our mother was. Perhaps I am more dark giant than sorceress. Perhaps that is why I am drawn to Taigh."

He sighed. "And you insist on this?"

It is my choice, as a woman. It is not yours. "Yes. I do."

Her brother stood, towering over her, his long hair following the line of his collar bones and cascading to the center of his chest. "Then I know my place."

Ahdia hesitated a moment, then threw herself into Korji's arms. "Thank you." Despite her arousal and tradition, this step terrified her. The idea of Korji refusing his duty would have made her reconsider.

She didn't have a father to stand with her. Ahdia had always hoped Korji would do it, but she'd never dared ask him to. Not when he had no hopes of a woman seeking his bed in the near future.

Please, let him find a female giant to sate his need.

* * * *

Taigh stared at the stars, his body complaining as it had for days. Self-release didn't quell it. Sleep didn't. When he slept, he woke from dreams of Ahdia, poised on the brink of a climax he couldn't claim.

Tonight would be no different. Taigh wondered how long he could endure this torture without going mad from it.

Gasps and muttered curses drew him from dark thoughts. Beneath the exclamations, he could hear two sets of footsteps. One was Korji, and he obviously wanted himself to be heard. The other was light...female.

Ahdia. He sat up abruptly, coming nose to glorious feminine core through her waist wrap. His mouth watered at her scent, and his cock demanded what it had no right to. Taigh tipped his head back, his eyes widening at the sight of her bare breasts, her nipples peaked and begging for a mouth.

"Ahdia?" Forming more of a question was physically impossible.

She lifted one leg and moved, straddling his thighs. With exaggerated care, Ahdia sank to her knees, bringing her breasts enticingly close to his lips.

"What are you asking?" If it involved printing, the gods were smiling on him.

Her brother spoke for her. "In the way of our people, a woman chooses when she wishes to share a man's bed. It is a great gift Ahdia offers you, giant. Do you intend to accept it, or should she offer it to another?"

Another? She is mine! Ahdia will give herself to no other. But she wasn't his. Yet. Using the press of her thigh against his, Taigh sensed her. *Not high cycle.* "I accept. You will not regret this."

His move to stand and take Ahdia to a private corner ended with Korji's blade to his throat. Taigh shot a startled look at the barbarian Warrior—half unclothed, his long hair loose and eyes wild.

"I will witness this, giant. In the way of our people."

Taigh bit back the retort that whatever ceremony they were following wasn't from 'their people.' The Warriors didn't do this. This was something they'd learned from the barbarians who'd raised them.

He swallowed down a half dozen curses and disrespectful names he wished to call Korji, as well. Though Ahdia's brother refused to use Taigh's given name, engaging in the same poor behavior would only upset Ahdia and drive her to another.

Korji continued, seemingly trying to force Taigh to a physical test of skills. "If you harm her... If you show Ahdia the least disrespect, you will no longer possess the parts to breach a woman."

"Your people take release this way?" he asked carefully.

Ahdia blushed, and she glanced up at Korji.

Her brother answered for her. "When the woman wishes it."

Taigh focused on Ahdia. "You wish this?" His mind soothed his bruised ego. It was a matter of trust. The Warriors had violated it within moments of meeting her.

She nodded once, timidly, as if she feared he would refuse her.

He shot a questioning look at his father. Taigh would do nearly anything Ahdia wished, but that didn't mean Gyr would approve.

The old lord fairly seethed in fury. At length, he offered a curt nod and growled Vesh away. Taigh's brother rose and loped into the trees.

Gyr remained. That was hardly ideal, but it was to be expected, given the circumstances. Korji had insinuated Taigh lacked self-control. By Warrior law, his father would be the judge of that.

Taigh turned his gaze to Ahdia. "As you wish."

She shot a nervous look at her brother, and the blade left Taigh's throat. The young *Blutjagdfrau* made no move toward Taigh, and her clasped hands trembled.

It was as if she feared his touch. *Or as if*—The truth seared him. This was the first time she was choosing to share a man's bed.

Or is it simply the difference in size between human men and Warriors that unnerves her?

Taigh didn't ask it. He would proceed as if she was intact. Slowly.

The tips of her nipples were too enticing to ignore. Taigh lowered his head and tasted one. It was a sweet exploration of one and then the other. He suckled at her blood mark, groaning at the spice of her skin, then returned to a nipple.

Ahdia's hands sought out the lines of his chest beneath his tunic, her breathing ragged. She moaned, her head dropping back.

Taigh broke away long enough to drag off his tunic. She brought her head forward again to watch him.

He didn't ask if she wanted him to continue. Her lowered eyelids and rising scent answered that.

Her hands circled the back of his head and urged him back to her chest. Taigh was less restrained. If Ahdia's tugging and low cries of pleasure were accurate indicators—and he didn't doubt they were—she enjoyed the change.

She lowered herself onto his lap, pulling the knots on his waist wrap free to bare his cock. Her heat and musk was a torture through her leather waist wrap.

Taigh released her breast and straightened. He cupped the back of her thighs and trailed his hands up until he was kneading the soft meat of her buttocks.

Ahdia's hands closed on his shoulders, and she stroked back and forth along the line of his cock. Taigh grasped the front of her wrap in one hand and wrenched it up, leaving them skin to skin. She went still, and her eyes slid shut on a whisper of air.

He closed on her lips, his heart pounding in excitement. Ahdia's hips shifted, spreading her cream over his length. Her lips molded to his, her breath teasing between the break in his and into his mouth. Taigh forced the air out of his lungs, returning the teasing.

Her lips parted on a moan, and Taigh dipped his tongue inside. She shifted closer, making tentative moves of her tongue against his.

Taigh let his eyes slip shut. Now that Ahdia had had a taste of his kiss, she was relentless. They came together in a searing combination of mouths and bodies in motion, their sounds rising beneath the sky as they ground sex to sex and chest to chest.

There was no mistaking the moment of her climax. If her sharp sounds of pleasure didn't indicate it clearly enough, her intoxicating scent would have.

Her mouth left Taigh's on a look of bliss. Any fear he had that she'd stop with her own climax and leave him wanting died with her frantic grinding against the leaking head of his cock.

"Taigh," she pleaded. "I offer."

He shivered in delight. There was no way to make his next move painless for an intact woman, so he did it quickly. Levering his cock further into her heat, Taigh thrust his hips up.

Ahdia didn't scream as women often did when breached for the first time. His mind numbly processed that it was probably a good thing she hadn't. He was certain Korji's blade would be at his throat again, if she had.

The tang of her maiden's blood made his head spin. Their kiss was slow and deep, their bodies locked together in torturous stillness.

Her first moves against him were tentative...testing. Ahdia pulled away from the kiss, stroking up and down more avidly.

Taigh laid back, grasping her hips, guiding her. He started thrusting again, her tight little body sheathing him.

Their sounds were sharp, their bodies slick and sliding against each other. Ahdia threw her head back, venting screams of pleasure.

Her body milked him, and the stars danced before his eyes. Taigh wished he could make it last longer, even as he gave himself up to his need to release.

He lost himself for long moments, his body buzzing in aftershocks. When Taigh came back to himself it was to the glorious feeling of Ahdia draped over him.

"Ahdia," Korji called out to her. "Are you ready to take your leave?"

Taigh's heart sank. He wrapped his arms around her, begging Ahdia to stay silently.

* * * *

Korji's question made little sense to her. Taigh's hands stroking her back and his cock, still hard and bucking inside her, made more.

"Taigh," she pleaded.

His cock jerked more forcefully against the walls of her channel, and he became larger still.

"You wish more of me?" he offered.

"Yes." It was a gasp, but it was an answer.

Taigh rolled her beneath him and stroked inside her. It was wonderful, shattering her mind into fragments that focused, here and there, on snips of sensation. His heated tool sensitized every fingerwidth of the area between her parted thighs. She wrapped her legs around his waist, wanting to hold to this feeling.

Until he'd kissed her, Ahdia had believed she'd never feel what other women did. Her heart had never sped at the sight of a man until she met Taigh. Her eyes had never lingered. Her thighs had never wet or her channel heated and begged to be filled.

Until I met Taigh.

Ahdia reveled in his touch. She hungered for more of him. She salivated to learn how long he could stay hard and pounding for her.

When the first tremors of unease hit her, Ahdia tried to push them away. Whatever it was, it was unwelcome.

The second wave stole her breath.

{He is coming. Hide, Ahdia. He is dangerous to you.}

That was enough to shock her out of the passionate blur she'd been locked in. Her mind unfettered, Ahdia felt it coming for her. It was dark, sinister... A vision of red, glowing eyes made her shiver.

Taigh faltered. "Ahdia? Is something wrong?"

"He is coming. We must run. Hide. Now, Taigh." It came out a series of halting breaths.

He jerked back, leaving her body in a rush. "What do you mean? Who is coming?"

"D-dark one. Creature, I believe. B-Beast."

Taigh reached for his clothing, his jaw tense. He looked around at his father, offering a nod that communicated an order to readiness. He fastened his waist wrap in efficient movements.

Ahdia looked past him to Korji, noting her brother's panning gaze. She thanked the goddess that they all seemed to believe her.

The amorphous threat solidified at her left, and Ahdia looked that direction. Her mind went from sluggish to racing as the dark cloud took shape. She shouted out Taigh's name, certain the creature meant to attack his unprotected back.

He turned, weapon in hand. The other hand went out to her, and Ahdia grasped it, pulling herself up with a yank from Taigh. She rose to her feet as he did.

"Behind me," he grumbled. Almost as an afterthought, Taigh shoved his tunic at her. "Wear that."

She stared at the interloper, the tunic held to her bare chest, her heart hammering, her muscles strangely weak. *A bird before a snake.*

Taigh grabbed her hand and tugged, and she stumbled into place behind him, trembling hard. Her channel ached, and she suspected the fluid winding down her inner thighs was blood and Taigh's seed rather than her excitement.

"Wait." The voice was little more than a growl. It brought to mind wild animals...predators that would feed on humans if hungry enough.

Motion on either side of her sent her closer to Taigh, and she hurried to pull his tunic on. That accomplished, Ahdia wrapped her arms around Taigh's chest, needing the solid feel of him to ground her.

"Hands away from my sister, creature."

Korji stood to Taigh's right and a step ahead of him. Gyr mirrored his position. Vesh came crashing out of the trees and stopped, his sacred weapon in hand.

Ahdia peeked out from around Taigh's shoulder, watching the creature swiveling his head to stare at Korji and then herself again.

"Two... I never knew there were two. Raji did not say..."

There was something in his expression that rattled her nerves.

Gyr motioned with his blade. "Leave us, foul one."

The creature seemed to overcome its shock. He shot a mocking smile at Gyr. "I see the Warriors have taken to voyeurism to entertain themselves," he taunted.

The old giant didn't react in anger. "The *Blutjagdfrau* does as she wishes. If she wishes protection from her enemies as she takes release, we humbly offer it. The fact that she requests our

116

protection only proves she is intelligent and aware. Now leave us, King of Lies."

Korji turned his head and shot at questioning look at Ahdia, then focused on their enemy again. "In the ways of our people, a woman is protected in such a situation unless she requests of her male relatives to leave her unprotected. If your laws do not include such protections for women, I find them barbaric."

It was a clear challenge, and Ahdia held her breath, expecting the creature's retaliation.

"I am your father, pup, and my daughter needs no protection from me." There was a bite of warning in that.

Ahdia's stomach twisted at the pronouncement. This foul creature had sired them? Her lips went numb, and she felt faint. Taigh's hand covered hers, offering silent comfort. She accepted it, grateful for his support in the face of so fierce an enemy.

Korji didn't back down. "I have no father. I am lord of my house, and I say my mother was right to hide my sister from you."

The creature cocked its head to one side and raked its gaze up and down Korji's form. "A man cannot be lord until he kills a Beast in battle. Or didn't the Warriors tell you that?"

"Then come be my first kill. I invite you."

It smiled, showing a mouthful of wolf-like fangs. Its eyes went from red-gold to glowing red. "An excellent idea."

Ahdia's breath caught in her throat, and her heart stuttered. *The creatures eat you, body and soul. He means to devour Korji.* "No." It came out a gasp.

Before Korji could close the distance between them, Gyr had done so. "The boy is under my protection, Veriel."

"I need no—"

"Protect your sister. Keep her between two or three at all times. Do not allow the Beast to find her back."

Korji nodded and turned to place Ahdia close between his broad back and Taigh's. A heartbeat later, Korji shifted to give Vesh a place in the ring of male bodies surrounding her. At any other time, Ahdia might have protested it. With the creature who'd sired them intent on her, she was more than willing to accept being penned in like a babe.

The sound of battle brought her attention back to the clashing enemies. Gyr moved nearly too quickly to be seen, but Veriel was faster. In moments, Gyr was in flight, tossed like a child's doll toward the horses.

Then the creature was gone. A fine mist hugged the ground where Veriel had stood moments earlier. At first Ahdia wasn't certain the movement she saw was real. The mist gained speed, moving steadily closer to her position.

It is of his *creation.* The feeling of it drawing nearer set her nerves on edge. Ahdia shied, trying to push the circle of men further. If they were intent on penning her, they should move with her.

"Be still," Taigh ordered. "He cannot touch you in this form."

The mist snaked around her legs. Instead of being cool as fog was, it was hot as a stone set in the sun. Ahdia yelped in surprise and tried to climb Korji's back.

Taigh grumbled. "Down! You will give him something to grasp."

Ahdia forced her feet to the ground, swallowing a sob. The last thing she wanted to do was touch the creature. The mist moved on, and she trembled, sobs rising in her throat. She swallowed them ruthlessly, unwilling to let the creature hear her upset.

Vesh disappeared with a grunt of pain before Ahdia saw any sign of Veriel. The young giant's blade landed at her feet, and Ahdia scooped it up just before Taigh would have stepped on it in his bid to close her in again. Though the blade had always been her brother's

118

gift from their mother, she could use a blade if the occasion called for it.

Gyr charged for them again, and Veriel met the giant lord halfway. The battle raged on.

"We should remove Ahdia," Korji suggested.

"Not yet," Taigh replied. "When it is safe."

"This is safe?" her brother demanded, sounding incredulous.

"Safer than horseback, where the Beast can reach her from nearly every side."

Korji grunted, a sign of his grudging agreement.

A movement in the distance brought her head up in that direction. Vesh bolted for the packs, threw things this way and that, and came up with a fresh blade.

He doesn't know where the one he lost is. Ahdia considered telling him. She'd heard Gyr say a giant benefitted in battle by having two blades.

{No. Keep the blade. You will need it.}

Yes, Raji. Thank you for your counsel.

Gyr went down with a grunt of pain, one hand pressed to his ribs. Ahdia winced, certain she would have to treat whatever damage was done to him later.

If he survives.

The Beast moved on to Vesh, bringing him down with a blow to the face. In the next heartbeat, he appeared at Ahdia's side.

She startled at his reach for her, lunging for Veriel with Vesh's blade. Their arms brushed, and she flew the opposite direction, dimly noting the rising scent of something noxious on the breeze as she crashed past the line of Warriors and left them behind.

The circle of men far away, Ahdia hit the ground hard and flipped to her feet. Veriel was nowhere to be seen, and her sense of him was muddled, as if he was everywhere at once. And nowhere at the same time.

The mist? But hidden from sight?

The three younger giants were on their feet and racing for her. Ahdia considered meeting them halfway, but a certainty that Veriel was waiting to attack her back in such an unguarded moment pinned her feet to the ground.

As if in confirmation, warmth at her back warned of an attack in the making. Ahdia whirled that direction and used the blade to strike.

There was a flicker of movement, and she struck again, the blade hitting bone, jerking, and sliding home. Before she could gauge the effectiveness of her blow, two other blades joined it.

Ahdia jumped back in shock, releasing the hilt of Vesh's blade. Taigh dragged her to his side, fury heating his skin and mixing with her anger and with Korji's.

Veriel looked down at his chest, seemingly stunned at the turn of events. When he looked up, his eyes were no longer glowing red. Instead, starlight lit silvery gray.

He smiled, a natural smile of human teeth. Still, Ahdia considered backing away from him. She took a calming breath and held her place between her twin and Taigh.

A laugh escaped the Beast's lips. "Well done. You both make your mother proud." His gaze trailed to Korji. "You are lord now." He cast a look of longing Ahdia's way. "Protect your sister."

"I always do," Korji grumbled in return.

Veriel took a step toward them, faltered, and dropped to his knees on the grass.

Taigh pulled his blade back. "Remove them. Let him bleed out. Give him peace."

"Peace?" Korji grumbled. "Why would such a creature deserve peace."

Vesh pulled the blade Ahdia had planted. "Because that is what we do. The Beasts know no peace but what we can provide."

Veriel's chin dropped down, and his body canted to one side.

Korji pulled his blade and let the Beast fall.

"Pack," Taigh ordered. "We have to move. Now. Before more come."

Ahdia snapped a look at her twin, noting his nod in relief. He bolted for the shelter, leaving her surrounded by the better trained Warriors.

Gyr appeared, leading a horse.

Taigh's horse.

He grasped Ahdia by the waist and settled her on the back of the horse, then he pushed Taigh after her. "Away," the elder giant ordered them. "We will be at your backs."

Taigh vaulted up after her, took the reins with his sacred weapon still clasped in his hand, and kicked his horse up to a run. Ahdia held to the reins below his hands, his chest pressed tight to her back.

She looked back as Korji bolted out of the shelter. Then Taigh turned into the trees, and her brother disappeared from view.

"Korji." Her heart stuttered. They'd never been separated.

Taigh answered her unspoken accusation. "He will be just behind us with whatever they can snatch up in the next few moments. You had to removed before more Beasts arrive."

"And if they attack while we are alone?"

"I can kill any Beast but Veriel without help." Taigh sounded supremely confident in that fact.

Ahdia nodded, but she peeked back again. Korji wasn't there. Indecision ate at her. Should she trust Taigh or not?

{Trust him, Ahdia. Taigh would do nothing to harm you.}

She nodded again. If her mother trusted Taigh, she would as well.

* * * *

The sound of a horse thundering away stopped Korji cold in the process of tying up Ahdia's sleeping roll. *They wouldn't.* But he knew they would dare take his sister from him.

He raced out of the shelter, catching sight of Ahdia disappearing into the trees, riding double with the damned giant she'd gone to for sex.

"Ahdia!" It was too late. She was gone. *I failed her.*

Not yet. He rushed toward his horse. If he followed quickly enough, he could catch them. *And kill the giant. Kill all of them.*

Gyr looked up at him. "Collect what you can. Only the essentials. We must leave here, but the sooner we do, the sooner we meet up with them. We will come back for the rest later."

He stopped, staring at the old giant in shock. Gyr sounded sincere. In the distance, Vesh tied sleeping rolls—his own and Taigh's—to his horse. No one made a move to attack Korji.

If they wanted to take Ahdia from me permanently, they would kill me.

"Korji!"

He nodded and sprinted to the shelter. *Only the essentials.* He secured the ties on both sleeping rolls and grabbed the two sacks of Ahdia's herbs. Anything else could be replaced simply. The sleeping rolls tossed onto one shoulder and the sacks on the other, he returned to the horses.

Gyr reached out and took the sleeping rolls, securing them for Korji. His heart eased a notch at that. He levered himself onto his mount, knotted the sacks together and slung them around the back of his neck.

Vesh pushed the creature's body onto the fire, and the flames started to lick at it.

Fire. The old tales said evil was destroyed by fire.

Gyr mounted up and met his eyes. "She is there, safe and waiting for us. You have my vow on that. We must move before more come, and Ahdia had to be well gone."

"I could have taken her," Korji reminded him.

"You wouldn't have known where to meet us."

That made more sense than Korji wished to admit. He grunted his agreement and waved Gyr on.

The pace the giants set was brutal, but Korji kept up with no difficulty. Time seemed to move too slowly. Just when Korji started to believe he was being led away from her, they broke from the trees, and she was there.

Ahdia looked up at their arrival, and her shoulders eased. She slipped from beneath Taigh's arm and ran for the horses.

Korji pulled up and dropped to his feet, catching his sister as she threw herself at him. Taigh rose from the side of the unlit fire he'd set, met Korji's eyes, and tipped his head. After a moment, Korji did the same.

She stroked her hands over his chest and arms, probably searching for any injuries she would have to attend to. Ahdia stroked a hand over one of the sacks and looked up at him. "You stopped to grab *these*?" she demanded.

"If any of us were injured, we would need them." He didn't add that he knew how much her healing meant to Ahdia. If she was angry with him, he would need a reason she couldn't argue.

She scowled at him, then sighed. "Next time, let me gather new herbs."

Korji lowered her to her feet. "As you wish."

Vesh took the reins from Korji's hands, tethered their horse with the others, and started removing the sleeping rolls. Taigh worked on lighting the fire.

Gyr approached them, his expression solemn. He bowed his head to Ahdia. "If the Beasts do not destroy it, we will collect the rest at sunrise. If they do, I will personally replace everything you have lost with all due haste."

Ahdia offered a shaky nod. Korji winced. Though they carried their most prized possessions with them, he knew there were things his sister would lament losing. "As will I," he added.

The old giant raised his blade, still coated in the creature's blood. "You have made your first kill, Korji."

"Then I am lord of my house now." That settled that.

His eyes shifted to Ahdia. "As did you."

She took a step closer to Korji. "Which means what?"

Gyr trailed his fingertip through the half-dried blood. "There is a ceremony I must do. It will not harm you. It announces you are Beast-killers. It is a rite of adulthood among the Warriors."

Korji nodded. "What must you do?"

"Draw the symbol of Syth at your brow and heart in the blood of your first kill. You can wash it off before it burns, of course."

He glared at Taigh, then turned his attention to Gyr. "Your young giant's symbol." Would this give Taigh some claim over Ahdia?

Gyr didn't flinch. "It is the symbol of the Stone's power. Those with the blood mark are tied to the Stone as Stone lord. Taigh will be Stone lord when Goven dies."

Korji considered that carefully. *They have not lied to me yet.* How long would he continue to mistrust them? "Very well, but you will perform this ceremony on me first." If it was a trick, he would taste the bitter magic and shield Ahdia from it.

"As you wish."

Chapter Seven

Ahdia pushed from her sleeping mat and headed for the shelter flap.

"Do you wish me to accompany you?" Korji asked.

Though she hadn't lain with Taigh since the night the Beast attacked, her brother knew her aim in rising this way. *He smells my arousal; he hears my breathing. Little as he has known of women, Korji recognizes what I want and probably who I want it from.*

"It is not right to ask you to do this," she admitted.

Korji rose and checked his blade. "You are my sister. I protect you. I have survived this long. I will survive a little longer."

"More than a little longer," she replied.

He didn't answer, making her fear for his state of mind.

Korji's hand closed on her shoulder. "If you want this giant..." He took what sounded like a calming breath. "This...Taigh, you take what you want from him. Let no one stop you."

"I do not know what I want from him," she admitted. Would a child be enough? Something told her it wouldn't be, but the thought of seeking more from a magical man with the power to bind her was terrifying.

"When you do, do not hesitate."

"And what happens to you then, Korji?"

He didn't hesitate. "You will not need me forever."

"Yes. I will." *If that is the cost of something more with Taigh, I cannot commit to more. Not until Korji finds a woman for himself.*

Korji's laugh was brittle.

Again, Ahdia considered how unfair it was to ask her brother to accompany her. *If I tell him not to come, he may believe I do not need him with me now.* It was unacceptable.

She turned into his arms, forcing a smile to her lips. "Well, I do need you now. How will I learn what I want from Taigh unless I go to him with the protection of my elder brother?"

Korji rolled his eyes, but the edges of his lips twitched up. "Then we should go."

* * * *

Taigh focused on Ahdia and Korji as they moved across the camp, her arm tucked in his. At first he believed Korji was escorting his sister while she relieved herself, but they headed straight for Taigh.

She was dressed, so he doubted Ahdia was seeking him out for the same reason she had the last time. *What other purpose would she have in coming to me?*

As if in answer, Ahdia released Korji's arm and rose on tiptoe, nestling her lips to Taigh's. Denying her was out of the question. Taigh wrapped his arms around her and parted her lips. In moments, they were locked in a wholly carnal embrace, hands mapping bodies, mouths sampling.

Duty intruded, and Taigh drew himself from the kiss. "Unless your brother is going to stand watch for me, we need to stop this." He didn't want to. Taigh cursed himself for saying it and possibly sending Ahdia away.

She trembled in his arms, hesitated, then shot Korji a pleading look.

"Go," Gyr grumbled. "The watch is mine." His lord appeared from the darkness.

The need to apologize for his dereliction of duty was pressing. *He has relieved me. I shouldn't waste time with useless words.* "My thanks, my lord."

Korji turned toward the fire, and Taigh snapped a look at Vesh's still body.

This isn't right. Vesh hasn't had a woman in half a moon. And I don't want him looking at Ahdia. "Perhaps we should use your shelter," he suggested.

Korji didn't turn back. "A woman comes to a man. It is presumptuous for a man to come to a woman's bed without her express invitation, giant...or to suggest that he would be welcome there."

Taigh's head spun. "I meant no disrespect." *Please, do not let me offend Ahdia. If she turns to Vesh, I will never recover from it.*

Ahdia looked up at him. "There is a reason you asked." She didn't question it.

His cheeks flamed, and Taigh forced himself to speak. "We find it..." *Choose a word carefully.* "...an insult to a woman to display her for other men." He nodded toward Vesh.

She followed his line of sight, shifting from foot to foot. "But the first time—"

"Your brother insinuated I lacked control. As my lord, my father was honor bound to stand as judge to it. Had I lacked control, he would have killed me himself."

Korji snorted. "He would have been too late."

"Which was right. As the head of Ahdia's family, it was your right to kill me, but had my father disagreed with your determination, it would have been his right to kill you for acting out of place."

"Head of..." Ahdia placed her hands on her waist and glared at Taigh. "No man rules me."

Korji turned toward them and smirked at Taigh over her shoulder.

Oh, gods! Now I've offended her. "Of course not, but he is supposed to be your protector."

"If I may..." Gyr interrupted them.

Ahdia visibly calmed herself. "Yes, Gyr?"

"May I suggest a compromise?"

She seemed confused by the pronouncement. "In what way?"

"If you may choose to come to Taigh's bed again, perhaps he should move his sleeping roll to beneath the shelter. That way, you will not be exposed to other men, and Taigh will not presume to come to your bed."

Korji didn't reply. Clearly, his role as protector did not equate to the role of lord he would have taken if he'd been raised by the Warriors.

Not that Ahdia would have accepted any man as her lord gracefully.

At last, she spoke. "Very well. Taigh, please collect your things. Korji and I will make a place for you in our shelter."

Her brother scowled, then nodded his agreement and headed for the shelter. Ahdia didn't follow him immediately.

Say something, idiot! "Thank you for this show of trust, Ahdia."

Her cheeks darkened. She opened her mouth to speak, closed it, and rushed to join her brother.

Taigh's move to collect his belongings ended at the sound of his father's voice.

"If she wants you, go to her. Any time she approaches you, go to her. Vesh and I will take on your duties, if necessary."

The order in that was unmistakable. As was his father's logic. Gyr hoped the young *Blutjagdfrau* was printing on his eldest son. While Taigh secretly hoped the same thing, this felt a little too much like baiting for his comfort.

* * * *

Ahdia ducked into the shelter and hurried to her sleeping roll. Korji stacked her herb packs against the head wall, then dragged his roll next to Ahdia's. The look of challenge he shot her said he expected her to argue sleeping between Taigh and her.

"Where else would I expect you to be, Korji?" she offered calmly.

He tipped his head, seemingly mollified.

Taigh entered their shelter, carrying the meager belongings he traveled with. Korji wasted no time, motioning to the far side of the shelter. Taigh didn't argue it. It took only heartbeats for him to arrange his possessions.

Ahdia watched him out of the corner of her eye, marveling at his attempts to avoid offending them. Taigh took as little of the space as possible and left most of the shelter for the rightful owners of it.

Taigh didn't presume to come to her. He didn't even motion for Ahdia to join him. Though his cock was hard and ready beneath his waist wrap, Taigh settled on his sleeping roll and removed his tunic, as if for rest.

The sight of him laid out and waiting for her was too enticing to let pass. Ahdia stripped off her chest wrap...then her waist wrap.

Taigh watched her, his expression hungry. His hands worked at his waist wrap, and he stripped off his boots, leaving himself as bare as she was. Still, he made no move toward her.

Korji thumped down onto his own sleeping roll and drew his blade, checking its cutting edge in what amounted to a warning for Taigh. Taigh didn't react to that, didn't even look Korji's way.

He has eyes only for me. That thought made her already-heated body throb in need for what Taigh alone could satisfy.

Ahdia crossed the space between them, bringing her lips down on Taigh's. He didn't hesitate. His mouth came at hers avidly, and his fingers went to work on her nipples, testing the peaks.

The need to have him fill her was maddening, and Ahdia left the kiss to ask it. Taigh smiled, and started to guide her over him.

Ahdia shook her head. "No. Like... Like the last time, when the Beast interrupted." Her cheeks burned at asking something so intimate. *But I want to feel him over me again. Why should I not have what I wish?*

After a moment of hesitation, Taigh nodded. He moved aside, turning to offer the sleeping roll to her.

Ahdia lowered herself to the woven surface, and Taigh followed her down.

His weight on her sent pleasant shards through her. Taigh was in no hurry to grant her request. He parted her lips, claiming her mouth while his rough hands traced the lines of her body.

Ahdia wrenched her mouth from his. "Taigh, please," she begged.

He eased his thigh between hers, and Ahdia spread for him, inviting him in. Taigh worked his length inside her with a groan. His muscles tightened down, and his eyes slid halfway shut.

Ahdia rose against him, panting out her plea again. Taigh retreated, and she whimpered in protest. His return forced half his length or more into her, and she gasped in pleasure.

"More?" There was a note of something that sounded suspiciously like amusement in Taigh's voice.

Though Ahdia would have liked to censure him for the presumption, she found his attitude endearing. "More," she agreed.

Again, he eased back, and she ground her fingernails into his arms. As if taking her hint, he pushed forward, impaling her with nearly his full length.

Whispers of pain warred with indescribable pleasure. The male fur around the base of his tool teased her with how close he was to being fully seated in her.

"Ahdia?" he prompted her.

"All of you," she breathed. Now.

Again, he retreated, and she let out a shout in frustration. At the next thrust, the fur teased at her seam, and Ahdia cried out harshly.

"Ahdia?" Korji inquired coolly.

She had to answer him, though forming the words to do so taxed her thinking mind. "So good," she managed.

Taigh held his ground, his cock offering whispers of movement in her sheath, taunting her with how right he felt there. Her head spun in pleasure, and her body trembled in need.

No wonder the women in the village sought this. If there was a way, Ahdia would choose to spend every heartbeat joined to Taigh thus.

"Ahdia?" He seemed to be asking a question, but she didn't understand what that might be.

She moaned, wiggled against him, threw her head back and arched up at the massage of his cock inside her. "Taigh, please." The words to ask for what she wanted were not in her vocabulary.

Taigh offered a snap of a nod and retreated slowly, easing back in at the same torturous pace. He performed the move again and again, his breathing going ragged as hers did.

At last, his hips sped, and his cock started slamming home of a purpose to bringing them both bliss. Ahdia grasped the meat of his buttocks, urging him on.

Her body was aflame, and every touch made the urge to take his length more powerful. The rise to climax was sweet torture, and she screamed at her pinnacle, her body going weak at the answering roar, at Taigh's seed filling her.

Her heart thundered behind her ribs, and Taigh sank over her, his weight a pleasant burden. There was something possessive in the move that unnerved her. Her breathing coming in short gasps, she pushed at his shoulder.

Taigh raised his head and stared at her, his eyes narrowing. "What is it?"

"I should return to my sleeping roll."

"Have I displeased you?" he asked.

Korji came to his feet. "She said—"

"No," Ahdia forced out. "No. I just..."

Taigh left her body and moved half a body length away. "As you wish, Ahdia. Always as you wish."

He sounded sincere, which only scrambled her emotions further. Ahdia stared at him for a long moment, then rushed to her sleeping roll, bypassing Korji's offered chest. She didn't want her brother's comfort. Ahdia wasn't certain why she felt the need for comfort, and the fact that she wanted Taigh's comfort instead of Korji's wasn't helping matters.

"Will you be well?" Taigh asked formally, seemingly searching for an answer she couldn't conceive of.

Korji tensed.

"Yes. Very well, thank you," Ahdia replied simply. Already, her breathing had eased, though her mind and body were still in a riot.

Taigh nodded and started pulling his clothing on. "I should return to my duties, then."

Ahdia wanted to call him back, but something told her it would be a mistake to. At a loss for anything constructive to say or do, she pulled the fur around her on the sleeping roll and curled to her side.

Taigh left the shelter, his gait stiff and purposeful, and she bit back tears.

Korji settled to his sleeping roll and touched her back through the fur. "Did he hurt you?"

"No. I don't... He confuses me, Korji," she admitted.

"If he harms you, I will kill him," he promised.

Though the thought chilled her, it was a comfort to know her brother was there for her. Ahdia turned into his arms and held tight to the single constant in her life.

* * * *

Taigh practically growled at his father when he returned to his post. Gyr raised an eyebrow, then decided to walk away without questioning Taigh about the situation.

Good thing. Given provocation, Taigh might have decided to court his lord's ire.

Damn their barbarian ways! Taigh didn't doubt that whatever had upset her wasn't something he could have been expected to know about. *And now she's likely decided I'm an inappropriate male.*

He ground his teeth, frustrated as much by the situation as he was by the need to be inside her again. *I have to learn her ways. I have to learn the things that are important to Ahdia.*

Most of all, he suspected he had to find a way to appease her brother. As long as Korji was adversarial, chances were that Ahdia would be slow to trust the Warriors.

* * * *

Late that night, Taigh sat by the fire. Though Vesh had relieved him and now stood watch, he knew there would be no sleep for him in the shelter with Ahdia. Nor did he wish to wake her in a bid to retrieve his sleeping roll.

Across the fire from him, his father slept deeply. Taigh wished he could be so lucky.

Movement from the direction of the shelter piqued his interest. Taigh closed his eyes and listened. His heart sped as he recognized Ahdia's light step.

She hesitated, pivoted, and made her way toward him. Taigh didn't look at her until she was seated next to him.

Ahdia scooped her hair behind her ear, revealing the ornamentation to him.

Again. Does she feel threatened? Does she feel she needs to remind me she's a woman of standing? "Are you well, Ahdia?"

She offered a shaky nod.

"You're not," he stated baldly.

Ahdia didn't argue it.

Taigh turned toward her. "Please...tell me what is wrong. I cannot help you unless—"

Her glance toward the shelter stopped him, and Taigh worked at it...to no avail.

He cupped her cheek and guided Ahdia's face back to his gently. "Whatever the problem is, I want to help."

Ahdia hesitated. She bit at her lower lip, dimpling the flesh slightly, as if she deliberated whether or not to trust him. Just when Taigh would have prompted her, she spoke.

"I must know that there is a chance for Korji at your village."

"I don't understand. Chance of what?" What was she afraid of?

Her gaze darted toward the shelter again, and her voice dropped to a whisper. "Will Korji be worthy of a woman's attentions among your...our kind? Will he be able to find one to come to his bed?"

"Can anyone make such a vow? If a woman finds him a worthy mate, she—"

Ahdia shook her head and motioned for a moment of silence. Taigh closed his mouth and waited. Clearly, he'd misunderstood her.

Gods, I want to understand her.

She looked up at him with pleading eyes. "I did not ask about a wife to share his life with forever. Will a woman choose to come to his bed?"

His repetition that no one could promise that died in his throat. Taigh shot a glance at the shelter. "Korji is in need of a woman's touch." He didn't question it.

Ahdia darkened. She didn't reply.

"How long has he been without?"

She remained silent.

Too long. Taigh replayed all the twins' stories, his heart stuttering. *The barbarian refugees believe carrying his child is a death sentence. Korji has never had a woman. Or rarely had one?* Taigh opened his mouth to ask that question, then snapped it shut again, certain Ahdia wouldn't answer it.

"Will they choose to?" she asked again.

"Yes. We have...ways of seeking pleasure without issue from it. Until he finds a mate, Korji would take part in it...if he wishes to." *How long has he been without a woman's touch? Has he ever experienced it?*

Surely, he had. If Korji hadn't, he would have gone mad in needing to.

But watching Ahdia take her pleasure while he cannot... That had to be almost more than the young Warrior could bear.

"Taigh?"

Her voice snapped him back to the conversation. "We will find a place soon. Vesh has need of female companionship, as well."

His father's voice came from the other side of the fire, startling Taigh. He hadn't realized the old man had woken. *How long has he been awake and listening to us?* It took a moment for his reply to sink in.

"Tomorrow. I know a place not far from here."

Ahdia smiled. In a whirlwind move, she placed a kiss on Taigh's lips and sprang to her feet. He was still reeling from his body's reaction to the innocent move that he almost missed her query.

"Will you be coming to the shelter soon?"

His cock ached at what might happen there. "In a moment." He suspected his father had something to say to him, and it was never wise to turn your back on a house lord.

She made her way back to the shelter, her backside swaying in a way that mesmerized Taigh. He dared not hope it was a promise of more.

His father sat up on his sleeping roll. "What do you know about this situation?" It wasn't a simple request.

Taigh forced himself to attend to the conversation, when he wanted to watch Ahdia until she disappeared from sight. *I want to follow her. Now.*

He cleared his throat and forced his mind to the subject at hand. "The barbarians believe a human woman cannot carry for a dark giant." Taigh chose to use their words for it, hoping to accentuate the cultural differences they were dealing with.

"I remember."

"I suspect Korji has rarely—if ever—had a woman's touch to console him. With Ahdia taking her release now, they no longer suffer the lack together."

Gyr grunted. "I concur. Tomorrow then. I will give you directions to lead Vesh and Korji in. It is very close to --"

"Me? I do not require—" His father's glare stopped him cold. Chastised, he waited for Gyr to finish his statement.

"If I take them, will Korji go?"

Taigh worked at that, nearly wincing at the answer. "No." If Taigh was the one left at camp with Ahdia, Korji would believe it some trick to get Ahdia into his bed without her brother's protection.

"Get some rest," Gyr ordered. "You will leave after morning meal."

Taigh made his way to the shelter, but Ahdia wasn't waiting on his sleeping roll. The young *Blutjagdfrau* was beneath her furs, one of her brother's large arms tossed over her as if to assure himself she would remain where he could protect her.

He retreated to his sleeping roll with a sigh. It was probably best that they not indulge again tonight. Once Korji had released his sexual tensions, he would surely calm about others doing the same.

Chapter Eight

Korji glanced back the direction they'd come for the fourth time, still torn about leaving Ahdia with the giants' lord. Though she'd insisted he go—hinted at a wondrous surprise—he wished she'd come with them instead of staying back at the camp with Gyr.

All he could see was the trail, trees, and Vesh lagging far behind them, of course.

Taigh pulled his mount to Korji's side. "She will be well. My father will guard her."

"If your father is anything like you, giant, I am certain he will not miss a movement she makes."

"Once one of our kind finds a wife, we do not watch other women. We do not share beds with other women. Only a Warrior that has lost his mate will seek out other women to find comfort from his curse, and my mother is very much alive and well.

"My father has a duty to protect Ahdia. I imagine he views her much as he would a daughter of his own, had he any daughters to compare her to." It was stated as a fact, without the slightest question or hesitation.

Korji considered that. He didn't doubt Taigh believed it to be true. At the same time, it was hard to envision any man being oblivious to his sister's charms. Even among the refugees, nearly every available man and some that had wives wanted her to share a bed with them.

He'd always suspected that she either refused them out of respect for Korji's challenges or in the belief that sex without chance of a child was a wasted venture. Now that he'd seen her with Taigh, Korji believed the magic giants and sorceresses shared had a sexual component, the same sex magic the hill people tried to mimic in their ceremonies.

That still didn't explain this outing. "Where are we going, giant? For what reason?"

He didn't answer immediately. "Consider this a sort of training. A pleasurable training, but one that is essential for you to learn."

"And that would be?" he challenged.

"We do not create young with anyone but a mate," he stated bluntly.

Korji ground his teeth. "I know well enough how to sate my male needs, giant. I require no training for that." What sort of man did Taigh think he was to offer such instruction?

"I'm certain you do. I must train you how to know a woman's cycle, so you can lay with her without fear of issue."

His cock stirred at the thought. "Lay with her fully without fear of it?" If he meant a woman's mouth or hand, Korji had had more than his share of that, and it did little more than his own hand did to stave off the madness for a female body. *I would rather go without than settle for that again.*

Though Korji would like to state that firmly, he knew his drives wouldn't allow it. Eventually, he would seek out a woman's touch, no matter how frustrating he found it.

The giant nodded, a sly smile on his face. "Fully."

Korji marveled at that. "And you know women who chance it, who trust implicitly that giant magic and honor will ensure them no issue?"

"My father gave me directions to such a place. There are others, closer to our village. There are women who seek out Warriors to fill their beds and bodies."

"And you have had such women?"

"Many times."

Lucky man. "Will you today?" For some reason, the thought of Taigh seeking another woman's body to fill while Ahdia was so taken with him seemed underhanded. There were no vows between the two, and men were not bound to hold themselves to one woman's bed without such vows. Still, he knew it would hurt Ahdia to find Taigh had gone to others to sate his needs.

Yes. That is it. I do not want him to hurt Ahdia.

"No." It was said with conviction.

"Why?"

Taigh shot him a look that called Korji an uneducated oaf and didn't offer a response.

Does he also worry about Ahdia's feelings? Or does Taigh see this as a threat to Ahdia choosing him as her vow-bound husband?

There was no answer forthcoming, so Korji turned his attention to thoughts of sinking his cock into a willing young woman. It was nearly enough to make him groan aloud, and it succeeded in bringing his cock to its full length.

If Taigh noticed Korji's need, he didn't mention it.

The time on horseback passed quickly, and a village came into view in the distance. Korji straightened, scanning his gaze over the inhabitants. Most of them seemed to be women.

As if Taigh was strolling through Korji's mind, he offered information to explain it. "Many of their men were killed in the wars. They tolerate few passing men as permanent additions to their community, and no human men I've met can match them in battle and force their acceptance."

"But they...lay with men? They choose to?"

Taigh shrugged. "Women have needs, just as men do. Beyond their physical needs to release sexual tension, they are rebuilding their society in the way they deem best. If they feel the purity of their culture is so important, who am I to say they are wrong? Foreign men would want to bring new ways into their village, but boys raised to men within the village know no other way of life."

Taigh's answer shocked him, but Korji tried not to show it. "Yes. I believe that is correct." His mind took another track, and Korji decided to follow it aloud. "Ahdia feels it worthwhile to preserve the culture we were raised in, as do I. Your culture or not, it is ours, and we preserve it as best we can."

The giant shot him a questioning look. "Am I disrespecting your culture in some way that distresses you? Or distresses Ahdia? Are any in our party?"

He took his time with forming an answer. "Sometimes. We hear when you refer to us as barbarians. We hear when you..." Korji searched Taigh's expression. "We hear you when you say it is odd that I sleep close enough to protect my sister."

Taigh nodded. "If you have heard it, you know it is not me saying it." He hesitated a moment. "I will speak to the others."

"Ahdia would appreciate it. As for the rest... Everything you do is new to us. We attempt not to disrespect your ways. Sometimes your ways seem dismissive of Ahdia's position and her will. And of mine."

"It is never my intent," Taigh offered, seemingly in apology.

"I believe that." He did. "But if you harm her or upset her, I will kill you in her name, your laws be damned."

Taigh pulled his horse to a halt at the edge of town, and Korji followed suit. When they were both dismounted and their horses secured to iron grazing rings, Taigh tipped his head in acknowledgement.

"I would expect nothing less."

Vesh appeared beside them. "Nothing less than what?"

Taigh ignored the question and waved Korji toward the gathering crowd of women. "Come. You have much to learn."

If only he knew.

That thought was short-lived. In moments, they were surrounded by women, young and old. Several of them tugged at Vesh, and he went with them, laughing at something one of them said.

One grasped Korji by the arm, testing his muscles. He stared at her, shocked by her sounds of enjoyment. The women in the refugee village had never reacted to him thus.

Taigh put up a hand, asking for a moment of peace. "I must take a moment to teach Korji our method of sensing a woman's cycle," he announced. "If the women of Shil would be so kind, we require your assistance in this."

An elder among the females sighed. "You are welcome to leave a young Warrior growing in a Shil belly." It sounded as if she was teasing Taigh.

The giant scowled at her. "You know why we cannot do that. Do I have the honor of addressing Javia?"

She bowed her head. "You do, Warrior."

"My name is Taigh. I believe you know my father, Gyr."

Her smile widened. "A few of the most enjoyable nights of my young days. Welcome to you and your men, Taigh." She clapped her hands. "Women of Shil! Formation, please. We aid our Warrior brothers."

The women rushed into two long lines, and Taigh motioned Korji to the closer end. The giant reached out and touched the woman's hand. After a moment, he nodded Korji to do the same with her opposite hand.

"Close your eyes," he instructed.

Korji shot him a sour look, then did so.

"Visualize the woman you touch, seek out what you can feel of her."

The sensation was so potent, Korji released her hand with a gasp of surprise.

"What did you feel?"

"A strong wind and the scent of ripe fruit." He opened his eyes and glanced Taigh's way.

The giant nodded his agreement. "That is the rushing of a woman into her fertile time."

The woman's expression crumpled.

As if Taigh understood, he squeezed her hand. "I am sorry, young one." He released her hand and turned toward Korji. "A woman in this time is not safe from issue. Our laws and the way the gods created us do not allow us to chance children that will not be raised with us to be trained and protected properly."

The young woman stomped off to join Javia. Taigh moved to the next one in line and repeated the motion. He nodded to Korji to do the same.

The sensation wasn't as overpowering that time. The wind was less striking, but the smell was as potent.

"Your determination?" Taigh asked.

"No," he guessed.

"Not as close but too close," he confirmed. "Another."

They moved down the line.

The next gave Korji the sensation of a gently-moving stream and the scent of flowers. "This is new. What does it mean?"

Taigh released her hand. "This one is in the stillness of her cycle. There is no fear of a child if you bed with her."

The woman in question fairly purred at the pronouncement. Korji barely stopped himself from licking his lips at the idea of bedding with the young beauty.

"Practice with more," Taigh directed him.

The next six passed in a blur. Two of them were high cycle or close to it. The other four were safe to bed. Korji's cock rose in arousal.

Five so far, and there are two hand more to check. He'd never dreamed of even one woman willing to bed with him, and there were so many here. The mad urge to spend the rest of his life in this village, siring and raising the young giants they so desperately wanted, had allure.

142

No. Ahdia needs me. And Taigh said there were other women like these. Perhaps, finding willing bodies to fill would not be so difficult at the giant village.

Taigh stopped checking the women with him, apparently content that Korji had learned the lesson well. The next four passed in a blur. Two were too close to chance, and two more were safe to bed.

Korji reached for the next woman and stopped in confusion. He tried again...and again. There was nothing. No stream and no wind...no fruit and no flowers.

"Is there a problem, Korji?" Taigh asked.

"The magic has failed me. I do not understand this." He looked over his shoulder, seeking an explanation.

Taigh reached out and took her hand. After a moment, he leaned down and kissed the young woman on the forehead. "My congratulations to you. May your babe be strong and healthy."

She let out a squeal and pressed her hands to her flat belly. "Thank you, Warrior."

Taigh smiled and turned to Korji. "A woman that gives no response is either carrying or does not cycle because of age or infirmity. Since this is a young and seemingly healthy woman, it is safe to assume she bears. You can bed with one, if she is willing, but you must be cautious if she carries, as you would have to be cautious with a virginal female."

As he has been cautious with Ahdia. His stillness on the sleeping roll made sense, in light of that knowledge.

"Warrior... If you have a moment?" an older female called from Javia's side.

Taigh turned and strode toward her. The woman whispered something Korji couldn't hear. Taigh nodded and said something in return, and the older woman hurried away.

Korji decided whatever it was wasn't his concern and returned to evaluating the women. In the end, he'd identified eleven possible bedmates.

Taigh appeared beside him. "Choose two," he instructed.

"Two?" Korji turned toward him, trying to understand the strange order. "Choose? Is it not—"

Taigh cut him off. "All those remaining are willing to bed with you. The choice of which ones to enjoy is yours."

Before Korji could question him further, Taigh continued. "But do not choose more than two. There is another form of training you will engage in today."

"Pleasurable training?" he pressed.

"I believe it will be."

* * * *

Korji had never dreamed of a scene the likes of the one he was engaged in. Two naked women bracketed him in a bed box full of furs and dry hay, one engaged in a heated kiss with him, the other untying his waist wrap.

The wrap parted, and the one he was kissing backed away. He turned his head and captured the lips of the other, moaning at the hands tracing his chest. He could sit between them like this for days.

"Mine first," the first he'd kissed insisted.

Before Korji could leave the kiss to question her, she was astride him, sheathing his cock in her tight channel. He thrust up with a shout of pleasure.

"Mmmm... He's big, Telya. He's so big and filling." With that, she started levering herself up and down his cock, taking what she wanted ruthlessly.

The mouth left his. Telya rounded his body, her sweet breasts pressed to his back. "It is too bad you cannot leave your seed in a fertile Shil. I should very much like a son of your kind to raise as a protector to my village."

It was so tempting, taking each of the women in turn, regardless of their ability to catch pregnant from it. Korji grasped the one before him at the waist and levered her up and down his length, imagining days of nothing but such joy.

Telya reached a hand around and touched the other woman's nipple. "So hard. He must be good, Melia. You rarely react so fiercely to a man's cock between your thighs."

Melia moaned, arching her back, driving her breast further into the other woman's hand. The change in position rubbed Korji's cock in a delightful way.

"That's better. Isn't it, Warrior?" Telya purred, nipping at his ear.

"Much," he agreed. The need to spend his seed rode him hard, but Korji held off, wanting to make this last.

Melia's sounds reached a crescendo, and she pressed down tight to his body, her sweet sheath milking him hard. Korji followed her into bliss with a roar, his entire body alive to the scents and textures of the woman on his lap.

She moved, leaving his sensitive length exposed to the chill air. A shiver of delight worked its way down Korji's body.

Before he could right his senses, Telya's mouth was wrapped around his cock, sucking ruthlessly. It was more avid and masterful than any mouth he'd had before, but it was still a woman's mouth. Korji had had more than his share of it. Why settle for hands and mouth, when slick sheaths beckoned?

"No," he grumbled. "There are more appealing places."

Telya sat up with a jerk, her eyes wide.

Do not let her refuse me now. Korji trailed his fingertips along her bare breasts. "I am sure you would prefer to sample what is between my legs in a more enjoyable position for you?" he hinted.

"You do not require time to recover?"

145

He stroked his ready cock. "Do I look to be in need of recovery time?"

She licked her lips. "I admit you do not."

Korji cupped her ass in his hand, massaging. Telya moaned and arched toward him.

It seemed she was leaving the choice of position to him, something no woman had done before. Dozens of positions others had engaged in circled in his mind, and Korji locked on one he'd always found appealing.

He guided Telya to the furs and knelt up between her thighs. She spread wider for him and tipped her hips up, moaning. Her position fit with what he needed. Korji wrapped his hands around her hips and lifted her higher, seating his cock at her nether lips, his heart pounding in anticipation.

Knowing she was a seasoned woman freed him to thrust deep inside her. Telya's inner muscles jerked against his length, and she gasped.

He watched her avidly, noting how she moved at every thrust, the sounds she vented, and the way her body reacted to his handling. It was glorious, more than he'd dreamed of all those nights alone with his fist to release him.

It was no harder to force Telya to climax than it was Melia, and his cock reacted fiercely to it, pouring out a fresh wave of his seed into her waiting body.

There was a potent moment of stillness in the aftermath of their sex. Then Melia ran a hand down Telya's chest and belly. Her fingers dipped between their joined bodies, first stroking at Telya's hood— bringing the other woman off the furs, her breathing ragged—then teasing at Korji's still-hard cock.

Her mouth pressed to Korji's, and his cock jerked in its ready sheath. Though he realized it was Melia's turn for a ride, he found he didn't want to leave Telya's body.

Her lips parted from his, and Melia smiled. "I enjoy watching you fuck Telya."

His cock jerked again, and Telya wiggled against him, gasping out pleas to continue.

"I suggest you give her what she wants."

"And then you?" he guessed.

Her smile was pure seduction. "Perhaps. Or perhaps you will continue to fuck her."

Telya cried out harshly, and Korji looked down, watching Melia's hand avidly. She was massaging Telya's hood, driving the other woman's body toward another peak.

He considered that. He'd chosen the two because they were very different in looks but had been standing with arms around each other, clearly a matched set. Korji's mind locked on the obvious conclusion. The two were lovers, and Melia preferred women to men, while Telya had more evenly-distributed tastes.

His body and mind both intrigued by the idea, Korji met Melia's eyes. "Perhaps we should share this delight."

She dipped her head and suckled at Telya's breast, setting off aftershocks that forced a gasp from Korji. His cock complaining, he joined in the play. Visions of them licking at the young woman between them...or of him taking her from behind as her lady lover did so had him riding the edges of another powerful release.

* * * *

Korji walked behind Taigh, nude and relaxed from his prolonged play with the two women. He'd left them in their bed together at Taigh's call, completely lost in each other's attentions. Taigh had taken the wrap from Korji's hands, promising to return it when his further training had been completed.

Women all over the village stopped to shoot admiring glances their way. That succeeded in bringing Korji's cock up again.

He'd never dared dream of women showing him such attention, and a far corner of his mind complained that Taigh had limited Korji to two.

I must learn their laws. What kind of laws allowed one man to order another not to take release willingly offered by women?

Taigh entered a structure near the center of the village, ducking to avoid the too-low crossbeam at the opening. Korji followed him in and stopped short, staring at the group of women waiting for them.

Korji shot a questioning look Taigh's way. Many of these women were ones they'd determined as not safe to bed with. If there was a way to avoid issue, why had they made such a show of testing and rejecting the women of the village who were fertile?

Taigh answered his questioning look with a glut of information. "These women are here to prepare you for the one you will bed. They will bathe you while another group prepare the woman."

"Prepare her for...? What, precisely, is this training, giant?"

His smile was wide. "A woman's first male is an important moment for her. You must be slow with her. Gentle. Bring her to orgasm and take her maidenhead. If you can, bring her over again."

Korji nodded solemnly. He had to do for this young woman what Taigh had done for Ahdia. "Will you be standing as her guard?"

Taigh seemed surprised by the question. "Do you feel I need to?"

"Of course not, but... Perhaps, we should offer it to put the young female at ease?"

"If you wish."

* * * *

To Korji's relief, Petra didn't want a guard while he took her barrier. He came to her, more than ready to do the job.

She sat, curled on the furs, her eyes wide and wild at the sight of him. Petra backed away at his approach, and Korji stopped and motioned for a moment of peace.

He squatted before her, compacting his formidable bulk into a less imposing presentation. "Are you certain you want this?"

Her confusion was impossible to mistake. "Why should I not?"

"But you fear me." Korji didn't question it.

She swallowed hard. "You are...very large." Her glance at his cock attested she didn't mean his height or the breadth of his shoulders.

He smiled. "A babe is much larger, and a woman manages that."

"Which hurts," she countered.

Korji tipped his head in agreement. "Would you prefer a smaller man for your first?"

Petra hesitated, then shook her head. He was about to question her when she offered an explanation.

"I have been told one of your kind will make this a day I will never forget. A woman deserves such a day. Does she not?"

"I would agree. If you allow me, I will endeavor to make this such a day for you."

Her nod came faster that time. Korji smiled, certain that educating the young woman would take most of the remaining day.

But it will be worth every moment. To both of us.

* * * *

Ahdia looked up at the returning men, torn as she'd been most of the day.

Korji walked at ease, smiling as she hadn't seen him for seasons. Vesh mirrored him. Taigh walked between them, laughing at something she couldn't hear from her position at the fireside.

Damn him. Her heart ached at that. Couldn't he look bored or annoyed or disappointed? Of course not.

He was male, and males took pleasure as often as they could and with as many women as they could.

She tried to reason that she had no cause to be angry with him. She'd come to his bed a few times. There were no vows between them.

Not that men always hold to those vows. More than a few vow-bound husbands had tried to entice Ahdia to sex with them.

I will kill Taigh if he does not.

Ahdia shook that thought away fiercely. When had she started considering making vows with Taigh?

As if she'd spoken his name aloud, the cur in question looked her way and offered a toothy grin. Ahdia rose and stalked the other direction. If he thought she was going to fawn over him after he'd bedded with other women, he was mad.

Ahdia headed for the shelter, then bypassed it. Taigh's sleeping roll was there, which meant he had the freedom to enter at will.

Why did I give him that freedom? But she knew the answer to that. She'd wanted to share his sleeping roll, and the idea of not doing so in sight of Vesh and his father had sounded appealing.

I should send him back to his family and out of my shelter. But if she did it this moment, he would glean the reason why and believe she had kind feelings toward him.

As if that were true!

Still, if she didn't eject him, he had freedom to enter at will, and her shelter held no particular privacy. Instead, she headed into the forest and sought out the plants she'd harvested only the day before. Her anger barely in check, she harvested more roughly than she normally would.

"What is wrong?" Korji asked.

Ahdia sighed but didn't reply.

"Does it distress you that I found solace in women?"

"No! How could you think such a thing of me?"

"*Something* is bothering you."

The truth that she cared what Taigh did irritated her, and her brother's sudden attention to details of what irritated her made it worse. "What gives you that idea?"

"You harvested enough of those herbs yesterday to last a year, and I have never seen you harvest with such an uncaring hand."

She turned to glare at him, noting his casual stance against a tree trunk. Ahdia started ordering the herbs in her hand. "These herbs fight winter illness. Who knows how large the giant village is?"

"Surely they have herbs growing there. Perhaps they also have a healer with her own stores of herbs."

"Perhaps not. 'Gather while the herbs are plentiful,' Zasha always said. Winter will be upon us all too soon."

"In more than two seasons," he countered. Korji didn't give her time to answer. "What is really troubling you?"

Ahdia picked at the herbs, trying to think of any excuse she could make to avoid admitting the truth to Korji. If he knew she was considering vows with Taigh, what would he say?

Her brother sighed deeply. "You care for the giant Taigh." He didn't question it.

She didn't answer his accusation.

It was not an accusation.

Then why did it feel like one?

"He did not enjoy the women at the village as Vesh and I did. The only time he laid a hand on them was to teach me how to take release without issue."

"How can you know?"

"I know. Even if he'd bathed as I did, he would reek of them."

She tried to make sense of that. Why had Taigh gone if not to indulge?

Korji settled next to her. "He told me when I asked that he had no plans of bedding with them...well before we reached the village."

"Why? Were there few women, and he felt your need greater?"

"There were many women willing to bed with us. More than the three of us could have tired of in half a moon."

She gaped at him. "So many?"

His smile was broad. "Do you want to know how many I had today? In just half a day?"

Yes. "No. Of course not."

Proving he saw through the lie, Korji laughed heartily. "Three. One was untouched before me. She *requested* I be her first, Ahdia."

Ahdia choked at that pronouncement. Korji was certainly making up for past lean times.

"I hear Vesh had five."

Her face burned.

"And still we turned away hands of women. But Taigh chose not a single one to bed with."

"Why?" she repeated.

"I do not know."

"Oh." Then it didn't mean anything. Her heart sank.

"I did learn something new, besides how to sense a woman."

"Really? What would that be?"

"When a giant takes vows with a woman, he remains her lover alone while she lives."

She stared at him, her heart pounding. "Truly?"

"So they tell me. They kill vow-breakers, and it seems that extends to breaking vows of oneship with a wife."

Ahdia wasn't certain if Korji was trying to tell her something of importance or if he was just imparting new stories of the giants to her. Before she could find a way to ask him, he shot her a searching look and questioned her.

"Do you think Taigh means to take vows with you?"

He hadn't asked if she was considering vows, saving her the need to decide if she wanted to or not. "No. He wouldn't? Would he? Knowing the vow is forever?"

Korji raised one eyebrow. "Wouldn't he?"

Ahdia had no idea if he would or not. How did a woman know such a thing?

Her brother pushed to his feet and offered his hand. She stared at it, confused by this move.

"Since you seem to be done gathering herbs, perhaps we should return to camp."

Though she suspected there was some trick in it, Ahdia complied.

Taigh looked up as they broke from the trees and offered her a smile that made butterflies take flight in her stomach.

The sound of Korji clearing his throat drew her attention. Her brother's smirk and his raised brow made his taunt more than clear to her.

Ahdia struck him in the chest, hooking his knee to land him hard on his backside. Before Korji could react, she was halfway to the shelter, his laughter chasing her down.

Other laughs erupted around the camp. A glance back at the men convinced her they were laughing at Korji and not at her.

Good thing for them. I could do the same to any of them.

Chapter Nine

"Ahdia has shared herself with you how many times?"

Taigh turned at the sound of his father's voice. "Seven occasions." It had been three days between the first time and the next, but since then, it had been more and more frequently—once a day, then more than once. They'd come together multiple times on more than one occasion, but his father knew that.

"And her cycle?"

His face burned at such an intimate question. "I have not taken her high cycle."

"Must I touch her and learn the answer for myself?" The threat didn't need to be stated clearer than that.

"A few days. After that, I will have to restrain myself. Perhaps...perhaps even tomorrow...for safety." Taigh had been dreading that coming event.

"If she comes to you fertile, give Ahdia whatever she wishes." There was an edge of command in that.

Taigh tried to force his mind to function. "The rules of sanction say—"

"She is a Warrior. The rules of sanction do not address female Warriors."

"But..." A thousand protests raced toward his lips, fighting to be first to emerge.

"For this war to end, Ahdia must reproduce. However that happens, it will." His expression warned of consequences for balking him. "Am I understood, Taigh?"

He can send me away and urge Ahdia to Vesh. Or to another male. That was unacceptable. "Yes, my lord. My blade is yours, my duty at your whim. I stand, a Warrior of Pol, yours to command." Perhaps pledging his allegiance to his lord would mollify his father.

As if in agreement, Gyr grunted and ambled away.

* * * *

Taigh looked up from the water, his mouth going dry at the sight of Ahdia dropping her wraps to the grass and entering the lake. His cock was hard that simply. One glance at her, and he was ready, even though her brother watched from the tree line.

She is on the cusp of high cycle. His father expected Taigh to take advantage of it, to plant a child outside of printing.

His mind and heart both protested it. This would be his child, and the gods knew he would go mad if denied either Ahdia or his son.

If it is not my son, it will be someone else's.

Unacceptable. He would gut any other man that looked at her.

Breaking the rules of sanction is also unacceptable.

They do not apply to her.

They apply to me! Perhaps she could choose to carry a child, but he could not create life without knowing she wanted it.

She reached his side and turned to face him. Ahdia's hot little hand circled his cock and started stroking. A pleased murmur left her lips.

Taigh reached between her thighs, circling her nub slowly. She tipped her head back and went on tiptoe, sampling his lips.

Ask her. If he asked, and Ahdia agreed, Taigh was breaking no rules of sanction.

"You realize you chance carrying my child," he reminded her. *Today. Tomorrow. Very soon.*

Ahdia's hand tightened and sped. While she didn't shy from the idea, it wasn't her agreement.

"Does it frighten you?"

"No."

Her answer slid over his lips, sending shocks of pleasure up his cock and causing his sac to tighten.

"Tell me why." After her mother, he'd been certain she'd fear his son killing her. "Why do you not fear carrying my child?"

"I am half giant. Zasha says a half giant will suffer no ill effects from carrying a giant's young."

Taigh resisted the urge to tell her Zasha had been wrong before. In this case, she was likely correct. Ahdia was a Warrior and would be hearty and fertile.

"And if you are correct... If I am all gian...Warrior, why should I fear carrying for my own kind? It was likely the flight from the Beasts that caused my mother's frailty."

"That is probably so." But it still wasn't enough. "You wish to carry my son?" he asked. It was more than the rules of sanction speaking. Taigh wanted to hear her say it.

Her hips jerked, and the intoxicating scent of her climax went to his head. Ahdia cried out.

"Yes. Oh yes, Taigh." She released his cock and planted her hands on his shoulders, hoisting her body up. "Now. Give me your child now."

His mind scattered. She'd said it. Ahdia had asked for one of the two things every Warrior lived to hear.

I want the other.

Soon. Take her now. Give her what she asked for.

Taigh sank his cock deep, and she moaned. Her wriggling against him was too much, and he started thrusting.

Tell her everything.

The words spilled out. "Warrior seed is very potent...and you will catch pregnant within days." It was a vow, one of the most solemn he could make.

Her breathing hitched.

"You have asked me for a child. That holds a particular magic over my kind."

"It does?" It came out in a series of gasps and hitches.

"Invite me to your bed, and I will be lodged inside you as much of the day and night as you allow." It was presumptuous to ask to come to her bed, but he needed her acceptance of him, in all ways, as much as he needed his next heartbeat.

Cries of delight rose from her. Ahdia levered herself up and down, swallowing his cock to the root. Taigh could stand no more. He emptied into her with a roar, setting off a second climax for Ahdia.

She dragged his mouth down to hers, ravenous. That was good. Now that she'd begged to carry for him, reining himself in would be difficult.

* * * *

Ahdia's body burned in need. She broke away from the kiss, her head spinning.

"My bed is open to you," she breathed. *By the gods, the thought of Taigh as a permanent addition to her bed was enough to set off flutters of excitement.*

He started to turn toward the shore.

"Not yet. Again here. Please, Taigh."

His mouth curved up in a wicked little smile, and he ground his thick cock inside her. "Say it again, Ahdia, and I will bed you wherever you wish."

"That I want you here or that you can share my bed?" She'd say either again, if he asked.

"That you want me to plant my son in you." His grinding stole her breath.

The magic. He wants me to cast the spell on him that will make him insatiable. He wants assurances that it will be his seed that fills my womb and not another's. "Do not tease," she replied.

His brow furrowed. "Tease?"

"You know only a dark giant can fill my womb with a child."

His hips tipped back and forth slowly, working his cock inside her. "To be honest, I do not know if that is true." There was a sad note in that, as if admitting it was something he felt would harm him, in the end.

"Zasha said a sorceress could carry for a human man, but a giant or half giant born of a sorceress could not. She said a common man's seed was so weak, it could not take root."

His thrusts became fiercer. "But you *want* to carry my child."

Forming words became difficult. "Yes. Yours." Ahdia had never found a common man more than passably notable. She'd never wanted to bed with one or considered the child one would give her exceptional, in any way.

And Taigh will give me a strong child. A child the likes of which I've never imagined having.

"Then you shall."

There were no words after that. Taigh put every muscle to the task of filling her channel with his cock...then his seed. In the wake of their joining, Ahdia sagged against him, energized even in her exhaustion.

"The next time will be in your bed," he informed her.

* * * *

Taigh came to consciousness slowly, blissfully aware of his nudity beneath Ahdia's fur coverings. They were curled together on her sleeping roll, Ahdia's back to his chest, her lush backside cradled to his ready cock.

He could hear his father and brother outside the shelter, preparing the morning meal and packing for the day of travel.

All day long, I will not be able to touch her. It was torture, now that she'd given him permission to sire a child with her.

We have not risen for travel yet. That thought firmly in mind, Taigh slid his hand from the breast he'd been cupping to her woman's curls.

She sighed and stretched against him. A moment later, her buttocks swiveled, seemingly investigating his readiness.

"That's right," he breathed.

He combed his fingers through her curls and sought out the nub of her pleasure. Her body heated against his fingertips, and her hips circled restlessly.

Taigh eased away from her, smiling at her moan. He positioned his cock at her seam, and she gasped out something that sounded vaguely like it was meant to be a word.

"Yes?" he prompted her.

Instead of answering, Ahdia forced herself onto him, taking the head inside.

"Oh, yes." In the next heartbeat, he was lodged deep inside her.

Ahdia shouted harshly, and her hand came up, her fist closing in the back of his hair.

Taigh thrust again and again, staking a claim on her in the only way he dared. If her culture was based on a woman's choice, what would happen if he dared follow his heart and ask for her choice of him as mate?

It would probably go badly.

Yet, holding it in was the hardest thing he'd ever done. Every instinct herded him toward asking her. He needed to bind her to him before his seed took root in her womb.

Ahdia ground her body to his, the flutters of her inner muscles becoming waves of climax. She screamed in pleasure, her body going rigid against his.

Taigh followed her over, his body and soul aching to ask her. He ground his teeth, reminding himself that he had to respect her culture and whatever vows between man and woman they made.

For a moment, her panting breathing was the only movement Ahdia made. Then she eased off of him and turned to Taigh.

The morning light streaming into her shelter, she straddled him and brought his cock to life again.

159

"Meal will soon be ready," Vesh called from the opposite wall of the shelter, not daring to approach the opening.

"No," Ahdia moaned. "It will wait."

"It will," Taigh agreed. He'd willingly give up all his meals to spend more time buried in her body.

Korji grumbled a curse. "It will wait a bit, but man does not live on a woman's cream alone." The rest was said so low that Taigh almost missed it. "Especially when he is not the one eating the cream."

Ahdia met Taigh's gaze, and he prayed she'd dismiss her brother. After a moment, she started stroking up and down his length.

After all this time, she still doesn't trust me. It was a bitter potion to swallow, especially in the throes of printing madness for her.

Chapter Ten

Ahdia stopped and stared, her mouth going dry.

Taigh stood, his waist wrap lifted, fisted in one hand while he relieved himself. It was an everyday act and a foul one at that, but just the sight of his beautiful cock had her hungry for more of him.

It is magic. He'd cast a spell on her. An angry little voice in the back of her mind opined she should fight it, fight him, learn how to break the spell, and leave him sorely disappointed.

{Remember Zasha's teachings.}

There was no way to best magic but with magic. Rajicorin had taken the secrets of her magic to the pyre with her. Even if, as Taigh attested, Ahdia had magic, she didn't know how to use it. Becoming invisible would not break his spell. There was no appropriate way to fight his magic.

If one could not fight magic, there was nothing to do but accept fate. She wanted to accept this particular fate.

Taigh finished his business and turned. He stared at her, his waist wrap tenting as he hardened.

Ahdia lifted her own, offering herself silently. She sank to the rock shelf behind her at his approach.

One of his hands settled against the wall next to her face. The other stroked between her thighs, spreading her cream over her nub.

"Are you offering yourself to me, Ahdia?"

"Yes."

"Without your brother standing guard over us? Do you trust me that much?"

"Yes. I do." It had little to do with trust, though, and everything to do with her drive to feel his length working her again. "Now, Taigh. Please."

He seated his length inside her in a single thrust. Ahdia shivered, drowned in pleasure that simply.

Pleasure taken illicitly, through the coercion of his magic.

"I don't care," she breathed.

Taigh stared at her, his hips working slowly: "About?"

"Whatever magic spell you've cast on me that makes me want you so intensely."

He shifted his hips back and forth more avidly, his expression starkly serious. "It is not *my* magic. It is ours together."

Yes, it was. Every touch made her hungrier for more of him.

His whispered words teased her face, and she drank them in greedily. "I burn in wanting you. I want to spend every day feasting between your thighs."

The memory of his feasting wrung a moan from her.

"Say you will be my woman, and I will start every day lapping at your cream, Ahdia."

It was a dark seduction. He wanted her vow to be his. Ahdia didn't question his purpose. Taigh was binding her in his magic. No doubt, once she was enslaved enough to say she was his, it would be unbreakable.

{Not his magic. Yours together. You bind him as well.}

How do I escape it? Ahdia had never tried to ask Raji for answers about her magic before. She wasn't certain it would work. Even as her mind formed the words, Ahdia's heart ached. If Raji told her how to break it, did she want to?

{You do not wish to escape it.} After a moment of guilty silence, her mother's voice continued. *{Taigh does not wish to escape it. He wishes to be bound to you.}*

"Ahdia? Will you be my woman?" There was a pleading in his expression that was at odds with the sure movements of his body.

162

{He will be unable to take other women, if you agree to be his. Not just vowed and honor bound to be yours but physically unable to choose another.}

Her fingers curled in his tunic at the idea of Taigh between another woman's legs. *I would geld him for daring. I would kill her for—*Her face flamed in the realization that she was jealous.

{He sees only you now. He will not stray from you.}

His sounds took on a fierce edge, and his Blutjagd burned against her skin.

{If you do not agree soon, he will have to banish himself from your sight. Even then, he will never be free of the magic. It will drive you both mad in wanting.}

The image of Taigh as a broken man was too much for her. "No," she breathed.

Taigh faltered, his face going shades paler, his expression pained.

Ahdia realized what he must think. Before he could react, she wrapped herself around him. "Yes. I will be your woman, Taigh."

His eyes went wide in seeming wonder. Buried deep inside her, his length jerked and then filled her with his male fluids.

The tension between them expanded, making her feel her skin was too tight. The air scorched in her lungs.

Taigh started moving again, herding Ahdia toward climax with precision.

"Say you are mine," she gasped out. Ahdia's breathing eased slightly as the question rushed toward him.

Her muddled mind searched for meaning in it. *It is our magic. Perhaps he must give his vow as well to complete the spell.*

And if he does not? Would she be the one to go insane in wanting?

"Only yours," he vowed. "I will be yours for as long as I live, Ahdia."

The tension shattered, and she screamed in the depth of sensation. Heat bubbled up inside her. Her mind argued that it could not be Taigh climaxing again, but the buffeting at her sheath confirmed it.

Taigh didn't stop. As if completing the spell broke something elemental free in them, they thrust hard and fast against each other, their sounds rising and falling.

At last, they lay panting together, tangled in the deep grass. They were sweat-soaked, and Ahdia was weak in exhaustion.

If the sun was an accurate indicator, they'd been locked together in sexual abandon for the entire break in their travels. She closed her eyes, trying to make sense of that.

"Ahdia? Are you well?" Korji's voice was tentative. Soothing.

"Rest," she offered numbly. "I need sleep. I cannot ride further today."

As if he agreed, Taigh's body moved in the slow, even cadence of deep and dreamless slumber beneath her cheek.

Gyr's voice was like a balm against her raw nerves. "Sleep, young one. We will guard you."

Ahdia had no clue if she managed to mumble her thanks before she succumbed to the need.

* * * *

Taigh woke to the feeling of Ahdia laying over him and smiled. They were mated, bound together by the Stone Herself. No one could part them. No one would dare try to.

He opened his eyes, startling at the sight of the tarp someone had erected over their sleeping bodies. *Most likely to protect us from the strong afternoon sun.* Still, the fact that they'd done so without disturbing him amazed Taigh.

It shouldn't. I've been half-mad for her for days. His sleep had been disrupted by dreams of sex unfinished for well over a quarter moon, though Ahdia had been sharing his bed for a good portion of that time. Many nights, he'd restrained himself from waking her to finish what the dreams hadn't by his duty to protect her alone.

Suffering much more time needing the seal and being denied, Taigh would surely have snapped. As it was, his starved body was making up for his lack of rest.

As if Ahdia was likewise afflicted, she sighed in her sleep and adjusted her body's fit to his.

Even if Taigh wanted to rise—*And I do not!*—he would have talked himself out of it, loath to lose this precious moment or disturb Ahdia's rest.

Sleep beckoned, and he let his eyes drift shut. A voice seemed to whisper assurances that they would not be moving on today and he could rest at ease; the other Warriors would protect them well.

Visions of Ahdia dressed in Mother's furs danced behind his eyes. *She is my woman. I should dress her in the finest I can.*

The last coherent thought he had was that he would have to send Vesh or his father to the nearest village to find appropriate cloth. *I can hardly surprise Ahdia if I go for it personally.*

Chapter Eleven

"What is it?" Ahdia eyed the fabric in Taigh's hand in confusion.

He offered his other hand. "Come with me." It wasn't a request.

She glanced at Korji, then let Taigh lead her into the trees.

Far from the others, he turned to her. "This is the type of wrap your mother would have worn. One of the three types. This is a chest wrap worn with a waist wrap like the one you already wear."

"And the others?" she asked.

"The second is worn instead of the waist wrap. It covers to the knees, but it is more difficult to wrap. The last is --"

"You wish me to wear this for what reason?"

"We are about to enter our lands. Common man or not, no man will dare approach you while you are clothed in such a wrap."

"But the amulet..." Words deserted her.

"The amulet means you are protected. This means you have a Warrior prepared to gut any man that presumes too much."

"And that male is you?" Her stomach squirmed in excitement. It was so new, she had hardly wrapped her mind around the idea that Taigh was her mate, bound to her by magic.

He tipped his head with a smug smile. "It is."

Rioting emotions fought for supremacy. Was she upset that he'd presumed to tell her what to wear? Saddened that she still wasn't his woman after all they'd shared? *Not until I wear his wrap!* Longing for something nameless? Frightened? Confused? *Most definitely confused.*

She touched her ear cuffs with trembling fingers.

The hand holding the cloth dipped slightly, and his smile dimmed. "Ahdia?"

"Why?" She pleaded for an answer to a question even she didn't fully understand.

His brow furrowed. "What are you asking?"

What am I asking? Ahdia blurted out the first question that appeared in her warring thoughts. "Are you ashamed of me?"

It was out before she could rein her tongue. Her cheeks burned, and tears stung at her eyes.

He paled, and the fabric slipped from between his fingers and fluttered to the ground between them. "No. By the gods, no. Never."

Ahdia fingered the edge of her chest wrap. "But my own clothing is not good enough for your woman. Is my past not acceptable? You want me to be—"

"No. I mean...of course you are. Ahdia, where did you get such an idea?"

"You met me in battle, Taigh. I was besting three men. Three! And...and...I have Korji for the times you are...h-hunting," she hitched out. "I have an a-amulet...and...and...I—"

"Ahdia." He reached for her, and she batted his hand away. "Ahdia, if you do not wish to wear the wraps, you do not have to. I only meant to keep you safe."

The change in him wrenched a sob from her. Before Ahdia realized what she intended, she was in Taigh's arms, venting tears into his chest.

A sound of surprise escaped his lips, and Taigh's arms tightened around her slightly. "Oh! Oh, Ahdia. I understand. I do."

"I do not," she admitted. Ahdia wiped her eyes with the back of her hand, sniffing in the miserable aftermath of tears, her stomach clenching and releasing most uncomfortably.

His hand traced the skin beneath her chest wrap to her belly. "Our son makes your emotions brittle."

Ahdia blinked in surprise. Then she laid a slap on his shoulder. "Perhaps our *daughter* simply dislikes overbearing men."

"And she will be as beautiful as her mother," he crooned.

"No woman is beautiful when she is crying." Ahdia didn't doubt that she was far from beautiful right now.

"No woman but you," Taigh corrected gently. With that, he scooped her into his arms and headed back to camp.

"Taigh?" Gyr called out. "Is something wrong?"

"We are slowing our pace," he replied. "And Ahdia will be resting while we prepare a meal for her."

"You are ordering me again," she grumbled, but Ahdia was so tired, it took effort to affect the right tone of warning.

"No, my precious beauty. I am offering."

Ahdia snuggled against his chest, letting her eyes slip shut. "Then I accept your offer."

"When we reach the village, I will be offering the gift of fur wraps. Please...accept those as well."

"Fur?" Gyr shouted after them. "*Mother's* furs?"

"If Ahdia wishes to wear them," he confirmed.

"You may show them to me," she whispered.

Taigh's chuckle overlapped with Gyr ordering Vesh to hunt for fresh game.

Chapter Twelve

"And there will be a Warrior standing watch somewhere along that ridge." Vesh pointed the way.

Ahdia searched the thick stand of trees but didn't see anyone. "Is he ghosting?"

Taigh answered. "He may be, but that is an incredible waste of energy when the trees will hide him well enough."

"Some young Warriors use the time to practice ghosting," Vesh shared.

Bird call split the air...the call of the soft blue bird and then the call of the red-chested one.

"That is the report announcing friends approaching," Gyr offered.

Ahdia met Korji's gaze, her heart hammering. *Friends. They announce us as friends.*

His smile was tense, and he offered a nod. She wondered if he was as unsure of their actual reception as she was.

Taigh reached around her body and covered her hand with his own. "You are Rajicorin's young."

She turned to face him. "But—"

"You are my mate, Ahdia. No one has the right to dismiss my mate. Not my lord, and not the Stone lord. I bring you to the village. Do you understand?"

Yes. She understood. That protected her, but what about Korji?

Before she could form the words to ask it, they'd passed through the narrow pass that forced them to ride single file. The village beyond was full of sturdy wooden structures...and teeming with villagers. Enough to rival the refugee village easily.

And all better trained for battle. That thought sent a shiver down her spine.

* * * *

"They've returned! Gyr and his sons have returned!"

Miriza left the pot of water behind and ran for the village, her heart skipping in excitement. Taigh was back, and she was old enough for him to ask for permission to take her to mate.

Dreams of Taigh taking her to his bed box had taunted her for more than a season. Though other Warriors had noticed her, Taigh was the one she wanted. *And women got what they wanted in the Warrior world...at least as far as men were concerned.*

She topped the hill and stopped cold, her smile and the dreams of Taigh fading together. He lifted a woman from the back of his horse. Taigh lowered his head and kissed the new arrival.

Most likely in announcement that she is his. Hopes that it was a new protected they'd saved from Beasts died a bitter death. Miriza cursed him silently and started to return to her work.

Taigh doesn't deserve my attention. There are plenty of other Warriors who would be overjoyed to have me show an interest. And she would do that. Some other lucky man would be hers, but she would make that one prove himself to her first.

Movement out of the corner of her eye drew her gaze back to the Warriors assembling below. She counted the horses again. There was an extra, but the woman had been riding double with Taigh.

Gyr dismounted, and she focused on the Warrior swinging off the back of the strange horse. Miriza gaped at him.

He was like no man she'd ever seen before. His hair was long; it reached halfway down his chest. A handful of fine braids framed his face, twinkles of color drawing her eyes to them. A blood mark stood out in stark contrast to his lightly tanned skin. Though it wasn't clear at this distance, she was sure it wasn't Syth.

Why would there be a need for two?

Miriza dimly noted that she was moving toward him, intent on a closer look at the mark. His head turned, and he watched her approach.

The blood mark took shape when she was nearly an arm's length away, and she reached out to brush her fingertips over it, heedless of how rude it was to presume to touch a stranger in such a manner. "Kor," she breathed.

"Korji," he grumbled.

It took a moment for his meaning to sink in. She drew her hand back and met his dark gaze. "Your name is Korji?"

He offered a simple, terse nod of his head.

The bear's paw. It suits him.

"Miriza!" Her father appeared at her side and drew her behind him, taking a protective stance she wanted to protest. Taigh and Gyr had brought him. He was a friend of the village and clearly a Warrior...though a stranger to her.

There was no time for that. In the next heartbeat, Gyr was calling Korji away.

* * * *

Korji took a calming breath, then turned toward the men gathering around him.

He resisted the urge to look at the woman who'd spoken to him. The dark giant who'd drawn her away was flaming in fury that Korji had dared speak to her.

His heart sank at the bald truth. *Nothing has changed. Not for me. Even among the dark giants, I will be denied the comforts every man craves. I should have stayed in Shil.* Perhaps he could return there, if this village proved unbearable.

Korji had barely spoken to her. He could only assume Miriza was the woman's name. It could very easily be a word in the giant's language he didn't know. *And I crave another moment in her presence already.*

He chanced another look at her, just in time to see the giant send her away. The woman moved stiffly, seemingly angry that the man was giving her orders.

The dark giant turned, looked from Korji to the woman and back again, and offered a glare that made it clear he would sooner kill Korji than see him with the young woman. Dejected, he turned toward Ahdia.

His sister looked nervous, an emotion she rarely found a use for. She pulled at her chest wrap, straightening it. Then she scooped her hair behind one ear, revealing the ceremonial ear cuff that pronounced her a woman of high standing in the village that had raised them.

As if in the attempt to soothe her, Taigh drew Ahdia to his chest. Korji ground his teeth. It had been his place to soothe her upsets before Taigh. What was his purpose now?

Hunting Beasts and nothing more. That was disheartening.

"Who is this Warrior, Gyr?" one dark giant asked.

Korji stiffened, more than aware that he was being evaluated. *Evaluated, and I have only the barest understanding of their laws. What happens if they find me lacking?*

But he knew the answer to that. Their laws demanded death or physical punishment for nearly every offense.

"Yes, Gyr, who indeed?" the one who'd pulled the woman away demanded.

That one will call for my death at the first provocation. If he is well thought of, he may succeed.

Part of him argued that he should simply assure the man he had no intentions of taking a woman that the laws said he could not have. *Raised by the barbarian refugees, I am still civilized enough to respect the laws of another tribe, as I must.*

Not to mention that such an assurance would make Korji seem weak. It might make the giant in question think he could order Korji around.

Gyr cleared his throat. "I believe we should speak with—"

"I am here, brother," a voice called out calmly.

The crowd parted to let a giant amble through. A mark that matched the one Taigh had graced his upper arm. That meant this man would be a formidable enemy, Korji was sure.

"An ally." His voice was low and calming.

Korji didn't reply to that. He wasn't certain if the man was using magic to read his thoughts or was proclaiming himself an ally.

The man surveyed Korji and then Ahdia. His gaze returned and fastened on Korji's name mark. His eyes widened. "You live," he breathed. "But where is Rajicorin?"

Korji opened his mouth to reply.

The scream of fury escaping the giant's mouth sent Korji back two steps. In a moment of realization, he knew this man saw all. He wielded magic that was chilling in its possible uses.

He has sorcerer in him. And he is angry. We never should have come here.

Korji moved to protect Ahdia. His sister stood, bathed in the giant's fury, wide-eyed, in the path of destruction that was on the verge of eruption.

Taigh didn't protest the presumption. He closed ranks, forming a human shield between the raging giant and Ahdia.

"Dead! My sister is dead!"

In the distance, women and children scattered. Korji grasped the hilt of his weapon, weighing the need to draw it. Only the fact that none of the others had stopped him from doing so.

He is our uncle, Rajicorin's brother. How would I react if I learned Ahdia was dead? The torturous moments when she had ghosted confirmed that it would be as bad as this or worse.

Gyr stepped between them, giving Korji his back as Korji was giving Ahdia his. "You knew that to be true, Goven," he soothed the man.

"No! The Stone would never say. I had hoped— But—" He glared at Korji.

He blames me. I was an infant, and he blames me? Korji's anger ignited at that.

Gyr waved him down. "They are your blood. They are Rajicorin's young."

Murmuring grew in the crowd. Giants shot wary looks at each other.

"And *his*." There was something cold and unforgiving in that. "They are not of my household."

Korji's ire bubbled its way toward a blast. "We are not responsible for the crimes of the one that sired us."

"Of course you aren't," Taigh attested.

The other giants were mixed in their response to that.

Goven opened his mouth to answer.

Ahdia recovered her wits. "Stop it. All of you, stop. You are being children. If you have the power to banish us, do so at sunrise. The barest courtesy one owes a weary guest is the night to recover."

"He does not have that power," Gyr assured her.

"Then still your tongue and go blow off your *Blutjagd* elsewhere. Anything you wish to discuss with us can be discussed when we are rested and you are reasonable. I intend to eat and rest after our long journey. If I have to go through you to do it, I will, Uncle."

Gyr shot her a bemused look, Taigh smiled, and Goven gaped at her.

Against his better judgment, Korji laughed. "She will, too. Never doubt Ahdia, when she is in a mood."

"She will not need to, nor would I allow her to," Taigh growled out. His expression promised death for Goven first.

Gyr nodded his agreement. Even Vesh tested his blade against the sheath. Korji crossed his arms over his chest.

Goven looked from face to face, turned, and stalked away.

Taigh turned and scooped Ahdia to his chest. He met Korji's gaze and nodded as if in thanks. "Come. My mother will have a place ready for all of us."

* * * *

Ahdia grasped a handful of Taigh's tunic, her head spinning wildly. The tang of Goven's *Blutjagd* grated at her already-abused nerves. In the distance, there were shouts and sounds of destruction.

Gyr started issuing orders. "Bir, Tivian... Arrange guards to protect our *Blutjagdfrau* until Goven blows off his loss."

Grumbled agreements followed.

Another Warrior offered his men, as well.

"Good. Work out the watch between you."

With that, they were in motion. The wooden shelter that Taigh carried her to was near the center of the village. He didn't hesitate in the main room. Ahdia had barely a glance at Gyr engaged in a heated kiss with what she would assume was Taigh's mother before she was whisked away into a secondary room and placed in a bed box.

The furs covered her, and Taigh traced the backs of his fingers along her chin.

"Would you like some water while we prepare a meal?"

She nodded weakly, her energy sapped by the tension in the air and Goven's sounds of anger. Taigh left without further question, and Ahdia let her eyes drift shut.

It seemed everyone was speaking at once. There were introductions, explanations... Harsh whispers passed on the outside of the walls, spreading the word that she carried Taigh's child. Footsteps moved away. She didn't doubt that the entire village would know who she and Korji were and the important details of their lives by the time the sun set.

Someone approached the bed, but it wasn't Taigh. Ahdia opened her eyes and met the questioning gaze of Gyr's mate.

The older woman offered a fine, smooth cup. "For you, *Blutjagdfrau.*"

She pushed to sitting and took it with a word of thanks. The water was cool and refreshing, and some of the lethargy left her limbs. Rejuvenated, she handed the cup back.

"The meal will be ready soon. Would you like some sweet bread now?"

Ahdia smiled. "Thank you, but no. I smell meat, and I am certain my child wishes to partake."

A nervous laugh escaped the other woman's lips. "Young Warriors usually do." She shifted from foot to foot nervously. "Is there anything you require, *Blutjagdfrau?*"

"For you not to use that title," she quipped in return.

The woman's brow furrowed in seeming confusion.

"My name is Ahdia. And yours is...?"

"Navia. I meant no offense. It is out of respect—"

"None is taken, but..." She sighed. Would everyone in the Warrior village go to extremes upon meeting her?

Navia sank to the edge of the bed box and waited for her to continue.

"I was led to believe Korji and I were coming home to our true family, Navia. Our uncle threatens us on sight, villagers challenge Korji, and people act as if I am...apart from them. I do not understand family acting this way."

She smiled and covered Ahdia's hand with one of her own. "I know just the thing."

"You do?"

176

"After we eat... I will send word, and the women of the village will welcome you properly."

Though she had no idea what that meant, Ahdia nodded her agreement.

* * * *

Ahdia followed Navia to one of the two central structures, Taigh, Gyr, Korji, and a hand of other men surrounding them. Some women walked ahead of them. Others rushed to catch up with the procession.

The shelter was larger than the rest, seemingly large enough to accommodate the whole of the village at once. Inside, she saw rock sitting places and several pools of water.

"A bathing area?" she asked.

Navia paused in the process of removing her knee-length wrap. "Yes. The pools vary in heat. The furthest there..." She motioned to the far wall and the smallest pool. "That one is the hottest. They become cooler as you move away from it. You should not go closer than two away from the hottest...in your condition."

She sounded much like Zasha had when she'd scolded Ahdia in her childhood. It warmed her to hear it. "Thank you for your counsel. I would not have known it."

The twittering of the other women paused at that. It took a moment for Ahdia to realize they were evaluating her.

"Remove your clothing and set it on one of the seats," Navia instructed.

Ahdia nearly shivered at the idea. She'd never been allowed to remove her chest wrap in the refugee village, even when she'd been bathing with only other women. *I removed it with Taigh. I removed it before the other Warriors when I first came to Taigh.*

There was no reason not to do so among the women of the Warrior village. That firmly in mind,

Ahdia removed her clothing and folded them on the closest flat rock, next to those Navia had left.

The silence around her put Ahdia's teeth on edge. Whispers rose. Among them, "Tes" was most prevalent.

Yes. Gyr said my aspect...my mark is Tes.

One of the younger women ran to the doorway and poked her head through the drape, probably reporting that information to the men outside.

Ahdia's face burned in embarrassment. Would every little thing about her illicit such a response?

Navia offered her hand, and Ahdia took it, still shaken.

"This is Ahdia, daughter of Rajicorin and Jotem. Mate of my eldest son, Taigh. Though she is known as *Blutjagdfrau*, she prefers the use of her name to her title."

As if that freed the others to address her directly, questions rose, overlapping each other.

"What happened to your mother? She was my friend, when we were young."

"One of the men said you killed Veriel. Is that true?"

"Do you ever wear boots?"

Navia put up a hand, demanding a halt, and the other women complied.

Her head spinning, Ahdia took a calming breath.

Navia guided her toward the pools. "Answer in comfort," she suggested. "Do you wish cool or warm?"

"Warm, please. I fear the long journey has taxed my muscles."

The water was a delight, and Ahdia sank into it with a sigh. After a moment of indulgence, she set out to answer their many questions.

"My mother died giving birth. I never knew her in life."

"Who raised you?" another interrupted.

"A healer that worked with my mother in the refugee village. Her name was Zasha. She was old and had no milk, so Korji and I were fed the milk of her goats instead of mother's milk.

"Korji learned from the men of our village, and I learned from Zasha."

There was a moment of silence. "And Veriel?"

"I wounded him, but since Korji, Taigh, and I all struck together, I cannot be certain which of us took the killing blow. I suspect it was Taigh, but my fighting knowledge is limited.

"I wear boots in cold weather, but I do not when the weather is warm."

A gray-haired woman snorted at that. "Taigh will be certain to order you to when he presents you with Mother's furs."

Ahdia glared at her. "Taigh does not order me. Do women in this village really accept being ordered about by men?"

There was a moment of silence, and even the young women running tidbits of knowledge to and from the drape went still and stony-faced.

"Of course not," another of the elder women decreed. "But men are men. Our men, especially, tend to take our protection to extremes."

"Since I was besting three men in battle when Taigh found me, I believe he has learned well how little I require protection."

The silence was more potent that time. One of the young women scrambled for the drape, seemingly bursting to share that news. From outside, the grumbling of the men was impossible to miss.

Another spoke up from the direction of the stone seats. "Your clothing is most striking. Will you continue to wear it in the village?"

Ahdia searched her out. "Taigh will offer me Mother's furs, but I believe I will wear my own clothing for work and nursing babes."

"Then you are carrying," another stated gleefully.

Ahdia's move to answer was overpowered by another question from the young one near the clothing. "Does Korji like this style of dress?"

"Miriza!" one of the women at Ahdia's back protested.

The young one blushed a deep red, but she raised her head proudly. "I am old enough to notice men," she countered.

The elder sighed. "Yes. Yes, you are."

Ahdia's mind worked quickly. Miriza's father might not approve of her choosing to dress as Ahdia did. If she'd noticed Korji, Ahdia was going to do everything she could to encourage the young woman.

"Korji notices style of dress very little. If you have interest in him, I believe that would be enough for him."

Her smile was shy and hopeful. The other young women shot looks between them, and none of them moved for the drape.

* * * *

Taigh guided Ahdia back to his parents' home, smiling at the sight of her wrapped in the woven he'd handed into the bathing hut for her. It covered more flesh than her own clothing did, though it left her blood mark and shoulders bare.

A few of the other men chanced a glance at the blood mark, but they looked away quickly enough when Taigh glared them down. She wasn't theirs to look at, certainly not theirs to touch.

Inside their hut, he led Ahdia to the room they shared. She shot him a smile that said she'd recovered from her earlier upset, and he laid a kiss on his lips.

Still, I have to make a statement to Goven. It is time to shame the old man into an apology. He fingered Ahdia's amulet, searching for the words to explain it to her.

She looked down at his hand and shied a step. "What are you doing?"

"I must replace this amulet with one of my own."

She wrapped her hand around it, shaking her head.

"Ahdia—"

"It was my mother's."

"Goven has spoken in anger, but he has renounced you. When he recovers, he will realize his mistake, but until then, we must shame him with his behavior."

"I cannot," she pleaded.

"It is necessary. It must be done. His crime cannot be left unchallenged."

"But it was my mother's," she repeated.

"I know, and Goven will return it."

"You cannot know that."

"If he refuses to, the entire village will rise up against him."

"I cannot chance it," she pleaded.

"Chance what?" She wasn't making sense. The one her mother wore or not, one amulet was like another. The only difference in them was in whose house they were attached to, and Rajicorin's house had renounced Ahdia.

She rubbed at the amulet, her hands shaking. Tears pooled in her eyes. "She speaks to me."

"Who speaks to you, Ahdia?"

"My mother. Through her amulet, she speaks to me."

Taigh had never heard of such a thing. Was it more barbarian mythology? "You mean you feel when the Beasts are near, as you did with Veriel. You have feelings that tell you when you run or hide or fight."

She shook her head, and one tear splashed onto her cheek. "I...hear her. She speaks to me. She tells me things...sometimes things I could not know without her."

He hesitated. "For instance."

181

"When you asked me to be yours, she told me what would happen if I continued to refuse what I wanted with you...or if I accepted it."

His heart pounded at that pronouncement. "What did she say?"

"She said you would be unable to take another woman, if I accepted you and—"

"I told Korji that."

"He did not tell me you would be unable...only that you would not. She did. She also said that my refusal would leave you broken...perhaps dying."

It was difficult to refute what she was saying, though he'd never heard of such a connection with the dead. "Has she always spoken to you?"

Her brow creased. "No. Only since my blood began to flow. Zasha said my sorceress powers unlocked when my blood began to flow and that was why I was able to commune with the dead."

The shadow of a memory taunted him. He'd heard that the Stone sometimes spoke directly to marked women, as it did to Stone lords.

"Taigh?"

"I suspect..." *No. I cannot tell her this until I am certain. She wants to believe it is her mother she hears.* "I suspect you will be able to speak to her with any amulet you wear. Let me exchange the one you wear and see if that is correct."

She hesitated. "She does not always speak to me. What if she does not immediately?"

"Then I will have to use a bit of trickery, but I will not take the amulet from you, if you cannot hear her with another."

He only hoped that Luven would play along and help Taigh in the bit of deception. Considering his friend's ire, it was nearly certain the young Warrior would aid Taigh in tricking his father.

Ahdia nodded and removed the amulet, her breathing going ragged. Taigh retrieved one from his pouch and settled it around her neck before he reached for the one she'd worn her entire life. Her hand tightened, then released the amulet to him.

She closed her eyes. After a moment, she chuckled. Her eyes opened again, gleaming in pleasure.

"You still hear her then?" he inquired.

Ahdia smiled. "She is still with me."

Taigh raised the amulet in salute, then made his way outside.

Luven waited for him, his tension showing in every muscle. "She agreed?" he asked.

"She did. If I was the sort to wish ill on another Warrior, I would send my belief that your father should choke on this." He placed the amulet in Luven's hand.

"He has my wish for it." After a moment of hesitation, he dropped his voice. "I could not help but overhear a bit of your mate's words..."

Taigh checked to be sure none of the other Warriors could overhear him. "Ahdia hears the Stone speak. She believes it is her mother's voice, and I will not tell her otherwise."

Luven ground his teeth. "My father is a fool."

He didn't argue that point. In the next moment, Luven disappeared with the amulet in hand.

Taigh made his way back to his bed, stopping short at the sight of Ahdia. She'd shed the woven wrap and was laid out, displayed in his bed.

Just for me. Taigh removed his clothing and joined her, parting his lips in a deep kiss. Before sunrise, the entire village would hear their passion and know that no man could stand between them.

Chapter Thirteen

Ahdia didn't question that Taigh wasn't in the bed box with her when she awakened. She stretched, working out the kinks of riding on horseback for so many weeks.

A movement in the room shocked her awake, and she pressed herself to the wall, holding the furs around her to cover her body. The shape of a man sitting in the center of the room coalesced from the mist of her waking vision.

It took a moment longer for his identity to settle in her mind and for Ahdia to react to it.

Goven.

She launched to her feet, wrapping the fur with the intent to flee for the nearest weapon she could find at his first movement.

"Don't go. I mean you no harm."

Ahdia hesitated and stared at him, waiting to see what her uncle would do next. Though she knew she could scream for her guards, Ahdia would save that for a mortal threat. There was little doubt her guards would kill Goven if she called out.

She shifted from foot to foot and scooped her hair behind her ear.

Goven's expression went wistful. "You are so like your mother."

"Am I? Zasha never told me I resembled her." Her heart ached at that. How shattering would it have been for Goven to see her arrive in the village?

"Zasha?"

"The healer who raised us."

He nodded, his expression sad. "You never knew her then?"

"Rajicorin?"

Goven managed a subdued 'yes.'

"No. We never had the honor of knowing our mother." The need to make peace for Korji ate at her.

Goven had sent a look that blamed her brother at him upon meeting them. "Korji came first. Had he been the only babe, she would have survived it. According to Zasha, my birth was...difficult."

She tensed, expecting the fury from him Goven had originally vented at Korji.

"Births are at times. The gods cannot say why some go badly and some go well."

Ahdia eased a bit. A potent silence fell between them, and the need to escape him rode her hard. He wasn't throwing off waves of Blutjagd, but his shoulders tensed and released as if he was considering attack.

"I was wrong to deny you and your brother. Forgive me. I was crazed in loss." He hesitated and peeked up at her. "It doesn't excuse me, of course."

She took a calming breath. "No doubt you were. I cannot fault you your anger and loss."

"I have some things that belonged to your mother. I thought you might like to have them."

Her heart skipped in excitement. "I *would* like that. There were so few things..." Ahdia stopped in the realization that she had her hand wrapped around the amulet. *But not my mother's amulet.*

"If you would accept it, I would offer your amulet back."

Anger rose in her. "It was my *mother's* amulet. Not mine."

"*Blutjagdfrau?*" one of the current shift of guards asked from the doorway.

Ahdia didn't turn to look at him. "I require no assistance. Thank you for your concern."

There was a moment of stillness, and Goven tipped his head, probably in response to a silent warning issued by her guards. They retreated but not far.

"I never meant for them to take it from you." That sounded like an apology.

"I gave it to them, Uncle. If you wanted no part of my brother and myself, I had no right to keep something with *your* mark upon it."

He winced. "Since your mate is also a Stone lord—"

"What do you mean to say?" she interrupted him.

Goven pushed to his feet, his head bowed. He pulled something from the pouch at his side, and she shied a step in the bed box, her breathing hitching in alarm.

Her mother's amulet hung from his hand. Ahdia stared at it, confused.

"I will understand if you refuse to wear it."

"Why would I refuse to wear what my mother gave me at birth?" In truth, she was glad he was willing to return it. Though Taigh claimed all amulets were the same, no other felt like her mother's amulet to her, her mother's voice speaking to her or not.

"It is yours." He took a step closer, offering it.

Ahdia took it with her free hand, watching him for any sign of attack.

"I would like to speak with you, if you are willing."

Her head spun at that pronouncement. "What have we been doing thus far?"

A weak laugh escaped his lips. "I understand you are a healer."

"I fail to see what that has to do with speaking. Do you suffer some ailment that requires my aid?" If he did, she would do her best for him. It was a pact with the gods that she would do so for anyone who needed aid.

He raised his head and met her eyes. "Your mother was also a healer."

"I know it." *Does he think I know nothing of my mother?*

"Would you like to see her garden?"

"Garden?"

Goven sighed. "You have traveled all these years. I forgot that."

"Not all of them. We moved on when the fighting got too close or game too scarce."

"A garden is a space where a healer grows herbs within the village. There were also places she collected certain herbs. I know them all."

Ahdia's heart tripped in excitement. "You will show me these places?"

"They are yours now."

She looked down at herself, her cheeks heating at the fact that she'd nearly suggested they leave immediately.

"Dress and eat. I will collect your mother's things and return with them soon."

Ahdia nodded enthusiastically. She couldn't wait to see the places her mother had held dear.

Goven headed for the main room.

"Uncle?"

He turned his head to look at her.

"Thank you for this."

With a tip of his head, he was gone.

* * * *

Ahdia pulled the fur cloak she'd found in her mother's belongings tighter around her body, blocking out the chill morning wind. Her mother's amulet was around her throat again, where it belonged.

The garden was easily five body-length's wide and twice as long. A stroll through it revealed many common healing plants, as well as cooking herbs and a few rare healing herbs she usually had to hunt and hope for.

She reached the far side of the garden, the side furthest from Goven's home. There, in the shade of the forest, was a barren spot.

Ahdia sank to her knees at the edge, running her hand over the dead grass. By the shape and size, she could tell it had once been one of the wooden huts most of the Warriors favored, but what could kill the land this way? Had it burned, the foliage would have overtaken the rich soil again.

"Ahdia, no," Goven called out.

She looked his direction and saw him running for her, his hand out and his eyes wild, her guards in his wake, their hands on their weapons. Confused at the gruff edge to his voice and their edge of *Blutjagd*, she rose to her feet and retreated from him.

He stopped, the guards flanking him, and motioned for a moment of peace. "Not the dead land. Please... Come away."

The crisp, brown grass scraped against her feet, and Ahdia looked down. She left the barren spot, but on the opposite side Goven stood on.

He breathed deeply and nodded.

Ahdia motioned to the spot. "What did this? It wasn't fire."

It seemed Goven didn't want to answer her, so Ahdia shot a questioning look at the elder of her two guards.

He tipped his head and started to speak. "It was their home...Rajicorin and Jotem, before he turned traitor. Goven ordered everything of Jotem's destroyed after Rajicorin disappeared, including their home. We burned it to the ground, but it was...unnatural. Nothing has grown here since."

Goven motioned her further away from the barren spot. "It is unnatural, Ahdia. Please, for the sake of yourself and your babe, do not tempt the Stone by going near it."

She nodded and distanced herself from the barren spot. With every step away from it she took, Goven's tensed muscles eased.

At last he spoke. "Would you like to see the other places she gathered?"

Her guards shot each other sour looks, but they didn't presume to tell her what to do.

"I would like that very much. Thank you, Uncle."

* * * *

Taigh stopped in the doorway to his parents' home, his heart stuttering at the lack of guards. When he hadn't seen them outside, he'd assumed his mother had offered them a meal and there were inside with Ahdia.

He vaulted into the room he shared with his mate, but the bed box was empty. A box he didn't recognize was in the corner of the room.

"Is she gone?" his father asked.

He turned back to the main room in time to see his mother coming in with a pitcher of water.

"Is Ahdia with you?"

She looked from man to man, spending an extra moment staring at Korji before she answered. "No. She's gone to see Raji's picking places with Goven."

Taigh's heart stuttered at that.

"Her guards are with her, of course," his mother hastened to add. "Goven has made no move against her."

Taigh cursed himself for leaving her with the guards. He'd wanted to discuss plans for the home that would be constructed for them, and he hadn't believed Goven would screw up his courage to offer an apology so quickly.

"We will find her," Gyr vowed. He turned to his mate. "Did they say which picking places?"

She seemed to replay their discussion before she replied. "No. But he did mention Rajicorin's garden. I would go there first."

Taigh ground out a word of thanks and headed out of the house, Korji and his father at his heels. He didn't doubt that Rajicorin's garden was the one adjoining Goven's home, though he'd never heard it referred to as such.

The dead lands. His heart stuttered at the idea of Ahdia so near that damned place. The stories of it were old, but it was said that Veriel had cursed the land, perhaps poisoned it with his foul blood. The last thing Taigh wanted was Ahdia anywhere near that place, especially while she carried his son in her womb.

There was no one in the garden, so Taigh headed for the forest, in the direction where he knew various healing plants grew. As an afterthought, he motioned toward the dead lands and issued a warning to Korji.

"Do not walk on the dead lands. They are cursed."

Korji's footsteps slowed. He grunted. "It seems not so cursed."

Taigh shot a look that direction and stopped short. The deep brown of dead, crushed plants was broken by vibrant green islands of color.

It took a moment for what he was seeing to sink in fully. "Footprints. I would almost swear they are footprints."

"We should find Ahdia," Korji reminded them.

"Yes. Yes, we should." But it was hard to tear his eyes off the foreign sight of growing plants in the dead lands.

A more welcome sight granted him when he turned away. Ahdia was emerging from the forest, walking side-by-side with Goven, her guards in her wake.

She looked up at them and smiled, and Taigh's breathing eased. Obviously, she had made peace with her uncle, and that was good for both of them.

Ahdia glanced toward the dead lands, and her smile disappeared. She broke from Goven and ran for it. Goven reached to stop her, and her guards grabbed him by the arms and pulled him back.

Taigh knew they acted precisely as they should have. *Still, I don't want her on the cursed land.* He scooped her up on one arm just before she could step into onto the dead grass.

She didn't fight him, though she shot Taigh a look of disbelief.

"You should not walk there," he informed her.

"But my magic heals it," Ahdia insisted. "See. Everywhere I touched is now whole and strong."

All the men turned to look at the change. Both guards released Goven in their shock. A few heartbeats later, they dropped to one knee and bowed to Ahdia.

Goven stood there, his mouth agape and moving as if he would like to say something but couldn't find the words.

Korji nodded. "So you've finally found your magic," he mused. "I suppose I shall have to call you 'sorceress' now." His lips curved in the shadow of a smile.

Ahdia smacked her brother's arm. "Take care that I do not prove it to you."

Taigh watched, spellbound, as the green areas spread, eradicating the brown.

Goven appeared at her side, intent on the new growth. "Nothing has grown here since Rajicorin left," he breathed.

"You said what was my mother's is now mine," Ahdia noted in a wistful, little voice.

"Yes. Yes, it is," her uncle agreed.

"Then the Goddess has given me a sign."

Taigh cleared his throat. "What does this sign mean?"

"When we make a home of our own, it must be here."

Gyr spoke up, clearly agitated by that idea. "The land is cursed. Who knows what will become of a babe born there."

"I know," she whispered. She stroked at the amulet she held inside her closed hand. "I know the curse is broken now. The land will be whole and its benefits plentiful."

Taigh didn't ask if the Stone had told her that was so or not. He nodded his agreement, revising his plans for their home. It wasn't where he'd planned to construct their home, but somehow, the idea of Ahdia surrounded by healing plants seemed right.

"Anything my mate wishes," he vowed.

Ahdia snuggled into his chest, nearly purring in happiness already.

* * * *

Korji turned to follow the others away from the garden of herbs that was now his sister's. The others were already past the nearest homes and well toward Gyr's house.

Goven called his name, and Korji stiffened. Whatever the old man wanted to say, it was surely something he didn't want to hear.

The Stone lord circled his position and faced him, his expression worn. "I owe you an apology, Korji."

"I require nothing of the sort from you." Only your distance.

"But it is owed to you, and so I offer it. I was angry and mourning the loss of my sister. I was wrong to refuse you and Ahdia. You are all I have left of Rajicorin. If your mother was here, she would have scarred me with my own weapons for treating you so shamefully."

Sisters have that way. Still, Korji wanted to admit no kinship to this man. He made to round the Stone lord and leave him behind.

"Korji!"

That snapped his patience and Korji turned on him. "I have no need of your family, Goven, Stone lord. I am lord of my own. I am well raised and not in need of a father, real or fostered. Gyr teaches me your ways well. I cannot fathom what you might believe I need you for."

The Stone lord blanched. "The blade you carry is old. I am a weapons-maker."

"It is serviceable, and it is mine. I know how to care for a blade."

"It is well cared for," Goven conceded. "But it is also the blade of a traitor, and it is worn."

"It was my mother's blade. She took it from the traitor and made it her own. Then she gave it to me. That is all I need to know."

"Let me replace it with a newer blade. You'll need two new blades, I'm sure. It seems you only have the one."

That was something Korji was willing to consider. Gyr had said he needed two blades to pin and kill a Beast most expediently.

Taking Korji's silence as acceptance, Goven pulled a gleaming blade from the back of his weapons belt and offered it to Korji. He took it, testing the weight and balance. It was superb.

The decoration on the hilt caught his attention, and Korji glared at Goven. He raised the blade between them, turned it downward, and threw it into the soft, growing ground at his uncle's feet. Goven flinched, but he didn't respond otherwise.

"You give me a blade with your seal on it, as if I do not know what that means?" Korji challenged him. "I am not of your house, Goven, Stone lord. I am lord of my own, and I will use blades with my own seal on it, or I will use none."

"The seal of a traitor? The seal of the King of Beasts and Destroyer of Lives?"

Korji showed Goven the blade he carried. "This blade killed that same traitor and gave me my place as lord of the house. It seems appropriate that I continue to carry it."

He swept past Goven and made his way to Gyr's home. The Stone lord didn't make an effort to stop him, and that was a relief. Given much more time in Goven's company, Korji might have tested the blade on the Stone lord himself.

Chapter Fourteen

"Father?"

Perit looked up from the weapons he was sharpening. "Yes, Miriza?"

She sighed. "Why do you dislike Korji so?"

His eyes widened. "I do not dislike him. Why would you say such a thing?"

"Then why do you discourage him from noticing me?"

His face darkened. "I would discourage any man from noticing you," he grumbled. "What father wants his daughter to leave him?"

"Mated to a Warrior, where would I go? We would be huts apart," she dismissed him.

Perit didn't reply to that.

Miriza sat at the table across from him, folding herself onto the straw-stuffed cushions. Her father didn't meet her gaze directly.

"You cannot keep me a little girl forever, father."

"I can try."

"And I can rebel," she reminded him.

He scowled at her, and Miriza shot him the smile that always won her way.

Perit went back to sharpening his weapons. "If Korji wishes to pursue you, he can ask me properly."

"While you give every indication that such a request would never be granted? You must be joking."

"Every man in the village knows what I expect."

"Korji was not raised in our village. He does not know what a gruff, unreasonable Warrior you can appear to those who do not know you."

He looked up at her, seemingly shocked by her candor. "Where did you learn to say such things to me?"

"Do you know...? In Korji's village, they are very civilized, I have heard."

He shot her a look that spoke of disbelief. "I see how civilized they are by how they dress," he shot back.

Miriza waved him off. "Because males and females do not see the need to waste cloth, you judge them uncivilized."

"And by what do you judge them civilized?" One thick brow went up in challenge.

"Their women do not take orders from men. Who a woman deems worthy to share her bed or become her mate is no man's choice."

Perit didn't answer that immediately. "I see. And you have found an interest in Korji. Is that it?"

"It is." She waited patiently for his answer.

Her father sighed. "I will speak with him at training tomorrow. I will inform him that I consider him a worthy suitor to your affections." He met her gaze, seemingly pained. "Will that make you happy?"

Miriza smiled widely. "Very happy, father. Very."

* * * *

Korji stepped back from the practice ring, putting his sacred weapon through the motions Taigh had taught him. When he'd been in the refugee village, he'd believed there was nothing he hadn't learned about fighting. No one could stand against him long. Here, he was little better than average and uneducated in so many things.

"Korji."

His muscles tightened at the sound of the unwelcome voice. He knew well enough who it was, and since Perit had never had a kind word for him, it was surely more of the same.

He didn't look up at the house lord. "Yes, Perit?" *I am a substandard Warrior and I will never be worthy of your daughter, no doubt.*

"You are improving nicely, I see."

Korji stopped his practice in shock at such unexpected praise. He turned to stare at Perit, wondering at his game.

"Of course, you were a strong Warrior when you arrived here, but you improve with every passing day."

He looked sincere, but there was no explanation for his words. "My thanks," Korji offered, at a loss to come up with anything better.

Perit didn't immediately continue, so Korji pivoted toward Gyr's home.

"I know you have noticed my daughter," he called after Korji.

He didn't look back. "I know the laws of sanction," he answered the accusation.

"If you were of a mind... I would not be adverse to the match."

Korji swiveled around to look at Miriza's father. "You mean that?"

"Warriors are not in the habit of lying, Korji. Should you wish to take my daughter as mate, I would not oppose you."

He considered that. "My thanks," he offered again.

Perit turned and made his way around the field toward the other house lords. Korji watched him go, confused at the reversal. After a moment, he started walking...not toward Gyr's home but rather toward his camp site. Until he understood this turn of events, he didn't feel equal to discussing it with Ahdia.

She can come to me now. Visions of Miriza walking toward him, clothed only in a waist wrap, made his cock ache.

His step slowed at a disturbing thought. *She can come to me, but will she choose to?*

* * * *

Miriza hurried to the practice field, her heart tripping in excitement. She was wearing the new wrap her father had given her for her passage to womanhood, and she'd tamed her hair and woven flowers in it, hoping to make the best impression she could on Korji.

Now she just had to hope the smoldering glances Korji shot her meant what she hoped they did. Before Taigh took Ahdia as his mate, she'd believed any Warrior would find her irresistible. Self-doubt was a constant companion now, it seemed. No one had asked her father for permission to approach her. Did any Warrior notice her?

Korji's reaction when she breached the edge of the field said he'd noticed her. His gaze trailed her movements, snapping away often, as if he felt he shouldn't be watching so avidly.

Emboldened, Miriza picked her away around the fight ring. Warriors moved aside for her. Some bowed their heads respectfully, and she offered the same in return.

Goven glanced at Korji out of the corner of his eye, bowed deeply to her and whispered a greeting to her. It took Miriza a moment to latch onto his words.

"Good day, Miriza, and good luck with him."

Her cheeks heated, and she offered a second tip of her head to the Stone lord. "My thanks, Goven."

She hurried along, her heart tripping at Korji's now-undivided attention to her movements. By the time she reached his side, she was breathless in anticipation.

Miriza dipped her knees a bit. "Good day, Korji," she offered brightly.

"Good day." He held himself stiff and looked around for something she couldn't name, seemingly confused or unnerved.

She'd hoped for more from him. A comment on her appearance, perhaps.

Finding words to continue was difficult. Miriza searched for something to say. "It is a beautiful day. Is it not?"

His brow furrowed, and he glanced at the sky. "I suppose. Warm weather is closing fast."

"I thought I might take a walk this evening."

His eyes shifted toward the opposite side of the fight ring, then skyward again. "It should be good weather for it."

Why is he still talking about the weather? Miriza continued on, hoping to make herself clear. "I enjoy walking by the cliff face." *There. He cannot misunderstand me now. Coming to his camp would only serve one aim.*

Korji shot another glance across the ring, and she turned to follow his line of sight. Most of the older lords were gathered there, but none of them seemed to be looking their way. She couldn't see anything that direction of interest.

"A woman should not walk to such a place without an escort," he suggested.

Miriza smiled and looked up at him. *Precisely what I had in mind.*

"Perhaps your father would care to escort you?"

Her smile faded. "My...father?" Did he find her completely unappealing and this was his way of saying it?

"A father should protect his daughter in such a situation. Do you not agree?"

There was an underlying tension in him she didn't understand. "I suppose," she offered carefully.

Korji smiled and turned his attention back to the fight ring. Miriza backed away, certain she'd been dismissed. Her head spinning, she made her way out of the training area.

At the top of the hill, she stopped to look at him. Korji's gaze followed her. That indicated an interest, but the tension in him seemed to belie it.

Which should I trust? How do I know?

* * * *

Korji headed for the practice field, cursing himself as ten types of fool. He'd waited for Miriza the night before, bathed and prepared to show her every possible comfort. He'd waited but she'd never appeared.

Two equally-unappealing possibilities had haunted him all morning. Either Miriza was playing at his need, perhaps even using his interest to make another jealous... He pushed that thought away, frustrated by it. He'd seen other women play such games, and he wouldn't have thought Miriza was that type.

The other possibility beckoned.

I've offended her somehow. That was more likely. The look Miriza had shot him when he'd suggested she ask her father to bring her to his camp had said he'd done something wrong. Perhaps women of the village were not open to men saying such things. If they found it presumptuous, he may have already destroyed any chance he had at sharing a bed with her.

That was a disheartening thought. Miriza was all Korji wanted. *And I will be denied again.* He didn't doubt it.

"Lord Korji!"

He turned toward the voice in surprise. He vaguely recognized Luven. They'd never spoken directly, but Korji knew the young giant was of Goven's line.

Korji tipped his head, inviting the young man to speak his mind.

Luven offered a leather-wrapped bundle, and Korji took it. He opened it, gaping at the four blades within. A check of the hilts showed Korji's goddess mark, coupled with the seal on his own blade. Mollified that Luven wasn't offering Goven's seal again, Korji tested the first blade. It was well-balanced and weighted well for battle.

"Very nice," he complimented Luven.

He offered a smile. "My father and I forged and etched them."

Korji wasn't certain what to make of that.

"My father offers his regards, Lord Korji."

"And you?"

Luven laughed. "Come. I think we should test your new blades."

Korji hesitated. "I will not be releasing my old blade, Luven. Not entirely." He waited for an explosion of the same sort of disdain Luven's father had voiced at the idea of Korji carrying the former King of Beast's blade.

Luven nodded sadly. "It was your mother's blade. I understand."

"Do you?" No one besides Ahdia and Taigh seemed to.

"Of course. We hold to the memories of those we love."

"But I never knew my mother." Was that why no one understood Korji clinging to her blade?

Luven clapped a hand on his shoulder. "You knew her. From what I hear, you and your sister knew your mother in a way few do."

He nodded, though he didn't understand.

"Time for training," Luven reminded him.

Korji followed him, enjoying the companionable silence between them.

Training was already well underway when they arrived. Korji watched the instruction, testing blade after blade he'd been gifted.

He looked up, spotting Goven across the field. For a moment, they stared at each other. Then Korji tipped his head in thanks. Goven's lips quirked up, and he returned the move.

It would be a long time before Korji was ready for more than passing courtesy, where Goven was concerned, but there was a chance for more. *Someday.*

Ahdia will be pleased to hear it.

Chapter Fifteen

"Is there a problem, Miriza?"

She looked up at Ahdia, blinking back what couldn't be mistaken for anything but a spate of tears, even to a passing observer, Miriza was sure.

The *Blutjagdfrau's* expression softened, and she sighed. "You want Korji."

The urge to lash out at her faded into misery. Ahdia wasn't the problem. Her oaf of a brother was. Miriza nodded.

Ahdia gathered the Mother's furs Taigh had insisted she wear on cool evenings around her legs and joined Miriza on the tree the young Warriors were cutting into cooking wood for the cooler months between their training sessions.

She surveyed Miriza for a long moment. "Your father has given permission for you to share Korji's bed. What is the difficulty?"

The words stuck in her throat.

"Miriza?" She cocked her head to one side.

"He does not want me," she blurted out. Her heart ached at the truth she'd dared not voice until now.

Ahdia's eyes widened, and she paled a notch. "He does."

"No! He does not. Korji does not want me, just as Taigh did not—"

"But he does," she insisted. "I know my brother well."

Miriza stared at the hands clasped in her lap. "Then why has he not pursued me?"

Her brow furrowed. "Pursued? I do not understand what you mean by that."

"Why has he not taken me to his sleeping roll, if he wants me so much?" she qualified, looking up at Ahdia.

Comprehension seeped into the her expression. "Have you ever asked him to? Have you offered yourself to Korji?"

Miriza hesitated. "What do you mean by that? My father gave his permission to—"

Ahdia reached out and patted her hand. "You forget that Korji and I were not raised in the Warrior village. We sometimes...do not understand your ways fully. It would seem this is one of those times. How does a male pursue a female?"

Her head spun at the reminder of their upbringing. How did the village that had raised him function? *Had he thought she hadn't wanted him?*

Gods, no! What if he gave up on her and chose another? "Never mind that. If Korji will act as he was raised... How does a man from your village indicate that he wishes a woman's company then?"

"He does not. The woman must approach him. Korji would never presume to...pursue a woman that had not already clearly indicated her interest in sharing his bed." She seemed to consider that. "Unless I explain your ways to him, of course. If you wish me to—"

"You mean... All this time, Korji has been waiting for me to...?" *To what? I need information.*

Ahdia nodded. "Yes. He has."

Gods, all this time wasted. She squeezed Ahdia's hand. "How? Please, tell me how a woman does such a thing."

"The sensibilities of the Warriors are too fragile for the proper ceremony. I understand your father would be unwilling to walk you, clothed only in a waist wrap, to Korji's bed and stand guard while he—"

"Taigh took you that way?" The impertinent question was out before Miriza could stop herself. Her cheeks flamed. "My apologies. Your time with Taigh is none of my concern."

The *Blutjagdfrau* laughed. "Of course, he did. It is the way of my... I know, the refugee village is not really my people, but it is hard to dismiss the things we were taught. Yes. Korji stood as my guard when I went to Taigh's bed."

Ahdia leaned toward her, shooting a conspiratorial look about as if making certain no one could overhear them. "Since you cannot perform the ceremony precisely, you will need to do something a little different."

But still offer myself to Korji.

No matter what it takes, he will be mine. "Tell me, please."

* * * *

The mad itch in Korji's body and mind had driven him beyond sanity. He thought of Miriza every moment of the day and night. He woke hard and needing and unable to find relief, even at his own hand. It was time to leave.

He hesitated with the tie downs for the sleeping roll in his hand, misery eating at him. *Damn her!* When Miriza's father had given his leave for a match between them, Korji had anticipated her soft, little body in his arms within a night or two. Ten nights later, she still hadn't appeared, and he could take no more.

"She has refused me." That hurt worse than training or battle injuries.

{No. She has not refused you. Miriza waits for you. She hungers for you. Go to her.}

Korji came to his senses—or as near to it as he could, in his incapacitated state—three steps closer to the village. "I am going mad." He knew Ahdia heard Rajicorin's voice, but he never had. It wasn't a man's magic to commune with the dead.

As if confirming his madness, Miriza stepped out of the shadows beneath the trees and walked toward him. Korji watched her come. If this apparition was madness, he didn't want to be sane.

It took a moment for his muddled mind to process the fact that she was unwinding her fancy wrap. He licked his lips, wondering if his madness would supply visions of her body to him as well.

She stopped a pace before him, her body tantalizingly warm. Without a sound, Miriza deposited the loose end of the wrap in his hand.

Korji stared at it, confused. It felt real. She felt real. But this ceremony held no meaning for him.

As if she'd heard that thought, Miriza spoke. "In the way of my people, it is your place to remove my clothing."

He nodded dumbly. His heart hammering, Korji unwrapped one loop...then a second, uncovering a pert little breast, already standing at attention for him. "What does this ceremony entail?" His aching cock wanted only one thing.

"It involves us sharing a sleeping roll."

His breathing went harsh in restraint, and Korji unwrapped two more loops, baring her feminine curls. "Where is your father?"

"Warriors do not accompany a daughter to a man's bed...or he to hers. His permission is as far as he goes." She moved a step closer, her nipple brushing his chest with each breath. "Of course, if you harm me, you will die on his blade. But there is no chance of that. Is there, Korji?"

"None." It was the most he could force out. Korji unwound loop after loop, then tossed the length of cloth away.

Miriza pulled the knots on his waist wrap free and let it drop to the grass. A little smile curved her lips into an enticing bow.

Her voice caressed his chest. "All that time I spent waiting for you to pursue me and claim me." Her gaze shifted toward his horse, and her eyes and mouth became wide 'o's in her surprise. Her cheeks darkened. "There is no way I am losing you now, Korji."

"None," he repeated. His mind in a spin, he managed a question. "Waiting for me to claim you?"

"In the way of the Warriors. I thought you would pursue me and lay claim to me as your own."

"How?"

Her fingertips feathered along his length in answer. "I had started to believe you did not want me."

Korji grasped her by the waist and pulled her flush to his rigid body. "Not want you? Are you mad?" Some Beast inside him wanted to push her to the grass and stake a barbaric claim the likes of which Tul's people would.

"If telling you I want you is the only way to have you..." Miriza swiveled her hips, rubbing her soft belly against his cock. "Then I am telling you clearly. Do not misunderstand me, Korji. I intend to have you, and I will pursue you, if that is the way women of your village would have indicated their needs."

Oh, you will have me little vixen. But—"Tell me what you are offering, Miriza." He trailed his lips along her forehead, drinking in her ready scent. In his madness, he would take whatever she offered. He would enslave himself to her whims.

She tipped her head back, whispering into his ear. "I am not content to be your tumble for the night, Korji."

His hands tightened at the idea of her thinking he'd want that, given the choice for something more. "Give me permission to spend every night in your bed, Miriza." Taigh had asked the same of Ahdia. It shouldn't shock Miriza to hear it.

"Your bed," she corrected. Her teeth nibbled at his earlobe. "Yes. I will spend every night in your bed."

"Mine" His cock leaked early fluids at the idea of her coming to his bed at all, let alone as a permanent addition to it.

She continued. "Then you will make me your woman and give me your sons to carry."

"Offer me that." A burn settled low in his belly and anticipation had him edgy and raw.

"I'll demand it, if you are so blind as to not know I want it already. I *will* be your woman, Korji, and you will never touch another."

Korji closed his mouth on hers, trying desperately to rein in his hunger.

Slowly. Take her slowly.

* * * *

Miriza's head spun at the taste of him in her mouth. She gasped, and he swept inside, his tongue dipping and twirling against hers. It was too much, and Miriza held to him, her knees quaking.

Korji guided her to his horse, and one hand left her body. The sleeping roll brushed the side of her breast, as he tucked it beneath his arm.

They moved away from his tethered mount, Miriza all but tripping over her own feet. The snapping sound of the roll unfurling set her heart pounding in excitement. In the next moment, she was in Korji's arms. Then the furs were at her back, and she was half-buried under his body.

The press of his bare chest against hers had her shivering in excitement.

Korji's head came back and he looked down at her, seemingly assessing something. Miriza opened her mouth to question his stillness, and he spoke.

"Are you untouched?"

"What do you—? How could you even *ask* such a thing?" What was he accusing?

Korji seemed stunned by her reaction, and the urge to strike him was pressing.

"I meant no offense, Miriza. How do your men ask?"

"Our men do *not* ask such a thing."

"Then how can they know to—?"

"They know our young women do not sleep with men unless...unless it is a man she intends to seal printing with."

"*All* of the women?"

That snapped her patience, and Miriza smacked him hard across the face.

"I don't want other women," he hastened to add.

Miriza crossed her arms over her breasts. *I suppose it is a good thing we haven't—*

"On my honor, Miriza. It is just... Where *do* men without wives --" Her intent to hit him again must have been clear on her face, because his eyes widened, and he motioned for peace. "I do not need to know what other men do to sate themselves."

By the Stone, you had best not even wonder such a thing.

He sighed and rolled to his back on the grass. "I meant no offense, Miriza. It was not something Taigh taught me about women in the village." He mumbled something under his breath that sounded of the belief he would never prove himself worthy of a woman like her.

Her anger abated, and Miriza eased her arms down her body. Korji really didn't understand their ways. It was one of the things she liked about him, so why would she discourage it?

At a loss to offer the apology he deserved, she reached out and touched his arm, seeking to close the distance she'd created between them.

He tensed for a moment, then turned his head to peek at her.

"Perhaps Taigh should have explained better," she agreed. *I will have to take him to task for that. Or have Ahdia do so.* "Our young women are not like the women the men seek out in other villages. The only women within the village who offer themselves to men that way are widows."

Korji nodded, seemingly committing it to memory. After a moment, he spoke. "Whether you refuse me or not, I will not be seeking out those widows."

That pronouncement warmed her heart, and a smile she was certain looked childish broke free. Miriza moved to his side, and Korji turned to meet her.

He hesitated, probably uncertain about what she was offering. Miriza tilted her head up and brushed her lips against his.

"Am I worthy to be your first?" he asked, his voice stiff and formal. "I mean...the one you take vows with? When you are ready for such a thing."

He is trying so hard not to anger me again. He must be printing to take such care. "I am ready for such a thing."

He seemed confused by her comment. "Are you still offering to let me...claim you and give you sons? To make unbreakable vows?"

She nodded and placed a hand over his cock, tracing his dimensions slowly. A shiver worked down his body.

"After I insulted you so grievously?"

"Did you mean to?"

"Mean to—? Insult you? Of course not!"

"Then it was Taigh's fault. Why should I change my mind over something that was not your doing?"

Miriza wrapped her hand around his cock, drawing a gasp from him. She licked her lips, ranging her hand up and down his ready length. He was big and ready, and she wanted him buried inside her and staking his claim.

His expression went potent in need. "I will be slow for you, Miriza."

"You will not."

Again, Korji seemed to be confused by her words.

"I do not want you to be slow. I want to feel your heat and vigor. You do want me to be happy, do you not?" Her bold demands of him were nothing she'd envisioned saying in her lifetime. There was something freeing in being expected to say such things to the man you wanted.

"I do not want to harm you."

The idea of him so impassioned that he had to worry about such a thing stoked her inner fire. "How long have you been needing me in your bed?"

At first, she thought he would refuse to answer. Then Korji sighed. "Since the moment I saw you approach me, I believe. When you touched my mark."

She'd suspected as much, but hearing Korji say it was thrilling. "Then you understand my urgency to have you deep inside me instead of having you touch me in careful caresses."

He moaned, and his cock jerked against her fingers. A small amount of his male fluids slid down the head to her hand.

"I have wanted you that long as well, Korji."

His lips came down on hers, parting Miriza's in a kiss that made her head swim. He worked her hand off his cock and turned her beneath him, pressing her hands to the sleeping roll beneath his.

"You wish me to claim you as my woman and fill you with my child?"

It was a challenge if she'd ever heard one, and one heard a lot of challenges when Warriors started to spar.

"Yes." It came out breathless, thanks to the kiss.

"Then vow to be mine, and you will have what you want."

Her nipples tightened at his order. "I vow it. I am yours."

Korji didn't smile, as some men might have if gifted that vow so quickly and simply. His expression was starkly serious, nearly feral in its intensity. Though all Warriors rode the edges of feral, this was more potent.

His mouth closed on hers again. By his kiss, Miriza could guess there would be no careful touching. His hair whispered around her cheeks.

His mouth left hers, and his lips trailed down her chin and throat. His breath warmed her collarbone.

His move to her breast was so fast, she hadn't anticipated it. Miriza rose up against his hold, forcing the whole of the areole and part of the globe into his mouth.

There was nothing careful about his handling. His suckling sent pleasant aches down her body, waking her sheath to potent readiness.

He alternated from breast to breast, sampling her body. Then he moved lower, his lips stroking down the join of her ribs, her belly, and pausing a moment at her woman's curls.

Before she could question him, he was suckling at her hood, bringing her up in an arch, hitching breaths escaping her trembling lips. Korji teased and tasted, driving Miriza to noisy release.

Bright stars danced before her eyes, and her mind seemed disconnected from her rioting body. Before her senses had a chance to right themselves, Korji's body was over hers, her legs spread wide around his, her wrists held to the sleeping roll beneath his hands.

His cock prodded at her seam, and Miriza gasped out pleas for more. In the next heartbeat, pain brought her to semi-awareness. His cock was deep inside her, stretching her virgin body around him.

Korji pressed kisses to her forehead, her temples, her eyes. "Calm, Miriza. Let me make you my woman."

His lips trailed along her face, and she turned to him, seeking his kiss. Korji didn't shy from the idea. Their mouths came together, and his cock jerked in response.

He didn't ask when she as ready for him to resume. Korji started moving, his cock retreating and returning, stirring the embers into fresh flames.

At last, his mouth left hers, and he thrust fast against her. Miriza's body reached for a second release, and she grasped at the meat of his buttocks, urging him on.

Her climax set off his, his heat traveling the length of her core, setting off aftershocks in its wake. Puffs of breath swirled between them, and Korji's cock bucked and shimmied within her body, releasing more of his seed.

"You are my woman, Miriza." Korji pushed himself up on one elbow and trailed his fingertips over her belly. "Soon. Very soon, you will carry my child."

"Your son." She smiled, envisioning a toddler Warrior with long braids framing his face, bare-chested as Korji usually was.

He shot her an unreadable look. "Goddess willing, but I would welcome a daughter as beautiful as her mother is. I know they are rare, but I would like to sire a daughter with you."

Miriza's face flushed at his praise. "We will have so many babies, the Stone Mother will have to grant us a daughter."

His gaze went hot and potent. In the next heartbeat, Miriza was on her hands and knees on the sleeping roll. Korji knelt behind her, one hand cupping a breast and the other guiding his cock into her body.

"Korji?" It came out a gasp, and Miriza reminded herself that she should pose more of a question if she wanted an answer.

Proving her wrong, her mate answered. "It is said this position encourages a child."

She nodded as he started stroking inside her. Though Miriza knew well enough that Warriors needed no special tricks to conceive children, she wanted Korji to teach her everything the village who'd raised him taught him about mating. As his mate, Miriza fully intended to enjoy Korji's culture and beliefs.

Chapter Sixteen

Miriza opened her eyes to the sight of the rough shelter Korji had erected during the night. Though she'd wanted to sleep with him beneath the stars, he'd argued they were too close to the village and the night too chill to sleep that way. He'd vowed to take her into the wilds with him in the heat of summer and fulfill her wish.

He wasn't on the sleeping roll with her, but he'd covered her with furs before he left the bed. She could hear movement outside and smell smoke and cooking food.

She stretched, too lazy to dress for the day after a night of energetic sex with her mate. Realization raised a giggle in her. There was no reason to dress. She was mate to a barbarian Warrior. That in mind, she chose the lightest fur of a size to wrap around herself and made her way out of the shelter.

Korji looked up at her and smiled, his eyes hot in promise, though she'd barely awoken.

Miriza settled next to him and snuggled into his bare chest. "How does the morning find my mate?" she asked.

"Hungry. In more ways than one, but we should feed the stomach's hungers first."

She sighed. "I suppose that is true." Her stomach was complaining at the wait to sample whatever it was he was cooking. She leaned forward to breathe in the mouthwatering scent.

Korji stirred it, chuckling darkly. "Rabbit stew with tubers and fresh herbs," he reported. "But it will need a bit of time to finish boiling."

"You had all of this?"

"Not the rabbit. I caught that early this morn."

Her jaw dropped at the fact that he'd hunted and cooked for her while she lay asleep.

One brow went up. "I believe I should catch more rabbits. Many more."

"You do?" What was he saying?

"You wish me to give you my son to carry. He will need wraps and soft furs to warm him."

"It sounds warm."

"The Warriors do not use rabbit furs for their babes?"

"Not for the wraps, but I believe we should."

"Your father will not take offense to having his daughter's children dressed as barbarians?" His shoulders tensed, though he didn't show any other outward sign of anger.

Miriza reached up and guided his face toward her, so she could meet his gaze directly. "Do you believe I want you to change for me? For him? For anyone?"

"Do you?"

She traced a finger down his chest. "Not at all." She considered another question. "Do you wish me to change for you?"

He hesitated, then shook his head in a negative show.

"You do."

A wry smile raised the corners of his lips. "The wrap you came to me in last night is beautiful, but it takes too long to get you naked in my arms."

She laughed. "I don't wear it all the time. My daily wraps are much easier to remove and to wrap."

"I would like to see them." His gaze flicked to her hair and away again.

Miriza touched the long, black strands, confused at what might upset him about it. His sister had long hair. Surely that meant the refugee village where he'd been raised favored the style. "What is it?"

"Nothing."

"No. There is something," she argued. When he didn't reply, Miriza pressed him for an answer. "Is there something your women would have done that—"

"*You* are my woman, Miriza. Until the day I die, I vow it."

"Yes, but... Is there something the women in the village that raised you would have done that would appeal?"

He peeked at her hair again, then smoothed a lock of her hair through his fingertips. His gaze was far away and full of longing. "It is something I would have done, had I made one of them my wife."

"What? Tell me please."

"I would have taken the beads from two of the braids in my hair and woven them into yours."

Her heart skipped in excitement. "Then do it. Or is there some reason you cannot—"

"I can, if you permit it."

"Does it have meaning?"

"It is my promise that all I own is yours. As I find more stones to make beads from, I give them to you." He smiled. "Given a long enough life together, I would see your entire head covered in beaded braids that show my devotion to you and my intent to protect you."

"Then you definitely should braid my hair with the beads, Korji."

He reached up and started unwinding the furthest braid from his face. "You will never regret vowing to be mine, Miriza."

I don't doubt that.

* * * *

Korji eased Miriza up and down the length of his cock, his body straining to release at every glance at the braids she'd allowed him to place in her hair.

The fur she'd wrapped herself in lay open around her as she rode his cock. He'd never seen anything so beautiful in his life.

Her sounds went sharp in announcement of her coming release, and Korji thrust deep as she liked him to. Her release spurred his, and they sat together, her impaled and snug in his lap, their breathing harsh in dwindling passion.

A sound in the tree line brought his head up. Whatever it was, it was big.

Most likely human. Or Warrior. Korji pulled the fur around her shoulders and wrapped her in it, motioning for silence as Miriza opened her mouth to speak.

She nodded and slid off his lap, and Korji fastened his waist wrap and came to one knee, recovering his blade from the fireside. All the while he scanned his gaze over the trees, watching for signs of someone moving.

When he saw it at last, he sighed and lowered the weapon. "Your father," he informed her.

To his surprise, Miriza didn't scramble for the damned long wrap she'd come to him in. Instead, she sat calmly, unclothed, save the fur wrapped around her.

"You do not wish to dress?" he asked, confused by her reaction.

"No. If my father intrudes on us, today of all days, he deserves no courtesies."

"He is not alone," he reported. "I believe Taigh and Ahdia are with him. And perhaps Gyr?" He knew the old buck was in the group.

At that pronouncement, she did rush for the shelter and her length of cloth. Though he didn't care for the time it took to disrobe her when she was wearing it, Korji sighed in relief that she wouldn't be meeting all the incoming men nude and fresh from his cock.

Just fresh from my cock. That sent a shiver of delight down his back.

He stood and crossed his camp site toward them, his hand on the hilt of his blade, just in case they came in looking for a fight.

Perit tipped his head. "Miriza is well?"

"Of course. She is also my...mate." Korji reminded himself to use their word for a wife of vows.

He nodded grimly. "When she did not return home, and Ahdia confirmed she'd reached your camp site safely..." He offered another nod.

Perit shifted a sack on his back. "We usually bring a gift of food to the new couple, but it looks as if you have already arranged a morning meal."

Korji straightened. "Of course. One provides for a mate."

"Indeed," Taigh interrupted their discussion. "But the whole village offers the gift of aiding in building the new couple's home in the days following their mating."

"Huts like yours?" he asked.

"If you wish. Is there another style of home you would prefer?"

Korji considered that. "The home I build is Miriza's. The choice of what she wants is hers."

Ahdia smiled. "I'm sure she would appreciate that."

"Appreciate what?" Miriza asked, emerging from the shelter.

His sister smiled widely and offered her hand to his wife. "Korji has left the choice of what kind of home we will build for you to you."

"I want a Zuragi home."

Korji stared at her, trying to understand why she would request such a thing. They had Zuragi among the refugees, and the structures were outrageously large.

Perit's face turned a fiery red. "Smaller, I would guess."

"No. A true Zuragi home."

"Miriza, those are built to hold a hand of families."

She took Ahdia's hand and folded the other into Korji's. "We will need the space for all the babies we will have."

Her father sputtered and stuttered.

Korji lifted her and fit Miriza to his body. She released Ahdia's hand to wrap her arms around him.

His heart light, he uttered the words he'd never thought he'd have the chance to. "Whatever my mate wants, my mate gets."

Raised to be his Own

Note to the readers:

Strange things happen when you're doing re-edits on an older work. In this case, I was reading Jörg's plans for Anna and Erin in the release of *Veriel's Tales II: Losing Regana,* and the following what-if struck me.

Knowing there were many beast wars and a "Veriel" in each war, what if a former Veriel came to a similar moment...the moment when he would attempt to steal back his lover and her female child to a Warrior? What if he managed to take the child and raise her, but the mother was left behind or killed, insuring that he could tell the young Warrior woman anything he wished of her past, her nature, and the nature of their connection? What would happen when she reached maturity?

Welcome to that vision.

Brenna

Chapter One

Ragath strolled out of her rooms and through the nearly-deserted keep. It was early, and she'd risen for the night before most of the household again.

One of her stomachaches had woken her. She'd asked Jonus about them, but he'd assured her many women suffered fleeting aches as they matured. There was no cause for concern...troublesome, but not dangerous.

They seemed to be occuring more often of late. She shivered in nervous energy; Jonus said that meant she would soon be ready to become his bride in more than name.

She nodded to one of the maids diligently performing her duties, either an early riser like herself or one who performed her duties in the day so as to remain unseen and out of the way.

All of the servants were female. Ragath had asked Jonus about it once, and he'd supplied that women weren't safe with more than one man about. Men were, by nature, destined to prey on unprotected females, to kill to take women from other men.

The only way to safeguard a woman was to send her into her future husband's keeping as a child, completely isolating her from other men, not even transporting her from household to household as she grew enough to be sexually appealing. What they could not see, the other males would not covet.

According to Jonus, Ragath had been in his care since infancy. Certainly, she had no memories of her mother and father. Jonus's household encompassed the whole of her memory.

The women in his employ had acted as nannies, wet nurses, and later as maids and confidants. Her every need was met, her every whim catered to. According to the maids, her clothing was the finest they had ever seen.

When she suffered her blood, her clothing was heavy enough and dark enough to hide the unsightly blood rags and any stains that might occur. When she wasn't, like now, her clothing was sheer, exposing her body to the man who would be her husband.

He hadn't touched her sexually yet, but that would come soon. She'd suffered her blood for four years, which meant she was of age for him to exercise his rights to her bed.

Ragath didn't fear the bedding. It was a natural step in a woman's life, and Jonus was an appealing male. Of course, she'd never seen a male besides him for comparison, but still he appealed to her.

What more could a woman ask for? Since females were not exposed to groups of men and permitted a choice in marriage, being attracted to your mate was all any woman could hope for, and the gods had granted Ragath that boon.

She headed for Jonus's rooms. There was nowhere in his household she was forbidden to tread, and the same applied to him. Only the servants had boundaries.

A strange sound stopped her short just outside the archway to his rooms. She worked at it. It almost sounded as if Jonus was in pain. Concerned, she hurried inside—and stopped short again.

The servant was one of her confidants, a girl only a year older than Ragath herself. At the moment, she was laid out on Jonus's weapons table, her legs circling Jonus's predictably nude body, her back arched to facilitate Jonus's suckling mouth latched onto her breast.

For a moment, Ragath stood there, hurt, betrayed, her emotions warring. Fury won out, and she launched at them, her fists clenched tight.

I will kill them. How dare they!

Jonus moved so fast, she could hardly track it. In the next moment, Ragath was pressed to the wall,

Jonus's body crowding hers, his hands fisted around her wrists, like the time he—

She forced that thought away. It was one of the few times he'd exercised his rights as lord of the keep and her body over her, and it was an experience she did not want to repeat.

His breath came in hot, little panting breaths that caused a disconcerting reaction in her traitor body.

"Leave us," Jonus ordered.

The skittering sounds would be the damned servant collecting her clothing and making good her escape. Her footsteps hesitated, and Ragath turned her head, glaring at the other woman. At least the bitch had the good grace to look pained and remorseful.

Jonus motioned his head sharply, and the servant fled, holding her gown to her body.

The moments passed in silence. Finally, Jonus addressed her.

"You wished to see me, Ragath?"

"I most certainly did *not* want to see you like that," she snapped back.

He sighed. "I have told you about men," he reasoned. "Men have hungers."

"Men are vermin. Men are insects."

Jonus smiled. He laughed at her insults. "Yes, we most certainly are. You are barely of an age to bed, Ragath. Be reasonable. I must have a way to sate myself until you accept me."

She wanted to deny it, but he had a point. How many times had she been told that males lacked control when faced with females? How cruel was it to see her daily, from the time she was an infant, and know he had to wait to touch her? How else could a male survive such a thing besides taking other females to his bed until he was free to claim his bride?

"And when I do accept you?" she challenged. "If men are such vermin, with no control when presented with the female body, will you continue to bed the servants, when you have mine?" If he said yes, he would certainly never have her willingly. Why should he?

His smile disappeared, and he shook his head solemnly. "When I have you, I will have no want or need of the others. You have my vow on that."

"But..." There was something left unsaid, she was sure.

He flattened his body to hers, letting Ragath feel the weight of his erect cock against her belly. "I will need your vow that you will be mine always."

She shook her head, confused by that pronouncement. "I am yours, Jonus. My parents struck the deal with you long ago." Even if she refused him, which was simply not done, where would she go? How would she? The bars and gates alone would trap her within the keep.

"No. *You* must choose. You must give your vow. The day you do, I will stop taking other women."

Ragath worked at that without return. What difference did her vow make? The deal had been struck without it. There was no way to rescind it. Females weren't permitted to show their faces outside the keeps, save when one was transported to her husband in infancy. What difference did her vow make?

"Your choice," Jonus repeated. "Are you prepared to make that choice?"

A sudden and unexpected fear made her lightheaded. Why had no one told her the question would be asked? Even knowing it was a foregone conclusion that she would be Jonus's, saying the words frightened her.

He nodded, his jaw tight in fury she could see like a dark cloud around him. "Then I will continue to seek out other—"

"No." The word was out before she could stop herself. She had no right to order Jonus about. He was her future husband, her master. He was lord of the keep and her body.

One brow went up in challenge. "You mean to accept me?" he asked calmly.

Gods, what a choice! "Why do you need that vow to bed me?" Perhaps if she understood his needs, it would come easier.

A smile curved his lips, and his cock jerked against her. "I do not need it to bed you."

Ragath shook her head. "I do not understand."

"I can bed you at any time you wish it."

"But—"

"A man has needs, Ragath. The only way to meet them all is to vow to be mine...and only mine...for all time. Until that time, if needs arise that you cannot or will not fulfill..."

She pulled at his hold, intent on striking him for saying something so hurtful. He held her easily, without exerting effort that she could see. She wasn't certain why she still tried to strike him. It wasn't as if she'd ever succeeded before.

"Will you choose to fulfill...some of my needs?" There was something dark and seductive in that.

Ragath considered it. "On one condition." She nearly winced at what she was saying. There had never been conditions between them before.

He tilted his head, his interest seemingly piqued by her choice of words. "And that is?"

"You will ask me for what it is you...need. If I cannot or will not provide it, you are free to seek it elsewhere, but not without asking me first." Her heart ached at the idea of refusing him, of sending him to another to sate what she should as bride sate, and it pounded in terror at the idea of making a vow to be his forever, though she had no idea why it would.

"Agreed." There was no hesitation in his answer. "At the moment, I need to taste. A woman's mouth, her breasts, her...sweet sheath. Will you offer me that?"

Her body reacted fiercely to the mental image his words created for her. "Yes. Taste."

His head titled and came down, his mouth playing at hers. He'd kissed her hands, forehead, and cheeks before. He'd brushed his lips against hers before she retired to bed every night since her blood started to flow.

This was different. His lips were soft; they played at hers as if seeking something she couldn't name.

He pulled back minutely. "Open for me."

She hesitated, confused by the request. Ragath parted her lips, shivering at his breath warming her mouth.

Jonus did the same, and his tongue emerged, dipping into her mouth, stroking her lips. Ragath captured it between her lips, stealing a kiss.

He moaned at the move, sliding his tongue free as if enjoying the sensation as much as she did. "That is right. Play with my mouth. Explore."

Encouraged, she repeated the move with his lower lip...then the upper. Ragath dipped her tongue between his lips, and Jonus snaked his own around it, setting off a firestorm of need.

In the next few heartbeats, their mouths meshed, lips wide open. Their tongues dueled and danced.

His hands loosened and left her wrists, caressing down her arms. When he cupped her breasts in his big hands, she took advantage of the freedom to lower her arms around his neck.

Her knees weakened in the passion washing over them. As if he could feel it, Jonus pulled away, guiding her further into the room.

Jonus didn't take her to his weapons table, as she'd feared he might. She was forbidden to touch the table or anything on it, and his displeasure when balked was a fearsome thing.

He took her to his bed.

His mouth left hers, and he started working the gown up her body. Her nudity wasn't a shocking thing. She was nude for her physical training, for sleep, and bathing. Jonus was not unwelcome at any of those activities, though he'd never shared her bed, to her knowledge. This was the first time she'd been disrobed with the idea that Jonus would execute his rights as husband.

The material slid over her head and extended arms, leaving her skin to skin with him. Ragath clenched her fists for a moment, reminding herself that he'd seen her nude form for her entire life.

Jonus tossed the gown away, and he lifted her to the bed, following her down. She'd been to his bed from time to time. When she was a child with nameless nightmares, she'd been encouraged to seek out his bed for comfort.

There was nothing comforting in this. It was hot and harsh, exciting and frightening.

Jonus took his time, sampling her lips...then the depths of her mouth. Sometime during the latter, a meal appeared silently on the bedside table. Part of her burned in jealousy that it might have been the same servant he'd been so engaged with; another hoped it was, so the bitch would see that Jonus was hers alone.

Left to her own devices, Ragath would have ignored the food, but Jonus demanded she eat. He watched her, his gaze hot with the promise of more. When she offered him food, he begged off, claiming he'd indulged earlier. All the while, the tension rose between them, the need to have him continued. At last, her stomach protested the idea of more. Not that she was full. Rather a strange ache and tremble made the thought of eating when she might be in Jonus's arms unpalatable.

As if he read the thought from her mind, Jonus turned her beneath him again. His lips parted hers, his kiss making her lightheaded.

Time lost all meaning. Ragath resorted to ordering what passed between them in rare moments of lucidity.

His mouth on her breasts brought her off the mattress and hard against him. Somewhere between there and the disconcerting play at her naval, the second meal arrived. She managed a few bites and a glass of wine, then she invited his kiss again.

Jonus was unhurried in his tasting, and her body rioted for more. Her breathing caught in her lungs at the first stroke of his tongue between her thighs. It escaped on a rush at the second.

Then he was everywhere, suckling at the forefront, tracing her woman's seam, licking from front to back. Strange sounds escaped her throat, and Ragath reached for him.

Her heart skittered at Jonus pinning her wrists to the mattress. Fear faded in light of his continued attention to her rising pleasure. Ragath forced her hips up, encouraging him.

His groan vibrated against her; the sensation tightened muscles all over her body and stilled her breath. The next suck on the sensitive bundle released that breath in a shout of surprise. The tension inside her rebounded, tightened, loosened again, more powerfully with each movement. Her head spun, and she moaned out her confusion. What was he doing to her?

His mouth left her, and Jonus snapped an order for someone to leave them. Ragath whimpered, her mind working at the truth that he'd spent the night tasting her, another corner arguing that it couldn't possibly be the late meal he'd been turning away.

He returned to her body, tasting more avidly, forcing her to a more powerful response than the last time. Her inner muscles clenched on emptiness, and she felt every finger-width of the channel Jonus would soon fill.

As if the thought summoned him, he levered himself over her, holding his weight up so his cock bobbed between them. Ragath stared at it—curious, frightened, ready yet not.

I should. He has given me such pleasure. And her channel was empty and aching for a filling.

No. It is too soon. Wait. The time is coming. Ragath didn't doubt it. It wasn't time to take him to her body.

Jonus grumbled a harsh curse. He knew. Would he seek out another female to do what she was uncertain about?

At a loss to stop him, she touched his cock. She'd only done so once before, when she'd been very young. At the time, it had sent Jonus into a rage, and she'd fled to her nurse's arms in confusion. This time, his hungry expression attested that the tension in his body was sexual in nature.

Encouraged, Ragath stroked him. Jonus shifted his weight, brought one hand to hers, and repositioned her hand. Once her fingers circled his girth, he guided her and squeezed her hand tighter where he needed it to be so, his breathing going ragged and his eyes red in arousal. When she'd learned what he wanted, he released her and left her to bring him pleasure.

His sounds were harsh, and his hips started moving. Ragath stared at him, stunned at his fierce hunger.

"Harder, Ragath. Make your hands tight as your virgin sheath will be."

She complied, and his eyes slid shut. His hips sped, and her body responded to it. Would he thrust into her as avidly? Cream flowed from her at the thought.

His hair swung wildly around his face, and his expression hardened. Then he roared, his male fluids splashing against her stomach and breasts. Ragath stared at it, shocked at the sight. There was so much, much more than she'd thought there would be.

"We will bed fully soon, Ragath," Jonus promised.

She nodded, touching the slick of his seed with trembling fingers. This was what would give her a child? What magic was there between a man and a woman?

Jonus used the linens on his bed to wipe the precious fluid away. Then he lifted her and carried her to her room.

The servants scrambled to do his bidding. Jonus passed Ragath into their hands with orders to bathe and feed her. Then he turned to leave.

"Wait," she called out. She'd refused to take him into her body. Was he off to sate himself in another? Perhaps in that damned servant he'd been playing with earlier?

He turned, offering her a smile. "Be at ease. I simply have business to deal with, Ragath. Sleep well."

"Will you join me?" It was a question she'd never asked before.

Jonus hesitated, for the first time in her memory seemingly uncertain. "Perhaps... I am weary, Ragath. Perhaps...another day would be better."

She nodded, feeling dismissed as she rarely had with Jonus.

He paused, shook his head as if to push away an unwelcome thought, then walked away.

"Lady Ragath?" one of the older servants called her.

She turned, noting the water being poured into the tub for her. All things considered, a bath might be the best thing. Ragath always thought best at the restful moments.

It was the perfect temperature, cool but not cold. Everything in her life was perfect.

Not everything.

Again, the servant's face was in her memories. Jonus often sent servants away to other duties in his holdings. If she asked, would he send that one away? But, he left the keep on business. Even if he sent the girl away, what was to stop him from sating himself in her when he was away?

My vow. He said he would take no others, if I gave the vow.

Not yet. The time is not right.

That meant accepting that he might bed others until she gave it. It was an imperfect solution.

Then again, if life were perfect, how boring would that be?

On that thought, she settled into the tub and closed her eyes. It had been years since she'd bathed herself, most likely since she'd started to bleed. It was Jonus's opinion that a lady should have to do as little for herself as possible. Hers was a life of leisure—reading, practice, and music, while others did the work. Bathing herself was something of a guilty pleasure.

Her servants had told her males sometimes chose to dismiss servants and bathed their brides themselves. Her heart ached that Jonus hadn't chosen to do so tonight.

She chided herself. Jonus had business to see to. He'd spent the entire night with her and would likely forego some of his sleep to see to the business he'd neglected.

What business is it? Perhaps he had to order troops or the overseer of his fields. Ragath had seen neither of those things, but she'd heard Jonus speak of them. Like everything else in her life, scores of others toiled while she amused herself...and Jonus.

Soft cloths stroked at her sensitized skin. The scents of herbal soaps and food tantalized her senses.

And it struck. The pain knotted her stomach as it rarely had, an intense, breath-stealing fist. She pitched forward around it, grunting, her teeth and eyes clenched tight.

The movement sent water splashing to the floor, and she shuddered. A wild need to run gripped her, but she couldn't walk like this, let alone run.

And where would I run? Why would I? There were no answers to those questions.

"Lady Ragath!"

Hands pulled at her, and she shook her head. It had to ease. It always eased.

"To the bed," one of the older women ordered. "Before she drowns."

That might have seemed extreme any other time, but this time, Ragath wasn't certain it was. The pain was worse than usual, and she was lightheaded in response. Hands supported her and stared to lift Ragath out of the water.

The pain intensified, a searing in her gut that doubled her fully. Her tenuous control in the face of pain shattered, and Ragath screamed. Tears pooled in her eyes and ran down her face.

It ended. Her muscles unknotted, and she went boneless in relief. The servants lifted her to the floor and wrapped her in a length of cloth.

Whispered conversations made no sense. The smell of food turned her abused stomach, and Ragath sent it away in a rough voice.

Probably at a loss for something better to do, they dried her and settled Ragath into her bed. Suddenly, Jonus joining her wasn't so important. She needed the sleep rushing toward her.

Chapter Two

The gut wrenching feeding nearly doubled Gaffin. He'd never felt it so acutely, and he wondered if it was the elder that made it so prominent in his senses.

Hirum met his gaze in the tandem ghosting the entire hunting party shared, pale, giving in to the need to curl around the sensation. So, it wasn't just Gaffin experiencing it.

Ebol's voice brought his head around, and he tried to focus on it, panting through the pain.

"The prisoner is our aim. She will be in one of these two rooms."

Gaffin stared at the rough map of the complex the former minion had provided, though he'd memorized it long ago.

"There will be no locks or doors to slow us once we are inside. The Mad Deceiver has forbidden such things, which will work to our favor."

The thought of the girl being held by the beast raised a fresh edge of Blutjagd in him. The servant hadn't been able to supply her age, and Gaffin's mind had locked on the image of a child becoming a woman.

"The main force will take this room."

The beast's lair. They had to send their oldest and best that direction, since the information on hand said the beast never shared the girl's bed.

He fisted his hand in a new spike of fury. *But, it said the young one sometimes shared the beast's bed.* Only the fact that there had been no sign of her maiden's blood kept him in control. Perhaps the Destroyer of Lives hadn't taken her barrier yet.

"Gaffin, your team will take the girl's room. If she is there, remove her as quickly as you can."

"Consider it done." If it killed him, Gaffin wasn't leaving the keep without the girl. The fact that the beast had perpetrated this tragedy so long was a stain on all of them. It would continue not another day.

Veriel had been careful to take his blood away from this stronghold...until recently. By all accounts, the elder's control was slipping. He was getting sloppy, making poor choices, from a strategic standpoint. But why?

The servant had postulated that every day the girl refused his advances, the beast became more dangerous. Such a thing made no sense. Beasts didn't need permission to take what they wanted. If it was not offered freely, they took it with a full measure of pain...or they used their formidable powers to seduce one to agreement. The girl's refusal would be a minor annoyance to the Mad Elder.

The feeding pain increased markedly, and Gaffin doubled with a gasp. Around him, the other Warriors did likewise.

The sound of a woman screaming in pain escaped the walls and gates of the keep. It was tortured, and it stoked Gaffin's need to hunt. He prayed the beast wasn't killing the girl to keep her from being freed or taking what he wanted in pain, as Gaffin had so recently postulated.

The pain subsided abruptly, and the screaming did likewise. Gaffin looked up in shock. He was on his knees, but he didn't remember crumpling. His face burned. He'd never succumbed to a beast's feeding that way before. Only the fact that three of the older men and one of the younger had as well calmed him. Whatever that was, it was powerful.

They waited for the sun to rise fully, then made their way to the gate the servant had indicated. She waited for them there, her face tense.

"The girl?" Ebol asked urgently.

"Asleep in her chamber."

Gaffin breathed a sigh of relief and then straightened. If she was in her chamber, she was his to free. It was a duty he would not fail at.

"The beast attacked her?" Niklus, his father, asked.

The servant hesitated, offering the key to Ebol. She shook her head. "No. A confidant of the girl's...another servant. But do not trouble yourself. She is dead."

"You saw it?" Broden inquired.

She hesitated. "No, but the master never lets one live that causes the young one pain."

Her acceptance of that fact was chilling. How many servants had caused the girl pain that she knew this?

"Yet he allows the young one to hear the screams of the other?" Hirum huffed. "Does that not harm her?" There'd been no coercion indicating that she might be in some unnatural sleep of the elder's making.

The servant's brow creased in confusion. "One he kills never has time to scream. The scream 'twas of the girl you seek."

"She saw it then," Gaffin grumbled. She would be terrorized. What woman faced with such things wouldn't be? What else had he expected?

Again, the servant denied it. "She knows when the master kills. He cannot hide it from her. Even in one of his sleeps, she feels the kill...or the feeding."

"Sensitive," one of the other Warriors gasped.

Gaffin didn't try to identify which one it was in his shock. It explained everything. It certainly explained why a beast would wish to possess the girl. If she could sense the beasts, she could sense the Warriors. It would be a tactical advantage to possess such a prize.

Broden and Ebol shot hard looks at Gaffin, and he bowed his head in response. If she was a sensitive, he would lay down his life to save her the least discomfort. None of them would leave the keep without her.

"And the beast?" Ebol asked the servant.

"I do not know. I could not excuse looking."

Ebol traded the amulet for the key, and the servant scurried away, her blessing already intact.

The Warriors didn't waste time. Sacred weapons in hand, they entered the keep. Chances were, the beast was sleeping in his chamber or gone to ground, but without sunlight inside the keep, he could rise to challenge them.

They would take any minions that resisted them silently and free the girl. Gods willing, they would either not encounter the elder at all or would send him to the Stone's punishment. That was why they'd come with so many in the first place.

*   *   *   *

Ragath opened her eyes at the noise from the archway. So, Jonus had returned from his business to join her. Perhaps he was worried by of her attack of stomach. Surely the servants had told him this one was worse than the others.

Her eyes took a moment to focus on the shape in the archway. Her mind took a moment longer to identify it. For a hand of heartbeats, they stared at each other, Ragath in stunned disbelief.

He moved, and she scrambled up the bed, holding the sheet to her body. *What a male cannot see, he will not covet.*

Gods, what do I do if he covets me?

Her mind spun sickly. How had the male gotten into the keep? Had he come for her? Where was Jonus? What would Jonus do if he took her away? What would Jonus do, if the male sated himself in her?

He took another step, his hands up in a calming gesture, words that made no sense crooning from his lips.

I have to escape him. I cannot let him fixate on me.

That in mind, Ragath vaulted to her feet, bolting for the archway with the sheet trailing behind her.

He had her wrapped in his arms before she made half the distance. Ragath screamed, beating at him, trying her best to escape his lecherous intentions.

The sheet slipped away, and she let it fall. She had to escape, naked or not. But to where? There were no doors she could bolt within the keep. All of those were placed to isolate them from the outside. She couldn't run there.

"Ani. Raga."

The endearments stopped her in her tracks. How would he know them? They were what Jonus called her for pet names. Not even her own parents would know that.

Once she stopped fighting, the strange male set her on her feet carefully and eased his hands away. Ragath turned to him, taking a shaky step back.

"How do you know those names?" she demanded. "Who told you?" Was there a traitor in the keep? Was that how he gained entrance?

He cocked his head to one side, his brow furrowed. Sounds that she was sure were words left his lips, but none of them were words she knew. Ragath bit her lip, working at that. Whatever language he spoke was not what she did. She'd never known there were multiple languages.

He tried again, and she shook her head hopelessly. She didn't even have enough of his language to tell him she didn't understand him properly.

He motioned up and down her body. When she stared at him without comprehension, he sighed and motioned to the shelves of clothing.

Ragath backed to them, wary, unwilling to give him her back. She reached around blindly and pulled down a gown. It nearly tore in her haste to get it on, and her breathing came in harsh gasps of air. The last thing she wanted was to be trapped in the fabric when he moved again.

His eyes widened, and he gaped at her. At a loss, Ragath looked down at herself. It was one of her fine gowns. Surely, he'd seen one before. She glanced up at him, shaking her head to indicate that she didn't understand.

* * * *

237

Gaffin took a calming breath. The gown she'd donned did nothing to cover her. That meant it did nothing to calm his raging lust.

This was no child. She was a woman, young but ripe and ready to be bride to some lucky man. Though he had no doubts his Warrior brethren could control their urges as he did, he could hardly travel with her unclothed this way. There had to be something more appropriate on hand.

He went to the shelves, and she retreated to the bed again. It wasn't an image he needed...her nearly nude on a surface built for sex.

I am stronger than my curse. That in mind, he pulled gown after gown down, grinding his teeth at the number of them that were the same material she currently wore. Surely, there was something that would cover her properly.

His muscles relaxed at the sight of a heavy gown. He carried it to her and motioned for her to put it on.

She took it from his hand, her nose wrinkling in distaste. The look she shot him said that he'd offended her somehow, though he couldn't imagine how. She held the garment over the floor and let it drop in a show of disdain.

"Gods alive, I cannot take you out like this," he pleaded.

There was no reaction from her. As he'd guessed, she didn't have knowledge of their language. The damned beast had certainly created an awkward situation.

Think! There had to be a way to get her to clothe herself. She wouldn't wear the heavy gown. Perhaps she would wear something else.

He started to strip off his tunic, and she bolted for the archway again, her eyes wide and full of terror. Gaffin caught her to his chest, pinning her to his body with the arm he'd freed from the tunic while he peeled it off one-handed.

She wriggled against him, which succeeded in bringing his cock up. Her sob caused it to shrink again.

Thank the gods!

Gaffin dragged his tunic over her head, and she stopped struggling in shock. She stared up at him, looking much more the child than the woman he knew her to be.

He threaded his free hand through the closer arm hole and circled her wrist, guiding her arm back through. She hesitated then pushed the other through on her own. Gaffin offered her a smile and released her.

She didn't move away from him. Instead, she smoothed the tunic down her stomach and thighs. After a moment, she pulled the edge to her nose and inhaled his scent. There was no reaction to that, one way or the other.

I have to teach her our language. There was no question about that. First and foremost, he had to learn what the beast was calling her.

Gaffin patted his chest, drawing her gaze up to him again. "Gaffin," he stated. He motioned to her, waiting for her reply.

She hesitated. Her small hand pressed to the hollow between her breasts. "Ragath."

He started to nod.

"Raga," she continued. "Ani." Her head cocked to one side as if questioning him.

That is why she stopped fighting me. She recognized the words. He nodded grimly.

"Gaffin," Hirum called out.

Ragath startled, hiding herself behind his body. She trembled, and her small hands circled his arm.

The other Warrior scowled. "Can you not control your curse better than that?"

She peeked out at him, and Hirum's jaw dropped. So, he felt the connection as well.

"Who is she?" There was a note of awe in his voice.

"Raga. The beast called her Ragath."

There was a moment of stillness. Then he went to one knee and bowed his head to her.

Ragath looked up at Gaffin in surprise. She ducked behind him again, her trembling more pronounced.

"She does not speak our language," Gaffin confided. "I may have to remove her by force." It was better to warn Hirum in advance, he supposed.

The younger man vaulted to his feet, offering a hand to her, as if she would accompany him without question. Ragath moved further around Gaffin's body with a squeal of distress.

"Gods only know what she's been told about us," Gaffin breathed.

* * * *

Good gods! Two males? A horror show of possibilities cascaded through her mind. Would they both expect her to sate them? The idea of Gaffin claiming her and taking her from Jonus was shocking enough, but this was more than her mind could handle.

Gaffin turned to her, taking her arm gently. He motioned toward the archway.

She shook her head, tears pooling in her eyes. There was a world of men out there, males who had no self-control when a female came into view. What would happen to her if she left the safety of the walls?

He grumbled something fierce and then scooped her over his shoulder, one large hand pressing down on the small of her back and the other gripping her ankles so she couldn't kick him. Ragath screamed in terror, beating her fists against his back. Tears escaped her eyes and wet his back.

Both males made soothing sounds. The other tried to touch her, and she swung her fist around, catching his cheekbone. He recoiled from the force of her blow.

Gaffin's snap turn made her dizzy. Whatever he said to the other sent him several more steps away. Then he turned and kept walking.

They passed the first gate, and Ragath choked. At the second, she reached out for it, desperate to stop them. Gaffin sidestepped, and her fingers skated off the metal bar closest to her.

"Stop. Please, stop," she begged them. The fact that they didn't understand her didn't matter. Ragath had to make them understand.

The intense light burned her eyes, and Ragath squeezed them shut in response. She reached out blindly, trying to find a handhold, anything that would keep Gaffin from taking her out of the keep and into the world of lecherous men. There was nothing.

Footsteps approached at a run. A sensation that announced Jonus was angry followed.

No. Not Jonus. Or, at least, not just Jonus. The feeling came from several directions at once, indicating that more than one person was angry.

Voices rose around her, a chorus of decidedly male voices. Her heart stuttered in response. The words flew fast and furious. Two were repeated several times, the pet names Jonus had for her.

She subsided into tears. There was no escaping this many. That was a given.

Gaffin settled her on her feet, wiping at her face with a soft cloth.

Ragath opened her eyes a slit, trying her best to focus in this damnable light. Shapes took solid form from the misty whole, and she counted them in mounting terror.

Nine. Oh, gods! No.

She scrambled closer to Gaffin. He'd stopped the second man in her room from touching her. Perhaps he would do the same for the others.

Assuming he is the strongest among them.

Her knees shook, and her head ached in the combination of crying, light, and the stresses of the night. Her breathing went ragged, and darkness took her. The shouts of distress faded away.

* * * *

Gaffin lifted Ragath to his chest. She'd retreated to him at every shock. Until she stated her mind, he would assume her choice of protector had been made.

"Is it true?" Ebol asked. "Has she the mark?"

"She has. I saw it."

"I want to see it for myself," Broden challenged.

Gaffin bristled at that. Not at the fact that Broden didn't believe him but rather at the fact that the other man expected Gaffin to strip her for their curiosity.

Then again, his tunic was overlarge for her; if he moved it aside, her shoulder would be clearly visible through the gown. He shifted her in his arms and did so.

Broden stared at it, swallowing hard. "Gods alive. Mieshen will be beside himself."

Gaffin's muscles tightened down a notch at the mention of Ragath's father. True, she was of the other man's household and subject to his rule, but she was also Raga. Being Raga meant she was destined to choose a mate from among the other Warriors.

Did her clinging to Gaffin mean he was her choice? Or was it only because she saw him first? Was it because he'd ordered Hirum to stand down, when she was so panicked? Without common language between them, there was no way for him to know her mind.

The only thing that was certain was her ease with Gaffin. Until she made a clear choice, he was her protector. He prepared to defend that interpretation.

"Gaffin?"

He looked around at Ebol, the eldest of their hunting party. "Yes?"

"The lady has named you protector. It is your lead."

His mouth went dry at that pronouncement. There were six Warriors older than himself present, two of them lords, one of them his own father. Yet they were deferring to his judgment. He'd been certain they would argue his place as protector.

Words stuck in his throat for a long moment. "Broden and Alri...find Mieshen."

The Warrior had gone into seclusion and rarely interacted with his brother Warriors. He would have been invited to join the hunting party if the beast had been any but Veriel. His control in the face of that particular beast would be an uncertain element and might have risked every man involved.

Gaffin glanced at Ragath, his heart aching. *All because you were stolen from him.*

"And?" his father continued.

She is mine. But she wasn't his, and that was the problem. "Ragath has named me her protector. Until Mieshen states otherwise, she stays with me. We move. The beast will pursue when night falls."

"You heard him," Ebol ordered. "Move."

* * * *

Ragath woke to the litany of soothing foreign words. She sighed, comforted, warm...protected. *Cherished.* Where that idea came from, she wasn't certain.

Her servants had always told her she should feel cherished, but she never had...until now.

A whisper of movement near her face brought a delight of scents: green growing things and aroused male. *Undeniably Gaffin.* She moved closer, seeking them.

The words continued, bathing her lips. Was he going to kiss her? They ended, and he moved...slowly, torturously.

At the limits of her endurance, Ragath levered herself up, sealing her mouth to his, her body in a riot. Gaffin growled, sending a shiver of delight down her body.

He wrenched away from her, and she startled, her eyes opening wide. His jaw was tense, and his muscles were strung tight. She'd often seen Jonus in such a mood, and she knew well enough that violence was on his mind.

What was I thinking? She'd been inviting him. What madness had struck her to do such a thing?

Ragath pressed a hand to her lips, shaking her head. What would she do if he took that as permission? Did he even live by the same laws Jonus did? Would he require her permission to bed her?

Surely not!

His muscles tightened down further, and her heart skittered in fear. She'd refused his quest for satiation. She'd angered him. What would he do next?

Gaffin visibly calmed himself, and she relaxed in response. He wasn't going to pounce on her. He wasn't going to force her.

At least not yet, her mind taunted.

He eased back, giving her space. Ragath didn't bolt from him. Something told her that with Gaffin was infinitely safer than outside the cloth room, where she could hear the other men milling about.

His hand went back, and it came around with a plate of food. Ragath stared at it. Was he offering it to her?

As if in answer, Gaffin extended it toward her. *"Eat."*

The word was unfamiliar. She took it, watching his face for signs that she'd interpreted his aim correctly. When the rough metal plate was in her hand, he nodded to it.

"Eat."

I have to learn to speak to him. She pointed to the food. *"Eat.* Food?"

His brow furrowed. She sighed and tried again.

Finally, an expression of realization settled on his face. He placed his fingers to his lips. *"Eat."*

She tried to make a logic stream that worked. Why was he telling her what lips or mouth was, when she wanted to know the word for food?

He sighed and reached to the plate, taking a bit of meat. He raised it to his lips. *"Eat."* Gaffin stared at the meat, probably working at whether it would be ruder to place it back for her or eat it himself. In the end, he popped it into his mouth and started chewing. *"Eat."*

Ragath nodded in understanding. He hadn't been offering her food. He'd been commanding her to eat it.

For a moment, she considered refusing the order. How dare he order her! Gaffin hadn't struck the deal with her father. He had no claim over her.

Her growling stomach made its opinion known. She sighed, her anger waning. Then she ate.

A strange movement against her chest had her looking for the cause. A heavy amulet rested on the end of a thong around her neck. The food stuck in her throat, and she coughed harshly.

Gaffin moved abruptly, rubbing his hand over her back. It was so solicitous, it made her head spin.

But, the amulet... She'd seen one like it before, of course. It would be the sign that she was Jonus's, when she made the vow to be his forever.

She raised her head, fingering the amulet in rising panic. If Gaffin gave her this, he considered her his own. He'd marked her as such.

I didn't give my vow.

Perhaps his laws are not the same as Jonus's. If that was so, what were his laws?

Gaffin placed his hand over the amulet, his expression one that brooked no argument.

She considered that. It was likely a warning not to remove the amulet. If the males he traveled with respected it, they might not touch her while she wore it. Other men might not. Ragath nodded. If anyone removed the amulet, it would be Jonus.

Or a male that bests this one in battle.

Chapter Three

Ragath stirred, looking around in the late daylight, her heart hammering.

It had been three days, and she knew the ways of the males well. They were awake and watchful through the night. No fires were lit in the darkness. After a time of rest and food that had been cooked in the waning sunlight, they traveled leisurely for the latter half of the night. They traveled hard in the pre-dawn and through half the day. Then they slept and ate. Only one stayed awake during those hours, a different one each day...never Gaffin, yet.

She didn't want Gaffin to be awake. If he was awake, he would do what he always did. He would sit with her, stare at her with those disconcerting eyes that made her want to invite him again.

That make me want to speak the damned vow to him.

Not that he would understand it, even if she did.

There was little enough chance that this would work. If Gaffin was awake, there would be none.

I am mad. Ragath didn't question that. Why was she considering this?

The answer was clear. Given much more time with Gaffin, she would beg to be his.

Whether she was or not, there was little chance Gaffin could defeat Jonus in battle. She'd seen Jonus train. He moved like lightning. He disappeared like ripples on water.

There was little chance he wasn't looking for her. Sooner or later, he'd find her. It was a safe wager he was close. If she ran from Gaffin, he might find her sooner...while she was still intact and not honor vowed to be Gaffin's. If she wasn't when he arrived, what he did to Gaffin would be akin to her nightmares, she was certain.

She hesitated at the cloth doorway, torn. She didn't want to be honor vowed to be Jonus's. Given the choice, she'd rather give herself to Gaffin. Was it fear of Jonus killing Gaffin that made her run? Was it simply the fear of being outside the walls that caused this irrational decision-making process?

At what point did I decide I was being irrational? Her anger spiked at that.

The sentry moved, coming to his feet as if danger approached.

He's seen me. Please, gods. Do not let him see me.

Moments passed, and he relaxed, shaking his head as if fatigued. Then he rose and started his walking tour of the camp.

Ragath knew the tour as well as she knew everything else about their ways. In moments, he would be out of line of sight of her.

When he was, she ducked down and moved quickly toward the tree line, taking care not to disturb the sleeping males. A savage glee lit in her. No one had seen her. Perhaps she would make it to Jonus after all.

The attack came without warning, a few body lengths into the trees. Arms circled her, and Ragath struggled with them.

A muttered word the males used often in their disgust or upset escaped him, and he clamped down tight on her and started carrying her. In their struggle, she'd lost track of direction. Was he carrying her toward Gaffin or away from him?

A sudden certainty that it was away struck her, and Ragath screamed. The plan of escaping Gaffin gone awry, she was safest with him. If this male planned to force her or otherwise harm her, Gaffin would surely stop it.

I pray.

The one holding her startled, and calming sounds left his lips, but he didn't release her. She opened her mouth to vent another scream.

Males hurtled at them, stopping her short in mid-intake of breath. Weapons were drawn, and her attacker dropped her.

Ragath made to bolt, but another arm circled her. She beat at him, venting the aborted scream.

A blade nestled to the man's throat, and he released her, putting his hands up in surrender. Frantic words left his throat. Some of them she recognized. Some were new.

Ragath stood in stunned shock, staring at the blade, too frightened to run again. A hand closed on her arm and drew her along the length of the one with the weapon clenched in it. She looked up...at Gaffin.

* * * *

His heart pounded in a combination of *Blutjagd* and fear. At her scream, Gaffin had been certain Veriel's minions were upon them. He hadn't expected to find Ragath in the midst of what appeared to be two of his brother Warriors attacking her.

"Explain," he demanded of Demin, couching the promise of death as her protector—and therefore judge—into that.

Ragath curled to his chest, trembling hard, her breaths hitching in terror that stoked his fury further.

"When the others took down Nev, she bolted. I was afraid she'd become lost or separated from us. I tried to explain, Gaffin, but she has no words to comprehend. And after her scare with Nev, I imagine... Well, I shudder to imagine what she thought my aim was in grabbing her that way." He darkened at the admission, clearly tortured by the situation, as Gaffin was himself.

"It is the truth," Ebol attested. "Demin was an arm's length from me when she screamed the first time. He was not with Nev."

Gaffin forced his arm back, nodding stiffly. "My apologies, my brother."

Demin took a deep breath, shaking his arms loose. "On my honor, I would never harm her. I swear it."

"I believe you." That settled, he turned to stand as judge to Nev.

The young man looked from man to man, swallowing hard as he met Gaffin's eyes. He was surrounded by Warriors barely leashing their *Blutjagd*. It was Hirum's blade at his throat, but the others were ready to gut him, if he moved a finger.

Gaffin took a calming breath before he spoke. "Explain this."

"She was escaping, Gaffin."

His heart stuttered at that. "What proof have you?" Had Ragath really been trying to escape him? Or was Nev trying to save his hide?

"She snuck out. She went to the woods."

"Perhaps she simply needed to relieve her bodily aches," he snapped. Most people did when waking.

"She was ghosting. Not perfectly. Not well, but ghosting," he insisted. "What other reason could she have for it but escape?"

Gaffin considered that. To ghost, she would have to want not to be seen. It was what set in motion the power to do so, in the first place.

He cupped her chin in thumb and forefinger, urging Ragath's face up. She stared at him, her expression unreadable. Yet again, he cursed the lack of language between them. Gaffin would have to accelerate their lessons.

He motioned impatiently at the deeper reaches of the woods, raising a questioning brow. He knew she recognized that as a request for information.

Ragath swallowed hard, glancing at the other men, then the trees...but not at Gaffin. "Needs," she grumbled the word he'd taught her to use when she needed to relieve her bowels or bladder.

Gaffin didn't doubt she'd lied to him. He didn't look away from her, challenging her to be truthful with him. To attempt, at least, to explain why she'd run.

This is new and frightening for her. Ragath needs time to build trust with us. He might never discover what had spooked her into this attempt. Veriel might have done any number of things that would echo into her dealings with Warriors.

He nodded. "Release Nev," he ordered. "She ran."

"What will we do about it?" Ebol inquired. "If she means to run—"

"She will not have the opportunity to run again," Gaffin vowed.

The Warriors' sounds of distress made his heart stutter. If they felt he was mishandling her, they could stand as judge and end him.

"Surely, you don't intend to bind her," his father protested.

"No. I intend to never leave her side."

"You do not now," Demin noted in obvious confusion.

"Until now, she has had a sleeping space an arm's length from mine. Now, she will sleep beneath my arm. There is no possibility she will leave the mat without me waking."

He expected protests at that. There were none.

One by one, his brother Warriors grunted or nodded their agreement. Ebol pronounced it "sensible."

* * * *

Ragath shivered at the hard cut of Gaffin's expression. He knew. He knew she'd lied to him. He knew she'd intended to escape...somehow.

His men wandered away to the camp, but Gaffin stayed with her. After a long moment, his hand circled her arm, and he guided her into the trees.

She looked back at the cloth room, panicked. She'd expected that he would claim her there. What would be his purpose in doing so in the trees? Would it be a brutal lesson not to attempt escape again?

Her foot caught on a tree root, and she stumbled. In a blur of motion, Gaffin was there, supporting her. He stared at her, his expressions shifting.

She wanted to question him, to learn what caused the pain in his expression, but there were no words for that. Ragath cursed it again.

Then they were in motion. Gaffin led her away from the camp and stopped.

Her breathing hitched, and she stared at his legged coverings, waiting for him to unfasten them as he did when he emptied his bladder. Soothing sounds brought her head up. Gaffin shook his head. Was he saying he didn't intend what she thought?

His hand retreated, and Gaffin motioned to the ground. Ragath looked that direction, confused. His voice rumbled out, a confusing mix of words, but it contained the word "needs."

She nodded. Ragath had used the excuse of needing to see to her bodily aches, and he was ordering her to do so.

Gaffin didn't turn his back as he usually would. It was a punishment for her lies and her attempt to escape him, she was certain. He didn't trust her as he had before.

That fact made her heart ache. What did it matter if he trusted her or not? She couldn't say for certain, but it did. Ragath opened her mouth to speak, then shut it again. What could she possibly say that he would understand?

"Needs," he repeated, probably believing she hadn't understood him the first time. It was said in a calm, patient voice, but nothing else about him could rightly be called calm. His muscles were strung tight, and his jaw clenched.

Ragath had learned long ago not to balk a man in this mood. She nodded, pulled her dress to her hips, and squatted to accomplish the task.

When the flow stopped, Gaffin offered his hand to help her to her feet. She took it, pausing halfway up, her eyes riveted on his erect length.

He tugged, and she stood, her senses in a riot. Did he plan to bed with her now that her needs had been seen to? There was no answer to that forthcoming, and so she followed him back to the camp, wound through the men settling back to sleep, and preceded him into the cloth room.

Her move to settle to her own bed met with the resistance of his arms circling her. Gaffin took a step toward his own, pulling her along.

Ragath resisted, trying to free her arm from his grip. Gaffin pulled her flush to his body, his cock long and hard against her belly. His breathing came in ragged blasts of air.

"Do not run from me."

She had no clue what that meant, but he said it slowly and clearly, as if he meant her to learn it. It was probably a warning not to fight him.

Ragath forced her muscles loose, her heart hammering as Gaffin eased her to the narrow woven mat. He didn't cover her with his body. Instead, he knelt beside her and urged her to her side. Then he laid behind Ragath, wrapping one large arm over her in a blatant sign of ownership to the other men...and perhaps to her.

She held herself stiff in his arms, waiting for him to punish her...or to claim her. Her traitor body heated at the latter possibility. What would it be like to be held beneath Gaffin as he thrust through her barrier as Jonus would have?

Gaffin's cock went hard against her back, promising that. Her breathing hitched. For long moments, she waited for the overt move toward what he wanted.

It didn't come. In time, her exhaustion won, and she slept in his arms.

Chapter Four

Gaffin sat his mount, Ragath across his legs. They would restock in the marketplace at Er and be on their way well before sundown.

Knowing the village was so close, Gaffin had reversed his usual orders for movement. The food the men ate on trail was good enough for them, but there was no reason to subject a woman to it. With winter approaching, the game was scarce, and despite trying, providing fresh food for Ragath had been difficult.

At first sight, the bright stalls drew her eyes. They widened, as if she was a child seeing such wonders for the first time.

He couldn't name what changed and made her so tense at first. Then it became clear to him. There were men, groups of men, drinking and sharing tales at an inn.

Ragath buried her face in his chest, pulling his cloak around her as if to hide herself from them. His mind worked quickly, piecing together similar attempts to hide herself from the sight of men. Hirum's arrival in her bed chamber had sent her to Gaffin's back. The sight of the nine Warriors had sent her into a faint. Every time she encountered new men, panic was the result.

What did she think would happen to her? What had the beast told her? There were no answers for that.

There was one thing he had to do. Now that she had been freed from Veriel, Ragath lived in a world full of men. She had to accept that.

Gaffin pulled his horse around, dismounted with Ragath in his arms, and tethered the animal. He settled her on her feet and eased his cloak from her fists.

On second thought... He removed his cloak and wrapped it around her, lending another layer of clothing to hide her slender legs from the men.

253

Ragath looked around, pressing closer to him. Gaffin took her arm, leading the way past the group of carousing men.

Their talking tapered off, and they stared. Gaffin bristled at that. Would all men have this reaction to her?

At his tensing, his brother Warriors closed ranks around them, to the sides and rear, leaving Ragath a clear range of vision while ensuring that no one would approach her.

She eased at that, shooting Gaffin a strained smile...in thanks, he was sure. He returned it, then set himself to the task of teaching her words.

The marketplace afforded them the opportunity to expand her knowledge in leaps and bounds. Like most Warriors, Ragath had a fine memory and rarely needed to hear a word more than twice to add it firmly to her grasp of the language.

It was a fine time. Ragath smiled and blushed.

Gaffin learned her favorite foods by watching what her eyes and hands sought out in the mix. Meat was harder than other foods; they had to expand her knowledge with vendors selling prepared foods, when it became apparent that she'd never seen raw meat before.

The live animals fascinated her, both those in water and farm stock. It didn't surprise Gaffin. Animals wouldn't tolerate close confinement with a beast, and until they'd freed her, Ragath had never formed memories of the world outside Veriel's keep.

Overall, this had been the best idea he'd had yet.

Her head turned, and she went rigid. That simply, every Warrior lit in *Blutjagd*.

Gaffin sought out some sign of danger. Had she seen a minion? Surely, she hadn't seen Veriel in a strong sun.

* * * *

Ragath stared at the group of women in horror. They walked toward the marketplace in a pack, no guards surrounding them as Gaffin's men surrounded her. Where were their men? What were they doing outside their keep?

A group of men at a weapons stall turned. Their sounds were sharp and full of sexual promise. More than one cock rose at the sight of them.

Still, the women came.

Ragath shook her head, certain that she knew what would come next. Women outside the protection of a keep were used by any man who spied them. The men might take turns with them, fight for them, harm the women in their lust and their drive to be first into their soft bodies. If a woman had no male protectors strong enough to hold them off, they did what they wished, when they wished.

She turned, trying to slip between the men behind her. She didn't want to see this. Ragath wanted to be well away before they started warring and fucking.

They closed ranks, and Gaffin took her arms. He shook his head, his eyes wide in concern. "Do not run."

She knew what that meant now, but didn't he understand? Ragath hadn't been raised in this violent world. She couldn't watch such things. She didn't want to see them. She didn't even want to know they existed.

"Do not run," he repeated.

The males' noises went to a high that warned the breaking point was coming. She ground her teeth, her head spinning in terror.

"Run," she insisted. "Gaffin...run!"

He nodded, scooping her to his chest. He set off at a sprint, shouting orders to the other men of his group. In moments, they were mounted and in motion, riding hard and fast toward the west.

Ragath held to him, sobbing in relief that she hadn't been forced to watch it happen, sobbing in agony for the women she'd left behind. Why hadn't she demanded they take the women with them? Had she been so selfish? That thought brought on a new spate of tears.

* * * *

Gaffin dismounted, carrying Ragath to the mat Ebol had laid out for them. She'd trembled and cried herself into a stupor, then fallen into a deep sleep, and he still had no clue what had spooked her so.

Something told him it was connected to the hoots and comments the young men in the crowd had sent at the women coming into the marketplace, but it had been a harmless show of appreciation for their beauty...a childish attempt at gaining the attention of one of the young women escorted by their mothers and grandmothers. Perhaps one of the women would have noticed. Perhaps one would be bride to the young man in the spring or summer.

Why that would disturb Ragath was a mystery. But, considering the fact he had no clue what the beast had done to her or told her, it was a mystery he had no hopes of unraveling soon.

Gaffin settled her on the mat, arranging his cloak to keep her warm. Even now, tremors wracked her form.

"What caused this?" Ebol asked, his voice low to preserve her restless slumber. "What did she see?"

"I cannot say. It may have been a minion, but I doubt it."

"You *doubt* it?" his father scoffed.

"I do not believe Ragath has been permitted sight of any man save Veriel in her life. Our ways are strange to her. They frighten her. I do not believe Veriel would have introduced her to a male minion. Remember the keep?"

There was a moment of contemplative silence.

Finally, Ebol grunted his agreement. "There were only women within. Not a single male guard."

"Can you imagine the trauma to Ragath when faced with a world full of men?" Gaffin was having a hard time imagining it himself.

"What should we do to counter it?" his father asked.

"Avoid places like the marketplace...for now. Let her become accustomed to our ways in the small groups of Warriors and families. Then introduce her to the world, when she has calmed to us."

"Sensible. For now, we should let her sleep and make her a hearty meal."

Gaffin nodded his agreement. Still, he wished he knew what Ragath had feared so acutely.

Chapter Five

The meal was a subdued affair. Ragath made no attempt at engaging in conversation. She hardly seemed aware of the conversation that did take place, of the worried looks the Warriors shot her.

Gaffin noted her wrinkled nose...the way she sniffed at her clothing and grimaced. She was a lady accustomed to comforts.

His cock aching at what he was considering, he left her for a moment and sought out his pack. The soap stone wasn't what he'd typically offer her, but it would do the job of cleaning away the dirt and sweat, and the cloth would cover and dry her, until her clothing dried.

Her eyes widened at the sight of his offering, and she vaulted to her feet. Ragath grasped the edge of his tunic and started to peel it back, revealing her body and reinforcing that she had no sense of modesty within the safety of their group.

Gaffin grasped her at the lower curve of her hips, stopping it there. Around the fire, heads snapped up, and *Blutjagd* rose. Ragath pulled from his hands, and he let her go.

He motioned the other Warriors down, and their ire faded. Ragath relaxed in response. Her gaze shifted to Gaffin, and she straightened proudly.

A tip of his head toward the other men caused the rising of a flush in her cheeks. She nodded, though he wasn't certain she understood his concerns.

Gaffin put his hand out. She hesitated and then stepped to his side, allowing him to wrap the hand around her arm.

"Gaffin," his father blustered. "Surely you do not mean to—"

"I have seen her nude before, Father. I will not take advantage of this situation."

There was no warning that he had best not. That went without saying.

258

* * * *

Gaffin led her to a gentle river that ran over smooth rocks. He motioned Ragath to the water, his eyes soft and inviting.

She took a moment to consider her situation. She had to wash her body and clothing and probably don them again while they were wet.

Or bathe in them.

Ragath discarded that idea. If she bathed in her clothing, she wouldn't properly clean her body, and she wanted to be clean.

Gaffin breathed her name, and she turned to look at him. He motioned to her clothing and spoke words that she hadn't learned yet.

Though he'd seen her in every possible state of dress and undress, including completely nude, disrobing before him now felt intimate, as if her nudity held some meaning it never had before. She hesitated, unsure.

When she started pulling off the clothing, Gaffin's eyes went hot and heavy-lidded. He took his tunic from her hand, then the gown Jonus had given her. Just when Ragath felt certain he would lean toward her and kiss her, he placed the soap in her hand and waved her into the river.

The water was cold and refreshing, and she glided in, reveling in the decadence of water so vast, with such natural, green scent about it. Ragath cupped handfuls up and wet her skin to make scrubbing away the dirt and sweat of their time traveling easier.

The soap was completely unlike the ones she'd been bathed with in Jonus's keep, but it did the job well, leaving her skin slick and her hair smooth. Ragath immersed herself several times, washing the slick away and leaving a light, woodsy scent behind.

There was something freeing in bathing herself, in not relying on servants to see to her needs. *I should*

259

have demanded this luxury long ago. But she'd forgotten how enjoyable it was.

A sound behind her brought her head around. Gaffin was knee deep in the river, wetting the clothing he'd taken from her again and again. She ambled to him and offered the soap. He took it with a smile and a nod, and she went back to her soaking, enjoying the push of the current on her skin. It was like a hundred fingers, soothing her.

Ragath stared at the rippling water, enchanted. She'd always loved the way water moved and felt.

A sliver of memory played at her mind, and she cupped her hand slightly. Ragath stared at it, her brow scrunched tight over narrowed eyes.

If I scoop the water and throw it thus... The droplets glittered like jewels and made a pleasing melody on the slowly-moving surface. She smiled and tried again and again. Laughter burst from her throat.

Small hands splashed water in her bath. Ragath aimed for the older nurses, giggling at their scowls of disapproval.

She'd enjoyed splashing as a child. How strange that she hadn't remembered it. Ragath sent another spray up, smiling. What was there not to enjoy?

The smack came without warning. Ragath stared at the rising bruise on her hand, stunned. The nurse struck her? She couldn't remember ever being struck before.

"No splashing, Ragath!" the nurse chided. "Look at the mess."

The other servants shied from the nurse, clearly horrified. Ragath scented their panic and reacted, screaming in confusion and fear.

She bit at her lower lip, trailing her fingers in the water. Was that why she'd stopped splashing water? Because a nurse had frightened her?

"Ragath? Is something wrong?"

"Ragath!"

Jonus appeared from nowhere, scooping her out of the tub. Ragath held to his shoulders, her little feet pressed to his broad chest, sobbing hysterically. Around her, there was absolute and chilling silence.

"Raga, my love," he breathed. "What—"

His question died off. Jonus raised Ragath's hand, his dark eyes widening. He laid a kiss over the bruise, whispering soothing words. Ragath laid her cheek against his shoulder, her breathing hitching.

Jonus turned to the nurse who'd struck her, picking her out flawlessly. The other servants backed away further, leaving that one alone at the center of the floor. Still, she stood her ground, straight and tall.

"You struck Ragath." It wasn't a question.

"The child—"

She made it no further. Jonus's backhanded smack sent her sprawling, sliding across the wet floor.

Ragath stared at her, shivering in the uncomfortable stillness. The nurse's head was at an odd angle, and her eyes stared at nothing in particular. Red mixed with the puddles of water, racing toward Jonus's bare feet.

Jonus whisked Ragath away to the safety of his bed.

She startled, looking at the water in mistrust. The setting sun turned the surface a fiery red and orange.

Blood. So much blood. I splashed...played...and Jonus killed her.

Ragath screamed at the thought, her mind rebelling.

* * * *

"Ragath? Is something wrong?"

She didn't seem to hear him. Ragath stared into space, her fingers stirring idly in the water.

Gaffin set her clothing on the rock he'd been using to beat his tunic and headed deeper into the water. Something wasn't right, and he wanted to be closer to Ragath in case it was a threat.

She shivered, her breathing coming in sharp gasps.

"Ragath?"

Again, there was no response.

She startled, her eyes darting back and forth, her head lowered. Was there something in the river?

Ragath screamed and surged toward him. She fought the water, fully opposite her smooth entry. Gaffin crossed the final distance and extended his hand, intent on guiding her around to his back. She scaled his body instead of allowing that.

He kicked beneath the water, expecting to encounter some sort of large eel or fish that had spooked her. There was nothing, just the pull of gently moving water.

"Ragath? What is it?"

Bits and pieces of words escaped her lips, in his language and hers.

Nothing that makes sense. He opened his mouth to speak again.

"Gaffin!"

He didn't turn toward Ebol's voice. There was little question that every Warrior in their hunting party had come running at her scream, and Ragath was nude with only his body blocking their view of her.

"The cloth," he ordered.

There was a flurry of activity and then the sounds of one man entering the water. The cloth appeared at his shoulder; the man holding it didn't step forward where he could see Ragath.

Gaffin considered his options. "Who are you?"

"Niklus," his father replied.

"Tuck the cloth around her."

"Gaffin!" It was little more than a shocked whisper.

"You are a mated man," Gaffin grumbled. "You won't have feelings for what you see. Wrap the cloth."

His father did so, his hands trembling, his eyes averted. When he was done, Gaffin offered a terse word of thanks and headed for shore.

"What caused this?" Ebol asked.

Gaffin ground his teeth in frustration. "Gods damned if I know, but I intend to find out."

Enough of not understanding what upset her. Every time Ragath screamed, it stopped his heart.

He took her directly to their shared sleeping mat and settled Ragath on it. She huddled in the cloth, shaking hard.

"Fish?" he asked, seeking to use words she understood.

Ragath stared at him, seemingly lost.

"In the water? A fish?"

Her head swiveled in a negative response.

"An eel?"

"N-no. No eel. No fish."

"What then?" It wasn't adequate to elicit an answer. Gaffin knew that before he noted that her look of confusion hadn't changed. He tried again. "What...makes you fear?"

"F-fear?" She shook her head, her brow furrowed.

Gaffin extended his hand and mimicked her trembling. He pressed a hand to his heart and then thumped it fast. "What makes you fear, Ragath? What makes you run now?"

Ragath paled. "Jonus."

He snapped a look at the setting sun, scanning for danger, reasoning himself out of it. If the Deceiver was near, why hadn't he attacked or tried to take her back?

"Here?" he demanded. If she said yes, he would order the move this moment.

She shook her head, her brow furrowed, as if he'd somehow misunderstood her.

Gaffin breathed a sigh of relief. "Something that reminds you of the beast." But how could he learn what it was to avoid it in the future? "Water?" No. She'd been so excited about bathing, so happy about being immersed.

Ragath visibly struggled with her limited vocabulary. "Water...no. Blood...on water."

The sunset reflected on the water perhaps. "You have *seen* blood on water with the beast?" He annunciated each word and watched for her response.

"Jonus—" she choked out. Ragath squeezed her eyes shut, then opened them and started again. "Jonus...slaughter woman."

He winced at the words she'd grasped on. It was probably precisely what she'd witnessed. Had she seen it the morning they'd rescued her? Did it matter?

Not really. She saw it. It didn't matter when she had.

Ragath continued, probably believing he wanted more information. She was correct, though he had no way of asking the many questions circling in his head.

"I..." She hesitated and then placed her flattened hand waist-height over the floor.

"You were young? A child?"

"Yes. Child. I was child."

Gods alive! Ragath had seen the beast kill a woman when she was just a child. He hardly knew where to begin trying to mend that trauma.

"I was in...bathe." She struggled to tell the tale.

"Bath," he whispered, correcting her usage automatically. Gaffin wanted to tell her to stop. He knew what she'd seen, more or less. *As a child!* It turned his stomach.

"I..." Her brow furrowed, and her hand moved aimlessly. It steadied. She cupped her hand and swept it around in an arc.

"Splash. You splashed." Before she regained the memories, she'd splashed in the river and laughed. He'd never seen her play before, and he'd been enchanted by it.

"I splashed, and she—"

"No." Hearing it would be a torture for him; telling it for her. Already, it was clear that she blamed herself for the woman's death, for some reason Gaffin couldn't understand. "I understand now."

Ragath looked up at him, pleading, seemingly the lost child she must have been all those years ago.

Gaffin knelt beside her, offering his chest for comfort. She pressed to him, letting him enfold her. They sat in silence until she slept.

He settled her on the sleeping mat, then stepped outside the pavilion. "You heard?" he asked no one in particular. The last thing he wanted to do was repeat it.

Ebol grunted an affirmative response.

Gaffin nodded and returned to the mat. Aching in body and spirit, he wrapped himself around her and sought out elusive sleep.

Chapter Six

Ragath snuggled against Gaffin's body. Unlike most mornings she woke in his arms, they were face to face instead of with Gaffin pressed to her back.

The cloth he'd wrapped around her had gapped open, leaving her pressed to his body. His clothing against her naked flesh was a wealth of sensation. His scent on her skin was strangely exciting, and the leather and cloth teased and tested her body.

His hand slid from her back to the curve of her buttocks and his arms tightened minutely, bringing her up against the length of his ready cock. Her gasp disappeared in the rumbling sound he made.

The fasteners on his leathers enticed her. What would he do if she was bold enough to undo them? To touch him as she'd touched Jonus? Would he do what Jonus had? Would he taste her? Allow her to spill his seed? Would he want more of her body?

Her body reacted to that thought. *She* wanted more.

As if he'd heard that thought, Gaffin's eyes opened. They were dilated in what she'd like to think was arousal. His cock moved between them, seemingly confirming it.

His head tilted, and he looked down at their touching bodies. His fingers flexed and tightened against her bottom, as if he was considering his next move.

I know what move I need him to make. Ragath trailed a hand down his chest and stomach, hinting at it gently.

Some back corner of her mind warned that Jonus would kill for as little as this. She was raised to be his own, marked as his, and she was making an illicit choice of another.

If Jonus cared to stop me, he should have kept me safe. I was taken by another. If all Gaffin is waiting for is a sign of my willingness, I will give it.

His hand left her back and clasped her wrist, stopping her a mere hand's width from his cock. He didn't order her to stop, but he jerked his head toward the flap of the cloth room they shared.

Not where the others can hear it. Not where they might want to partake, as well. Her face heating, she nodded her agreement. Silently, she cursed men. Would there ever be a time and place they would be free to enjoy each other?

Gaffin's retreat and the way he yanked the cloth shut around her body spoke his doubts.

Or perhaps he has no intentions of claiming me. She shivered at that thought, staring at his back disappearing through the flap. Gaffin didn't seem disinterested, but she knew well enough that not all men gave in to their innate urges to bed a woman fully.

If that was true, what would be his reason for denying himself?

* * * *

Gaffin swallowed down a scream of frustration. They didn't have enough words to discuss what Ragath's aim had been in touching him, and teaching her those words would be an inappropriate intimacy.

Still, her actions taunted him.

Had she wanted to compare his body to the beast's? If, as he believed, she had never seen a man, besides the foul one, it might be simple curiosity driving her. If it was, would the others support him letting her examine him.

My sanity will not support it. There was little question of that.

Worse...or better, what if her interest was personal? If he raised the possibility with her, it would be accused he was taking unfair advantage of his place to convince her to him.

Torn between duty and need, he pulled her dried clothing down from the pavilion lines and returned to the flap. Cursing himself, he shoved them through and waited for Ragath to retrieve them. Praying she would remember to put on both layers, he turned his back.

That wrenched a wince from him. There wasn't a single pair of eyes in the camp that weren't locked on him and assessing.

Of course. I stormed out here, stamping down Blutjagd, reeking of arousal and woman. There was little question that they were already speculating on what happened inside the pavilion. Perhaps, they were reconsidering their stand on Ragath sharing a mat with him.

I have done nothing wrong!

Yet, his mind taunted. The hand on her ass, holding her to his erection, had hardly been innocent.

But unconscious. He'd been asleep.

And dreaming of Ragath riding that same cock. If he allowed himself too long to consider that, he'd be turning himself over for judgment.

The movement behind him, had him glancing to make sure she was dressed before he allowed the others to see her. Both the beast's gown and his tunic in place, he relinquished his position at the flap and headed for the fire.

* * * *

"Practice? Training?"

Gaffin turned to Ragath, noting her excitement in surprise.

Of course! The beast had to have allowed her physical training, though by the way she avoided their weapons, it was a safe wager Veriel hadn't allowed battle training.

"You wish to practice?" he asked in a slow, even voice. "To train with the men?"

She nodded.

He waved her toward the meadow they were using, his mind buzzing. Ragath was a Warrior; she would require physical activity to quell the *Blutjagd*, as any male Warrior would. Leaving her at the edge of the area, Gaffin headed for Ebol to discuss how to carry out training a female without injuring her.

"Gaffin!"

His drawn weapon thumped to the grass as he whirled around and launched toward Ragath, landing hard on his knees. Only after he had his hands around her hips did his mind process that her dress and his tunic were gathered beneath his palms, her legs bare to just below her feminine curls.

Gaffin forced the fabric down her thighs, averting his eyes by silent reminders of his duty alone. A rebellious corner of his mind protested the move.

"Practice," she protested, her cheeks going crimson and her eyes hard. "Train, Gaffin."

"Oh, gods." His answer came out rasping and unsteady.

"What is it?" his father asked.

He released the dress to her ankles and motioned for Ragath to be still. "She cannot train in a dress or tunic, but she must train, as we all do." As it was, they'd delayed training until the strain of it was beating at them. It was likely beating at her, as well.

There was a moment of silence.

Ebol managed speech first. "What are you suggesting?"

Gaffin swallowed the lump in his throat. "When—when we reach the keep, I will teach her to wear a boy's leathers."

"We have nothing that small here," Niklus reminded him.

"Obviously." Everyone in the group was a seasoned Warrior, fully grown into his muscle and more than twice Ragath's size.

Gaffin pushed to his feet, looking at Ebol and Niklus instead of Ragath. Considering what he intended, looking at her would be problematic. "For now...she has to train."

"Nude?" his father choked.

"You have another suggestion?" Gaffin raised an eyebrow in challenge.

The Warriors looked at each other nervously, and Gaffin noted that more than a few of them had come erect.

His face burned at the idea of all of them seeing her unclothed. "Alone. I will oversee."

For a tense moment, Gaffin thought they'd protest. Surely, someone would claim he was abusing his position to get a sexual thrill.

Instead, they nodded their agreement. Tension Gaffin hadn't realized he harbored seeped from his muscles.

He motioned Ragath to follow him and led her to a spot over the hill from where the other men were training. Somehow, he was certain they were finding it hard to concentrate on that task, knowing what was going on behind the hill.

He stopped deep in the bowl of the meadow. "Now...train," he managed.

Ragath tipped her head back, glancing at the top of the hill. After a moment, she nodded and stripped off her newly-washed clothing. Gaffin tried to normalize his breathing, but his base needs were drowning out his thinking mind.

He licked his lips at the sight of Ragath securing her hair back with a strip of leather Hirum had given her to do the job while she rode. The move pushed her breasts forward and curved her back, placing her on display.

She shortened the thong the amulet hung on. Gaffin hadn't even considered the possibility that she might try to remove it, but she hadn't.

That accomplished, Ragath glided through the grass to a place near the center of the bowl.

Her first moves were stretches. Her supple body folded and unfolded, individual muscles tightening and flexing.

Forcing himself not to move was all Gaffin could manage. His cock lay heavy against his belly, and his head spun lightly in the combination of his strangled breathing and increased heart rate.

The next moves were strength exercises. Ragath supported herself in any number of positions and undulated slowly from feet to hands and back again, exposing herself to him in the process.

Gaffin's cock wept against his leathers, complaining at the confinement. It ached in demand for release. If he dared tempt fate and the rules of sanction, he'd take his cock in hand and end this torture...while she watched or ignored it. He didn't care which, though his cock had a definite preference.

Just when he thought it could get no worse, Ragath erupted into motion. Wheels of her body, hand to hand and foot to foot, gave way to flips, feet to hands and back again, one-handed and no-handed flips in all directions, rolls, vaults, and all manner of maneuvers Gaffin had no name for.

At some indeterminate point in time, Gaffin realized he was gaping and forced his mouth shut. He was also a few steps closer to her. Gaffin backed to his former position, using the tree behind him as a guidepost. He sent up a prayer to Tes that she hadn't noticed the change.

This was insanity. Vow or not, more of this would drive Gaffin mad. Already, his bespelled body argued to break sanctions his mind knew all too well.

He locked his muscles down, his feet shoulder-width apart, his arms crossed over his chest. Only his attention was allowed to roam.

It didn't. Looking away from Ragath was inconceivable. When her "training" ended, it took Gaffin's lust-soaked mind a hand of heartbeats to acknowledge the change.

She moved toward him, soaked in sweat, her skin glistening as it might during heated sex.

That is not an image I need to indulge in.

The beast's gown covered her first, and Gaffin cursed himself his envy that Veriel had been gifted this sight daily.

It is no gift; it is torture. How could so intemperate a being deny himself when Gaffin hardly could? When mated Warriors could hardly deny themselves with the want for her riding them?

What if he didn't?

Gaffin opened his mouth to ask it, then snapped it shut. His own reaction if the Destroyer of Lives had abused her aside, Ragath had suffered the beast's memories only the night before. Did he want to chance another miserable memory for her?

No. Stand down, Gaffin.

In the next heartbeat, Ragath gave him something else to occupy his uncertain sanity. His tunic smoothed over the damned gown, she appeared at his side.

Gaffin followed her line of sight, the blood rushing in every extremity in realization. She was staring at his erection, her expression moving from uncertainty to interest to hunger and back.

He didn't discourage her appraisal. Perhaps she would find peace in the knowledge that a male could come erect and not do whatever it was the Deceiver had made her believe was natural for an aroused male to do.

Ragath didn't attempt to touch him, and Gaffin reminded himself that he should thank the gods for it.

If she touched him, he would surely have his answer of how far the beast had ventured sexually with Ragath.

I have to stop thinking about this. "We should go."

Her gaze snapped to his face. Whatever she saw sent her two steps further away. Ragath straightened, her chin came up, and she nodded.

Gaffin waved her ahead of him, half in expectation that she'd be afraid to have him at her back. As if in opposition to his line of thinking, Ragath turned and preceded him up the hill.

It didn't help. Instead of staring at her mouth and breasts, Gaffin found himself staring at her swinging backside. He dragged his gaze away over and over, cursing his Warrior memory for detail in three languages.

Reaching the camp both helped and hindered him.

It helped, because it gave him ample reason to find other places to fix his attention.

It hindered him, because that attention was drawn to the Warriors averting their eyes. Even the older, mated men seemed to have trouble looking at either Ragath or Gaffin.

Ragath paused at the fireside and reached for a skin of water. Hirum handed it up to her without turning his head. She hurried to the pavilion and darted inside.

Gaffin didn't question why she fled. From the moment he'd come back into camp, reeking of musk, the others' bodies had gone into a frenzy of the same. There was no doubt that every man in camp was hard and wanting.

He wasted even less time speculating that Ragath was unnerved by the reaction, perhaps fearful that they would choose not to control their urges.

He wanted to demonstrate that control. His body was less accommodating. Gaffin panted back his arousal.

His father's hand closed on his shoulder. "Do you need self-release?"

Gaffin shook his head. He staggered to the closest tree and dug his fingertips into the bark until they ached.

"You do," Niklus insisted.

"No. If I do—" Gaffin looked at the pavilion, his face and neck heating in more than arousal. "My sanity will not stand for using memories of her to accomplish it."

Several of the Warriors winced at the blunt statement.

"I understand," Niklus assured him.

"When we reach the keep, I am teaching her to wear a boy's leathers for training," Gaffin decreed.

His father leaned closer. "Until then?"

"We have four days. We are not training again. None of us are. Not until she wears leathers."

Niklus groaned. "It was that difficult?"

Gaffin ran her fingers through his sweat-soaked hair. "I need...water."

"Water!"

Hirum scrambled to comply.

Gaffin pushed him away. "No. Not that." He staggered around and bolted for the river. He plunged into the water, grinding his teeth at the brain-clearing cold.

He dunked his head once...then again. When Gaffin dragged himself out, he was numb, exhausted, and still erect.

* * * *

Gaffin startled at the sound of a vicious curse. If it had been one of the men, it wouldn't have affected him, but it was Ragath who'd uttered it.

He turned to her, his face heating at the fact that she was still squatting to see to her bodily needs. Gaffin had only watched once, after Ragath had run from him. Worse, he hadn't fully recovered from watching her train that morning.

Forcing speech was difficult. "Ragath?"

"I need..." She faltered, shooting Gaffin a panicked look.

"What? What do you need?" His heart was hammering, and he wasn't certain why it was.

"Blood...clothes?"

"Blood rags?" Was she cycling, or was it something else? Ragath wasn't calm, as most women were about a moon time event.

She nodded. "Blood..." She gasped. "Rags."

Solve the puzzle later. Serve her needs.

"Hirum!" Gaffin only called for him, because he knew the young Warrior was close.

Sounds of Hirum crashing through the wood drew near.

"Stop there and listen."

He obeyed, and silence filled the void between them. "Listening, Gaffin."

"We need blood rags. Quickly. Go to camp and scavenge spare tunics. Scavenge anything our men carry to accommodate her."

Hirum moved the opposite direction as quickly as he'd come. Gaffin turned back to Ragath.

She'd stripped off her clothing and donned just his tunic. The beast's gown was folded neatly and pressed to her chest. Ragath squatted there, taking slow, even breaths.

Gaffin noted that in rising concern. True, he'd only been around his mother and sister during their blood time, but he'd never seen such an outward sign of pain.

He knelt next to her, lifting the edge of his tunic. Ragath pushed back, her face paling another notch.

"I wish to see," he soothed her.

Ragath shook her head and tightened her grip on the tunic.

A dozen distasteful possibilities fought for his attention. Had Veriel drank the blood of victims in front of her? Had the Destroyer of Lives insisted on

275

drinking her moon blood, leading Ragath to believe Gaffin might wish to indulge in the same perversion?

Don't think about that! "I have to check."

"Check?"

"How much blood you are losing?" he qualified.

Ragath looked down, then grimaced. "More than some. Less than others."

Gaffin nodded. "Is it... Is it your moon time?" *What if Veriel planted a child? What if she is rejecting it?*

Well, that would be for the best, but Ragath was a woman. She would grieve a lost child, half-beast or not. Ragath wasn't a trained Warrior. She wouldn't know what a monster Veriel's young would be.

"What? My...my moon?" She glanced to the sky, assuring herself that the moon was not in the sunlit expanse. Her eyes pleaded for answers.

At a loss to explain it with their limited shared language, Gaffin reached for her hand. She stared at his hand, trembling.

"Give me your hand. Just your hand, Ragath."

She complied, her fingers cold. Gaffin gripped her hand and sensed her. His breath escaped in a ragged rush.

"Cycling," he breathed. *Thank the gods, she is cycling normally.* If Veriel had planted his seed, rejecting the infant or not, she wouldn't be.

"Gaffin," Hirum called out. "The blood rags?" He didn't dare to approach since he'd been warned not to earlier.

With one last gentle squeeze, Gaffin released her hand and stood. "Stay," he requested.

Ragath offered a tense nod, and he hurried off to collect the first blood rag.

Hirem offered a broad smile, and Gaffin returned it. Despite their many failures, this was one they *hadn't* made.

Chapter Seven

The keep was built into the side of a mountain. There was no indication how large or small it was. If the corridors connected to tunnels, as she suspected they might, the structure might go on for miles. The thought warmed her for reasons Ragath couldn't name.

Gaffin took her arm gently, leading her toward the heavy doors. Before they reached them, one opened and someone launched toward her.

Ragath shied, then stopped in surprise. The approaching person was a woman.

She stopped and yelled out something. Another appeared. Several young men and children followed.

Before Ragath recovered enough to question Gaffin, the older woman wrapped Ragath in her arms and squeezed, speaking fast. Ragath allowed it, though she shot Gaffin a look requesting answers.

He launched into a rushed speech that Ragath caught little of. Her name and pet names were included, as was the term "beast." Aside from the fact that he was explaining her presence here, little more made an impression. Somewhere in there, she thought she heard the word "bath," but she couldn't be certain how it fit with the rest.

At his words, the woman stiffened. A moment later, she released Ragath and stepped back, her expression pained. Ragath reached for her, in need of a woman's companionship. As if she understood, the woman drew Ragath to her side.

Gaffin kept speaking. Ragath caught odd words in the mix, nothing that made sense in combination.

The woman nodded grimly and led her into the keep. Ragath looked back, meeting Gaffin's gaze for a long moment. He nodded his agreement and then went back to giving orders to his men.

Inside, the younger boys scattered, leaving Ragath with the two women. They didn't hesitate. In moments, Ragath was deep within the keep and moving deeper.

Torches lit the way, soft light that made Ragath feel immediately at home. She shivered at that; she didn't want to feel at home here. Not like the "home" she'd shared with Jonus, at any rate. Would this place be like that keep?

No. She stopped short, taking a step back. The women stared at her, then each other, seemingly confused. Ragath's heart pounded in apprehension. They reached for her, and she jerked away.

"Gaffin," she requested. She'd wanted the companionship of women, but she needed the security of Gaffin in this strange place.

The younger woman motioned for her to stay and bolted back the way they'd come. Ragath retreated to a close corner, shaking though she couldn't state why she did. The other didn't approach her. Soothing sounds left her lips, but she kept her distance.

Gaffin came barreling toward her, and Ragath launched herself at him. He was solid and familiar, and she held on tight, on her toes so her face nestled to his throat.

His breath stirred her hair. "What makes you fear?" he whispered.

Explaining it was impossible. All that mattered was that Gaffin was with her. "Stay. Do not run." It wasn't the correct way to ask it, she was sure.

He nodded. "Come. There is a bathing chamber."

Ragath loosened her grip on his tunic and settled to the flats of her feet. Gaffin planted a hand on her lower back and guided her further into the rock, the two women in their wake.

The bathing chamber was large enough that the entire company she'd seen so far could conceivably use it at the same time. Something told her that wasn't so.

Or will not be when I am here. What gave her that idea was beyond her comprehension.

Gaffin motioned for her to continue, then retreated to the doorway.

She started removing her clothing, and the older woman reached to take them. Ragath swallowed a sour wave. Were these to be her new servants?

I do not want servants. Moving deliberately, Ragath stripped down and tossed the clothing to the closest carved bench instead.

The move seemed to confuse them, but no one complained. The younger offered Ragath a comb but didn't attempt to groom her hair. Confident that they understood her wishes, Ragath took it and set about untangling the half day of travel.

Soap and a cloth for drying appeared on the bench that ringed the pool of steaming water, and Ragath shot a look at the other two women. Neither one ordered her toward the water. Rather, they were busy stripping off their own clothing and wading in without her.

No servant would do that. With a sigh of relief, Ragath went back to her hair. When it was tamed, she ambled to the bench, set the comb on it, and retrieved the soap.

The water was so hot, she initially shied. Ragath dipped her foot in, testing the heat. After a moment, it was comfortable, and she waded further in. The floor dropped off faster, and she went from her knees to her waist with a gasp of surprise and a splash.

Her cheeks flaming and heart pounding, she glanced at the other two women. Adults did not splash. Would they be angry? Would they think her clumsy? Neither seemed to notice her error, and Ragath forced her heart to slow.

Bathing in the hot water was a decadent experience. Ragath sank to her knees, reveling in the moment. Had there ever been a more perfect moment in her life?

The memory of Gaffin's mouth meshed with her own brought a flush she hoped the others would attribute to the heat. She opened her eyes and looked his way, but Gaffin had his back turned.

It was a fine back, strong and broad, but she missed seeing him from the front already. His eyes were soft and inviting. His lips were full and dark. And his cock... She was certain his cock was hard inside his leathers.

What would it be like to stroke him as she had Jonus? Would he make the same sounds or different ones? She felt certain his eyes would—

"Ragath?"

She snapped her head around, staring at the elder woman. Gods, what had she been thinking? Did the others know? Did they disapprove of such things? Women had no say in what men they belonged to. They had no preference.

I have a preference.

The younger pressed a hand to her chest. "Elee. My name is Elee, Ragath."

"Elee," she repeated. It was a pretty name, and the girl was pretty.

She waved to the elder. "Nara."

Ragath nodded. She tipped her head to the first. "Elee." And the elder. "Nara."

Nara took over. "I am Gaffin's *mother.*"

Her brow furrowing in confusion, Ragath repeated the last word as a question.

Nara seemed to consider that. She cradled her arms as one would to hold a babe. "Gaffin." She tipped her head toward the baby. "My Gaffin."

"Mother," the man in question growled. "Please."

A laugh bubbled up. Ragath tried to hold it in, but it burst free. She clapped a hand over her mouth and shot a look at Gaffin. He was inspecting the cave roof, his face bright red. That was all it took to send Ragath into spasms of laughter.

The momentary twinge of fear that something bad was coming melted away. Jonus wasn't here. He wasn't here to be jealous that someone else had made her smile or made her laugh.

A sob mixed with the laughter at that. How lonely it was, even surrounded by people, when only Jonus was allowed to make her happy.

* * * *

Gaffin shook his head.

On one hand, it was good to hear Ragath laugh. He heard it seldom. After her life with the beast, that was to be expected.

But she is laughing at me. At the image of me as a babe at my mother's breast. It stung. He preferred the image of himself as a strong protector.

Only because she clings to me, and I get to feel her body against mine. Gods but that was both damning and true.

Her expression changed, an indefinable sadness welling in her eyes. Her laugh went brittle, then stopped. There was a moment of tense silence. She sighed and went back to bathing.

The rush of feet caught his attention, and Gaffin turned to peer down the corridor. The young boys were heading toward him at a run. His mind working through the possibilities, Gaffin ordered a halt. They obeyed, staring up at him from their varying heights.

"Goff and Ran, you are too old to bathe with the women. Wait until they leave the bathing room." At twelve and fourteen, they were beginning to look like men, and he felt certain that would be too much for Ragath's sensibilities.

The two stared at him, shocked. Gaffin added a warning look, and they turned back.

They shouldn't be shocked. Ragath is not a woman of our house. Even then, the only man who bathed with a woman was her mate. Children bathed whenever they liked, though older children or women always accompanied babies and toddlers into the bath.

"And us?" Turl piped up, his bright four-year-old eyes expectant.

Gaffin cleared the way and motioned the other three—all under the age of eight—into the bathing chamber. They rushed past with all the exuberance of youth, shouting and running.

Ragath turned to look at them and caught a faceful of water. She sputtered, reared back, and lost her balance. Gaffin tensed as she disappeared under the water, but she was back up in a moment, wiping the water from her face.

The boys didn't seem to realize the havoc they'd caused. They splashed and dunked each other, their noises echoing off the stone walls and roof.

For a long moment, Ragath stared at them, her brow furrowed and mouth set in a thin line. She flinched at the splashes that connected with her.

Turl turned and saw her. A mischievous smile curving his lips, he aimed a splash for her.

Ragath smiled. Her eyes narrowed in challenge. Her return splash showered the child and left him sputtering in surprise. Then she laughed.

Scenting a competition in the making, the other boys joined in, and the water battle began in earnest. Elee took Ragath's side, though it seemed the young Ani had no need of her aid. Gaffin chuckled at the squeals and warnings, the laughter and riotous play.

Thank the gods. I thought I'd never see it.

* * * *

Ragath wrapped her arms around herself, another of Gaffin's tunics momentarily taking the place of her gown. This one was longer and reached past her knees, and it was infinitely better than the blood gown they'd tried to convince her to wear. It didn't carry his scent, as the other tunic had, and that was a loss.

Gaffin stopped and motioned to a chamber. "I bed here," he announced.

She turned to enter, and he took her arm, shaking his head. Gaffin guided her down the corridor, past a hand of chambers. He stopped again.

"You and Elee bed here."

Ragath swallowed a heavy lump. "Here?" She looked back the way they'd come. He was banishing her from his bed? A blade of disappointment lodged in her chest.

"I will be there if you need me," he promised.

The last morning with Jonus flashed through her mind. He'd refused to share her bed, as well. Gaffin was no better, no matter what kind thoughts she'd had about him.

She glared at him, turned on her heel, and stormed into the room he'd indicated was hers. The furs on one bed smelled sweet and fresh, so she flopped down on it, relatively certain it was the one intended for her.

"Ragath?"

She motioned him away, stung by his callous dismissal.

"Ragath, what is wrong?"

She called him a handful of foul names in the language he didn't speak. Gaffin deserved no better from her. In fact, if she knew the words in his own language, she'd make certain he understood them.

At last, he withdrew.

Ragath waited a few heartbeats, then glanced back at the empty archway. *Damn him!* Why did so simple a thing make her feel doubly rejected?

* * * *

Gaffin turned toward the young women's sleeping chamber again, hesitated, and doubled back. It seemed he would never know what would upset Ragath next or why it would.

The only thing he was certain about was that she was brutally angry with him. Her *Blutjagd* had been hot and potent, and whatever she'd replied to him in the beast's language had not be a compliment.

"Problem, Gaffin?" his father asked.

He ground his teeth for a moment, then forced his jaw to unclench. "She's angry at me."

"Angry? Well, that is an improvement over her usual upset."

"Is it? You didn't feel her *Blutjagd* burn your skin." *And hate yourself for making her react that way.* But saying that would give away too much of his feelings for her.

"Oh, that was hers? Impressive."

He turned, fighting not to say something his father would take offense to. The sight of the leathers in Niklus's hands made his mouth go dry. They were small enough for a boy of ten.

Or Ragath. Just the thought of her body filling the leather sent tremors of delight through his stomach.

His father cleared his throat. "Will these—"

"Yes. I believe they will do nicely."

"Elee can instruct her." He shifted nervously. "Ragath will allow that, will she not?"

Gaffin took the leathers from his father's hands, considering it. "I cannot say for certain," he admitted. "I will let Elee attempt it."

Finding his sister didn't take long. Every Warrior, cursed and not yet so, would be aware of the females around him. With Elee in tow, he returned to Ragath.

Without turning to look at him, Ragath started spouting that damned language again, grumbling what were probably curses at him.

He ignored it. "Ragath, I have brought training clothes."

She stopped talking and went still. Slowly, her head turned, and she stared at the leathers. Lines creased the skin between her eyebrows.

Abruptly, Gaffin felt the need to explain. "You must dress to train, Ragath. It is necessary. Do you understand?"

"In..." She motioned to the leathers.

"Yes, in leathers. It is the only appropriate way." He hoped she wouldn't refuse as she'd refused a woman's gowns.

She looked down at her body, confused or sad for some reason he couldn't name but wished he could. Ever since they'd arrived at the bastion, she'd been volatile.

Ragath looked at Elee, pleading for something. Gaffin turned to look at his sister, questioning silently.

She waved him away, taking the leathers from his hands. "Go."

"I need to understand her upset," he whispered harshly.

Elee's look was the long-suffering variety women often shot males when they felt the males were being obtuse. "Go. I will tell you what I can...later."

Grumbling curses, he retreated to the turn of the corridor outside. After a moment, Ragath's face appeared in the doorway.

"Go, Gaffin!" his sister shouted out.

As if in agreement, Ragath waved him away.

He left, striding for the cooking chamber in search of food, no longer bothering to grumble the string of profanity he needed to vent.

* * * *

Ragath shivered at Gaffin's fury. She recognized the feeling of it, though Ragath didn't understand why she could feel the anger of Jonus and the Warrior men when she didn't seem to feel it from her nurses and other servants. Never from another woman, in fact, even when it was clear they were angry.

She didn't understand what she'd done to displease Gaffin so either.

"Come," Elee invited her.

She took one look at the leathers he wanted her to wear and burst into tears.

Elee stared at her for a moment, seemingly shocked. The older woman dropped the leathers to her own bed and guided Ragath to the one intended for her. Once they were both seated, Elee wrapped her arms around Ragath.

"What has Gaffin done?" she asked, slowing her speech to allow Ragath to understand her words.

Her first attempt at answering came out in the language Elee didn't speak. Ragath took a calming breath and tried to find words in the correct one again.

"What makes Gaffin..." She had no word for it. Ragath made an angry face.

Elee looked toward the corridor, then back, her brow furrowed. "Angry? Gaffin is not angry."

"I have..." *Damn, but it is difficult to speak coherently with so many words missing.*

"Confused?" Elee guessed.

She shook her head.

"Well, you have confused Gaffin, but it is not what you meant to ask."

Ragath stared at her, at a loss for how she could have confused Gaffin. Surely, she'd been clear enough.

"Distressed him?"

She considered it and shook her head in a negative response. The Warriors had used that word to refer to Ragath many times. Distressed was akin to fearful, and Gaffin was anything but fearful.

"Displeased?" Elee continued.

Pleased was a word that Gaffin used to ask if something was to her liking. Displeased, as she understood it, would be something that was not to the liking of the individual. "Yes. Displeased. I...displeased Gaffin."

Elee sighed. "I do not believe so."

"Believe?" *So many words to learn.*

"No, Ragath. Gaffin is not displeased with you."

He is. There was no question that he was, but there was no way to make Elee see it. Ragath sighed at the impossibility of making her see that she must have.

"How?"

It wasn't a word she knew...again.

Elee continued, probably seeing her confusion. "You believe you have displeased Gaffin. What has he done to make you believe such a thing?"

She was starting to understand the word "believe." Answering the question was difficult, though. *Start with the simple facts.* "Gaffin tells me to bed here."

Elee motioned for her to continue.

"Not with Gaffin."

She glanced at the corridor for a long moment, then swiveled her head back to gaze at Ragath. "You are accustomed to sleeping with Gaffin?"

"Sleeping?"

Elee seemed to consider something carefully, probably trying to choose words she knew Ragath understood, as Gaffin often did. "You bed with Gaffin?"

Ragath pulled her knees to her chest. "Before." She waved back over her shoulder. "Then." She'd felt safe in Gaffin's bed. "And..." She motioned toward the leathers. Fury spiked hot in her. She wanted to rip them, burn them, anything to destroy the insulting piece of clothing.

"I do not understand," Elee offered carefully.

How can I explain something this complex? I need to learn the language. I need instruction in everything. She opened her mouth to ask Elee to teach her. Since it seemed Gaffin had no intentions of doing so, now that they'd reached his home—

"What clothing did you wear to train before the leathers?"

Ragath glanced down her body, stared at Elee, and shook her head.

Elee's confusion melted into shock. Her cheeks darkened in an unnamable emotion. "N-no clothing?"

"That displeases you?" She hadn't meant to anger his family. What would happen if they refused her their home? Where would she go? Would she have any protection?

"No. Not at all."

Ragath relaxed at that. It sounded sincere.

So did Jonus. He wasn't.

Not the time to consider that. "It displeases Gaffin." That was the problem, of course. Tears stung at her eyes, and she wiped them away miserably.

Elee's eyes went wide, and she took several choppy breaths. "I doubt it."

Ragath stared at her through the fog of tears. "Doubt?"

"Seeing you...unclothed does not displease Gaffin."

So much so that he wants me to dress as a man. That thought burned more than her anger. It seared at her heart. "I...believe it did not, before..." She motioned to the leathers again.

When she'd trained in the nude, Gaffin had been affected enough. His cock had been long and heavy and his scent enticing.

Not enough. If it had been enough, he would have bedded me. That is what men do.

As if Elee heard every thought she had on the subject, she shook her head. "No, Ragath. Gaffin is not displeased with you."

"But, he—"

"No. Gaffin must do these things. There are laws... You understand laws? Rules? Sanctions?"

Gaffin used those terms. When he gave her orders to be obeyed, he sometimes said them. She nodded. It meant things that were not to be disobeyed.

"Do not run."

She focused on Elee's rush of words.

"Our father and the other Warriors... There are rules. Gaffin must do these things or he breaks the rules."

"Then?" she questioned. "Before...home?" Ragath didn't have enough words to ask the question properly.

Elee seemed to understand well enough. "Outside, the rules are different. You had to be safe."

Though "different" was a new word, Ragath thought she understood it. Not the same. Here, Gaffin had different rules to follow. She nodded.

Elee sighed in relief. "Will you wear the leathers?"

Ragath scowled at them. "Rules?" she asked. The more she heard of rules, the less she liked them.

"Yes. Rules."

"Teach me to wear leathers."

Elee smiled her encouragement.

* * * *

Gaffin looked up at Elee, his heart pounding at the sour look she shot him. Never one to mince words, she had ones for this situation.

"You are a careless fool, brother."

"There is no anticipating what will upset Ragath. I have tried, Elee."

She breezed past him, her expression one that both dismissed him and chastised him. "I understood it well enough."

"Then it is a female concern," he shot back.

"If you had any sense, you would understand it."

"Then tell me."

"Why should I?"

"I need to understand her," he reminded his errant sister.

"For your duty or for yourself?"

His breath caught at what she was hinting at, and he narrowly avoided looking around guiltily to see if anyone had overheard it. Suggesting he was being inappropriately intimate with Ragath could see him dead. It was better to act as if he didn't understand it. "You are saying what now? Riddles? Games?"

A little harrumph of sound was her only answer for a moment. At last, Elee turned and met his gaze, an alien stern look for him. "If you truly mean that, you will never understand her, and you do not deserve to. If you are playing coy with me... Well, you are a careless fool to play such games."

His   heart   stuttered.   Surely,   he   was misunderstanding her. Elee couldn't mean that she felt he was playing coy with Ragath, that he was playing with the young Ani's emotions in such a way.

Before he could ask it, Ragath ambled into the room, tying a knot to secure the smaller tunic Elee had provided at her waist. His mouth went dry at the sight of the boys' leathers outlining her. They left nothing to the imagination, while they covered the actual body beneath.

Not that Gaffin needed an imagination. He'd seen her delectable body enough times to have memorized every line of it. At the reminder, his cock surged up.

A soft cough from Elee brought Ragath's head around, and the young woman stared at his state of arousal. Her   red-rimmed   eyes   went   soft   and considering. A small smile pulled up at her lips, and Gaffin felt it hard to breathe.

She is interested in how men react, compared to beasts, he reminded himself. It could be nothing more. His sanity wouldn't stand for it to be more.

"Where do I train, Gaffin?" Ragath asked.

His heart in his throat, he led the way to the empty training room. All the while, he tried to work out how to keep the other men from watching her train. Even in the leathers, this would be an assault on any adult male in her vicinity.

Perhaps on youths, as well.

Chapter Eight

Gaffin stared at Mieshen across the table, noting the other Warrior's nervous movements.

"You are certain?" he asked. "The girl is really my child?"

"The Stone confirms that Ragath is your daughter."

"And she..." His jaw tightened. "Did the beast..."

Gaffin understood his reluctance to ask the question. "She has known...some of the beast's touch," he offered carefully.

Mieshen pushed to his feet, dragging his hands through his hair. His Blutjagd burned hot and fierce.

"I do not believe she has been...pierced of yet." Gods, how did one discuss such a matter with a father?

There was no response for a long moment. "You are not certain." His voice was tortured and heavy in guilt, Gaffin was sure.

"As certain as I can be without..." He let the rest remain unsaid.

Mieshen nodded.

"The beast raised Ragath with..." *Delicately.* "...strange ideas. She does odd things that you may find unnerving."

"Odd? What do you mean by—" Mieshen's jaw dropped, and his eyes went wide and wild.

Gaffin didn't question that Ragath was behind him. Nor did he question that she wasn't dressed appropriately. Again.

He turned, snatching the length of cloth from the shelf beside him. Ragath startled at the move, then settled as he wrapped it around her over the damnable gown. Her cheeks darkened, and she shot him a sheepish look.

Her head turned, and her gaze locked on Mieshen. She gathered the cloth closer around her, moving to place Gaffin between them.

Mieshen watched the move, his eyes pained. "What is...that...that..." He motioned, seemingly at a loss for words.

Gaffin sighed. "The beast dressed her in such gowns."

Her father's face lost all color.

It is better that he hear the worst now. "As near as I am able to tell, she only wore something heavier when she bled. I have taught her to wear a tunic over the gown...when she remembers to do so, but within a permanent structure, she seldom does. At least she remembers to wear leathers for training."

Little good that it did Gaffin's sanity, but something was better than nude, he supposed. His mind argued that he was lying to himself.

Mieshen staggered to the chair and slumped into it, looking to the roof with tears in his eyes. "She had no protection. All of those years with the beast, and I was not there to protect her."

* * * *

Ragath stared at the new male in interest she could find no good reason for. There was something about him. He was different than the others, but it was in some way she couldn't name, wholly unlike the ways Gaffin was different than the others.

She touched Gaffin's arm, and he turned to her, his eyes questioning. At a loss to ask for specific information about him, she decided to indicate whatever he could impart with their limited shared language.

Ragath pointed to the stricken man, hoping Gaffin would understand her.

His eyes shifted from her to the male and back again. She prayed he didn't think she was showing a preference of some sort.

"Father," he stated simply.

That made no sense. Gaffin's father was deep in the keep with his woman, Nara. She looked that direction, confused. Her knowledge of the things a man and woman did together were not extensive, but she knew only one man could be father to a child. How could he have two?

Gaffin drew her face back. He shook his head slowly. "No." He motioned to the other male. "Mieshen."

"Mieshen," she repeated, pointing to the male.

He nodded solemnly. "Mieshen...Ragath's father."

Ice settled in her stomach at that. Mieshen was her father? That meant he'd struck the deal with Jonus to sell her to her future husband. Was he here to strike a deal to return her to Jonus?

No. I will not go. I cannot go.

She bolted.

Gaffin caught up with her before she was out of the big meeting room. She held to him, searching for the words to tell him she wanted to be his and not Jonus's.

Women do not have a choice in whose they are. Their fathers strike the deal.

She sobbed at that. Was this why Gaffin never claimed her? Did he want riches to give her back to Jonus and needed to prove her unmolested to gain his prize? At that, she struck his shoulder. If it was true, she'd gut him herself.

Soothing sounds surrounded her.

Mieshen—her father—asked something about her upset, but he spoke too fast for her to catch every word she knew.

Gaffin waved at him, motioning for a moment of silence. He raised her chin, forcing her gaze to his. Then he spoke.

"Do not run," he reminded her.

She shook her head, then shot a look at Mieshen to make certain he wasn't close enough to touch her. To her relief, he was still at the center of the room.

Gaffin spoke slowly, enunciating every word. "Why-do-you-fear-Mieshen?"

The words to explain it seemed lost in her mind. "Mieshen...bring..." She motioned to herself, cursing her inability to focus on the correct word to identify herself in her panic. "Jonus." She didn't look at the man in question to see if he was angered that she was defying him, perhaps denying him some prize in the second delivery of her to Jonus.

"What?" Gaffin shook his head. "Mieshen will *not* bring you to...Jonus."

She knew he hated saying that name, though she didn't understand why. He'd tried to teach her to say another for her former master, but the sounds wouldn't come reliably to her mouth. Sometimes, she managed the second term he used...beast.

"Mieshen bring...me..." *That is the correct term.* "To beast."

"No. I promise you, he would never do that."

Ragath shook her head, tears pooling in her eyes. How could she make him understand that Mieshen had already done so once? Did he not know it? Or was Gaffin lying as well?

She calmed herself, searching out every word she knew, every one he'd taught her while they'd traveled and here at his keep. She spoke slowly, trying to recreate the sounds faithfully, so there would be no misunderstanding.

"Mieshen..." She motioned to him to emphasize her point. "*Father*...sell...me to Jonus."

She watched Gaffin's face go pale in satisfaction. So, he hadn't known it. The question remained, what would he do about it now that he knew?

Before he could respond to her statement, Mieshen was in motion. An unholy howl escaped his lips. The chair he'd been sitting in splintered against the far wall, and being in the room with his anger was like scorching her skin on a close fire.

Ragath pressed to Gaffin, swallowing a scream of fear.

She'd seen Jonus in a fury like this once, when one of her nurses had cut her while arranging her hair. It had been a simple accident; Ragath had been fidgeting as children do, and the bone pins had points. He'd beaten the servant to unconsciousness. Ragath hadn't seen it; another servant had whisked her away at nearly the first blow, but she'd been told the servant had been evicted from the keep...once she woke from that beating. More than once, Ragath had suspected Jonus had killed the poor woman instead, but there was no way to know.

She'd prayed never to see it again. But now Mieshen was in a similar fury. A low whine escaped her throat. Every instinct said to stay with Gaffin, but something else warned her to run.

As if making the decision for her, Gaffin pushed her to his back, stepping between them. "Stay there," he ordered. "Do not run."

* * * *

Gods, what would go wrong next?

Gaffin cursed himself for not attempting to get the story of what she believed to be her life from Ragath before she met her father. He'd expected a lie Veriel had told her, but he hadn't expected the lie that her own father had sold her to the beast.

That lie had pushed Mieshen past endurance. If Veriel was here now, he would lose—for the first time—in single combat.

His father launched into the room, stopped, and stared. "What in the gods' names is this?" he demanded.

"Veriel's lies to Ragath," he replied simply. "I did not know what he'd told her...about her father." He tipped his head to Mieshen.

"Take her away. It may take hours to burn off this much *Blutjagd*."

Another chair fell prey to his fury.

Gaffin nodded. "Probably best." He guided Ragath into the deeper reaches, not toward the sleeping rooms but rather toward the Stone room. Why he made that choice, he couldn't say, but he did.

It was a testament to Mieshen's madness that he didn't notice them leaving. His father was correct. It might be hours before this abated.

In the meantime, Gaffin had to explain this to Ragath as best he could.

He settled her on a mat in the blue glow of the Stone and knelt facing her. Ragath stared at the Stone as if fixated. His heart stuttered at that. If she touched the Stone in innocent exploration, the gods only knew what it would do to her.

"Do not touch," he warned her. "Never touch. A rule, Ragath. A law that must never be broken."

She nodded grimly and looked away from it, stealing peeks out of the corner of her eyes.

"Now... Mieshen did *not* sell you to the beast."

She sobbed, nodding fiercely.

Gaffin sighed. "No. The beast told you that."

Ragath stared at him, seemingly confused.

Not enough of the words she knows. "He...lied." *Gods, I need words she knows.*

"Father sold me," she insisted.

Has she never questioned anything she's been told? Probably not. Veriel wouldn't have encouraged it.

"Father sold me!"

"No, Ragath. Father did not sell you. The beast took you."

Her brow furrowed, though he knew she had a grasp of almost everything he'd said.

Take. It is not a word she knows. "Stay."

She nodded.

Gaffin rose, marched to the weapons cabinet, grasped a sacred weapon, and turned to her. "Take. Took," he corrected himself. Small distinctions in sound were important to her.

When she didn't reply to that, he continued.

"The beast *took* you. He took you from your father...in battle."

Ragath stared at him, seemingly without comprehension. "Battle. Jonus..." She swallowed hard. "Jonus *battle* Father Mieshen?"

He nodded. She understood half of it. Her expression said she didn't understand the rest.

Gaffin returned to her, at a loss to explain *take* clearly. She understood *battle. That is it!*

He offered the weapon to her. Ragath shot him a panicked look and shook her head.

Of course. Veriel forbade her to use weapons. He would have. Though she was female, Ragath was a Warrior. The beast wouldn't want her trained to fight him, though he'd allowed her physical activity to relieve her *Blutjagd.* She seemed to have been trained in speed and acrobatic skills only and practiced at them as the men trained to fight. It was ingenious but deplorable.

Gaffin eased one of Ragath's hands away from her chest and pried her fist open. He settled the hilt in her hand and closed her fingers around it.

"Give," he stated.

She pushed the weapon back at him. He retrieved it carefully, watching as she rubbed at her wrist. In a moment of clarity, he realized Veriel had injured her for touching a weapon. He pushed that away before it could launch him into a fury.

"You gave the weapon to me," he supplied calmly. "Give. Gave. I gave the weapon to you. You gave the weapon to me."

Ragath nodded, her breathing hitching. "Gave," she repeated.

"Mieshen did not *give* you to the beast. Mieshen did not *sell* you to the beast. Veriel—Jonus took you in battle."

She shot him a weary look. "Took?"

Gaffin offered her the weapon again.

Her hands shaking, Ragath held it as he'd instructed. She looked up at him. "You...gave...me the weapon."

He smiled his encouragement. "Yes."

She tried to offer it back. Gaffin shook his head. Ragath looked at the weapon, turning it in her hand to examine the lines of it.

Gaffin snatched it from her hand, and Ragath recoiled, tripped over her feet, and landed on her backside on the mat. The fabric he'd wrapped around her gapped open, baring her body to him.

Hating himself for it, Gaffin stood over her, the weapon in hand. "Take," he growled. "Took. I took the weapon from you, Ragath."

She stared at it, trembling hard. "Took," she gasped out.

Gaffin tossed the weapon away, kneeling before her. Ragath didn't right herself immediately. She closed the fabric first, then she pushed to sitting. When she was buried inside the shield of the fabric, he chanced speaking again.

"The beast *took* you from Mieshen," he repeated.

Her face went a shade paler at that.

He let her digest that much. Her calculation was palpable. Gaffin didn't push her. She would come to the decision to believe or disbelieve on her own.

"Women...go...buy...market," she mused.

"Yes. Women do go to the market to buy things," he corrected her grammar. He had no clue what that had to do with the subject at hand.

"Jonus..." Her breathing hitched. "...lentae."

"Lentaen," he corrected automatically, as if he was teaching a young Warrior. His jaw dropped in realization, and her gaze snapped to his.

Gaffin slipped into the language of the ancients. "Yes, the beast lied." He spoke slowly, hoping he was interpreting it correctly.

She did the same. "Your women are not...prisoners in the keep."

Her pronunciation was strange, so strange that he only understood her when she slowed her speech to a snail's pace for him. It was as if she was using an older root version of the language, perhaps the version Veriel would have used when he was the traitor god and not the traitor beast.

"Never," he assured her.

"Your women walk in the sun. Men do not..."

"What are you asking? Our women do walk in the sun, as you have, since we freed you. As do our men." She didn't think they were beasts, did she?

"Men do not...attack them, if they go outside the keep? Without their men?"

His jaw tightened. "I would gut any man that did," he informed her. "But no. There is little danger of that."

Ragath didn't reply. After a moment, a tear fell to her cheek. Then a second. She looked at him, her eyes tortured. Then the sobs started.

Gaffin wrapped his arms around her, letting her cry into his chest. Knowing that she would understand him, he used the language of the ancients to soothe her.

She started pulling at the dress the beast had given her, and the sound of tearing fabric mingled with her grunts. *Blutjagd* flamed around her. "Get it off," she grumbled. "I will not wear it a moment longer."

Sounds of someone approaching nearly stopped Gaffin's heart. He dragged Ragath behind the shelter of his body, blocking the view the interloper would have of her.

"Gaffin? Ragath?" Elee called out.

"Get a dress she can wear, Elee. Get one quickly."

In moments, Ragath would be nude and pressed to his body. The ripping got louder. Elee rushed toward the room she shared with Ragath.

She was back a few moments later, and she tossed the dress his direction. Elee stared for only a moment before she bolted away again.

The dress in tatters around her, Ragath allowed Gaffin to ease the new one on. Then she sank into his arms and held on tight.

* * * *

A sound brought Ragath's head around. She stared up at the man who was reported to be her father...lost, hating him, fearing him.

"Ragath?" Mieshen reached for her.

The memory of his uncontrolled fury sent her skittering behind Gaffin.

He swore fluently. "Gods damn it! I did not sell her to that damned beast," he complained in the other language Gaffin spoke.

Gaffin switched to her primary language, but he didn't speak to her, confirming that Mieshen also spoke it. "She knows that now. My apologies for that shock. I never thought to ask it."

Mieshen's response was so fast...and in that same strange dialect of the language Gaffin used, she couldn't follow it.

"Slowly. Ragath speaks a version of the language of the ancients, but she cannot understand you, unless you speak very slowly."

"She...understands?"

Irked by his patronizing pace, she fired back an answer. "I understand without your damned—"

"Slowly, Ragath," Gaffin reminded her.

She took a calming breath and offered each word clearly. "Yes, I understand you."

"I was told she had no language in common."

Gaffin nodded. "As you can hear, her accent is nearly indecipherable at speed. Until she spoke a single word clearly, I had no clue to what language she was using."

Ragath sighed, burying her face in the back of his tunic.

Mieshen directed his next comment to her. "I understand you have chosen Gaffin as your protector," he intoned. There was something harsh in that, as if he disapproved.

"Yes. I have."

"Then you are refusing to return home with me."

She raised her head, staring at him. Now she knew why she feared him. Like Jonus, this man had power over her. She didn't doubt it.

Still, he asked. "Yes, I am refusing to leave here." She held her breath, waiting for his response, ready to spring away if he went into another fury.

Mieshen went to one knee and bowed his head. "For losing you in battle, I deserve no better," he opined. "Still, if you would allow me, I would like to spend time with you. Here, when you are comfortable with the idea." There was a plea in that, as if he would not be allowed that much without her permission.

"Y-yes. If Gaffin is with me." After his fit of temper, there was no way she would meet with Mieshen alone.

Mieshen nodded. "Gaffin, may I speak with you alone? Just for a moment?"

He nodded and rose, following Mieshen toward the corridor. Halfway there, he turned, his expression a warning. Gaffin motioned to the glowing stone. "Do *not* touch," he reminded her.

A snicker escaped Mieshen's mouth, and Gaffin turned on him, issuing a silent warning. Her father put up a hand for peace and turned away.

* * * *

Gaffin stood in the corridor, careful to keep himself between Mieshen and Ragath. He rested his hand on the hilt of his weapon in warning, just in case the old man intended to unleash another spate of *Blutjagd* on him.

Losing a daughter this way had to be nearly as crushing for him as her initial loss had been. Gaffin

301

was certain Mieshen was planning to point out that the law was on his side, and he would only wait so long to take custody of his daughter again.

That was one thing Gaffin would fight with all he was worth. After the horror of her life with the beast, no one would forcibly take Ragath anywhere she didn't want to go.

Mieshen glanced toward the doorway to the Stone room, his face strangely calm. "She trusts you." He switched away from the language of the ancients, probably to ensure that Ragath wouldn't be able to follow their discussion if she spied on them.

"She does. I cannot explain it. Ragath trusted me nearly on sight, and I cannot account for it."

There was a moment of silence. "Has she shown a preference for any man yet?"

"Not particularly," he admitted. *Gods, do not let him bring men in to try and force her to a match.*

Mieshen stared at him. "You are blind, Gaffin."

He searched for the words to adequately express his outrage at that statement.

"She shows a preference for you. Can you not see it?"

Gaffin looked toward the Stone room, his face burning at the accusation. He'd like to deny it, but it was true, and he was taken with her.

Mieshen's voice was a whisper, directly behind him. "If she shows willingness to be your mate, do it."

His heart pounded. "You would freely give me leave to pursue Ragath as mate."

"Not to pursue. To accept her, when she is ready to trust you that much."

He nodded, turning his face back to her father. It was a rare show of trust. "I will not pursue her," he vowed.

Mieshen offered his hand in agreement. "I trust you will not."

Chapter Nine

Gaffin heard the movement in the corridor and startled awake. The footsteps were light, too light to be a Warrior or a clumsy child. They were too smooth to be one of the older women. It was Ragath. He slipped from bed silently and donned a short set of training leathers.

She moved again, not toward the outer reaches of the keep but rather toward the deeper. Gaffin shook his muscles loose. As long as she was heading into the keep, he was content. Anything else was curiosity or investigation.

The Stone! He rushed after her. Though Ragath hadn't disobeyed him in almost half a moon, she'd continued to show a marked interest in the Stone. This wasn't a mistake he couldn't chance her taking.

Ragath didn't go to the Stone room. Gaffin found her in the training room instead, dressed in her leathers but not stretching or whirling about the room. He didn't announce himself; Gaffin wanted to see what she'd choose to do if left to decide for herself.

Her hand extended, stopped a finger's width from the hilt of a training weapon, and retreated to her chest. Ragath took a deep breath and extended her hand again. She caressed the length of the blade with a shaking hand, her breathing easing when there was no attack imminent.

Gaffin shifted to the right, watching her. *What did the beast do to her? What atrocity made her fear a blade so palpably?* If he cut her with it, she bore no scars to show it, not even the lines of something the beast healed with his powers.

Her teeth made little indentations in her lower lip. After a moment, she lifted the weapon from the shelf. Again, her breathing roughened at the move. It took a moment longer to ease this time.

He smiled. Ragath was taking control of her life, rejecting the harsh lessons the Deceiver had taught her, one at a time.

She whirled toward him as if Gaffin had made a sound, though he knew he hadn't. He expected her to drop the blade at the sight of him, but her hand tightened on the hilt.

Yes. You are a Warrior. This is your birthright.

* * * *

Ragath stared at him, waiting for Gaffin to make his move. Would he try to take the weapon from her? Would he crush her arm in his fist until something snapped inside and she couldn't move it for weeks? Until it had to be splinted for ten days? Until she could hardly bear to eat or move from bed? Until she woke crying, night after night?

I will kill him before I suffer that again. Her hand tightened in preparation to use the weapon against him.

Gaffin's smile didn't falter at the implied threat. He stood there, his arms crossed over his bare chest. A tense moment later, he moved, and she sidestepped to a more defensible position.

"Weapons are for men. Women do not battle, Ragath. It is a kindness I show you. The penalty for using a weapon against me is death. I prefer a gentle lesson." His eyes had been cold and hard.

Gentle. She nearly snorted at that. *I will never suffer such a lesson again.*

Ragath brought the weapon up and adopted an attack stance she'd seen Jonus use in his training. Gaffin nodded and ambled to the shelf. He took down another weapon slowly...reverently and turned to her.

She let out a breath in a gasp, a breath she hadn't realized she'd been holding. Her hands trembled in the possibility that he might intend to cut her as lesson. She moved into a more aggressive stance, one Jonus launched what she believed were his most deadly attacks from. Perhaps Gaffin would reconsider if he believed she could harm him in return.

"Hold the weapon like this." Gaffin didn't attack. Instead, he rotated his hand back and forth, demonstrating his grip.

Ragath hesitated, then looked at her own grip, adjusting it to match his as closely as possible.

"Do not ever turn your attention from an opponent."

She startled, bringing the weapon around with the new grip, taking the stance she'd chosen to unnerve him with feigned expertise.

He hadn't moved, despite her lapse. "Very good, Ragath. Now...show me what you know."

"What I know? Of battle? The training I have seen the beast engage in?" Too late, she realized she was admitting she had no personal knowledge of battle. *It would be best if he thought I have.* He would be less likely to hurt her then.

His eyes narrowed.

What have I done? I should have lied about my prowess. One guilty look at Gaffin later, she conceded that she didn't want to lie to him.

"If that is what you know, that is what I wish to see," he offered diplomatically.

Ragath called to mind one of the battle forms Jonus practiced and started to follow it. Instructions flowed from Gaffin's mouth, directing and correcting her execution.

"Keep that elbow up." He motioned to it.

"Do not overextend your arm. It compromises your balance and opens you to attack.

"Good form. Excellent kick. Higher next time.

"Again. Faster this time." He cocked his head to one side as if in consideration.

"Keep your movements close to the body, a snap of movement and return."

Time and again, she repeated the form, until Gaffin called a halt and proclaimed it perfect. Pride welled in her at that. She'd done well at something Jonus had denied her. Gaffin's voice drew her back to the present.

"Do you know another?" His expression was encouraging.

"A few. Not as well," she admitted.

A smile curved up the corners of his lush lips. "You will," he vowed. "I will teach you the forms. All of the forms, but we will start with the ones you know."

* * * *

"Like this," Gaffin instructed. He caught Ragath's leg, raising her thigh until was parallel with the floor.

Ragath's heart skipped a beat, and she stared at his hand. If it slipped just a little higher, Gaffin would be touching her slit through the fighting leathers.

Her body heated and moistened in response to his proximity. Gaffin went still, his breathing harsh. His hand moved minutely, and she licked her lips.

"Do you..." His hand moved again...only a finger's width closer.

Ragath looked up at him, her heart hammering at the stark hunger in his eyes. "Yes." It came out a strangled whisper.

Gaffin moved, putting a body length between them. "Again," he ordered.

Tears stung at her eyes, and she started to question his abrupt withdrawal.

"Gaffin?"

She stiffened at the sound of Niklus's voice.

Gaffin nodded, though whether in confirmation or soothing she couldn't say. "Now... Ragath, demonstrate for my father. All the forms you have knowledge of."

"But I—"

"Your best," he soothed her. "It takes Warriors a year to train."

"Train?" There was a snap in his voice and the burn of anger pouring off him in waves.

Ragath winced. Like Jonus, Niklus didn't approve of her training as a Warrior.

Gaffin shot a quelling look at his father, and the old man's *Blutjagd* settled.

"Show him." Gaffin's voice stayed calm and encouraging.

She moved into position, checked her stance, then focused on the forms. Blocking out the lord and any other distractions, Ragath transitioned from form to form smoothly. In the end, she looked to Gaffin for a reaction.

He smiled, and his eyes glittered.

Niklus was slower to respond. "It is...wonderful. Gaffin, why did you keep this from me?"

"Ragath has only just agreed to train for battle. I encouraged her interest, of course."

"Immediately," his father decreed. "I will—"

"No." The word was out before Ragath could rein in her errant tongue.

Both men stared at her.

Ragath swallowed hard. "I wish..." She glanced at the glowing stone, then forced her attention to Niklus. "I wish Gaffin to train me." She closed her hand into a fist around the hilt of the weapon, preparing herself for the lord's outrage at her demand.

The older man swiveled his head, moving his gaze from his son to Ragath and back again, his expression unreadable. "Of course, Ragath. If that is your wish, Gaffin will train you."

"T-thank you." She shivered at the tension between them. "May I rest now, Gaffin?"

"As you wish. You have worked hard tonight. Perhaps after a day of rest, you could join the—"

"No."

Two pairs of eyes flicked toward each other and then focused on her.

"I... Not yet. The men...stare." Her cheeks burned. They would surely think her a frightened child.

"In the night then," Gaffin conceded. "When you are more comfortable, we will join the men."

She nodded and then glanced at Niklus. His stillness made her uneasy, though no *Blutjagd* burned in him. At last, he nodded his approval grimly.

Ragath passed the weapon into Gaffin's hand and fled to the room she shared with Elee. In the silence, she burrowed under the furs without removing her leathers.

Her stomach squirmed in excitement. Gaffin would train her in the night. Alone. If tonight was any indication, who knew what might happen without interruptions?

* * * *

"Is she warming to you?"

Gaffin ground his teeth at the memory of her scenting body. Had she been nude for training, his father would have found them in a very different position.

"A bit," he admitted.

"Yes."

Ragath's whisper taunted him. Had she been accepting him as a lover? Or had she been saying she understood his instructions? Given a few more moments, he might have been certain.

"Be cautious, Gaffin. If the others believe you have convinced her..." He raked a hand through his hair, mussing the curls more than he smoothed them. "The move to a more intimate relationship must be hers." Niklus jerked his head toward the empty corridor.

Gaffin let his attention stray that direction. "I understand."

He did. Gaffin couldn't even hint at what he wanted. There could be no assumptions. No chances.

Until Ragath said she wanted him as a lover or mate, he would have to keep his errant cock in his leathers.

His semi-erect length added that he had to do something to relieve his present discomfort. When he did, there was no question what his fantasy would be.

Chapter Ten

"Like this, Ragath."

He stepped up behind her, one hand on her hip and the other on her weapon arm. His scent was sublime, and she didn't have to look around at Gaffin's cock to know it was pressing to his leathers.

"Do not overextend. Rock your weight from flat forward and back again. Do not reach your arm further than..." He eased her arm into a slightly bent position. "Here."

She did so, acutely aware of how he moved with her. All it would take would be an extra movement back toward her heels and—

She gasped in pleasure at the proof that he was aroused by her. *By something,* she taunted herself. Perhaps it was a normal male reaction to being close to a woman, as Jonus had attested. Perhaps the beast had only given in to it, because he was a beast. Perhaps a man that didn't find her attractive would have no interest in doing so.

Gaffin went still, his ragged breathing buffeting her ear.

Ragath took the opportunity to rock back and forth, as if she was still practicing what he'd meant to teach her. She added movements to the left and right, playing at testing her balance while she invited him to let loose his control and ask her to share his bed.

He let her brush against his body, his grip tightening a notch. It wasn't painful, as Jonus's grip sometimes was. There was something encouraging in the movement.

Gaffin released her and backed off a few steps, and she turned to him. He didn't look at her. He didn't invite her to his bed, as she'd hoped he would.

"We should stop for now," he informed her.

Her heart crumpled again. While her dreams were driving her mad, the only man she wanted to take the need away showed no interest in it.

Acting unaffected took all her remaining calm. "Of course." She hurried to the bathing pool, hoping the heat would calm her jangled nerves.

It wouldn't of course. Nothing did. Nothing could except one disinterested man.

* * * *

Gaffin sparred with his cousin Ries, his mind half on the training and half on the woman that was such a bittersweet distraction.

Damn this! The punch he landed was harder than it had to be, and Ries winced and bounced out of range.

He'd given his word not to pursue her, but it was likely to drive him mad. If Mieshen had given him leave to pursue Ragath, Gaffin wouldn't be playing this maddening game. He'd already have told the young Ani how he felt and either gotten her agreement to what he wanted or been free to break printing.

Her innocent movements and words were driving him mad with the belief that she was interested, but there was no sign of her upset at being rebuffed when he could take no more of it. When he broke training with her, she always accepted and left without distress.

She goes on to her amusements, while I am in misery. She never asks to spend more time with me. She never seeks me out for companionship. He cursed his decision to encourage Elee to be Ragath's confidant.

Ries made a move to round Gaffin, probably feeling he would be safe somewhere other than in front of Gaffin's fists.

Gaffin swept his cousin's feet and laid the killing punch. Still, his blood burned in an edge of *Blutjagd* that refused to be silenced. "Another," he grumbled, offering a hand to aid Ries to his feet.

"I think you need a night in a woman's bed instead," Ries opined, taking advantage of the boost to his feet.

Fury lit in Gaffin, and he shoved Ries against the wall. Before he could pull back his arm to strike again, his father was there, ordering a halt.

"Go to bed and sleep, Gaffin."

As if he could. His rest time was full of erotic dreams of Ragath, near-climaxes from which there were no sweet release, asleep or awake.

On some level, Ries was correct. Gaffin definitely needed a woman in his bed, but the only woman that could please him now hadn't given more than the faintest indication that she saw him as a prospective mate or lover.

Niklus appeared before him, his eyes so knowing that Gaffin was forced to look away. His father's voice went to a soothing low.

"You train twice a day, Gaffin. You do not sleep often enough or long enough. Sleep. That is an order from your lord." There was a warning couched in that last statement.

Gaffin growled out an acceptance and stalked away, his muscles strung tight. Sleep? There would be no sleep for him.

There would be no sanity for him until he either sealed printing with her or broke printing entirely.

Perhaps I should attempt self-release again. It hadn't worked in days, but maybe the gods would show him mercy and allow it to work for him.

"And perhaps Veriel will impale himself on his own blade, as well." The chances of either were as likely.

Chapter Eleven

Ragath stared at the ceiling, her nerves jumping so much she couldn't sleep. Every night, Gaffin showed her to the chamber she shared with Elee and took his leave. He'd never even hinted at taking her to his bed.

For that matter, she'd all but begged him to bed with her in practice, and he'd sent her away. His musk screamed his interest, yet he sought no roads toward the goal.

It would serve him right if I found another interested man.

But, damn him, she didn't want someone else. On that thought, she punched the furs beneath her and rolled over.

"Problem, Ragath?" Elee kept her voice low and her words slow for Ragath's comfort.

Realization came in a flash. Jonus had lied to her about so many things. What if the rules for bedding a woman were different than she'd believed all this time?

"Ragath?"

She launched in before she could talk herself out of so intimate a discussion. Elee was a woman, after all. She could be a confidant.

"How do your women...*our* women tell a man she would like to...to bed with him?" Her face burned at the audacity of the question.

Elee moved, crossing the floor between their beds and settling on the edge of Ragath's. "You are not like other women, Ragath."

She turned, stunned by that comment. "I am like you. Miesh... My father is a Warrior, like your father is."

There was a moment of silence. "You are blessed by the Stone. Touched by it. I am not. I would need my father's permission to bed with a man."

Ragath bit her lower lip. Mieshen's permission? Gods, what were the chances of that? Not high, she'd wager.

Elee continued. "You need merely choose a man, and he is yours."

"Choose? Women do not choose. Men choose, and women may..." Her face darkened. "That is not so. Is it?"

"Men show an interest to be sure. Men may indicate an interest, with the father's permission...if such a man sought a woman like myself. You..."

Her heart hammered in her chest. "Yes? What about me?"

Elee's smile widened. "No man would dare approach you without your leave to do so, but they need not ask your father's permission."

Ragath tried to find the reason in that. "Because I am Stone touched? But... I have *not* touched the Stone. Gaffin told me not to. Never to. It is a rule, Elee."

The young woman laughed, then sobered. "No. You must not touch the Stone directly. Gaffin is correct about that. The Stone...chose you, Ragath. It marked you with the sign of the gods."

She reached back, touching the mark. She'd seen it in mirrors so many times, but Jonus—"The beast Veriel lied about that as well, I suppose. He said it was his mark, and he'd placed it on me as a babe to show his ownership."

Elee grimaced and looked toward the corridor. "Gods, do not tell the men that."

"Why?"

She looked back, seemingly picking her words carefully. "It is sacrilege, and the men will be upset to hear you say it."

Ragath nodded, filing the information away for future encounters with them. Still, she had no answer to her question. "So, how does a woman like me tell a man she wishes to bed with him? How do I know if the man has interest in it, if he will not say?"

Elee smiled brightly. "If the man is the one I believe it is, he has interest. How do you tell him?" She giggled, then leaned closer. "Listen well, Ragath."

* * * *

Gaffin came to consciousness slowly. There was something different...not wrong, precisely, but different.

He shivered in the evening air. The chill bumps rising on his thighs were the first indication that something was amiss. Where was the cover he'd gone to sleep with?

Gaffin ranged his hand about, searching for it. What he encountered was vastly different.

The soft globe of a breast filled his hand. He froze, cupping it, too stunned to withdraw.

I do not have to withdraw. Mieshen has given his leave, if Ragath proves amenable to the idea of mating. That in mind, Gaffin stroked her.

Ragath moaned, arching into his touch. Her nipples came to tight little points against his hands, and her scent intensified.

He sensed her cycle, groaning at her timing. If he did this, she would likely catch pregnant.

She shied. "You have no interest in me?" There were tears hidden behind the words.

"Oh yes. I do have interest." He lowered his head, laying a lick on the tip of one rigid nipple.

"Then you will lay with me?" she asked. "Bed with me?"

His cock surged up at her direct question of it. *Gods, she is offering to be my lover.*

She is not sealed as my mate. I cannot chance a child with her. "I will lay with you, but I cannot breach your body with my cock."

There was a tense moment of silence. "Cannot? Elee said any Warrior I offered to could, if he had interest and I did. Do you lie? Or does she?"

"Neither...but... We have laws, Ragath. Rules."

"Elee said the laws and rules did not apply to me, as they do to her."

"This one does, but Elee would not know to mention it."

Ragath drew away, sitting up next to him, seemingly seeking space. "What law? What rule?"

He pushed to sitting, meeting her eyes in the near total darkness within the keep. "We may only create life with a woman sealed to us as mate."

An edge of *Blutjagd* burned in her skin. "And how do you seal a mate to you?"

"You must promise to be mine always."

She swallowed hard, and a shiver worked over her form.

"What is wrong?"

Ragath remained silent.

"Ragath? What is it?"

"Veriel asked the same of me. I did not promise it, of course," she hastened to add.

A vicious string of curses left his mouth. "And so you will not offer that promise to me, even if I wait years for it," he guessed. Already, his printing was driving Gaffin mad, and he was doomed to failure, because the damned beast had played at Warrior for this one thing.

She wrapped herself around him, seemingly seeking comfort. Gaffin let her and even managed an awkward attempt at patting her back, but he couldn't force words forth.

Her breath teased his ear, heating his blood in an indecent show of his mounting printing madness. No matter his vows, he would have to leave her soon.

"I promise to be yours always. Only yours, Gaffin."

He pulled back, gaping at her. "You mean that?"

Her hand circled his cock, stroking him in a manner he tried to ignore was all too knowing. "I... Yes, I will be yours alone. Please—"

He captured her lips in a fierce kiss. Some corner of his mind argued that he should be slow for her.

Her heated responses refuted it nicely. Her tongue danced with his in a way that reinforced the beast had done this, at least.

Gaffin had to know what he'd never dared ask before. He broke off the kiss. "What have you experienced of a man, Ragath?"

She laid her head on his shoulder, her hand working him. "He tasted, as men taste a woman."

"And you?"

Her hand tightened a bit, and she made a concerted effort at his pleasure. "This." It was said in a wary little voice, as if she expected his displeasure for having known so much of a man.

Beast. It was the beast she touched and who touched her.

I must put her at ease. The only way to do that would be to put the beast out of his own mind and give them both pleasure.

For that, he had to give her a new experience. He slid his hand between her thighs and started circling her nub. Ragath rose against him, seeking more, seeking his fill.

She begged for him. Gaffin guided her to the bed, easing her hand from his cock. He made a more concerted effort at her pleasure, moaning at her sweet sounds.

"Gaffin, please."

"Please, what?" he teased.

"Fill the aching emptiness." Gods, but she was blunt, and there was nothing like it on the furs.

"Soon."

He could tell her release was beating at her. Her eyes slid shut, and her head rocked back. She panted, arched, opened her mouth to suck in air—

And he moved, filling her in a single stroke and then freezing against the gates to her womb.

Her eyes opened wide, and the breath hitched in. In the next instant, her body started contracting around him and the scream ripped forth. Her hands clawed at his back, giving him the same sort of pleasure-pain she was experiencing.

The scent of her blood went to his head, driving Gaffin on. He started moving, slowly at first, savoring her continuing contractions. Then he was pounding, venting his possession in grunts, as an animal might.

Another scream split the air...then a battle cry.

Gaffin jerked upright, dragging Ragath along with him. His move to turn on the intruder ended with a groan of delight as she settled onto his cock and started levering herself up and down his length, oblivious to their audience.

"Gods," his father choked out. "My apologies."

Ragath's legs encircled him, and his father bumped his way out of the chamber. Gaffin was torn between the urge to gut him for daring to look at Ragath and the soul-deep need to spend deep inside his mate.

The need to spend won out. Her mouth meshed with his, and his seed rushed into her body.

He'd heard sealing soothed the madness, but as far as Gaffin could tell, it had done nothing of the sort.

Perhaps her fertility affects me. Whatever the case might be, he wanted her again immediately.

Ragath broke off the kiss, biting her lip, her hips shifting to move his still-hard cock in her. "This is the claim," she breathed.

Gaffin liked the sound of that...claiming her as his own. He pressed her into the mattress and pinned her arms down. "I claim you," he growled. "You are mine, Ragath."

She rose against his thrusts, her sounds deepening again. "Yours," she panted out. "Only yours."

"No!"

Gaffin startled, his senses going wild with the proximity of a beast. Before he could turn, claws cut

318

into his shoulder, and he found himself flying through space and into the cavern wall.

* * * *

Ragath forced her eyes to focus, her heart skittering at the sight of Jonus. She pressed her thighs together on the mixture of sex fluids and blood, sending a silent challenge that she would never be the beast's woman.

His hands fisted, and his teeth lengthened into the fangs Gaffin had told her the beast had. She'd never seen them before, but she'd suspected he'd been hiding more than his liaisons with her servants long before she saw evidence of it.

Jonus didn't address her. He made a sound of disgust at the sight of Gaffin's amulet. Then he turned toward the downed Warrior, wicked-looking claws appearing at the ends of his fingers.

There was no question what he intended. Ragath didn't hesitate. She grasped the weapon hung on the far side of Gaffin's bed and flipped across the room in one-handed arcs of her body, landing between them.

Jonus made as if to push her aside, and Ragath struck, sliding the dagger into the spot that her mind told her was right with a scream of fury. The Warriors rushing toward them stopped at the archway, gaping in surprise.

The beast staggered back, pulling the weapon from his chest. Ragath tensed to move, planning how to turn a flip into an offensive attack.

Before she could do so, Niklus was there, giving her his back as he wrenched the weapon from Jonus's fingers. "You may not wield the weapon, foul one," he growled. "You are unworthy."

There was a moment of silence, broken only by harsh breathing from everyone in the room.

The foul stench of the beast filled the chamber, a rancid cloud that made Ragath's eyes water and her lungs complain. So, this was what he truly was. This was the creature that had stolen her away from her father and imprisoned Ragath with stone and gates and lies about who and what she was. She hated him.

Jonus looked up at her over Niklus's shoulder. His fangs were gone, and a strained smile pulled up at his lips. "I have always loved you, Ragath."

Her stomach clenched at that pronouncement. "You show it poorly," she offered in return.

He collapsed to his knees. "No doubt." He wheezed the concession. "I always have." He started up at her, his eyes rolled back in his head, and he pitched backward.

Ragath turned to Gaffin, kneeling at his side, trusting that Niklus would protect them both. He didn't answer her call, and a mixture of hopelessness and anger bubbled up in her.

Gaffin couldn't be gone. Not now, when she'd finally promised to be his.

One of the men draped a fur around Ragath.

Ries motioned her aside and started to poke and prod at Gaffin. He smiled grimly. "Gaffin will need mending, but he will survive it."

She sobbed in relief. "Fetch my gown. I wish to help."

It wasn't until the gown settled in her hand that she realized she'd given an order and been obeyed. It was hard to conceive of, but she was master of her own body and space. Ragath savored it.

* * * *

Gaffin groaned at the aches and pains spearing him here and there. His head felt as if it had been split in two. His shoulder and chest felt as if he'd taken one of his grandfather's hardest hits in his early training. Bruises made themselves known over most of his body.

Over my back. Someone attacked my back? Only a beast would—

The elder!

He came up with a shout that was half warning and half pain. Hands stopped him, and Gaffin panted and ground his teeth.

The pull at his shoulder was stitches. Only his family would extend that kindness.

As if in confirmation, his father's voice rumbled out. "Slowly. Don't tear the mending out."

Stitches... That took time. How much time? What did the beast do to Ragath?

His heart aching, he opened his eyes. He let out his breath on a word of thanks for Tes and Ani at the sight of her. Ragath appeared whole and unharmed.

Gaffin reached for her, stroking a hand along her cheek. "Are you well?" There might be amulet bruises he couldn't see.

She nodded. "Are you?"

The hands eased away. Only his father's remained, steadying him while Gaffin's head spun lightly.

"Confused," he admitted. He couldn't reconcile what the beast had done to him so quickly that he'd had no chance to retaliate.

A mark on her forehead caught his attention, and he reached for it. It was akin to a burn or abrasion.

Beast blood.

The outline of the mark of Syth took shape. Realization came slowly, at about the same time Ragath darkened and averted her eyes.

She killed him. The only reason his father would paint the blood seals was if Ragath had made a kill.

She saved me. Gaffin didn't doubt that. The elder would have been intent on the goal of ending him.

At a loss for words, he cupped her head in his good hand and pulled her into a kiss. Ragath met him avidly. Her scent rose, and his cock did as well.

She's fertile. The need to take advantage of that again was impossible to ignore.

"Gaffin," his father whispered harshly.

He broke from the kiss, making a sharp movement with his hand. "Leave us."

"Your injuries?" Ragath suggested.

"The blood needs cleaned away. Mine and yours." It was a challenge to the others. Gaffin had shed her blood. Ragath was his and no one else's, and he would bathe her in the traditional manner in sign of it.

"You'll hurt yourself," she protested weakly.

"I wasn't done with you," he informed her. "Not by a long, hard..." He nuzzled her lips. "...march."

Ragath gasped at that. "Leave us." There was a bite of order in that.

No one questioned her. No one wasted time in complying. The bathing chamber was empty in moments.

She kissed him, pulling her gown up between them.

Gaffin drew away. "Remove it. I want to see you."

In a heartbeat, she'd flung it away. The matching symbol covered her heart. He kissed lightly at it, prompting a shiver from her.

"First I bathe you," he informed her. "Then I finish claiming you."

"Now...please."

"No. It is traditional that I bathe you."

"Traditional?"

He repeated it in the language of the ancients, and she nodded.

Gaffin used his good arm to lift her from the floor. His head was fuzzy and complained at the movement, but his responsibility for Ragath keep him focused enough to stand and wade into the pool with her.

He settled her on her feet in water that reached her mid-thigh and sank to his knees before her. Cupping handfuls of hot water, he started stroking away the blood from her inner thighs and along her seam.

Ragath moaned at the contact, her head pitching back and her hips forward. It was too much temptation for Gaffin. He would have what was his alone.

He buried his face between her legs, licking and suckling at her ready body, tasting the faint traces of his earlier possession. Her hands closed in his hair, and her legs trembled.

"Gaffin, please." It came out a rough whisper.

He eased away minutely, burning with the need to send a message that Ragath was his. "You still wish to have me claim you? You still wish to be mine always?"

"Yes."

His printing blazed at that, and he pulled Ragath to her knees, chest to chest in the pool with him. The water splashed up around them, but she didn't flinch from it as she often did.

"You are mine," he informed her. "You will never belong to another man." *Not now. Not ever.*

Her answer turned to a scream of pleasure at his thrust into her body. Gaffin pinned her wrists together behind her back with his weaker hand, using the stronger to guide her up and down his length.

It wasn't enough. He had to be deeper. Gaffin drew her to the smooth lip of the pool and lifted Ragath to it. Once she was settled, he pinned down her arms as he had in his bed.

They came together hard and fast, voices echoing off the stone walls. Her legs wrapped around him, and Gaffin ground his teeth. The next time, he would hold them open for their joining.

She is fertile. She is mine. He had no doubts that she'd carry his son before this need to show his strength abated. Once that was accomplished, there would be no doubt whose woman she was.

She may have been tricked into thinking she was the beast's woman, but she was born and raised to be mine.

With that, they climaxed, a long, loud announcement that nothing would part them.

The End

The Stone Alphabet

Ani (birth/the mother)- Regana first Lady Kreuzträger, Jayde Marie Albright

Baroo (thunder)- Olbrecht first Lord Kaufmann

Dobler (twin peace-bringer)- Ditrich first Lord Jäger

Fih (twin war)- Geldric/the beast Cerran, Cody König-Armen

Geil (iron)- Bryon König-Kaufmann

Hir (the cool wood)- Gerhardus first Lord Landwirt

Iol (immovable ice)- Redulf/the beast Carstol

Jee (justice)- Mikel of Crossbearer-König and all descendants thereof

Kor (the bear)- Corwyn of König-Maher

Len (mountain)- Wilhelmus first Lord Maher

Mul (flowing water)- Mitchell König-Farmer

Nul (stealth of the night)- Bertolf/the beast Draden

Ori (the sun)- Pauwel first Lord Kreuzträger, Hunter Lord Crossbearer-König

Pol (the horse)- Dado/the beast Lorian

Reg (intensity of the fire)- Jörg/the beast Veriel

Syth (the Stone lord)- Master Trainer Sibold, Gawen first Lord Schwertträger, Etienne Lord Kaufmann, Joseph Lord Armen, Carrick Lord Armen, Corwyn Lord Hunter, Lewis of Maher

Tes (stars and moon)- Kevin König-Smith

Vin (wind)- Cunczel first Lord Schmied

Wul (the wolf)- Tilbrand/the beast Resten

Zel (ending/death)- Erin of Crossbearer-König, Kaitlyn "Katie" of König-Maher, Skye of König-Armen, Victorious Ellen "Vick/Vicky" of König-Smith, Margaret Elizabeth "Maggie" König-Farmer, Colette "Lettie" Kong-Kaufmann

About the Author

Brenna Lyons wears many hats, sometimes all on the same day: former president of EPIC, author of more than 100 published works, owner of Fireborn Publishing, columnist, special needs teacher, wife, mother...and member in good standing of more than 60 writing advocacy groups.

In her first ten years published in novel-length, she's won 3 EPIC e-Book Awards (out of 15 finalists) and finaled for 3 PEARLS (including one Honorable Mention, second to NY Times Bestseller Angela Knight), 2 CAPAS, and a Dream Realm Award. She's also taken Spinetingler's Book of the Year for 2007.

Brenna writes in 26 established worlds plus stand-alones, poetry, articles and essays. She's a bestseller in indie/e fantasy and horror, straight genre and cross-genres thereof. Brenna has been termed "one of the most deviant erotic minds in the publishing world...not for the weak." (Rachelle for Fallen Angels Reviews) Milieu-heavy dark work is practically Brenna's calling card, with or without the erotic content.

She teaches classes in everything from POV studies to advanced editing, networking to marketing. Brenna enjoys hearing from people who read her work and can be reached by e-mail.

Website: http://www.brennalyons.com/

Facebook: http://www.facebook.com/brenna.lyons

Email: brennalyons4168@live.com

Also by this Author

Available from *Fireborn Publishing*

KEIF'S DEN AND PACK
Keif's Pack
Mother of the Keif
Keif's Den (Coming Soon)

PROPHECY
Prophecy: Revelations
Prophecy: Rapture
The Prophet's Mate
Prophecy: Rampage - Meet Gavin
Prophecy: Rampage (Coming Soon)

THE FANTASY CLUB
The Consort

Beyond the Veil
Fairy Wishes (Coming Soon)
Mine for the Night
Once in a Blue Moon
Overtime Pay
Stay With Me
The Fire God's Woman
The Punishment of Phoebus Apollo
Werewolf U

Available from *Phaze Books*

ANGEL-WING SAGA
Sons of Heaven: Beldon
Daughters of Man: Prize Match
Sons of Heaven: Unexpected Mates
Daughters of Man: Claiming a Princess

BRIDE BALL
Bride Ball
Poison, Lies, and No-Win Choices

COLOR OF LOVE
The Color of Love

FIRE AND ICE
Magmon's Hunger
Magmon's Lover

INSTINCT SERIES
Animal Instincts

KEGIN SERIES
Conquest
The Last of Fion's Daughters
Last Chance for Love
Rites of Mating
In Her Ladyship's Service
Matchmaker's Misery

KIELAN SERIES
The Lady's Lowborn Lover
Time Currents
Cubed

NIGHT WARRIORS
Night Warriors
Will of the Stone
Bearing Armen
Hunter's Moon
Maher Men
Choosing a Mate/Starting a War
Raised to Be His Own
Veriel's Tales I: Crossbearer Turned
Veriel's Tales II: Losing Regana
Blutjagdfrau Lost
The Warrior's Man
Damsel in Distress

STAR MAGES
The Master's Lover

XXAN WAR
Daahan Rising
Crossbred Son
Raashh Decisions

Enslaved
All I Want for Christmas is You
Fates Magic
All's Fair...
Black Sail
Mama's Tales
Dream Walk
Unexpected Daddy
Phaze in Verse
We Shall Live Again
May the Best Man Win
Nevermore
Marked
And It Was Good

Available from *Mundania Press*

STAR MAGES
Written in the Stars

Fairy Dreams
Monsters of Myth Anthology

Available from *Under the Moon*

RENEGADES SERIES
TYGERS
Renegade's Run
Max Sec

URBAN GRIMM

Catch Me, If You Can
Three Wishes
Temptation of Eve

With Great Power
Undead in Blue
Evil Overlords Union Issue #1 Anthology
Undead Embrace
"Playing Games" in *Forbidden Love: Bad Boys*
"Marked" in *Forbidden Love: Wicked Women*
"The Master's Lover" in *Forbidden Love: Sacred Bands*

Available from ***Logical Lust***

"Mine for the Night" in *The Cougar Book* Anthology

Available from ***Coming Together Charity Anthologies***

INSTINCT SERIES
"Foundling" in *Coming Together: Into the Light* Anthology

"Claim Mate" (available separately and as part of the *Coming Together: Against the Odds* Anthology)
"The Fire God's Woman" in *Coming Together: Under Fire* Anthology

Available ***self-published***

KEGIN SERIES
Earth-Born Lord
Graham: Training the Earth-Born Lord

NIGHT WARRIORS
Claiming a Lady
Stone Lord
Mother's Son

COLOR OF LOVE
A Safe Heart

Snapshots from a Poet's Life

Award-Winning Books

EPPIE/EPIC eBOOK AWARDS WINNERS
Coming Together: Against the Odds- 2010
Time Currents- 2010
Coming Together: Into the Light- 2011

EPPIE/EPIC eBOOK AWARDS FINALISTS
Fion's Daughter- 2004
Collected Poems: Book One- 2005 (now titled *Snapshots of a Poet's Life*)
Renegade's Run- 2005
Rites of Mating- 2006
All I Want for Christmas- 2006
Phaze in Verse- 2008
"The Fire God's Woman" in Coming Together: Under Fire- 2009
Three Wishes- 2010
Matchmaker's Misery- 2010
The Cougar Book- 2011
The Master's Lover- 2011
Bride Ball- 2011

DREAM REALM AWARDS FINALIST
Last Chance for Love- 2003

PEARL HONORABLE MENTION
Night Warriors- 2004

PEARL FINALISTS
Schente Night- 2003 (now included in *The Last of Fion's Daughters*)
König Cursebreakers- 2004 (now titled *Will of the Stone*)

JOYFULLY REVIEWED BEST BOOKS OF 2010
Written in the Stars- 2010

SPINETINGLER'S BOOK OF THE YEAR 2007

NOBODY: An Anthology of Dark Fiction- 2007 (Brenna's pieces of the anthology can be found in *Beyond the Veil*)

TRS's CAPA FINALISTS
Ultimate Warriors- 2004 (Brenna's portion is now available as *With Great Power*)
Written in the Stars

LOVE ROMANCE AND MORE CAFÉ BOOK OF THE YEAR RUNNER UP
Last Chance for Love- 2008

ROAD TO ROMANCE REVIEWERS' CHOICE AWARD
Prophecy: Revelations- 2004

LOVE ROMANCES REVIEWERS' CHOICE AWARD
Black Sail- 2003

ROMANCE JUNKIES BOOK CLUB STAFF PICK
TYGERS- 2003

FALLEN ANGELS ROMANCE RECOMMENDED READ
*Devon's Price-*2005 (now available in *Bearing Armen*)

JOYFULLY RECOMMENDED READ
Fairy Dreams- 2008
The Last of Fion's Daughters- 2009

TREBLE HEART FINALIST
Prophecy: Revelations- 2003